OTTO
Danish-American

a novel by
W. Rosser Wilson

No part of this publication may be reproduced
in whole or in part, or stored in a retrieval system,
or transmitted in any form or by any means,
electronic, mechanical, photocopying, recording,
or otherwise, without written permission of the author,
except for the inclusion of brief quotations in a review.
For information regarding permission, please write to:
info@barringerpublishing.com

Text and Illustrations copyright ©2010 by W. Rosser Wilson
All rights reserved.

Barringer Publishing, Naples, Florida
www.barringerpublishing.com
Cover, graphics, layout design by Lisa Camp
Editing by Elizabeth Heath and James Barrow

ISBN: 978-0-9828425-1-5

Library of Congress Cataloging-in-Publication Data
Otto Danish-American/W. Rosser Wilson

Printed in U.S.A.

This book is a work of fiction.
Names, characters, places and incidents are
products of the author's imagination or are used fictitiously.
Any resembence to actual events or locales or persons
living or dead is entirely coincidental.

*** ½ - great character story 9-2019

For Carleen,
I hope you like it —
Pass it on, please, to any
friends who might enjoy it
Bill

Dedication

For my wife Julie and the children.
In memory of Anne, Otto and Peter.

Acknowledgements:

Thanks to schoolmate Tim Holland for suggestions for and editing the first draft. Also, thanks to Jette Williams and husband Peter for acting as my authorities on things Danish. Thanks to Joanne Schultz, Joyce Hartwick, David Wilson and Fran Dattilo for reading the manuscript. And special thanks to Suzi and Don Weinert for advice and encouragement. Finally, thanks to Jeff Schlesinger and Elizabeth Heath at Barringer Publishing for their professionalism.

Chapter 1

Denmark September, 1927

And so Otto began his story. "Uncle Erik, it was hot as Hell out there and they lined up the whole class shoulder to shoulder at the edge of a cow pasture. An officer fired a pistol in the air and shouted: 'Drop down and go! Belly crawl you miserable bastards across that pasture! Keep your heads down or I'll shoot you in the ass myself.' More shouting, shots here and there. We didn't know what they were firing at. I crawled like mad, tried to stay away from the instructors because we had heard—avoid the cow pies, the officers would love put a boot to your head and shove your face in it." Otto looked across the table at the silent figure who sat, arms crossed, balanced on the back legs of an ancient wooden chair. "Halfway across I saw it, straight ahead, a fresh pile of cow dung. I shifted to the right to go around. A lieutenant saw it too and trotted over and yelled, 'Damn you, soldier, crawl straight, stay on your line, go on!' That thing was perfect for what he wanted it for, still slimy and crawling with flies. He had his boot ready. Not me, I said to myself, you're not putting my face in that crap. I stopped. If it had been hard and dry I might have gone on, but I wasn't crawling through that smelly goo for anybody, not for God Almighty Himself. The imperious little prick stood right over me and shouted again, 'go on you insubordinate bastard straight on, there will be no cowards in this unit!' I looked at it and my mind snapped. I wasn't taking this. That's when I stood up!"

Filtered through dusty window glass, the last rays of a September sunset on Jutland filled the ancient farm kitchen with a drowsy, yellow half-light. Otto, his angry story spilled, cradled the glass of warm beer in his hands and looked across the wooden tabletop that had been rubbed smooth over time by a thousand elbows. There was no response. Erik, who's once handsome face, now cracked and grooved and rust-red from years farming in the harsh Danish winds, didn't move. He only listened, an idle smile drawn through two days of blond stubble, unsure how to interpret what he had heard.

"It's a game with them," Otto began again, "the instructors at the Academy. They thought it up years ago. Like an initiation that has no purpose other than to see how many underclassmen they can make crawl through manure pretending there's barbed wire and machine gun fire overhead. 'No turning back, no matter what.' Shouting, whistles blowing, pistol shots, egging us on. This is the introduction for us to the hardships of battle. Some introduction, crawling through cow shit." He paused and studied the rings his glass made on the worn wood. "Of course the real objective was for them to have a laugh over drinks at the officers' mess that night. 'Give Otto Nielsen an A in field maneuvers; he crawled through shit and, by God, if I didn't make him eat it too!'"

"Who cares what the bastard orders, crawl around, Otto, for God's sake? What can he do to you?"

"Uncle Erik he's shouting in my face, 'that's an order, soldier!' The faculty calls us 'soldier' from the day we enter the Royal Academy. That's sure a joke. It was straight ahead or straight to the brig. I wasn't going either place. It became a shouting match and my arm was cocked. I was ready to flatten him."

"The others, did they crawl through?

"Probably, everyone unlucky enough to come up to one did, but most of the pies were old and dry."

"Were they looking for something more, see how badly you wanted the Academy and the army? Or just looking to give you a taste of war?" His uncle spoke softly, his smile gone and his eyes probing. Realizing his accidental play on words, the smile returned.

"Yeah, a taste all right. For more than a year I've put up with that damn place and I stayed on, getting by, doing the minimum. But my face pressed in manure, no, that's the limit. When I stood up it was a declaration: I'm leaving, I'm finished with the Academy. I walked off the field and that ass ran along behind me, right on my heels shouting, 'Stop, come back here and get down this instant!' I could feel his stinking breath on my neck and I knew there were fifty of my classmates watching me, begging me: 'Come on Otto, turn around, pop him one, punch the crap out of him.' I almost did. I could have killed him right then and there."

Otto took another swallow of beer. "So, there is nothing left for me there. I was ordered to report to the commanding officer. Instead I went to my room, packed my things, and came out here."

"And that's it? That's all?" Otto could smell the dried sweat from his uncle's dirty shirt. His uncle's hands were thick and black dirt was caked under the short square nails. "You didn't go home, back to Arhus, see your folks, tell your father what happened? Why you quit? You came straight to the farm?"

"You know my father, he always takes the other side, argues with me even if he knows I'm right. Being objective he calls it, testing theories. To him being objective amounts to issuing orders. There would have been another shouting match. 'Go back now!' he would have hollered. I didn't need that. This damned dream of his, this dream he had for me to go to the Royal Military Academy, become an officer, what crap. 'Otto,' he says, in so many words, 'do what I never took the trouble to do, make me proud. It's up to you now Otto to carry on the Nielsen family military heritage' … that conveniently skipped his generation. 'Live by those eternal soldierly ideals: sacrifice, honor, duty … Be like your great uncle, the remarkable General Otto Nielsen, the family hero who died in Africa bravely defending Denmark by observing the Boer war' … probably from a safe distance. Uncle Erik, you want to know what have I learned about the military? Three things: there's low pay, hours of boredom and lots to drink."

The sun had dropped below the horizon and the room had darkened. Otto took the last swallow of beer and watched the foam slide down to the bottom of the glass before he banged it down on the table. "So Uncle Erik, go home? No! It wasn't worth the fight. And I might not have been able to control myself."

Erik leaned forward and locked eyes, "You know that lieutenant did you a big favor. He gave you the excuse you needed." With those words Otto stood and flung his arms out, his hands bumping the wide, rough boards of the low ceiling. "You're right. I'm through! It was perfect!"

His uncle rose to his feet and stretched. Ten o'clock and the house and barns were quiet, eight hours until milking time. With a pat on the back he pushed Otto toward the ladder to the attic. "Things are always hard here. Your grandparents would starve before they would turn you away but don't take advantage. Tomorrow we go to work."

At the top of the ladder Otto fumbled through the dark and fell onto the narrow bed without undressing. He rolled up in a blanket and pulled it to his chin. The weather had suddenly turned cold for September and the ancient walls surrounding the rough wooden window frame, though chinked with mortar, let the insistent wind through. He recalled the first words he had heard the first day at the Academy, while standing at attention in a rough line-up with his classmates on the parade grounds: "Denmark's battles are won or lost in the hearts of the Academy's graduates, you men." The commandant in his dress uniform paused after that sentence and appeared to look each man in the eye, letting that message sink in. In the attic Otto felt the heat from a surge of blood to his cheeks. He had quit, made a rash decision, abandoned friendships, thrown away the opportunity for a military career that he had assumed would be his. Rolling on his side he whispered thoughts as they came to him into the darkness, softly making the argument for his actions, new thoughts he had never legitimized before, words he had heard shouted by the pacifists from soapboxes in the parks of Copenhagen that he had dismissed, even cursed: "war is idiocy … a failure of reason … organized debauchery," and so on. His mind replayed grainy images from newsreels, pictures of the carnage of the Great War, the bodies, eyes and mouths gapping, half buried in the mud in the trenches at Ypres, the Somme and Verdun. Within a few moments his mind's work was done. He, Otto Nielsen, he pronounced into the gloom would not become a small cog in a military machine. Life had too much to offer to spend it, and perhaps to lose it, senselessly. What was done was done and to Hell with it. To Hell with the Academy! Then sleep came quickly.

For as long as Otto could remember summers were spent at the ancient farm. Scarred by centuries of storms off the Skagerrak and North Sea, the farmhouse looked south across pastureland and grazing herds to a hedge of trees and beyond to the white church tower that marked the village. Above, the clouds scurried across Jutland, whipped on by the interminable coastal winds. A few steps outside the kitchen door lay a garden of vegetables and flowers that grew in neat rows tended by his grandmother, on her knees in her garden dress and big brimmed hat. Praying with seed, she called it. The rich soil, tilled by uncounted generations before her, produced such an abundance that an extra market basket filled with peas and cabbage, larkspur and lilac, or whatever had flourished that week would be the tithe to the village church. Against the house, by the thick gray wall by the heavy wooden door stood a jumble of brightly colored hollyhock, and though neglected, every spring the flowers shot skyward in celebration of a new season. These joyful hollyhocks against the rough wall made the picture that came to Otto whenever, years later, his thoughts traveled back to Denmark. At the front of the house facing the road were the barns, attached on the right the milking barn, and on the left, the wagon barn, which together formed the wings that cradled the courtyard. Out from the courtyard the long driveway connected to the village road and the world beyond.

The old house and dairy farm were the ancestral home of his mother's parents, Hans and Bente Larsen that provided relief every summer from the stresses of city life for Astrid, their only daughter and for Otto and his brother, Jorgen. Thought too pretty and bright to be a farmer's wife, Astride was sent at seventeen to Copenhagen to study to be a teacher where she could improve her prospects for a good marriage and comfortable life. Her brother Erik, his prospects predetermined, remained behind to work the farm. In Copenhagen, as hoped, Astride met and married Peder Nielsen, considered an excellent catch as he had advanced at a young age to the position of head teller of the Arhus branch of Den Danske-Union Bank; an important post as Arhus was the second largest city in Denmark. For Astride the city's university, theater, art, music, and café life could have provided great joy; however, it afforded no pleasure to head teller Nielsen whose interests were limited to commerce and banking, and as a result, Astrid found herself prosperous but housebound, a prisoner in a sterile marriage. Peder disliked the farm as well and traveled there only from a perceived sense of duty. When Peder made the requisite trip to the farm, his misdirected energy was put to pacing the creaking boards of the small parlor. Not removing his white shirt and tie, his suit jacket neatly folded over the back of a chair, he rued the burdensome disruption of his regulated life, protesting to the empty room that duty called him back home. Within a day or two, swamped by concerns about the bank, the missed meetings, and fears that aggressive junior managers jockeyed for his position, he would solemnly announce at dinner his return to Arhus was imperative and that he had hired a car to pick him up in the morning. In the later years he didn't travel to the farm at all and his absence went unfelt.

For Astride the sight of the old barns and the prospects of kitchen and garden wakened the pleasures of her youth. She put city clothes aside, adopting a simple farm dress and apron. In the evening she played the old piano and sang, avoiding the stuck keys while the family told stories or played cards and the boys argued with Uncle Erik about his barefaced cheating. Afterward, if not too late, they would read out loud often from the Bible, unless Old Hans was awake. "Put away that useless book; it's for women," he would say.

The farm, 30 kilometers east of Holstebro in Jutland, had passed through uncounted generations of Larsens to the present, and thus the fertile soil, and the family who worked it, had never been separated. Years earlier his grandfather, in a whispered voice, ominous and grave, told Otto, then a wide-eyed boy, that since the time they had been Viking warriors the Larsens had sprung from the earth to work this land, and when done and buried on the hill at the end of the pasture merely lay there passing time, waiting to come back and toil again, the farm literally their Heaven and Hell. The others laughed at the preposterous tale, understanding it to be another of the droll old fabulist's inventions, but Otto believed it then and always, because he could find no greater truth that could replace it.

By the second day back, working alongside Erik, Otto had once again found the rhythm for throwing hay up on the wagon as they passed up and down the mowed field. The Academy's food had fueled his growth to a height of over six feet and had broadened his shoulders, so that a fork full of grass required little effort no matter how high the wagon pile. Since boyhood he had tried to emulate Erik, who in fact he resembled: blond and rugged. His uncle, a man who despite sick cows, deluge and broken machinery, persevered with steely humor and faith that tomorrow would somehow be better. It rarely was.

Otto broke the silence. His mind had replayed the events a few days before at the Academy. "You know what it was like there?" Otto began, upset that Erik thought him weak. More than any person alive, it was Erik's opinion of him that mattered, his brusque advice that had always given direction to Otto for what a strong man would do. He was certain had Erik been in that situation he would have hit the lieutenant and taken the consequences. Impelled to make his case for leaving the academy stronger, Otto went on. "March miles till exhausted, drill for hours, stand out in the rain, snow, freeze, roast—I—had no problem with that; I expected that, there was no humiliation there." They stood by the wagon leaning on the forks. Otto looked for words a farmer would sympathize with, could understand. Humiliation, that was the issue, the final straw; that's what he couldn't stomach. He took a chance. "And there were the unbearable times we stood in dress uniform at attention against the wall at official receptions and dinners, unable to move, like a potted palm, back aching, watching, not flinching. Reduced to an ornament, a piece of scenery! Humiliating!" The last word he added in case his uncle didn't get the point.

"Otto, for God's sake, stop your carping." Their eyes met. "You weren't cut out for it, so that's that. Figure out what you want … school, farm, who cares, whatever. Make a choice that can make you happy. That's life's important lesson, the goal, to be happy isn't it?" They returned to haying wordless until the lunch bell reached them across the fields. As they walked in Erik softened, "I'm stuck here. I'm not suited for anything else. Don't make your life a melodrama. You have to do what you have to do."

Midday dinner, the usual farm fare, included roast chicken carved by old Hans into chunks and forked onto the plates that he then passed around the kitchen table. This was followed around the table by a bowl of boiled potatoes and then a bowl of carrots slid along the smooth wood and shoveled out with large wooden spoons. Bent into the food, they had begun eating before Bente took her seat across from Hans. Before sitting, she leaned in to place in the center of the table a chipped clay pitcher stuffed with the last of the season's sunflowers she had made no effort to arrange. They ate to the laments of old Hans repeating his complaints of how nineteen twenty-seven was going to be worse than twenty-six because of the goddamned Social Democrats and their schemes that always meant more and more taxes. Then he began grousing about the German inflation affecting farm exports and depressing the Danish economy. "They want everything we've got, those damn Germans, they wouldn't know what a fair price is if it bit them in the ass." As a boy Otto had rolled his eyes up at these rants but today the old man brought the lesson home, saying they needed cash, and told Bente and Erik to pick out four of the worst milkers to sell for meat. At that moment, as if timed to coincide with the end of the meal, the wall phone rang. Erik, without looking up from his plate muttered, stabbing at the last piece of carrot, "Otto, you get it, we know who it is."

Chapter 2

Years earlier, the directors of Den Danske-Union Bank, seated in leather bound chairs surrounding a conference table, immersed in the haze of cigar smoke, discussed a fateful promotion. Should the young head teller at the Arhus Bank, Peder Nielsen, recently identified as an organizational and administrative prodigy, be promoted further and so early in his career? Following a brief discussion and with a perfunctory show of hands the ambitious functionary rose to the position of Branch Manager. Upon receiving the news, Nielsen, delighted, for the first and only time in his life, danced, albeit about his office floor. By the last step of this awkward jig he had decided to grow a bristly mustache, a pot scrubber, to age his boyish face and harden his countenance to better match the fierce determination that burned at the center of his soul. From this point on, he vowed he would demand of the bank's staff unfailing punctuality and exactness and the respect due their new, commanding supervisor. Any recalcitrant would be shown the door. And for almost twenty years since that momentous day, the Arhus branch of Den Dansk-Union Bank stood strong, unshaken by the incoming and out flowing tides of financial boom and bust, solid as a rock in war and peace; Nielsen's branch was cited as a model among banks for its regimentation, militaristic discipline and flawless accuracy. This happenstance, this providential decision was the fruition of the Board of Director's lucky stumble upon an uncommonly obsessive personality they chanced to hire and promote on a whim. And, fearing his annoying presence in Copenhagen, they kept him continually sidelined in Arhus, far away, allowing him only the briefest contact with senior management and never with the Board.

So on an exhilarating morning, the business of the bank humming below as he watched the panting message boys run up and down the marble stairs from the teller's booths and loan officer's desks to his office on the balcony, Peder took a phone call. Smiling, he waved his assistant away and leaned back in his chair. On the end of the line he heard the voice of the Royal Military Academy's Chief Administrative Officer. The words of praise for his son he expected did not come, but rather solemn, unhappy words that abruptly collapsed his smile and blanched his face white. After short initial pleasantries the officer reported that during recent field maneuvers Peder's son, Otto, had disobeyed a direct order and then without permission had left the Academy. Responding with disbelief, Peder blurted, "My son behaved in such an appalling manner?" Pressed, the officer assured him he had, and worse: Peder inferred from the officer's tone that he, Peder Nielsen, was in part to blame, as he had been responsible for the upbringing that resulted in this "insolent disregard for authority." Peder extended repeated obsequious apologizes to the Academy staff on Otto's behalf and quietly replaced the phone in the cradle. Following a stunned silence, he erupted with a battery of shouted orders to his cowering assistant, canceling all afternoon meetings, no more messages, and keep everyone out! His mind awhirl, he sought answers, pacing his office, while he considered stratagems, tossing out, modifying, reshaping the words he would fling at Otto to undo this "outrageous calamity." In time his anger cooled and he resolved he would listen first, hear his errant son out, whom for the moment, as an act of unbounded charity, he would consider to have suffered a temporary failure of judgment. Then, having listened to Otto, he would reason and convince the boy of the wisdom of going back, and offer to help set matters aright with the Academy as best he could. In this frame of mind Peder had every intention of standing by his son and would provide the benefit of his experience and moral courage. He would "stiffen him up," or so he planned. Now satisfied that prudence could be relied upon to overcome all obstacles, he determined the prospects for a happy result to be good. Relying on his relationship with his son, which he believed to be at its core loving, he cleared his throat, and smiling once again, asked the bank's operator to put the call through to the farm.

"Otto, what ever did you do? The Academy called—said you were cited for insubordination and had left the school? This couldn't be true?"

"The Academy is not for me." Otto modulated his voice carefully, keeping it steady.

"How so?" The calm response.

"I can't fit in, comply with the demands they make."

"You are not considering leaving, are you?"

"I've left already, I took my things and quit for good. It's over."

The words, despite the quiet, respectful tone, presented a rare challenge to Peder's dream and absolute authority, an authority he had strictly maintained through the years at the bank and at home over his sons, Otto and poor Jorgen. His response was violent, an uncontrollable release of the suppressed anger and shame he had spent most of the morning stifling.

"Otto, you can't leave. It's family heritage. Go back there tomorrow! Do you hear?"

"I hear, father. I'm not going back."

Then the shouts came. "Are you telling me you can't you take it? The Academy is too tough for you? Are you that soft?" He paused for several seconds waiting for an answer. Otto could hear his father's breaths whistling through the hairs of his nose. Then Peder bellowed into the phone. "For God's sake, Otto, Nielsens never quit! Get back there! Your great uncle never quit!"

"He didn't have to, he shit himself to death!"

"He suffered from dysentery, died for Denmark in the line of duty! Otto you are a goddamned quitter!"

"Go to Hell." Otto said slowly and distinctly into the receiver. Grandmother at the sink did not react, as if she hadn't heard, carefully stacking the dishes so they would drain on the wooden sideboard. Old Hans had gone back out to the barn. Erik, alone at the table, gasped, "Jesus, Otto."

There was a long pause. Having spoken those spiteful words to his son, Peder recognized his mission had failed utterly. Shocked by Otto's curse, he was incapable of considering any concession. The words in effect had cut both ways, stunning the speaker and hearer alike joined in this internecine battle of wills.

"Okay, Otto, have it your way … certainly you have no concern that your contumacy reflects harshly on me."

Contumacy, what the Hell is that Otto thought? His father's stilted language, trying to impress whoever might be listening, had always annoyed him. A longer pause and Otto was content to wait, to see what he would propose, silently calculating what options might be left realizing there were essentially none.

In a voice lowered by anger and frustration Peder growled, "You made your decision. I can't help you any longer. No, it's more than that, I *won't* help a quitter any longer, any quitter. Go find a job and a room someplace and support yourself! Go to work, see how you like it!" And as an afterthought he murmured, "Needless to say, this will upset your mother terribly when I tell her. Let her know where you are."

Otto didn't answer. He would follow these orders as he had no alternative, but they were of little consequence as they amounted to what he expected. He could hear the whistling breaths puffing quicker and moved the phone back from his ear.

"Damn you Otto! I have enough trouble running the bank without this!" The phone clicked, slammed down at the other end. The relief came to Otto like a warm shower, a sunburst, like every pleasurable thing he had ever known.

"What did he say?" Erik asked suppressing a laugh.

"Upset I didn't follow his damned plan; but, as always, he sends you his very best." Otto replied blowing Erik a kiss.

"You know what Otto? He would have crawled through the cow shit."

"He would have rolled in it."

• • •

The farm work, the desultory hours spent in the barns and fields milking, mucking out, planting and haying, brought the unexpected pleasure of sweat and achy muscles bulking up Otto's arms and rippling his back like that of a sea-hardened oarsman. No instructions, no need for them, tasks were taught by example as the jobs were simple enough, see it once and do it—harness the team, shovel the muck. Erik's easy banter made time irrelevant, filled as it was with tall stories about the characters from surrounding farms that regularly drove carts into a ditch or tumbled drunk from a hay loft. In essence, during those days, Erik, a story-telling pedagogue, passed to Otto the fundamental tool of Otto's future stock and trade, that of a good story teller and host. There were unspoken economic lessons as well, less happily learned, as sharp and clear as the patches of white sunlight that squeezed through cracks in the barn wall to mark the barn floor. Laboring in barns and fields led to little prosperity; hard work and monetary return on a farm did not equate—the returns were meager.

On the cold, windy nights huddled beneath a thick comforter in the drafty farmhouse loft, Otto thoughts turned to dreams of home. The house in Arhus sat among the towering trees and conventional homes of Sjaellandsgade. From the Lutheran Church at the far end of the street, the house and its occupants were watched over by the ever-vigilant Pastor Svensen. At Peder's insistence the family attended church Sunday, rain or shine, despite Otto and Jorgen's pleas for relief. Peder's role as bank manager and pillar of the community demanded that he present his family as an example of flawless, indeed inspiring, behavior and harmonious stability. The result: as a child Otto suffered hours of condemnation to hard church benches where the agony was partially relieved by swinging his feet and rocking from cheek to cheek while playing with his fingers or leafing through the hymnal and accepting as absolute truth, despite the torture, snatches of the stern lessons from the lengthy homilies that managed to pierce the perfect boredom.

Among his earliest memories of the good days, Otto recalled how his mother each morning would loop back the window curtains of the house and fill the rooms with bright light and what little warmth the winter sun gave up, tend the plants set on the windowsills, arrange the schedule for the maid, plan the meals with the cook, and several afternoons a week give piano lessons or tutor neighbor children … and at every excuse organize children's parties. After school, Otto and Jorgen and their friends were free to run about the house, thump up and down the stairs, saturate the house with noisy play until Peder opened and slammed the door at five-twenty sharp, having marched double-time the ten blocks from the bank to the house. Before he had removed his coat, order was restored, or red-faced, he shouted for quiet. After dinner he followed his routine, a stroll to the parlor to read the evening paper while Astrid stayed behind with the boys at the dining table to correct their schoolwork. This is how life had been until the winter of 1918, when Otto's brother Jorgen, two days after his fifteenth birthday contracted influenza, the "Spanish flu."

Jorgen was a small boy with brick-red hair that refused to lie down, uneven, widely spaced teeth, pencil-thin arms and legs, and a chest so anemic that the skin, like glistening white paper, stuck to his ribs. Though three years older from the start he was frail and sickly and had been quickly surpassed by Otto in size and strength. The doctors, flummoxed, described his medical condition as "failure to thrive", a term they coined, as the medical books provided none. Yet despite this, Jorgen was carefree, unconcerned about his health, serving as the self-appointed family jokester, playing small pranks and spending hours practicing card and magic tricks. Exercise impossible, at school Jorgen became a boyhood authority on sports, committing to memory an encyclopedic tabulation of names and statistics from the national football (soccer) teams, world track records and a flawless listing of boxing champions, past and present, in every weight class. This sorrowful ailing son, her first born, Astrid loved absolutely and when Jorgen's condition declined, as it often did, she nursed him with boundless compassion, working to the point of exhaustion, unable to rest until she had returned him to his customary state of poor but stable health. This sickly son posed an embarrassment for Peder from the start, a constant reminder of a genetic mutation, a weak, imperfect and unacceptable product of his seed, best hidden and ignored. Therefore, Otto, the second son, became the family's future standard bearer and, taken aside by his father one snowy day in the quiet of the family library, told with great solemnity that from that point forward he was obligated to emulate the life of his granduncle, the General, making it clear to Otto he had no choice but to pursue a soldier's career. Otto, unprepared and unschooled in military life, accepted the call unquestioned and offered no resistance, imagining only the best.

Jorgen's final illness began with what appeared to be a cold with a deep cough that despite steam treatments and codeine syrup grew productive of ropy, green phlegm. After days and nights, the boy, flushed with chills and fever and gasping for breath, had used all the strength his emaciated frame could muster and finally gave up the struggle and died wrapped in Astrid's arms. In the tomblike house his father stood stiffly by, in a world apart, silent, feigning grief and unable even in those most grievous of moments to embrace or comfort his mourning wife. Finally the words came, the affected sentiments and the pretence of love he thought appropriate for the occasion; words she knew he had practiced and were unfelt. They repelled her. They were worse than none at all. Otto learned years afterward when she spoke of that day those words consumed her with hatred. It had finally come to that between them, husband and wife; and she screamed at Peder: "If you feel compelled to speak of Jorgen, say what you really think—that it is good for the family that Jorgen is dead! That finally the hereditary blight had been erased and the blemish on this family removed! Good riddance!" And from that time forward she turned her back on him.

For Peder, the funeral and burial at the farm forced another unplanned disruption in his schedule. Meetings with important clients were canceled and his compulsively clear desk became stacked with papers. In the winter mist by the grave, on the low hill at the end of the field, Peder's sober demeanor displayed no perceptible change as he stood, dry-eyed, arms crossed with the grieving family for the short funeral service.

Following the final benediction, as far as Otto could recall, his father never spoke of Jorgen again. The house in Arhus remained morose, dark and loveless; the curtains left closed to block the light, and Astrid left the plants unattended and unwatered until withered, they were thrown in the trash.

For twelve-year old Otto, Jorgen's death arose in him an understanding of mortality. The word death, as with all children, had been devoid of meaning or emotion, as in Otto's experience death was limited to fairytale demons killed by the heroes of bedtime stories. And the graveyard on the hill at the end of the field, as his grandfather's fable went, was until then, just a depository for their sleeping Norse ancestors. Now, with Jorgen among them it became a manifestly personal place, to where, Otto came to understand he would at some very distant, unimaginable time, come. There, he told himself, he would be reunited with his brother, in a place where they would lay together awaiting the reawakening.

Otto was fourteen when Peder announced during an otherwise silent dinner that his remaining son would be sent to military boarding school. This news Otto received without protest, or feelings of rejection, or enthusiasm, merely with uneasy relief as the prospects seemed less bleak than life in the house on Sjaellandsgade. He recalled, now years later bundled in blankets in the frigid farm attic, how his father, picking his words, went on to say the decision was in good part based on the necessity to correct what he perceived in his surviving son as "indulgent and undisciplined behavior," traits that Peder intimated were due to the unsavory influence of his Uncle Erik during the long summer visits at the farm. Respectful of Astrid's feeling for her brother, Peder spoke in awkward circumlocutions, trying as indirectly as the Danish language permitted to say essentially he thought Erik a country bumpkin with a penchant for drinking and joking. The words, though carefully picked, drove Astrid with her food from the table. Peder took no notice. He continued to Otto, that the school would serve "to impart good habits of study and prepare him for a respectable life befitting his goal," and now that his mother had "finished her meal" he could express directly to Otto that he expected the military school "to quickly dilute his uncle's influence and make a proper man of him."

The recollection of that conversation summoned a laugh from Otto that he barked out into the dark attic air. Fallen from grace, and since that September phone call in essence disowned, he now worked alongside Erik, the arch despoiler and his father's nemesis. Otto had Erik to thank for his consignment to boarding school where the faculty did indeed impart the firm, structured environment his father sought.

The school was a dismal place. Located half a day's travel from Arhus, it consisted of a single large three-story, stucco building, unadorned by shrubs or trees to soften the sharp corners. Remote and foreboding it stood alone on a flat grassy plain that served as drill grounds and playing fields. The classrooms, library, and the dining hall made up the main floor. The formal dining hall, dimly lit by massive iron chandeliers that hung like storm clouds above the room, was paneled in dark oak with an encircling carved cornice painted with the armorial insignia of Danish heraldry. The other decoration centered in the far wall at the end of the room, a portrait of King Christian the Tenth. Though admired, this mustachioed paragon of Danish manhood stood as an irresistible target for biscuits hurled by laughing schoolboys when faculty monitors were absent. Otto was convinced, had he been there, the King would have thrown the first one himself. The second and third floors held the sleeping quarters, four boys to a room furnished with badly scratched metal framed beds with sagging springs and a thin mattresses, foot lockers, and against the wall, ink stained wooden desks with a single reading lamp and a wooden chair that screeched when moved on the bare wooden floor. A bachelor-teacher housemaster lived in a small apartment on the ground floor and though charged with maintaining order and enforcing lights-out, rarely made evening inspections. The married faculty lived down the road from the main hall in a row of neat cottages.

Prior to the car trip to the school Otto had no notion of what attending boarding school would involve, but from the first day forward he found the experience positive. Inspections taught a habit for neatness, the uniform taught good grooming and care for clothes, the creases mainly. He studied Latin, German, algebra, geometry, and history. Most important, with the realization that all the boys there had been placed in this militaristic atmosphere to break their boyhood spirit, Otto did not feel alone. Certainly Otto's father's objective, the subjugation of his personality to a purposeful life … a goal that necessitated the obliteration of humor and spontaneity in favor of realignment to a requisite sense of purpose, was in that atmosphere easily thwarted. The boys banded together in their resolve not to succumb. So surrounded by dozens of rowdy schoolmates, no amount of study, marching and running about the athletic fields could discourage the horseplay once the pressure was off. Spirits suppressed during the day soared at night after study hours.

Of his teachers, Otto admired one enough to emulate. A history teacher, a Dane, who had volunteered for duty with the British Army in the Great War and fought only to be in a fight. A Viking at heart ordered by the British to the trenches along the Marne, he inspired Otto with the notion that military life could be grand and exciting, an adventure, particularly when surrounded by comrades of similar bent, warriors, champions, heroes. And so without further contemplation, and conjuring up beer hall victory parties, songs and dancing girls, Otto applied to and was subsequently admitted to the Royal Danish Military Academy. At this point Otto was excited to fulfill his father's plan and for a brief time their stars came into alignment, until confronted by the fateful field maneuvers in the cow pasture.

Wrapped in the comforter against the cold, Otto had no recourse but to reconsider what this newly contrived life could provide. It would be easy to stay on the farm, except he already had concluded farm life would not satisfy him. The hard work didn't trouble him but the fact was reinforced daily that money could not be made at farming, certainly not enough to satisfy his plans for the life he imagined ahead—a life with a comfortable house, a car, and a white collar job, in essence an existence totally removed from the farm with city clothes, sophisticated friends and interesting conversation. The decision grew stronger with each passing night and he planned, come spring, he would leave for Copenhagen.

The bright sunny June morning made for a propitious day to start a quest. Erik offered no advice, just small talk as the truck bumped along the country road, past farms toward the village to the shed that served as the bus stop. Otto swung down with his satchel and after a handshake and a wave watched the truck back around and turn toward the farm, disappearing into the dust beyond a rise. He was off to Copenhagen. It was the twenty-fifth of June in his nineteenth year.

Chapter 3

The university students had scattered from Copenhagen to every corner of Denmark and Europe for the summer and rooms for rent were plentiful. Otto, walking near the university, spotted a yellowed sign in the window of an old house advertizing a room for rent on the first floor with a separate entrance. It amounted to little more than a dusty monk's cell, furnished with a single bed, a straight wooden chair that he used as a clothes rack, a dim lamp on a small bedside table and a window curtain he could slide closed to block the view in from passersby. A spotted, threadbare rug lay over a small portion of the wooden floor. On the bed, woolen blankets and sheets covered a horsehair mattress with stained blue and white ticking. He shared a bathroom down the hall. Humble as these circumstances were, by comparison to the attic at the farm, this was luxury. And for Otto, with no limitations upon his time, the absolute freedom without a single commitment to concern him, life became unbelievably splendid: a feeling he had never known. The first few days Otto spent wandering the city, browsing the university's great library and exploring bookstalls, cafes, and shops. They were the best ever.

Erik paid Otto a modest amount for ten months labor, a token, Erik explained sadly, but enough he said, to give Otto a start; and only since he had great need of it, did Otto accept. Astrid sent money from her household accounts, tucked in letters that contained scraps of news from Arhus and a proposal that until he had become suitably settled he stay with the Larsens, cousins in Copenhagen. Otto had no interest in this. He began a search for work, walking in a regular pattern up and down the streets, stopping at every establishment that looked as though it might pay a decent wage. After several days and a short interview with the manager, he was hired as the night clerk at a small hotel, *The Dahlberg House*, where he was entrusted with the front desk five nights a week and from there charged with oversight of the lobby from eleven until seven in the morning. The small income from this work supported his modest room and board with some to spare. The hotel, five stories high, held forty-two rooms and welcomed the world with a worn, disheveled elegance, like a pretty girl past her prime with mussed hair, nothing some cosmetic changes such as fresh paint and new lobby furnishings wouldn't fix. The hotel housed a few permanent residents but most of the trade Otto found to be tightfisted transients, primarily salesmen and frugal German tourists who sought inexpensive lodgings. The ground floor, in addition to the lobby and registration desk, included the hotel lounge and a small, quiet bar.

At this point, owing to the nightshift, his life became reordered. Returning from the hotel, he slept for four or five hours until the sunshine leaked around the curtain, filled the room, and pushed him up and out to the streets. He picked through used bookstores and gathered a small library of select books, the ones that had been alien to a military science curriculum—literature, philosophy, art, and most importantly, business. The remainder of the day he spent at self-instruction, reading stretched out on the grass in a park or nursing a glass of beer at an outdoor café or because of the frequent rains that summer, in his room curled on the bed.

After several weeks a package arrived from Arhus containing clothes, a small cake and a note detailing his relationship to his distant Larsen cousins. Otto, Astrid wrote, had met them as a boy. He remembered the trip to the large house with a broad lawn and spreading trees bent by slushy snow. They had come by cab and as they approached, his father became tense, making little dry coughs and drumming his fingers on his knee. It was a Sunday afternoon; a maid greeted them at the door. The house felt warm, and smelled of cider and cinnamon. Gilt framed paintings hung on the walls, heavy drapes hung about the windows, oriental carpets covered the floors, and fires blazed in the gigantic hearths in the parlor and dining room. Mostly he remembered the house as very large and the cousins very rich. His father in the entryway, stiff and deferential, bowed as he shook hands with the host and taking the hostess's hand, bowed more deeply and kissed it. His mother hid her annoyance and remained smiley and breezy, kissing her cousins hello. After all the years, Otto couldn't picture his cousins Niels Larsen nor his wife, whose name he could not recall; but the children, Kirsten and Hans, dressed in what he took to be their Sunday church clothes, he did remember. Hans was a few years older, perhaps eleven, and Kirsten a few years younger. Hans showed Otto and Jorgen his collection of lead soldiers made up of hundreds of every rank, men on horseback, artillerists by small canon, the dead and wounded infantrymen scattered among the carefully arranged battle formations on the floor of his room; Napoleon's army facing the British at Waterloo, he bragged, just as they were that fateful morning. Otto recalled Kirsten. She had long blond hair, wore a red velvet dress and white knee socks and she excited feelings in him he was too young to understand. She sat humming on the edge of a chair, swinging her feet, and he watched her every chance he could, although he didn't want to talk to her. So, these many years later, wishing to please his mother and his interest in seeing them piqued by the memories, he phoned the Larsen home from the reservation desk at the hotel. The maid who answered informed him, as though he should have known, that the family always spent six weeks at their summer house on the coast and would return mid August. Call back then, and added clearly miffed, at a decent hour please.

The hotel supplied him with a uniform: a long formal black coat, gray striped trousers, white shirt and gray tie. The clothing outdated, a throwback to the hotel's fancier, halcyon days seemed no longer appropriate. He stood most of the night behind the reception desk hanging up room keys, filing, sorting the mail. Despite the hour, clientele arrived from the late trains and ferries: tired German or Scandinavian businessmen, some tourists, and occasionally a "Mr. and Mrs. So and So." He made it a game to look for wedding rings but the suspect women, better at these games than he, kept their hands below the desk out of his view. He could converse easily in German and Swedish to provide directions and keys, but his rudimentary English and French obliged him to point and write room numbers on a slip of paper. He had been cautioned under no circumstances to admit to the lobby, and especially to the rooms beyond, the prostitutes who walked the nearby streets—a rule he bent, allowing the nicely dressed, escorted ones into the bar but never upstairs, although he realized once in a while they slipped by if his back was turned. Laughing on the way out, they would give him a smile and a little wave good-bye. Finally, he was to keep the lobby neat and free of loiterers, this task facilitated by his six foot two, farm-hardened frame. Most of the offenders responded to a smiling request to leave, but now and then a drunk from the bar required a firm grip on the arm and a push out the doorway to the street.

Within a few weeks, Kurt, the bartender, a retired detective from Copenhagen's police force, took notice of the young clerk and elected himself as Otto's self-appointed late night advisor and confidant in areas involving the practical matters of life, a void in Otto's education he instantly recognized. A ruddy-faced widower with time to kill, heavyset, gregarious and shrewd, Kurt had worked behind the bar for years. His uniform included a short red jacket, bow tie and black pants. He claimed to shake the best cocktails in Copenhagen, an artist with liquors in addition to the standard European fare of beer and wine. If the hour was late and he enjoyed the patron and the prospects looked good for a healthy tip, he served as the after-hours cook, preparing eggs and bacon. Unaccompanied regulars and strangers he engaged in talk, and Otto saw with the aid of spirits that he could pry out deeply hidden, scandalous tales before the drinkers realized what they had said. Therefore whatever facts regarding life in Copenhagen Kurt had not encountered in sixty-five years he learned of over the bar: details of Copenhagen's business triumphs and failures, marital infidelities, and his favorite, his specialty, crimes. When the bar closed and if the lobby had emptied and Otto was free, Kurt would sprawl on the lobby sofa, arms stretched along the sofa back and legs spread apart, and pass on to Otto embellished recounts of what he had drawn out that night. In the empty morning hours, stories of the comings and goings of Copenhagen animated the city for Otto with characters from all walks of life, filling in the streets, rooming houses and mansions with clowns and thieves, the righteous and the profane, exposing Otto to what he could have only imagined. If the reservation desk remained quiet after Kurt left, Otto took out a book to study until the morning papers arrived, and then, opening to the business pages he struggled to interpret the financial numbers that he was convinced hid from all but the most brilliant or well-connected the clues to stock market fortunes.

When Otto opened the door to his room one mid-August day following an afternoon reading on a sunny bench in the park by the Mineralogisk Museum, he saw a note-sized envelope on heavy linen paper that had been slipped under the door. Addressed to **Mr. Otto Nielsen** in elegant handwriting on informal stationary, it held an invitation to dinner at the home of Mr. and Mrs. Niels Larsen at 4 p.m. Sunday, August twenty-second. His mother's part in this was clear. Determined that Otto know them, she had made the connection with the cousins that he, now settled and comfortable, had decided to neglect. He called that evening and the same uppity servant said she would make a note of his acceptance.

Peering out the open window of the cab as it approached, he recognized the house he had visited many years before. The degree of affluence, he then too innocent to grasp, this day produced an echo in him of the perturbation his father had felt. An iron spike fence surrounded the expanse of lawn that held tall park-like trees standing guard over the stone house built in a style more English than Danish, with a gray slate roof, narrow embrasure windows with leaded sashes, and under a Norman arch, a large oaken door that brandished a heavy iron knocker in the form of a lion's head and an immense iron latch strong enough to withstand axe blows. He knocked. A portly middle aged man in a tan linen sport coat and brown trousers swung open the door and with a broad smile haled him, "Well, Otto, do come in!" His cousin turned gesturing with an open palm to his wife standing behind him, "And of course you remember Ulla." In truth Otto didn't remember her at all and certainly not her fetching looks, though Otto assured his cousin that he did. In that instant she set a standard for beauty and style that Otto would not forget; the appropriate compliment for any man of means, very desirable, absolutely necessary and undeniably pleasurable.

Niels sung out down the stone walled hallway in a baritone big enough to fill a cathedral, "Otto is here!" The words brought an abrupt stop to music Otto recognized as the Polonaise someone hammered out on the piano with excessive vigor. He followed Niels into the vaulted living room, where Hans, now a gangly six feet tall and dressed in tennis clothes, lay on the leather sofa reading before the fireplace, above which hung an immense full-length portrait of Niels and Ulla looking out across the room with such enormous majesty that Otto felt a immediate sense of fealty. Hans stood and brushed away a sprig of unruly hair from his brow as he extended his hand. Otto learned Hans, now an engineer, had come home on a break from Sweden where he worked. Kirsten swung about on the stool before the grand piano, surveyed Otto with a glance and gave him a gentle smile and a small soft hand to shake. The long, blond tresses Otto remembered were styled to a fashionable cut that framed her tanned face that he found uncommonly pretty. The summer dress, tailored to fit her form, displayed an athletic figure and dispelled any remaining disinclination he had for coming.

The maid served dinner to the family at a small dining table just large enough for six, located in a windowed alcove adjoining the main dining room, which in keeping with the grandeur of the house, held a table Otto estimated could comfortably seat twenty-five. In the alcove, Otto was positioned so he could overlook the gardens and lawns to the side and rear of the house. Kirsten and Hans sat across from him. Ulla, to his left, began by asking about his grandparents, mother and uncle, and his father and the bank and so on, noting how sorry she was that so much time had passed since they had seen them and how terribly neglectful she had been; but now that he was here in Copenhagen and they would be visiting, the families must get together. Balancing jellied consommé on his spoon, Otto wondered how to get it to his mouth without spilling while trying to look at Cousin Ulla with each query and answer, agreeing that a meeting would be wonderful, although recalling his father's torment at that long past visit, he doubted another visit was in the offing. He decided that leaning forward, pigeon-like with each bite, awkward as it appeared, would be the best choice rather than risk splattering the quivering goo in his lap, which, adding insult to injury, he detested and could barely swallow. From the corner of his eye he noted cousin Niels, who most certainly must be versed in the proper technique for eating jellied soups, leaned forward as well—and on top of it all, this process was complicated by an irrepressible urge to look across the table at Kirsten. After the soup course, the stolen looks became more manageable and more numerous. Feigning interest in the gardens over her shoulders, his eyes bobbed back and forth from the garden glancing off her face, down the sensuous curve of her neck, drawn irresistibly to the outline of her breasts that rose and fell with each breath. Beneath the thin cloth with a slight squint to improve his focus, he thought he could catch the outline of her nipples, which made his glances uncontrollable. Kirsten cast her luminous blue eyes down and never met his gaze as it flashed by. Niels tore Otto's attention away. Holding out a bottle at arms length so Otto could read the label, asked if this wine met his standards. Otto, whose knowledge of wine amounted to red with meat and white with fowl, thought best to nod his approval, fearing his voice would crack with apprehension at being so imperiously tested. Beer was his drink and he ranked himself among the authorities there. Uncertain if he had approved a dreck or not, he vowed in the future no facts applicable to wine or any like matters important to the social class to which he now began to aspire would go unstudied. The wine splashed clear as garnet into the crystal ware and to Otto's untrained palate it made the perfect accompaniment for the roast lamb, julienne vegetables and the miniature potatoes that until he tasted them he failed to recognize. They were the size of large grapes and skittered away from the tines of his fork as he chased them around his plate. Hans ate in mouthfuls, finished quickly, stood, and with a stifled belch, hurried off to a tennis match.

The conversation began to flow easily after the second glass of wine. Kirsten left her wine untouched and spoke of concerts and sailing and shopping at the new shoe store that opened in town while they were away. Otto relaxed, stretched his feet beneath the table, brushing against Kirsten's calf and the sudden touch, unexpected and electrifying as an exposed wire, recoiled his legs with such force he jerked upright. Kirsten made no reaction, though he thought he detected a wisp of a smile. Her eyes did not seek his. By dessert he overcame the initial startle of her touch and emboldened by a third glass of wine, Otto ventured his foot out again seeking another touch, a message that might induce a look and smile. Advancing it inch-by-inch across the carpeted space under the table he suffered the disappointment that her legs were tucked under her chair secured well beyond his reach.

Cousin Niels placed his silverware across his dessert plate, looked up, settled back in his chair and in a serious tone that required a suitable answer asked, "Well Otto, what are you up to?" meaning, Otto deduced, his work and study, not the location of his feet which he quickly retrieved. A natural inquiry and Otto had anticipated it. Certain his mother had provided more information to Niels than his address and that, like any successful businessman and practiced negotiator, Niels knew the answer to the question before it had been asked, Otto sought to offer the truth, improved as best he could under the circumstances. He explained that he had withdrawn from the Royal Military Academy last fall after a little more than a year and had stayed at the farm to help his grandparents and uncle until this June and, when the spring planting was done, had come to

Copenhagen to learn business. He sat back, relieved the words had come smoothly without hesitation, but wondering if they had been effective.

"And so? Where and how?" His cousin persisted, his face drawn, his gaze fixed on Otto's face.

Otto explained that he had a room near the university so that he could audit courses, especially business ones, and in order to pay his expenses he clerked nights at a small hotel.

"Otto, that's not a proper way to proceed." His cousin replied; a statement of fact, sympathetically put, and though not a question, the pronouncement required an answer.

Otto didn't presume to ask his cousin what he thought to be "proper." He knew the answer: matriculate formally at the university and earn a degree, but he wouldn't denounce his father and tell the raw truth that he had been cut off by the angry bastard. Loyalty overcame the inclination and he suppressed the details of how he had been disowned and left to forage for learning on his own, and that this haphazard program of a so-called business education forced upon him by these circumstances was his only recourse. So, ashamed of a father, Otto evaded the question, and said with a smile, "I see it as a start. For the time being I read everything I can get my hands on … constantly," and trusted that this enthusiastic description of self-study would convey an understanding of his fierce determination to succeed or, better yet, that his cousin could discern the truth behind it all, making matters easier. At that moment, looking about, it came to Otto that the near forgotten visit to this house as a boy had introduced him to what money in abundance could provide and planted in him the early seed, heavily nourished today: the inexhaustible desire for all the trappings of wealth. That desire would shape his destiny. Here today clearly the first lesson was: when wealthy you needn't crawl over shit, it would not be expected of you. Someday he vowed he would have all this and more.

His cousin did not read his mind and spoke in a total disconnect as if thinking out loud, oblivious to listeners. "Your decision to leave the Academy sounds impetuous," he said. "Certainly it is better to change directions at your age, but putting myself in your shoes, you must have a degree, engineering, science—something useful." Without waiting for a reply, and as if signaled by the clank of the cup in the saucer following a sip of coffee, he changed subjects. "With the various factions taking advantage of the German inflation," he said, "I think Germany is in for more troubled times. Cousin Ulla and I have a business trip planned there but we are uncomfortable about the goings on…and may cut it short." He looked up and smiled at her, unquestionably making a concession to her wishes and she smiled back as if to say, cutting it short it will be. Otto tried to sound well informed. "The papers say that Social Democrat's victory over the Communists looks good for Germany, certainly much better for the economy," he said, leaning forward and studying Niels' face for an indication of agreement.

"You are right there," his cousin replied and gave up this subject as well. The rectangles of sunshine on the carpet had lengthened and the effects of the wine in the doldrums of the late afternoon led to a prolonged silence.

Kirsten studied her nails. Cousin Ulla broke into the silence by inquiring again about Cousin Astrid. Otto added she had become a substitute teacher in the elementary school and repeated that she still had not recovered from her grief years after Jorgen's death. These repetitive words ended the dinner. The family stood and walked single file to the sitting room.

It was time to leave. Ulla, in the entry hall holding the door, suggested that while she and Niels were traveling Kirsten and Otto might use their tickets to the Royal Theater. Otto accepted quickly as he knew enough about women and their artful manipulation of social parings and calendars that his sweet cousin would never dare make such an important suggestion without discussion and Kirsten's approval. They were to meet ten minutes before the play at the ticket window in two days. He had passed a muster of some kind.

• • •

Kurt lounged on one of the leather sofas in the lobby. It was eleven thirty and the place was empty. Otto sat on the arm and looked down on the barkeep.

"So who did you say your cousins were?" he asked, yawning, fighting sleep.

"Niels Larsen, import-export business."

"No shit?"

"No shit. What?"

"He's a major player! The company made buckets of money during the war, probably by selling to both sides. His name comes up in the bar a lot. Even in this economy and so on, the word is they still make out very well." A smile came over his face. "Did he offer you a job?" The subject matter was waking Kurt up.

"No."

"Too bad. He could put you on easy street. Why don't you ask him?"

"He thinks I need a formal education, engineering, science, things he could use," Otto replied, repeating what his cousin had said. Besides, Otto considered that asking now might jeopardize the developing relationship with Kirsten, at this point a more urgent objective.

"If you screw your courage up, don't forget your old pal here."

Chapter 4

Otto came early, Kirsten late. He picked up the tickets and stood pressed against the lobby wall by the ticket window where he could watch her come in, scanning the crowd on his toes, planning his hello, expecting at any moment to see her thread through the chattering crowd. Half an hour passed and then the brass doors to the theater swung open and the crowd poured into the theater, and the lobby like a drained aquarium, hushed to silent. He felt abandoned and flustered. The clerk at the ticket window gave him a puzzled look and slammed the little door shut. Kirsten had stood him up! Her nails at dinner held more interest than his remarks about the German economy. How could he have been so stupid? She hadn't raised her eyes to look at him. Not from modesty or reticence as he had thought but from boredom. He could hear that the play had begun. In the empty lobby the answer why she had not come became clear. He heard her imaginary voice shout in his ear, "Hush up, you're a damned fool. Some expert!" Otto looked at his watch and relying on the small chance that some mishap had held her up, decided he would endure another ten minutes before leaving. Taking a posture of sham nonchalance he wandered about, hands clasped behind his back, studying every detail of the lobby posters that pictured scenes from some future play, bending over to read the small print of the minor cast listings, reading names he had no intention of remembering, his mind in a fog, unfocused beyond any comprehension, as if looking at hieroglyphics.

She came through the door and smiled when she saw him as though her tardiness was of no consequence and might well have been expected. A white shawl covered her bare shoulders and fluttered back over her blue dress as she glided across the lobby.

"Otto, you are not interested in this silly play, are you?" she said, ignoring his "Hello."

"No, not at all, most certainly not."

"Let's go to Tivoli, to one of the open air places."

They walked. The evening was warm, a fresh breeze off the Oresund swept down from the scattered clouds above, cooling the streets filled with strollers. She took his arm when they reached Longangstraede. In the park they waited at the entrance of a café under an old tree festooned with small lights. A table came open, and as they moved toward it, he felt her breast brush against his arm. Nothing indiscreet, just a brush, but no accident he was convinced. She glanced about for familiar faces as they passed between the tables and to his great relief she recognized no one. He ordered Rhine wine. She removed her white summer gloves, pulling them off finger by finger, and inclined her head, squinting at him as if studying a piece of art she might buy, imagining how she could use it, where it would fit. The light from the lamps strung among the branches above sparkled in her sun bleached hair and lit the string of pearls that glowed white against the tan skin of her neck.

"Tell me about the Military Academy, I've always been interested in that," she said, giving him a smile for encouragement. He knew her reason for the question, she wanted to know why he had left; had he been thrown out, disgraced himself in some way, and if he refused to talk she would conclude that he had been involved in some indiscretion that was beyond explanation or forgiveness. He obliged her with the tale of the cow dropping and found her so sympathetic that she reached for his hand, her gold charm bracelet making small clicks on the metal table top, her eyes drawing his eyes to hers in an expression of understanding, even compassion. Life for Otto as he knew it, untroubled and orderly, changed at that instant. She aroused the most primal of cravings; he wanted her in the most fundamental of ways, thoughts of a single-minded objective erupted, obliterating any orderly thought processes in his mind. Totally unpracticed in the affairs of the heart, or more to the point, seduction, his school boy preparation amounted to only whispered fantasies about the hoped for result, but they provided no practical instructions on the art of attainment. The objective, he thought, would require care, reading of subtle signals, but mainly reliance on his intuition, his only resource, inadequate as that was. Success lay on the narrow path between audacity and timidity. He had no choice but to proceed because he had little control over this feral thing or understanding of how to keep it in check. He would tread lightly, look for an opening, and push ahead on any pathways she left open.

The conversation drifted to details about families, summer vacations, and the farm where he spent his summer. She told of the big house by the coast where she spent her summers, croquet on the lawn and the secret midnight swims at the beach that set his imagination aflame. She spoke of the *nouveaux riches* who had bought houses and moved next door there. And how her mother snubbed them and how that had bothered her. He consoled her, telling her he understood, but in truth was thrilled her sympathies were with the self-made people, as the *nouveaux riches* were precisely the people he yearned to join.

"Tell me about your work," she said with genuine interest.

"As you know I'm the night clerk at the Dahlberg House," he began, "it's a small hotel near Fiolstraede, forty rooms, mostly business travelers. There is a bar and lounge and they attract some unusual fellows." Her inquisitive look encouraged him, and since the evening had gone well thus far, he decided to hint at his intentions with an amusing story and study her reaction to it. "There is one special customer, a very successful businessman from Malmo, Bjorn somebody, who returns every month for three days, and each time with a different woman that he signs for on the register as his wife. I of course make no indication that I notice. These women are always lovely, one more splendid than the next. But he has a problem. After a few drinks he can't remember the new lady's name. Last month after three tries, the lady stood and shouted 'my name is Inga, can't you remember that!' and she poured a glass of wine on his head, turned and walked out. He didn't flinch; it was beautiful, he just sat there, absolute aplomb, Chablis running down his face dripping off his chin onto the bar. And then what did he do, he ordered the lady another drink! 'In case she comes back,' he said, 'she'll need more ammunition!' A typical Swede! Indomitable! And, you know what? This week he was back with a new one!" Kirsten seemed amused. Otto was proud of the words "aplomb" and "indomitable" and mused to himself that the boarding school vocabulary list had paid off—when her question abruptly brought him back to reality.

"You admire this man?" Her smile hadn't faded, but he noted her eyes had narrowed, as if she was trying to see something through a haze. The Swede was rich, tough, self-made and had his choice of beautiful women.

Admired? Otto thought; if he had a word to describe his feelings, he would have used revered.

"Oh, no, not at all. He's such a cad!" He said with emphasis. "I just thought it an amusing story."

"Indomitable, because he bested the women?"

"No, I meant it like pigheaded, not fazed by common sense. Keeps coming back, doesn't recognize defeat."

"You do idolize him Otto, don't deny it."

She had picked up on his implied meaning and turned it about knowing he could neither speak of his intentions for telling the story nor confess to his admiration for the womanizer. He had lied ineptly and she recognized that before her sat a rank beginner, and she, schooled in wiles of the beautiful and rich now took control of the relationship. He attempted to regain the initiative directing the conversation once again to neutral ground.

"When do you start school?"

She was matter of fact. "In ten days I go to Paris. I'll be living for a year with a French family, attending the Sorbonne, perfecting my French." He fought to keep the reaction from his face, leaning back into the shadows and lifting his glass for another drink of wine. She looked at her watch and remarked that the play must be getting out soon. Carl was to meet her outside the theater after the play.

"Who's Carl?" He asked trying to sound unmoved but fearing she had plans to meet someone else. Carl, she explained, was her father's driver. Leaving Tivoli, Otto took her hand. They strolled without talking. The theater was dark, the play long over. A lone car waited in front. With a brief hug, a squeeze of his hand, a wave through the car window, she was gone.

Kurt sat in his usual spot on the couch in the lobby when Otto walked in. After a short review of the time with Kirsten that evening, Kurt interjected, "Did she tell you her grandfather committed suicide in that summer house?" Otto shook his head 'no', not certain this was something he wanted to hear. "Yeah, the old man shot himself sitting in his overcoat at his desk out there in the middle of winter. Left a note apologizing to his wife, saying he couldn't go on. A police detail went looking for him when he hadn't come home. They found him stone cold, frozen stiff as a board; they couldn't even straighten him out. Finally they carried him out sitting in the chair. The company was going under from the inflation, new taxes, competition. The old man couldn't take the stress of loosing it." Kurt had an intimate knowledge of the family, apparently he knew as much or more than Kirsten did. "Niels took it over. I heard it was real touch and go for him but he put it back together, refinancing, new loans and so forth. The guy knows finance, and I hear he's a very tough negotiator, always gets his way."

It was another one of the nights that Kurt sapped of his resolve to leave and dreading the thought of an empty house, stayed on to talk. The bar had become, for all practical purposes, his refuge. He held court there, trading stories, making friends, greeting old ones; never bored or lonely. He poured good drinks that ensured a healthy clientele—if management only knew how good. Otto admired him. Not because he had money or women, in fact he had neither, but because he was master of his fate, in control of his life. As Otto saw it, Kurt had achieved his primary goal, happiness. In fact the best kind of happiness, the self-generated kind that was not reliant in any way on external parameters. Kurt accepted his lot with no change required; a fellow who sought nothing more emotionally, physically, or financially. And bartending, Otto saw that the job suited him, menial as it was, he had taken it to the level of an art form, made a true profession of it. With a gift for words that flowed effortlessly and a mind that could take a position and defend it with skill, and without offending, what a lawyer he would have made!

But Kurt's principle avocation was that of listener and this skill Otto took to heart. Drinks aside, that's how Kurt made friends. He lent a sympathetic ear to downfallen clients, had a talent for bucking them up. But most importantly, the bar was his listening post. Here patrons would confide. Little bits of information, here and there, Kurt put together with other bits he had remembered and then assembled a picture of what was going on around Copenhagen. He learned about events in business and politics, long before the news reached the newspapers if ever they did: like the closely held secret that old man Larsen's death was not natural as the papers reported, that he had shot himself. It was clear to Otto little happened in Copenhagen that escaped him, especially when his old friends from the police force came in. Many times Otto watched Kurt pay for their drinks to induce them to linger and talk. If he had traded on the information he drew out what a fortune could have been made—an important lesson!

"No, she made no mention of her grandfather," Otto replied, "and I sure didn't see any hint of financial problems."

"Well, I understand her brother, what's his name, Hans, works for a firm in Stockholm and will come back to the company one day to run it."

To avoid comment Otto stared through the lobby windows out to the nearly empty streets. Kurt noting Otto to be lost in thought, left.

Otto settled in for the evening shift at the front desk just as the phone rang. "Otto, it's been two days and you haven't called." The voice teased, not a schoolgirl tease, but soft and friendly. He leaned back in his chair, smiling at the ceiling as he picked his words, as if a lexicon was printed there. He needed the right combination so as not to appear uninterested on one hand or over-anxious on the other. Before he could answer, Kirsten went on, "I'm tired of packing, why don't you come out here tomorrow for lunch?"

"What time?" was all he managed to get out.

"Eleven." And she was gone.

In the morning he filled the communal tub for a hot bath, washed his hair and slicked it down with a brush, shaved, trimmed his nails and put on the sport clothes he had bought for just such an occasion. Pushing the bicycle that leaned against the wall of his room out to the street he started for the Larsen house. He rode slowly through patches of broken sunlight along a path shaded by trees and cooled by the breezes off the Oresund. It was a beautiful day for anything, and high on anticipation he let his mind drift, not knowing what direction lunch and the afternoon would take. In twenty minutes he pushed the bicycle along the front walk and leaned it against the porch railing. Kirsten answered his knock. She wore a light robe with a sash at the waist and slippers. Smiling, she beckoned him inside. "Daddy gave cook and maid a holiday while they are traveling," she said, anticipating questions he might have as to their whereabouts. "So you will have to put up with what I put together. Probably make us both ill."

She led him to the right, through the dining room and on through a large pantry with cabinets filled to the ceiling with plates and glassware and then into the large kitchen. A rectangular metal-topped worktable filled the center of the room. An icebox stood next to a refrigerator against the outer wall, an apparent testament to the cook's lack of faith in the reliability of the new electrical appliance. There was a double-sided stone sink and opposite it a large, black stove. The stove was cold. Kirsten picked up a tray she had prepared from the sideboard and turning out of the kitchen led Otto down a short passage to a room, large and to his surprise, windowless, which clearly was planned as a space for servants, but he realized had been appropriated by the family. There were bookshelves on two walls haphazardly filled with books, magazines, and family photographs; and on the other walls hung paintings of landscapes set in ornamental gold frames. Two commodious chairs flanked by side tables and floor lamps extended from the corners. A dark red oriental rug covered the floor. A comfortable looking overstuffed couch with end tables took up the space before the remaining wall and Otto took a seat there. She placed the tray with a plate of cheese, sliced meats, crackers and two glasses of wine before him on a butler's table. Lunch was served.

Kirsten walked around the table, and sat down beside him; grazing his arms and thighs with movement that broke open the sash of her robe, exposing a band of the shear, white silk slip; and he could see, by the light and dark that filtered through the thin cloth, there was nothing beneath. She turned her face up, he accepted the invitation, and kissed her. Not a word spoken, the ardor of her response encouraged him and she, anticipating his confusion, favored his advances, then resisting gently for a moment, then submitting, using the momentary torments to heightened their desire. The softness of her body surprised him, and as his hand moved the cloth away and drifted about, from the pliant peaks of her breasts to the steamy valley that lay open between her thighs; the sensate beauty of her nakedness brought an intensity beyond any he had known. If absolute beauty could be sensation, he had found it and she welcomed it. Her fingers danced down his buttons, opening his clothes, inviting his participation in her state of undress. Soon he lay over her and in response to an upturn of her hips, they slipped together, joined in slick rhythm soon accompanied by her barely perceptible shudders. The exquisite caress that wrapped him he hoped would never end; but too soon a perverse impulse deep in his member's base called for release, and he pulled free.

He was immediately ashamed. How badly did he fail, he wondered, but embarrassed would not ask? Though he would never have told her so, this was his first; and like a potent drug, the experience addicted immediately. With an understanding smile she smoothed his essence over her belly, and looked into his eyes, sat up and leaned forward, gave him a soft kiss, stood, stretched, closed her robe and concluded he was easy.

Lunch now was an afterthought and had the tray not sat before them, the idea would have been abandoned. She talked of all the packing she had left to do and laughed about how she would never get all the clothes she needed in two suitcases and, thank heavens, a trunk that would be sent after her. She handed Otto a cracker with cheese while talking on about Paris, heedless of the distress these offhand words produced in her smitten lover. Clearly she was unmoved by any significance these glorious past moments had for him, moments that he would have given the world to repeat in triumph, as the victor, unrelenting driving until she became exhausted and begged him to stop. Although he remained rational enough to realize her plans to go had been made long before, he thought he would explode listening to them and if he spoke he would just prolong the agony. So he sat silent. Besides, what could he say? Talk of his business courses or small plans that would have bored them both? Talk of the weather seemed less dull. What they had begun, for that day, was past revisiting. Kirsten would return to her packing and Otto, relieved she provided an excuse, departed, but not before arranging with a sequel in mind to meet her at the sidewalk café at the Hotel D'Angleterre in two days. She needed to shop.

That afternoon he lay on his bed watching shadows creep across the ceiling, and thoughts of her restored his erection, which in addition to his recollections of the perfect morning, stirred up the sediment from the recesses of his soul a murky cloud of guilt. He had broken one of the tenants of strict Protestantism. That much he understood, but the question was one of degree. The Ten Commandments provided the structure on which he was expected to model his life and each Sunday as a small boy they had been inculcated and reinforced with the threat of eternal damnation if abandoned. Murder, thievery, and lying were simple concepts, and as a child he had understood those. But sexual conduct was another matter—more complex, more desirable, and far more likely. Adultery, the only commandment that concerned sex, had no description of the boundaries, what this commandment truly encompassed, and finally, how lenient would be God's interpretation? The literal meaning was clear, but details, even in the most oblique, whispered terms, were resolutely avoided in church, and at home. Despite his lack of religious inclination, he was fearful … as the only God he knew, the God of Martin Luther, was uncompromising and probably not, as he yearned for that afternoon, a God who would understand. The oft sung hymn, *A Mighty Fortress is Our God,* Luther's hymn, described the Devil's power, and as a small boy scared the Hell out of him. The message was simple, be good or be damned!

Taking a rational approach, Otto searched his memory for any instruction on the limits of sexual conduct he had received. As a child when he had come upon his mother undressed she would cover herself. There, lesson one, the sight of the female body forbidden. As a seven year old he had broken that rule behind the barn one summer afternoon with Johanne, a young girl from the farm across the road. The sight of her bare body, the line between her thighs that ended where the creases above her legs all pointed at the same magical place—that image became imprinted on Otto's brain as it had with all males since time immemorial: indelible and erotic. He could see it now, plain as day. He wondered if she remembered his prepubescent "thing" as well. The whole episode lasted ten seconds before she ran home. He never told anyone.

His father, incapable of discussing sex, never mentioned the subject. His mother's only related advice was that he should respect women, whatever that meant. The basic mechanics of copulation could not be lost on anyone who had spent time on a farm. In grade school the subject was covered by a short chapter in a science book illustrated with stick people. The stick man had a stick erection with dashes coming out. There was no stick woman, only dashes going into a line drawing of a uterus. Real sex education began in boarding school, taught after hours by a boy who had four sisters and knew about menses. Otto didn't believe him at first. Then he learned there were whores. You could buy sex! Wonderful! Another boy had a deck of playing cards from Hamburg stolen from his older brother, fifty-two nudes. Passed around again and again, the deck became shorter and shorter. During these reflections Otto concluded that his father, a schoolboy himself, must have depended on the fact that boys educate themselves and thereby excused himself from the unsavory duty.

To a roommate who entered the school for the final year, Otto owed a special debt. 'Buzzy' Harnsworth, son of an English diplomat and Danish mother, awaked one morning with an erection, leapt from bed, applied a ruler and in a loud voice announced the measurement. Over the following week, the application of rulers became a morning ritual for occupants of the third floor, and the measurements, many fanciful, were called up and down the hall. Otto found, to his relief, he had nothing to worry about. Thus ended his review, and still unable to define the limits of Godly tolerance, he concluded damnation or not, there would be no alteration in his plans to his pursue these pleasures and he returned to his dreams of the next meeting with Kirsten.

"She played you like a fiddle," Kurt laughed. Seated on the couch, he looked around to ensure the lobby was empty. The rain soaked street shone like gun metal in the reflected light from the window. It was almost midnight.

"It's the oldest game in the world, and women have always been the master of it. Brains over brawn, that's what I've always said. From the days of the caveman they figured out how to make us think we were in charge. Run out there and spear a tiger for supper, Sonny Boy, and out they'd go, hoping to get something in return." He paused, anticipating

Otto might defend himself at this point. With no response, he continued. "Otto, look at your situation here. She had it planned to the last detail, to the minute, probably days in advance. It came naturally to her. You didn't have a chance. Like a fly in a web. Going for lunch—you were lunch!" He leaned back on the couch, laughing, head turning from side to side, muttering "rich, rich."

"Yeah, I was a happy fly," Otto retorted, trying to save some respect, though he enjoyed the joke.

"What happened when you met her the other day?"

"Nothing."

"Nothing! What do you mean, nothing?"

"As you say, my plans fell through. I wanted to take her back to my room, but after some conversation at the sidewalk café—and I did drop big hints—she said she absolutely had to do some last minute shopping. So shopping we went. And then she left."

Kurt twisted the knife once more.

"Where's she now?"

"Paris." This subject was exhausted. Otto changed it.

"What's the story with the fellow from Malmo who shows up every month or so with a different wife?" Otto asked.

"Bjorn? That son-of-a-bitch. Rich as Hell. He owns a hardwood lumber business, sells to furniture manufacturers. Makes sales-calls on customers here in Denmark and Germany. The ladies? The lady that comes every once in a while, she's one of his secretaries; I don't know where he gets the other ones. Most are real nice, but you're thinking of the one who dumped the drink. Never saw her again. He never mentions it."

"Is he married?" Otto asked.

"Told me his wife's unable, you know what I mean." The tone of his voice implied he thought the truth amounted to something more than inability.

"Does that make it okay?" Otto had come to trust Kurt's opinions on most matters though this area, morality, was new. He needed an answer.

"Who am I to judge? Adultery? You could say as long as it doesn't do any harm, what's the difference? But sometimes it could spell serious trouble, I've certainly seen that." Kurt paused as his mind conjured up some domestic crimes too gruesome to describe. "As far as I can tell, what he's up to isn't too bad as long as he isn't caught or better yet if his wife doesn't care or one of the ladies doesn't think it amounts to more than it does." Kurt leaned back in the couch and spread his arms across the back. "And who knows what she may be up to, maybe the same thing. It's a two-sided thing; the ladies have to come from somewhere. Who might they be cheating on?" Kurt paused again, recalling some of the bar's customers. "It's pretty common as a matter of fact. There are a lot worse things, I suppose."

"So you see no problem with it?"

"It's not for me, but who knows."

"Do you think God has a problem with it?"

"Now Otto, that's way too deep for me."

"What about what I've been up to?

"Shit Otto, that's nothing. I don't think God would even notice."

Kurt swung his body off the couch and headed for the door.

Chapter 5

Shortly following Kirsten's departure, Otto filled an empty afternoon writing a thoughtful, soul baring letter to his mother, the first in several years, and upon reading it she recognized his loneliness and wrote back that day that she didn't know why Paris was such an attraction for Kirsten, she could learn French perfectly well in Denmark; and furthermore, why should Paris be called the City of Light, certainly Copenhagen deserved that title, and since Kirsten had abandoned the city (and Otto as well, which she left unsaid), he should go out and enjoy himself. He read the letter without reaction, his comprehension impervious to any suggestions that would lift him from his melancholy, despite the fact that three days of rainy weather had cleared and Copenhagen became once again splendidly beautiful; the afternoon sunlight caught by the windows along the walking streets tossed about flashing through the crystalline air, the leaves on the park trees, shined by the rains, shimmered red and gold in the soft breezes; the open squares that bulged with young people had not an empty seat at the tables beneath the bright red and white umbrellas.

Otto roamed with no sense of order, mechanically exploring dark consoling places: the used bookshops where he mindlessly pawed through the dusty shelves and bins finding an occasional gem, the dimly lit antiques shops where, though he had no intention of a purchase, the relics formed up memories that helped the time to pass, and his final refuge, the indoor cafes where amidst the bustle he sat alone, reviewing the audit list he would take at the University. The business school concept was new and though he had heard it had become popular at several universities, he had no concrete knowledge of what the curriculum should be and therefore, forced to design a program, he registered for lectures he determined useful for the study of business consisting primarily of Economics and Accounting. However, soon after the classes began he became caught up in the spellbinding biographies of the great businessmen and studied at the registration desk in the gray hours of early mornings the stories of Ford, Rockefeller, Nobel, Rothschild and Krupp as well as Denmark's own titans F.L. Smidth and also Moeller. He scoured the pages for hints of the methods for their success, carefully writing down what he thought relevant in a small notebook he bought for the purpose. He admitted freely to himself, his goal now, was to become very rich. The vague dreams he first allowed himself to have in the cold farmhouse attic became enlarged following the visit to his cousin's home and since his time with Kirsten took on fresh urgency and heightened resolve. It was very clear that Kirsten could not marry a man of moderate means. One afternoon shopping with her had underscored that.

Again the sermons of Pastor Svensen plagued him. The painful recollections of the fiery denouncement of riches from the pulpit had followed him like a hungry beggar on his long walks down the cobbled streets of Old Town and along the canal where gradually he worked things through: no matter the heavenly consequences, the pursuit of wealth would be the path he would follow. Acquired wealth, he rationalized, was but the byproduct of success and served only as a marker, a measurement of the hard work and the perseverance required. And once obtained, he concluded, wealth had innumerable uses beyond mere pleasure—good works: majestic gifts to the poor, to schools, to libraries and museums. Yes, he assured himself, here was the answer to all this discomfort: the practice of philanthropy, generosity on a grand scale! This had to be God's answer too! For Otto's conscience his future beneficence, planned generosity , it would serve as deific balm; this must be the repayment expected by the Almighty for temporal success, and therefore it followed, these worldly alms would be acceptable in the firmament. Heaven's gates remained open. At last that was settled.

That Tuesday Otto sat at his desk and began a letter filled with news, rewritten, crossed out and edited; he refined paragraphs and pages over the course of a week. Letter writing, ignored as an onerous duty required during his school days, now became an intense struggle as he hungered to compose something of merit with pen on paper: appealing, amusing, and newsy. Something that would hold her attention long enough to trick her imagination into believing him clever. He drafted five pages filled with everyday events that he embellished with glowing adjectives and multiple exclamation points: the classes he sat in on, small trips about the city, a few of the inconsequential people he had met during his wanderings, and best of all, selected stories from the bar, carefully edited. Not until the last sentence did he mention he missed her, although, that essentially was all the letter said. He signed it "Sincerely, Otto" and mailed it that afternoon to the address she had given him. The following day he found a light pink envelope in his mailbox. Inside, on a page of perfumed paper covered on both sides in stylized script, there was a description the train trip and the French family with whom she was staying and ending, as her classes were to begin in the morning, with a hasty "Must go, Love, Kirsten"

His face lit on fire. What an imbecile he was, "sincerely"! My God, he thought, how could he have been so stilted, so formal, so unaffectionate, so stupid? Desperate, he wrote back immediately, filling one sheet between salutation and signature with scraps of information, whatever entered his head, a chance meeting and a found book, but ending with the sign off, written conspicuously large, "Love, Otto." He walked directly to the post office and mailed it. He waited more than a month for a reply. She wrote describing her classes and how wonderful Paris was. That was her last letter.

Unfortunately for Otto, this was not a time in Europe for the fulfillment of dreams for financial success. The devastation of the Great War, and the cold economic reality produced by the crippling German inflation created in Denmark only lost jobs and pay cuts. Business at the proud Dahlberg, in better times brisk, had declined to a trickle, leaving the once pleasant lobby shabby and frequently empty. In better days the hotel had been worthy of royalty. But now, the windows in the past hung with sweeping red velvet draperies were now barren, the chandeliers and sconces, since management removed half the bulbs, glowed dimly, and the dance floor where couples once twirled to Viennese waltzes were scuffed and unvarnished. The hotel had sunk beneath the economic miasma of war and recession. Now the lobby was occupied by beleaguered travelers with their tattered luggage sitting on the worn furniture, and the few employees that stayed on, desperate to hold on to the jobs remaining, accepted one reduction after another, Otto among them. As long as Kurt remained, Otto told himself, he would work and if need be for nothing.

Despite the humble wages, Otto felt fortunate, not so much for the employment, but because the hours suited him. Before sunrise he read and after returning to his room for a good morning's sleep, he was free to prowl the city and attend one or two classes a week. Kurt's salary, Otto later learned, had not been reduced, but raised by the owners who were thankful that at least the bar remained a reliable source of kroner.

Still not a word from Kirsten, though in December he found in his generally empty mailbox an invitation to a Christmas party from his cousins providing him with the excuse he needed to call the house, eager to talk with her. The brusque maid, whose voice he could identify and had hoped to avoid, answered and noted down his name, and made no attempt to conceal her pleasure in telling him that Miss Larsen's schedule anticipated her arrival the day before the party.

Otto took a cab. The Christmas lights from the windows of the brightly-lit house reflected off the snow, and the heavy wooden door that ordinarily stood defiant against intruders stood open, permitting a broken rectangle of light from within to spill out, illuminating the arriving guests. His cousins stood in the entryway welcoming their friends and handing the lady's wraps and gentlemen's coats off to the bustling servants, and then pointed guests toward the baronial living room on the left. After a few pleasantries with Niels and Ulla, Otto walked into the room warmed by an immense Yule log blazing in the fireplace. The grand space, redolent of the mingled scents of burning wood, perfume, Christmas spices and pine bows held a throng of people dressed in evening clothes, standing about engaged in banal conversations. Otto knew no one and absent the desire to see Kirsten would not have endured the agony of chatter with strangers with whom he held no common interests, relevance or status. He spoke of the weather with a stylish woman in a long red silk dress and wearing ruby and diamond combs in her hair, while her husband, disinterested, fondled his drink and rocked back and forth on his heels. At last, at the far end of the room standing in a group near the Christmas tree he had caught sight of Kirsten, as she with a sidewise glance, recognized him. Her smile invited him over and she welcomed him with the briefest of hugs, the stiffness of which failed to dampen the passion that had been fueled by months of molten memories and suppressed desire. He clasped her hand between his warmly, and to his dismay, she withdrew it immediately and turned to introduce Robert, a houseguest, an American with doughy skin and crooked teeth with whom she made a point of speaking French. Unsophisticated as Otto was in the unspoken language of courtship, the cool gesture, an affront beyond his wildest imaginings, could not be lost on him. He could not fathom a reason for her interest in this interloper other than, of course, the gift of Mammon, wealth. Speaking in Danish she made the introduction to Otto to which Robert, not comprehending a word nodded devotedly. Reading Otto's mind she could have called him a dolt, a flaming asshole, and smiling he would have shaken Otto's hand; but she didn't. Otto hid the shame he felt from his forwardness and the intensity of his anger he felt during the nonsensical conversation with the American he attempted using kindergarten English. Betrayed, rejected, relegated to the human trash heap, his breath became ragged, and within a minute he managed to utter a clumsy excuse for moving away, something about he would go for a drink, that she, wide-eye with feigned disbelief, accepted.

As he threaded through the room toward the door, Cousin Niels raised a hand, interrupting his escape in order to inquire how Otto's studies were progressing. As Otto listed his courses Niels' eyes scoured the room nodding to a guest here, raising his glass to another over there. With a shrug and a remark to the effect that if Otto qualified for a degree he should inquire about a position with the company, Niels walked away. That evening Otto felt shipwrecked, and like a drowning man he would hold on to this impromptu offer, a piece of verbal flotsam, all that could be salvaged from this disastrous night.

Kirsten watched him walk away as she bit into a Christmas sweet. She considered her liaisons as nothing serious. An heiress to what for the time was substantial wealth, she did not suffer rebuff from those with whose hearts she so carelessly toyed. She regarded these amorous dalliances as practice to sharpen her skills for enticement and reaffirm her powers of seduction, games to be played biding the time until she would face the more serious challenge of finding a suitable match, a man who would be a proper addition to the proud Larsen legacy. So she thought, tomorrow or the next day she would make it right with Otto; a few happy, well chosen, oblivious words would be all that it would take to lead him on again, ignoring what was foremost, his failure to understand. After all, for the time being, he served as a perfect escort, tall and handsome and with a stripling body that would satisfy that certain desire from time to time. And with the amusing stories he told and the grand appearance he made on her arm served to generate the envy of her friends, and that she found especially delicious. She could not bear to toss him away, but limitations were limitations, though for now, those pecuniary considerations could wait.

It was a cold, moonlit night. As matter of thrift, with his hands stuffed into the pockets of his overcoat and bent into the wind that blew off the frigid water, Otto walked the several miles back to the hotel. It was nine-thirty when he reached the hotel bar.

"Back early?" The words, an intentional barb, were spoken with mock cheer. Kurt could read the anger in Otto's face as soon as he entered and relished the opportunity to needle his young friend and expected a vigorous, informative retort, for this was the old barman's game. Time had made him a master and at the heart of it, Kurt as barroom psychologist prodded for news of lives he studied from afar, a voyeur, enjoying a peak into another world now and then. His method applied this night with all the subtlety of a hammer blow came accompanied by a gesture of goodwill in the form of a glass of beer slid over the bar. That would open Otto up. Otto shoved the beer back, spilling some, and Kurt made a ritual of carefully wiping it up before he poured the rest in the sink. Otto asked for hot wine and wrapped his cold hands around the mug.

"No go?" Kurt fished again for news.

"Bitch!" Otto cursed, "She brought a rich American home for the holidays." At that point Otto assumed all Americans that traveled to Paris to be incredibly rich.

"Wasn't some friend of the family?" Kurt asked, knowing it wasn't the case.

"No. Kirsten held his hand."

"Oh, a 'him'," Kurt said pretending surprise.

Otto had finished taking bait. Staring down at the steam rising from the red liquid he muttered. "I'm going to Arhus for Christmas. My father has softened some."

"What the Hell," Kurt observed.

• • •

The melting sleet that fell like icy tears fueled Otto's dejection. When he approached the door in Arhus and his mother drying her hands on a dishtowel answered his knock, he struggled to make a small smile. When she embraced him he could feel her bones through her clothes, the warm, soft body he had snuggled against as a child now shrunken and withered, parched and made frail by time. Gone, left to memory, the mother of his childhood who gave him hot baths and wrapped him in thick, fragrant towels.

Determined that Christmas be celebrated Astrid had assembled the same arrangements of pine branches, ribbons and balls that each year she had hung about the mantle and woven through the uprights of the staircase. She bought a small tree that Otto placed in the corner by the window and they decorated it together before pulling back the drapes so it could be seen from the street. When they finished, they sat at the end of the dining room table, sipping coffee, talking softly, a small plate of cookies between them. She asked about his work, courses, and the cousins. They all were well, he told her, including Kirsten, making no special mention of her by lumping her with the others. He could not speak about her without the jealous frustration boiling up and pouring forth and destroying whatever pleasantry remained. The room, in the dreary afternoon light, the dark wood paneled walls, the heavy walnut furniture, the brown seat covers and window drapes, depressed him. After their words had run out, his mother stood and cleared the coffee cups and cookie plate, remarking with a sigh that his father would be home in an hour. A small pile of wrapped gifts was stacked on an otherwise barren buffet. Otto would have preferred to be back in Copenhagen, alone in his sparse room with his books.

He climbed the stairs, tossed his suitcase on his boyhood bed and threw his coat over a chair. He opened the door to Jorgen's room. Nothing had been removed, it sat unchanged. Jorgen's rock collection and lead soldiers stood still on the windowsills, his books arranged as he left them on the shelves, and his clothes hung in the closet. Otto ran his finger over the bedside table, marking the dust. Returning to the living room, Otto lit a match to the paper and kindling in the fireplace and watched absentmindedly while the logs caught fire, then walked to the kitchen. His mother stood peeling potatoes; the cook and maid, no longer necessary in the small household, had been discharged.

When he came next to her, she said, "Otto, you know I never loved him. Not like young people today love and marry."

"How do you mean?"

"It was expected then—the convention, he was eligible, I was eligible."

"Never loved him?"

"I knew it when I married him. I tried to love him, I thought I could, but along came Jorgen and you and I had my own world. I didn't need him any longer. For years we tolerated one another, a kind of awkward, empty relationship. When Jorgen died I began to hate and now, as if it could be possible, I hate him all the more because of how he treats you. He comes home, asks what's for supper, and sits with his paper. I let him be." She turned to take a pan from beneath the stove and when she stood, Otto saw the tears that had formed. "If he didn't come home I wouldn't notice. If he died I'd have more feeling for a dead fish. If he went away with another woman, found a mistress, I would celebrate. But who would be fool enough to have him?" She laughed weakly. "I shouldn't be saying these things to you, he's your father. I'm sorry, Otto," Turning, looking him in the eye, she said. "No, Otto, now it's beyond hate; all the passion has drained now. I don't know the word for how empty I feel."

They heard the front door open and close, the sounds of an overcoat being shed and hung in the closet, and a throat clearing. She dried her hands on her apron and blotted the tears from her cheeks. Otto, prepared for any adversity the moment might bring, felt a tightening of his jaw. Peder entered the room and said "good evening" to them both as they stood there, then took an uncomfortable step toward Otto and put out his hand to shake, all the while looking at the floor. No nastiness, no caustic words, only stilted formality that Otto accepted, satisfied to have any greeting. His father then withdrew with his newspaper under his arm, passing through the dining room to his chair before the fire.

At dinner that evening a small revelation; Otto found the conversation proceeded without the customary atmosphere of an interrogation. His father, the Grand Inquisitor of his youth, the uncompromising Torquemada de Arhus, no longer sat in judgment but made casual talk, safe subjects and no mention of the banishment, or an apology, or explanation for why it was lifted. Otto surmised his mother had prevailed, had argued for the Christmas together. Otto had earned acceptance of some sort. With dessert and coffee, Peder turned the conversation to a more serious matter.

The bank was in trouble. No surprise, Otto thought. Banks everywhere were in trouble. A second disclosure, however, was more troubling. In a voice flat and barely audible, Peder spoke, his shoulders slumped and as if speaking to his plate said that he was under investigation. His hand shook with a fine tremor that rattled the saucer as he set his cup down. His face was ashen when he looked up and Otto detected a rim of tear on his lower lids.

"Bad loans." He said.

"You review all the loans don't you?" Otto asked.

"These were hidden from me. Of course, I insist on signing off on everything!" The mounting anger vitalized him. His back stiffened once again and his voice strengthened. "They forged my signature! And lied about it! Boundless perfidy!"

Otto pressed his father, curious. "So the investigators believe them, not you?"

Peder shouted, "Otto, do you think I'm naïve or stupid! I run the bank! I picked up the unexplained losses! I called our auditors! I found the bad accounts!"

"Then it's not a problem; fire those responsible."

With a sarcastic plea Peder taunted, "Don't you get it? They are gone, fired! My signature is the problem! My career! It went on under my nose!"

Peder searched Otto's eyes, seeking a sign of understanding. There had been too much said before for compassion now. Astride's hand had been three inches from his father's. A small act of tenderness to put her hand on his was beyond her. The three sat at the table silently for several minutes until Peder pushed his chair back and without a word more went up the stairs. Otto helped his mother clear the table and wash the dishes.

"What do you think?" Otto asked, as she had remained silent during the tirade about the bank.

"I don't know what to think," the emotionless, untrusting answer.

The next evening they celebrated Christmas by the fireplace, quietly exchanging unwrapped gifts. Otto thought of Kirsten and imagined her seated on the floor with her legs tucked under a long skirt, colorful scraps of torn wrapping paper scattered about her on the rug, the servants bustling around the large house, the food, the countless delicious smells, the drinks, the toasts, and the laughter. Astrid gave Otto a box of stationary and pen, a reminder, she said, that she lived for his letters, and a heavy wool sweater she had knit because he had mentioned that his room was drafty. Otto had brought jellies for his mother and a belt for his father. There was no further talk of the bank or the loans. Following church Christmas morning he began the trip to back Copenhagen, welcoming, once again his freedom.

Chapter 6

Otto had been back in Copenhagen for a day. The bar closed for the night, Kurt had gone, and at eleven fifty the phone at the registration desk rang and the ring ricocheted about the marble walls of the empty lobby with such intensity that he dropped his book and dived for the receiver, grabbing it to shut it down.

"Otto, where did you go? I looked around and you were gone. I missed you." He was stunned by her insouciance. Was she blind to his wounding? Masking the depth of his feelings, suppressing the urge to shout, he remained mute. Undeterred by the icy silence she went on, her voice playful, as if nothing of concern had happened, as if their friendship and their intimacy, the significance of which he never fully understood, could go on, unchanged. Pressed finally to fill a lengthening pause, he said that he felt sick. It was an unplanned lie and Kirsten knew instinctively it was not true.

"Well, I didn't want to leave without saying good-bye. I'll miss you, you know."

Otto ignored her tempting that he had begun to understand to be calculating and cold. He had suffered her whims for too long, and finally had overcome their effects and preferred neglect to this reiteration. She had taken him for a fool and wanted him back for a stand-by, an infuriating position he was far too proud to accept. "Will you write?" she asked, seeking to measure his anger.

He vowed he would never write and said, "Of course." This lie lifted his spirits.

"How are your parents?" she persisted, sustaining the conversation, to which he replied, "They're fine." Looking out across the barren lobby, he told her a line had formed at the registration desk and that he had to go. Lying was infectious and it felt good.

The remainder of the winter and spring passed quickly. The one letter from Kirsten, despite the pledge to himself, he answered. Kurt had reminded him not to burn his bridges and if he wanted a job, write. He did.

That spring Otto regularly nodded off in the Economics and Accounting lectures that he found overly detailed and filled with minutia, and he soon awakened to the fact that for him they held little relevance to what he envisioned business to be—buying and selling, bargaining, making friendships and deals on a handshake—not laboring blurry-eyed over debit and credit columns. He stopped attending. The history courses, essentially the study of politics and war, provided what he thought to be a more important fundamental lesson, the better guide to shape his destiny. Underlying the dates and facts, the lesson unmistakable, always there, like a constant drum beat: right or wrong, good or bad, deserving or not, the financially strong win—not only in war and business, but in day to day dealings—and, as he had experienced that dismal holiday night, in affairs of the heart. And what had made Kirsten's friend, that corpulent American, desirable? Nothing more than money. Money provided his power, and money and power thus joined are rarely separated. Not talent, nor brilliance, nor looks; none of these alone could replace money. That was a fact and because of that—he would fight for it, a lifetime quest.

Astrid moved to the farm for the summer and within a week called Otto with the news that his grandfather was spitting up blood and she thought him gravely ill. The man he knew as a rough, unrelenting farmer, a fierce battler of the cursed winds and rain and frigid summers; the man who since childhood Otto had regarded as the embodiment of the Viking warrior, was stricken.

Otto's praise for the old man and his forbearers was repeated once too often for Kurt, sending him into a rant, "In that case you are descended from a thug!" he said, pronouncing "thug" in a throaty voice, half spittle half air. "Otto, your goddamned ancestors were not nice guys, they murdered the helpless, pillaged, stole gold, silver, and the plate from monasteries for Pete's sake. Yet, let me surprise you, I say despite that, may God in all his goodness and mercy bless them! Yes, God bless them! For they also stole the women, and only the beautiful ones!" A lascivious smile crossed his thick face. "So, in spite of all the carnage, what a big favor they did us! Otto, look at the Scandinavian women. You can walk ten blocks in Copenhagen before you see a bad looking one, and she's probably a tourist. Try that in Paris or London." Waxing proud of his barroom observation, he laughed. "But, how the Vikings are viewed depends entirely on who's writing the history. They won so we make them our heroes, otherwise we would be damned mum about them." Otto delighted that unprompted, Kurt had affirmed his conclusions that the world belongs to the daring and strong, and not withstanding the church's teachings, it would be a long time before the meek would inherit it.

When word came that Old Hans was bedridden, Otto took a few days off and traveled to the farm. Ruggedly august, tall and bald, Hans had looked out on the world through clear blue eyes set deep in a face dominated by a nose that stood like a bastion for the determined soul within. He emanated power. He was not one to be toyed with. Brusque but fair, he lived as a natural leader among the local farmers and carried their fight to the regional agricultural regulators. But that afternoon when Otto entered the sickroom, he was staggered by what the disease had accomplished. How shrunken and enfeebled Hans looked wrapped by blankets and propped up against pillows. Wracked with fever, his face, blue-gray, glistened with perspiration through several days' growth of white whiskers. The sunken cheeks moved in and puffed out as he worked to breathe. "What the Hell are you doing here?" the old man croaked with a hint of a smile. The sickroom air smelled fetid from his breath.

"Came to see you," said Otto who, overcome by the smell, felt a rush of nausea.

"You have better things to do." The remark took the last of the old man's breath and was followed by a series of deep rumbling coughs producing large globs of blood-streaked sputum that he fought to get up and out of his lungs and spit into a towel. Then he turned wide-eyed toward Otto, mouth agape, unable to pull the next breath in. Otto thought he would die then and there. Finally it came, a long sucking breath accompanied by a high-pitched whistle from his chest, and relieved, the old farmer settled back in the pillows and stared at those gathered about. His fiery eyes danced about from one to the next and without a word he said death did not scare him. Slowly his lids came down and he drifted asleep, the only sign of life the rattle of mucous in his throat.

In the morning the country doctor made his rounds and sat on the bed and thumped Han's chest and listened to the raucous breaths and said because of the bloody coughs he figured the old man had lung cancer and an accompanying pneumonia. Without embellishment or emotion he said in his experience the situation was hopeless. In the days that followed Astrid and Bente flittered in and out of the sickroom, changing Han's sweaty nightshirt, fluffing up the pillows behind his back, and setting up a tray of food, mostly thick soup and bread that Hans dipped and ate aimlessly. When his patience was taxed, Hans would growl that he didn't like their gallywagging and force them out of the room to be content to listen for his calls from the kitchen or if sensing he was asleep, slip in to pull the covers over him and bring fresh water.

They spoke softly in the kitchen so that any ominous sound or unusual quiet from the sick room would be noticed. Erik asked, "So Otto how is Copenhagen?" as he passed a bowl of vegetables across the kitchen table. Otto spoke of his work and his studies. After a pause his mother began, "Otto, your father has premonitions, afraid he will be dismissed from the bank. He doesn't sleep well any more. Worries all the time." Otto looked at his mother, unable to reply other than with a nod. At that moment he noted that the low light of the kitchen erased all the lines of age and care from her face, and he recalled the wedding picture that sat in the silver frame on her dresser in Arhus of a pretty young woman looking expectantly out at the world smiling, as if the future could hold for her nothing but happiness and light. How wonderful she looked years ago, a Viking prize. And how different life had been.

At ten the next morning a gentle rap on the door announced the arrival of the village church's assiduous shepherd, Pastor Hansen. He shortened his awkwardly tall body with a stoop, a humble posture he assumed as a young minister and now, with age, he had been frozen into. His face, that bore a perpetual look of concern, was distinguished by an inordinately long nose and jaw that in combination with large, syrupy eyes gave him the look of a fagged horse. In a voice, hushed and obsequious, he made inquiry about the patient and then wringing his bony hands before his chest took reverential steps toward the sickroom, entering with great solemnity. The family gathered behind him at the end of the bed. The old man opened his eyes and glared.

"What the Hell are you doing here?" The old Viking's voice, strengthened by sleep, was stronger than it had been the evening before. The Pastor, if perturbed, did not show it other than by a brief swallow to wet his throat in preparation for his words.

"I came to pray with you."

"Oh, bullshit!" came the shout, followed by a chorus of coughs that Otto realized were self-induced by the old farmer, who despite his final illness, remained the church's most formidable apostate. Writhing with exaggerated breathlessness, Hans clutched at the collar of his nightshirt and ripped it open in a heroic effort to drive the do-gooder away, but to no avail.

Pastor Hansen would not leave nor be silenced. He waited for the paroxysms of coughing to subside and began, "The Lord is my Shepherd, I shall not want…" The psalm was met with a surprisingly vigorous waving of the patient's right arm and had it been long enough, it would have had the desired effect of batting the minister away. More furious coughing ensued. This time it had no effect other than that Pastor Hansen raised his voice to a near shout and finished…"and I shall dwell in the house of the Lord forever." Unsuccessful with the deathbed conversion, the village's shepherd turned to the respectful group assembled at the end of the bed. "Please join me in the Lord's Prayer." Otto felt a blush spread over his face, ashamed to stand before his grandfather participating in a prayer his grandfather did not want. Uncle Erik pretended that he didn't know it and mumbled a word or two. His grandfather clamped his eyes closed, as if they could shut out the sound.

Following the prayer session, Pastor Hansen stayed for coffee and cake in the kitchen. Erik disappeared out to the barn.

When the Reverend left, Otto looked into his grandfather's room. The old man had a smile on his face. He had enjoyed every moment of the encounter.

"Who let that stupid ass in? He's just looking for something to eat."

If Otto had any doubt of his ancestry it was confirmed at that moment. When the time came, Old Hans would joyfully join the rest of the "thugs" up there in Valhalla.

"Otto, you go back to your job, we'll call you," his mother said. Otto endured the old man's scoffs at his pitiful expressions of good-bye until, finally forced by the protest over any further sentiment; he retreated to the bedroom door and with a final wave, left for Copenhagen.

Chapter 7

The call to Otto came a week later with word that his grandfather had dozed off and then drifted on during that afternoon. On the phone, Astrid, emotionless, reported the news dryly so as not to oblige Otto to come for the funeral, though she knew he could not stay away.

Driving back from the bus stop, Erik turned the truck off the road onto the long driveway and encountered a line of trucks, cars, tractors, tractors with wagons, horse drawn wagons, literally every type of farm vehicle. "Shit, Otto, these clowns smell free food and drink. The old man would have shooed them away, told them to get their asses out!" Otto and Erik made their way to the door past the men that milled about in the courtyard, and squeezed through the crowded parlor to the kitchen where they found the women had gathered. The place smelled of cooking; the kitchen and dining tables laden with covered dishes, breads and cake. In his grandfather's bedroom a plain wooden coffin rested on saw horses. No flowers, only his sweat-stained hat lay on top. Grandmother standing at the sink, her back curved as if the years there had changed her slight form to fit, scrubbed furiously at a pot as if that would make the time pass quickly. The light from the window turned the loose stands of her gray hair to silver as they moved and flitted about in the sun. She wore an everyday dress, no pretenses, even this day. The ladies busied themselves arranging and rearranging the food on the table and talking quietly about a recent unexpected pregnancy or the last farm to fail. Pastor Hansen arrived, and almost as a parting of the Red Sea made his way through the hushed women to the small woman at the sink.

"Bente, he is in a better place now," he said in an unctuous voice barely above a whisper. She turned drying her hands in her apron, but did not answer. He placed both his hands upon her shoulders and looked down at her with his long, mournful face and held this position for what Otto thought was an eternity; she never looked up or said a word. With a somber sigh, he dropped his arms and announced, "Let us get started." Acting on this signal, Uncle Erik and three neighbors carried the coffin to the hay wagon hitched to the tractor, and led the slow procession to the grave.

The neighbors followed in silence, walking through the grass to the ancient family burial ground in the trees on the small hill at the end of the field. It was a warm day, cumulous clouds drifted across the sky; a gentle breeze stirred the leaves, insects buzzed about. Otto caught up with his mother and walked by her side, his father walked behind. The grave had been dug the evening before by Erik and several neighbors, the fresh soil piled there smelled sweet. The coffin, lowered on two ropes clunked on the bottom of the pit, and Pastor Hansen assumed his position behind the grave. It was a good day to be buried, the ground was soft and warm, the weather pleasant. The farm folk had come to say good-bye to a sick old friend who, contrary to Christian doctrine, believed he was returning to the soil from which he had arisen and would arise again, recycling as regularly as the seasons after a few years of rest. Curious to hear what words the Pastor would say over the remains of the old iconoclast, the farm folk crowded in to catch every word. Otto thought how bitterly cold it had been when his brother was placed in the grave a few paces away; the weather that day had suited as well.

"Dear Lord we are gathered here to commit to your bounteous forgiveness your servant Hans...." The Pastor's eyes rolled toward the heavens in prayer, his voice up an octave, rising and falling, imploring the Almighty for help in this most serious of unrepentant cases. As if the old man could have willed it from the grave, there was a furious bout of coughing from a farmer at the edge of the gathering, prompting a lengthy pause in the fervent graveside entreaty. Otto smiled and raised his eyes from the ground and carefully scanned the bowed heads to identify the cougher. He knew his grandfather would never ask for forgiveness especially if, in Pastor Hansen's opinion, he needed it. In fact, Otto wondered if the Pastor would truly want to share Heaven with such a confirmed nonbeliever and if, in truth, he secretly hoped his prayers would not be answered. Clearing his throat, the Pastor resumed and preached on for several minutes more before he commended Hans' soul to God's merciful care and finished with a mighty flourish, drawing his voice down to bottom of his throat for a protracted "aahhmenn." Otto walked in silence with his mother and grandmother back to the house, accompanied by Pastor Hansen and trailed by those gathered at the grave site, except for Uncle Erik and several helpers who filled in the grave.

The wide floor boards groaned as the house filled with the funeral goers, filled not only side to side, but top to bottom, as the heads of the tall men brushed the low ceilings. Mourners spilled out from the kitchen and doors. Grandmother sat at the kitchen table and oversaw the serving of the food. The Pastor paid his respects and quietly left. Upon his departure, the bottles of schnapps the men folk had hidden for just this moment came out. Glasses and cups were pressed into service and the farmhouse turned noisy with talk and laughter. Pedersen, the farmer from down the road, making a toast to Han's soul, cheerfully gulped the clear liquor and following the "here, heres", shouted how old Hans would love this! Absolutely true if someone else paid for it, Otto thought. Later the ladies washed dishes and cleaned up the remaining food. In a few hours the last of the guests were gone, the farm road emptied, and the house quiet once more. The farm would not be the same. The finality of death settled like a thick mist over the small family that sat at the table that evening. Grandmother retired, his side of the bed would be cold. Otto knew only now would she let herself cry.

In the morning Otto and his father traveled to Arhus together. Astrid remained on the farm. On the train his father broke a long silence.

Leaning toward Otto who sat across in the compartment, Peder spoke in a low voice, not wanting passengers near them to hear. "Your mother and I are estranged. She wants to live at the farm."

"Since when?" Otto was not surprised, as their only connection had been the boys. She had no reason to remain in Arhus.

"I don't know, since the investigation began maybe. I've been preoccupied with that." Peder said, and raised his newspaper, ending the conversation with a virtual wall of newsprint.

Hadn't he seen it coming? Even as a child Otto sensed the rift, the long periods of silence, the abrupt leavings, the occasional caustic remarks. Though too young to understand why or take sides; he felt it. The house on Sjaelland Street had not been a sanctuary that drew Peder home at the end of the day. He came home at night to a fine house and a model family because that was the accepted pattern for bankers, what bankers did. This claim of bewilderment was incredible; it was he who created the tension with his stiff bearing and needless regimentation. And now to protest ignorance? Otto's fists had curled over the armrest, his nails dug into the cloth, and he turned to watch the county side pass, unable to look across at the sorry man whose sole source of happiness derived from bank profits and ordering subordinates about; all else amounted to an intrusion into this world. Otto fought the temptation to reach across and take him by the collar and shake the self-centered bastard, shout in his face. "Yes father, she went to the farm to be free of you! And every summer she had gone from school out to school in with Jorgen and me to escape the dismal, empty life you provided!"

Otto held his tongue until they were off the train and on the platform in Arhus, and asked with more than a hint of sarcasm, "Well father, just what do you think I can do?" The question did not have the caustic ring he had intended. Peder stopped to let the crowd pass them. "You ask me what you can do? What you can do! You could say something to her!" and without a word more he walked away. Otto let him go.

In Copenhagen, Otto found Kurt in the bar and the bartender listened then asked, "Why weren't you more forceful, push him around, rough him up, punch him in the nose, let him know how pissed you are?"

"Punch my father? I backed away, made the practical choice. I should have said more but more words wouldn't have changed a thing; you can't tell him anything. I'm not proud of that." Otto took a long sip of beer and after a moment. "You're right, Kurt, I backed out of a fight, I should have let him have it."

Kurt, enjoying this, sided with him. "Then again, maybe you did do the right thing. You treated him with kindness, the Christian thing, the dutiful son and all that crap."

"You've been in fights?" Otto asked, getting him off the subject.

"Came with the police job. After one or two they don't seem a big thing. You're a big guy; I don't think you would lose many."

"You are telling me to pick fights?"

"I'm telling you to stand firm, step up Mr. Viking man."

Chapter 8

They came weekly—slapdash, newsy little notes from his mother bursting with excitement at having been released from the hopeless marriage. She wrote the details of her new life, baking bread, the weather, grandmother's good health that she attributed to lots of sleep and vegetables and that Erik had hired a helper. They missed old Hans, especially the rants and raves over the dinners that she said were on the quiet side now; but the farm for the moment was doing all right, no sick cows and the price of milk steady. She had taken a position in a local doctor's office as secretary making appointments and keeping the books, and as assistant, a job that consisted mainly of holding struggling babies and children so the doctor could look at their ears and tonsils. The work made her feel useful but there was an unexpected benefit, she met old friends and school chums, most of whom had "a rearrangement of their outer dimensions" but thinking and attitudes seemed resistant to change. The letters avoided mention of Peder and she reaffirmed her decision in each letter that the move to the farm was permanent; reconciliation was not a consideration. Otto wondered if his father had tried.

For Otto's part, that summer he had seen Kirsten occasionally but the painful rift here was too great to mend. Despite his desperate double-entendres laden with sexual innuendo which he thought she could not misunderstand, Otto was unable to awaken any passion. Her coldness forced Otto to the unhappy conclusion that he should persist in this awkward friendship only in the interest of a dreamed for job. Nor did he understand her interest in him, of carrying on in this platonic way, the intermittent invitations and phone calls. All his plans for rendezvous in parks and cafes followed by stolen moments in his room, of undressing her, spilling her clothes about the floor, abandoned –- and thus resigned, he concluded that seeing her occasionally would be the best he could manage, although even years later, the memory of every detail of that bygone luncheon never faded.

Left with time on his hands Otto completed work on the final paper required for the semester and with that ended his studies for the year. He had written on the problems associated with the current European trade agreements and thought cousin Niels would be impressed and planned to show the paper to him— assuming that once Niels read it, he would recognize that here was a young man who had a profound understanding of the economic realities of Europe, and who as a consequence, would be a valuable asset to any business dealing in international trade, especially his. Otto planned to mail it to his cousin's office in the morning.

That evening, entering the hotel at eleven, Otto heard shouts and curses from the bar and strode in to investigate. The lone customer, a large gray haired man wearing a business suit, had reached over the bar and held Kurt by the shirtfront with his right hand and his left cocked ready to swing the ham-sized fist that wavered above his shoulder with Kurt's panicked face the target. Otto, giving no thought to what was required, trotted up behind the assailant, tapped him on the shoulder, and when he turned, slammed a fist into his stomach, and as he doubled over with a breathy grunt, Otto pounded a right fist against his jaw. The man staggered, his glasses skittered down the bar; he wavered for a moment then fell straight backward, his head bounced off the brass foot rail with the sound of a thumped pumpkin before striking the floor.

Kurt, eyes wide, stood on his toes and bent over the bar. "Jesus Christ, Otto."

"You told me I should step up to a fight, well there, I saved you."

"So you started with this guy? Do you know who the Hell he is?" Kurt was shouting, red faced, blue veins showing in his face and neck.

"No, but he was big and angry and was about to smash your face in. You wouldn't want me to pick on somebody small, would you?" Otto added quickly hoping some humor might improve the situation.

Kurt scurried around the bar, tucking his shirtfront back in his trousers. "That happens to be Anders Jacobsen. He's a big cheese, a lawyer, has a lot of friends, not the kind you would want to meet, spends his days floating around the city courts, defends all the riff raff that gets pulled in, petty criminals, muggers and thieves, people like that. They all know he's the lawyer to get. Sleazy as shit."

A moan came from the floor and the injured lawyer, pulling his knees under him pushed off his elbows and with a groan sat up. Kurt and Otto grabbed him under the arms and pulled him up onto a chair where he sat bent at the waist, head between his knees, rocking back and forth, open mouthed, blood and saliva dripping onto the floor off a flaccid lower lip. With a thick hand he rubbed the welt rising on the back of his head.

Kurt handed him a glass of water to wash his mouth out, but it became apparent that the water simply ran down the front of his shirt dribbling onto the floor into the widening puddle of blood and spit. The lawyer was unable to close his mouth.

Kurt and Otto stood helplessly by until Jacobsen stood, still bewildered and with a crazed look struggled to focus on them. Putting a handkerchief against his chin to catch the bloody drool he muttered, "Oou assterds" and stumbled out onto the dark street.

Kurt stammered, stating what had become obvious to them both. "Jesus Otto, you broke his jaw! Of all people you had to punch him!"

Otto took a seat at the bar rubbing his right hand. "Kurt, tell me what choice did I have? He was ready to pound you and that guy is big. He could have killed you."

Kurt walked behind the bar and drew two beers.

"What the Hell led to this?" Otto asked.

"He came in here tonight for the first time and recognized me. I arrested the dumb bastard for assault ten years ago. He's a mean drunk, aggressive, you saw that. He got drunk back then, beat up his girlfriend; messed her up good. She presses charges so we go get him and bring him back to the station house. So then, he claims, while he was being held we went back to his apartment, rifled through his stuff and stole some money he had in his desk."

"That happens?"

"Occasionally. There are crooked cops, you know."

"Was money stolen?"

"I doubt it. He had been around the block a few times and knew how to get back at us. There was an investigation. No proof, there was no record of a police officer having been in the apartment. It went away."

"So he came in here drunk tonight and recognized you?" Otto said, still trying to put it all together.

"Yeah, he doesn't forget old debts." Kurt paused for a moment and changed the subject, going back to the problem at hand. "But Otto, we need a story. As soon as he gets that jaw taken care of, he will have you, and probably me, charged."

"Shit. What do we do?"

"Tell the truth," Kurt could not contain his smile, "But with embellishments, of course."

"Embellishments?"

"We have to be the first to report this, that's important, like the good little citizens we are. Here's what we say, which is pretty true. 'He came into the bar and recognized me, and after a few more drinks became belligerent, reached over the bar and grabbed me. That's when you came in and thought that I was in grave danger and after he took a swing at you, you hit him. Better yet use the expression 'mortal danger', emphasize it, and emphasize that he swung first. Of course, his story will be that you sucker punched him, but who would believe a sweet university student would do a thing like that, particularly when Jacobsen has a prior arrest for assault. The judges know what he is capable of."

Kurt called and within half an hour police officers, old friends, arrived and following handshakes and a few laughs and they took a report of the incident. Kurt made them read their notes back insisting that he wanted them to get it right. They had not heard about the injured lawyer or from the hospital but would make some calls to see how Jacobsen was doing.

Several days later Otto was charged. He hired a lawyer Kurt recommended based on "this guy does a lot of this kind of work and knows all the tricks."

At the top of the stairs on the second floor of an old building near the courthouse Otto faced a long hallway. There were scuffed wooden doors every twenty feet or so, and on the third door on the left at the end of the hall he found a tarnished brass plate that identified this as the law offices of Arne Knudsen, Esq. He knocked, and from within received shouted instructions to enter. The outer door opened into a small waiting area just wide enough for a window and two straight-backed wooden chairs opposite. A worn rug covered the floor. Picture hooks without pictures stood out on the wall. Otto looked at them twice to make sure they weren't bugs, then figured the pictures were stolen. From behind a closed door leading to the office beyond Knudsen bellowed further instructions in a hoarse voice. "Take a seat!" Otto sat, and having no choice, looked through the dirt-streaked glass at pigeons preening on the window ledge and beyond at the courthouse across the street. He had a sense of doom; in that building he would meet his fate.

The office smelled of tobacco. Smoke seeped under the office door and mixed with the residual odor of underarm sweat from earlier clients whom Otto imagined to be dirty little men, felons, purse-snatchers and muggers. Before long the muffled voice in the inner office lapsed, followed by the sharp click of a hand piece placed roughly back into the cradle of a phone. Then a shout, "Okay, come in." Arne Knudsen, coatless, stood as Otto entered. He was stooped, about fifty, brown hair fell over his forehead, his face rounded and his skin, rough as a grater, was pitted by acne. His tie pulled open hung askew over a rumpled white shirt and his trousers dangling from suspenders followed him up like a hammock strung under the paunch of his gut. No smile or extended hand, the only greeting a nod toward a chair. Otto introduced himself, but continued to stand while Knudsen stood and thumbed through the papers scattered on his desk, giving Otto a moment to look about at the scratched metal filing cabinets and ochre walls on which were hung, with no attempt at arrangement or symmetry, several large elaborately scrolled diplomas and smaller gilt-framed awards. At last Knudsen pulled a sheet from the pile with some notes scrawled in blue ink and laid it in front of him on the desk. The remainder of the desk was taken up with an ashtray filled to overflowing with crushed cigarette butts, a phone and file folders. And without looking up as he sat, he said, "Sit down." Otto sat.

"I spoke with Kurt. He filled me in, but I need to hear the story from you. Because people ramble, I'll ask the questions rather than let you blither on." Knudsen bent over the desk with a sigh, pen poised awkwardly in his left hand while the other steadied the corner of the paper like a school child. "What did you hear going on in the bar before you went in?"

Otto was on practiced ground. "Angry shouts, curses, I couldn't make out the words." He felt as though there was nothing in this statement that would contradict anything that Kurt might have told Knudsen.

"What did you see when you entered the bar?"

"I saw this man reaching over the bar; he had Kurt with both hands by the collar of his shirt, pulling him up on the bar and choking him."

"This was Jacobsen?"

"Yes, Jacobsen, and he was yelling 'I'm going to break your goddamned neck.' He is a big guy and I thought he would do it."

"You thought Kurt was in danger of serious injury?"

"Mortal danger, absolutely. If I hadn't shown up just then who knows what would have happened."

"Then what?"

"I yelled, 'Hey mister, let him go!'"

"Where were you then?"

"Right behind him."

"And?"

"He swung around, threw a punch that just missed my face, so I hit him in the stomach and jaw. He fell and hit his head on the brass foot rail. We helped him up, tried to give him some water and offered to take him to the hospital. He refused, called us 'bastards' and walked out."

"And Kurt called the authorities?"

"Yes, right away because we were very worried about him, that he might be injured and all. Asked them to check the hospitals."

"Did you know how badly injured he was?"

"We were worried that maybe his jaw was broken."

"And Kurt has told you the background to all this?

"Yes"

Knudsen scribbled a few notes and sat back and looked at Otto.

"I know Jacobsen, his jaw is broken and he has been out of court for a week now. I heard they've got his jaw wired together so he can barely talk and has to eat by sucking soup through his teeth."

Otto hadn't realized the seriousness of the injury never having seen a broken jaw or the treatment. He did now.

The lawyer continued. "He's a mean son of bitch, as you have seen, and would be inclined to push this as far as he can. However, you have a retired policeman with a good record as a witness to confirm your description of the events. That's a big help. Next, we even have a motive for the attack on Kurt. Finally, Jacobsen has had that assault charge in the past, which, incidentally, he beat." He looked out over Otto's head, eyes unfocused, lost in thought, gently tapping the cap of his pen on the desktop. "Jacobsen knows these things as well as we do. What I'll do is talk to him. As I don't think he will get the kind of satisfaction he wants in a courtroom, you understand, he'll probably drop the charge. Save himself the trouble." His eyes searched Otto's face for any indication of understanding.

"Do you think that's likely, drop the charges?" Otto was delighted that the matter might be so easily resolved.

"Well, in a manner of speaking." Knudsen paused and after a moment went on. He did attack Kurt, you came to Kurt's aid, both of you testify to the same thing. You are clean-cut with no record, there's no reason you would attack him without provocation. That would be hard to beat,

Jacobsen knows it, your word against his, and it would be likely that he would come out of it with his reputation damaged again. It might even wash him up, legally, law practice wise." He paused and thought it over again and then stood up. "I'll work on it." and extended a pudgy hand as a parting gesture.

Otto grabbed his coat, hurried out the door and bounded down the office building stairs out to the street. He felt like running, skipping. All those hours he had spent worrying over this; the concern that had driven his thoughts whenever he wasn't busy, when he tried to sleep, all suddenly calmed. He took long strides, his legs stretching out in celebration. Just a promised victory, but he was certain Knudsen could talk sense into Jacobsen; make him see how futile his case would be. Otto gave no thought to the justice of the matter, ignoring that this case amounted to a moral morass as both parties were at fault, and it appeared that the worst transgressors and apparent victors would win based on lies. His pace slowed while he considered this as he turned up the block toward Kurt's apartment. How do courts get to the truth, when the 'truth' amounts to who has the most believable story and is the more convincing liar? If the truth were to come out in court, Jacobsen would win — except that only three people know what the truth is and two would lie convincingly. Jacobsen understood that. Otto had never been in a courtroom, but began to appreciate that the proceedings were simply a performance, and sometimes the real facts came out, sometimes not. He surmised what is deemed justice often amounts to a guess by a judge or jury. The punch had given him an education.

Kurt's apartment was located in a small four story building on the corner of a side street. The place was sparsely furnished which made it appear larger than it was. The sitting room to the left of the entry held a sofa, end tables and an easy chair. Kurt's opened newspaper lay on the floor beside it. A wide doorway led to a small dining room with lace curtains that filtered the sunlight that nourished the potted plants and highlighted the dusty tabletop clearly unused since Kurt's wife had died. Otto followed Kurt through a swinging door to the kitchen and took a chair at the kitchen table. Kurt carried over cups and a pot of coffee.

"What did Arne say?" he asked, looking at Otto as he poured.

"Said he thought he could get Jacobsen to drop the charge." Otto declared with relish. Kurt's earnest expression did not change.

"Yeah, that's what I think will happen, but you realize that's not the end of it. Jacobsen will find a way to settle up. He always does. It won't be right away, that would make him the obvious culprit. He'll bide his time, but I know him and his friends too well to think there won't be a nasty reprisal." He looked Otto in the eye to make sure that he understood. Otto's smile dissolved as he began to understand that a court case, or the lack of one, was just a preliminary to Jacobsen's retaliation, or as he now saw it, Jacobsen's brand of justice. Arne Knudsen's words came back to him. "I don't think he will get the satisfaction he wants in a courtroom." Now he did understand what he had been told. The streetwise attorney had given him a warning he had been too guileless to recognize.

"God, Kurt, what a mess."

"One thing leads to another." Kurt shrugged. "Now we've got to watch our backs. Don't expect to see Jacobsen. He knows plenty of people to do his dirty work. If you are alone at night, especially on the streets, don't let anyone get near you."

As if a switch were thrown Kurt's dark demeanor changed and a smile crossed his chubby red face. "Buck up, it'll be ok. He got what was coming to him. A lot of people have been wanting to do that." Kurt stood, slapped Otto on the back, and carried the cups to the sink. "Gotta get dressed for work, see you at the bar."

Chapter 9

The bank teetered near insolvency. In addition to the miscreants who hid the bad loans, all non-essential employees had been dismissed, hours had been shortened, and every conceivable effort made to prop up the bank's strapped borrowers. Still the monthly balance sheets worsened. Peder, exhausted, had run out of ideas. The proud Vice–President and Manager of the Arhus branch of the Den Danske-Union Bank now came and went by the back entrance, avoiding the staff, no longer making assignments and inspecting. Instead, he quietly retreated to his corner office to sit alone. Behind the closed door he reviewed the daily ledgers and found they meant less and less as day after day waves of bad numbers came in that were so oppressive that for the past few weeks he could not focus his eyes on them. Finally he didn't bother to review them at all; he merely sat insensate, unthinking, studying for hours the paint on the wall opposite longing for the day to end. But before leaving each afternoon he forced himself to walk down to the floor of the bank to buck up the remaining tellers and officers with a forced smile and an encouraging word or two. "The crisis has bottomed out, soon it will be ending," he would say. Then he made the walk home, erect and brisk as ever, the only outward change, his hat brim pulled down to conceal the dejection from those he might pass.

Since Astrid had gone, he stopped at a small restaurant, always taking a table in the rear where he supped, shielded behind the evening paper, searching as he ate for some hint of encouraging financial news. Finding none, he would leave the paper behind and walk the remainder of the way home to the desolate house, carefully hang his coat, and go directly to the liquor cabinet. Within an hour he was drunk, asleep, a liquor bottle and empty glass on the floor by the chair. In the early hours of the morning, two or three, he would awaken cold and stiff, take himself up the stairs to the bedroom and fall, fully clothed, onto the bed. In the morning it was an effort to shave. His hands shook, making it difficult not to cut the haggard face looking back from the mirror. Dressed, again he set out for the bank, once more his stride erect and brisk, posturing for the neighbors, a pretense that nothing had changed. Work, once the central purpose of his life had become a dread, yet he carried on trying to avoid what he feared most: the dishonor of dismissal.

In mid-June a knock on his office door announced three members of the Board of Directors and following a few pleasantries, the life and career he had expected to live out ended at fifty-three. Peder was fired. He walked around his desk to close the office door behind them as they left, placed the wastebasket where his chair had been and methodically poured the contents of each drawer in it, saving nothing. Then he took the office keys from his key ring, dropped them on the desk and gently pulled the door shut behind him, his demeanor expressionless should he pass by someone as he walked out the back entrance.

• • •

The phone at the registration desk rang at the moment Otto arrived.

"Otto, your father has been fired." His mother's voice announced.

"Over the investigation?" he inquired.

"He blames national economic problems."

"What do you want me to do?" He asked though he knew the reason for the call. She was passing on a responsibility on that she no longer accepted.

"Otto, please, when you have a chance go to Arhus and check on him. I think he is drinking."

• • •

Not knowing what he would encounter, Otto informed his father of his plan to visit. He arrived at four in the afternoon. Peder met him at the door neatly dressed, hair combed, shaved, moustache trimmed, suit pressed, tie carefully knotted, outwardly unchanged. "So, Otto, to what do I owe this pleasure?" Peder began; the sarcasm divulged the tension he felt but no open hostility. He maintained his composure.

"Mother was concerned about your health." Otto answered stepping inside looking about.

"As I thought!" Peder snapped with more than a hint of bitterness. "I'm doing fine, you can tell her that!"

Seated in the living room, his father sought the offense, taking the opening gambit in the verbal game, turning the tables. "So, Otto, what do you propose to do with yourself?" he inquired, leaning forward to press for an answer.

"I'm finishing up my business studies." Otto looked up. Their eyes met. It was no business of his father's and he felt no obligation to open a topic that exposed a lack of planning, that incidentally, Peder had played a large part in. Peder would not be deterred.

"And to what end?"

Without thinking, partly in jest, Otto replied, "To get rich, of course."

"And how do you propose to do that in Denmark?" His father, accepting the answer at face value, sought to analyze the practicality of the resolution, and saw, based on his recent experience, little opportunity.

Searching for an answer and led by the underlying supposition of his father's question, Otto replied again off-handedly, "I'll go to America!" He had given the idea some thought but surprised himself for making that comeback. He was further surprised by his father's reaction.

"That's a good idea! If I were your age that's just what I would do!" Peder smiled for the first time, energized by the dream.

Following dinner Otto turned in. Peder stayed up to read the paper. In the morning Otto found him asleep in the chair where he had left him, a vodka bottle tucked partway underneath. The pressed suit rumpled and creased, the coat crushed against the back pillow, the cuff of his pants worked up around the calves of thin white legs exposed during a glacial over-night slide. He lay sprawled spread-legged and open-mouthed. As he sensed Otto's presence, his eyes opened, his mouth closed and shaking his head, "God dammit." He swore. Otto had not heard his father curse before. Peder thought swearing sinful, and equally importantly, a sign of weakness and a poor vocabulary.

"You've been drinking."

"So what!"

"You've got to stop!" Otto replied in a near shout.

"What the Hell for, my life is over, it helps me sleep!" he wailed.

"You'll kill yourself."

"I told you, Otto, I don't care!" He shouted; his face reddened as he struggled, pushing down with his arms to get up from the chair.

"What about mother?" Otto shouted back, backing away from his advancing father.

Peder screamed, "What about her? You're asking me 'what about her'? She left me, that's what about her! Yes, Otto, that's over, too! Do I make it plain enough for you!" and reaching out with both hands gave Otto a push backwards, causing him to stumble. "Now did you see what you came here to see? Huh? A miserable broken down old drunk? Get the Hell out!" The pushes continued, shoving Otto toward the door. A good push from Otto would have sent him crashing across the room into the furniture, but Otto couldn't break that ancient taboo. He simply left, his toilet kit and pajamas forgotten upstairs, and after he pulled the door shut he heard the empty liquor bottle shatter against it.

That night, returning to work, Otto found a note from the manager on the registration desk that said simply. "Kurt is in the hospital. Come in early tomorrow and take care of the bar."

Chapter 10

In the morning when his duties at the reception desk had ended, Otto burst out the door of the hotel and sprinted headlong for the hospital, his imagination aflame with images of beatings, stabbings, shootings and Kurt lying in a hospital bed, bandaged and bloody, moaning, dying or worse his naked body purple and green lying on an icy marble slab in the hospital basement. News of a heart attack or stroke would be good news; but he hoped, for Kurt's sake, it would be the flu or a bad bout of indigestion to which Kurt was prone. Having dashed through the empty streets in the early morning mists of Copenhagen, Otto stood panting before the information desk in the lobby of the hospital.

"Is he a relative? Only relatives can visit before visiting hours," the elderly lady in the pink smock seated behind the card file asked sweetly.

"Yes. He's my uncle," Otto assured her.

"Well then, he is in Ward 3B, second bed on the left." Her instructions told him Kurt at least was alive, but he feared she knew, as her directions were precise as to the number of the bed and the side of the ward it was on, that Kurt was in such terrible shape, that his face would be unrecognizable, or that he suffered from multiple fractures or stab wounds. Otto took the stairs by two. Ward B, a twelve-bed ward on the right hand side of the hall, was a long rectangular room with a solarium at the end. Down each side the curtains had been drawn around the beds creating a waving wall of blue cloth that nurses ducked through carrying pans and bedding. Five or six white-coated doctors stood in the middle of the room talking, and unmindful of the nurse's activity, they failed to move aside, forcing the nurses to detour around them. Otto eased in, and as he was unchallenged, parted the curtain at the second bed on the left. He found Kurt sitting upright braced by pillows, his face and arms cut and bruised and a thick band of white tape encircled his chest. A matronly nurse bent over him carefully dabbing the cuts on his face with wet gauzes. Kurt, seeing Otto, winked, reached around, patted her bottom and told her she was beautiful. She gave his cracked ribs an expert push with the desired effect; it brought his hand back and he was silenced. When the nurse left, they talked.

"I wasn't careful enough. It was my own fault. Going home the other night after work I was jumped by five or six Russian or Polish sailors, judging by their curses. They beat the crap out of me; broke a couple of ribs. But at least my jaw isn't broke. I think I got the better of the deal."

"Jacobsen?"

"I'm sure. They tried to make it look like a robbery. They took my wallet. I only had a few kroner. But this is an old device. He sends a man to the docks to hire some sailors to do a job like this. They get back on board ship and are gone the next day. They've made some money; he has a job done; all nice and tidy."

"I should watch out." Otto thought out loud.

"Nah, you don't have much to worry about, for quite a while anyway. The attack on me, it could be said, was a random theft, nothing that would necessarily point to anyone. But if you are attacked as well, that creates a pattern that points to Jacobsen. He's too wily for that. He got the person he wanted most. That'll be it for now." Kurt winced as he tried to change position. Otto helped him move up on the pillows and told him he was to fill in for Kurt at the bar. "There's a book next to the cash register that tells how to mix some of the newer drinks for the sophisticates, especially the occasional Americans, otherwise it's simple." Kurt added.

"Speaking of Americans, you know, my father thinks I should go to America, better opportunities and all." Otto emphasized his father's role in the matter, not wanting to appear motivated by fear of Jacobsen.

"You and about fifty million others." Kurt sniggered and looked around the ward. Most of the curtains had been drawn back and the daily activities of nursing care could be observed. "You ought stay right here and work on meeting some of these horny nurses. Look at the tits on that one. She'd help you get rid of your cockamamie ideas." Otto's eyes swept about the ward alighting for a second or two on several of the young ones.

Kurt's remark, "Fifty million others" had an effect opposite than intended. It set up a challenge that Otto thought he could meet and his mind drifted to elsewhere: to New York, Chicago, San Francisco. How fine the opportunities would be there. He was a good catch for any country: smart, ambitious, a business education and presentable looking. Getting there couldn't be that tough, look at all the losers that make it?

• • •

The room at the American consulate was small with just enough space for a desk that faced the door and two chairs. The walls were concrete.

American and Danish flags hung down the poles that stood in the corners. There was nothing to personalize the office; no pictures, diplomas, or nick knacks, just a nameplate near the front edge of the desk identifying the junior officer, and in this instance a Mr. Ronald Witmer. Otto sat in a chair opposite. Dressed in a dark suit, white shirt, blue tie, Mr. Witmer was a model mid-level bureaucrat. About forty, bald; the thin mustache that traced along his upper lip gave Otto the impression he was better fitted for slicing salami.

This was Otto's second visit. Witmer took a thin folder from the file drawer of the desk with the care appropriate for the Magna Carta, placed the folder before him, and with the flat of his hand repeatedly smoothed out the single page it contained as he studied it. In time he looked up with a practiced look of disappointment. Otto felt his spirits drop and concluded the remainder of the visit would serve only to fill the slot in Witmer's appointment schedule. "Mr. Nielsen we have several problems with your application." he began in heavily accented Danish. "We found that a charge of assault had been made against you by the Copenhagen police. This, I am afraid, is tantamount to a disqualification."

"Yes, but the charges were not pressed."

Witmer switched to English as a back and forth discussion would get beyond his familiarity with the Danish language. He would make Otto struggle. Otto felt his face heat in anger, his English was poor; and he thought, if this dimwit couldn't speak the language of my country he shouldn't be here.

"That doesn't matter."

Otto understood that much, but failed to comprehend fully the remaining remarks "There is the second problem; you didn't mention the assault charge on your application. The United States government considers that a very serious omission,"They spoke a few more sentences in English. Finally Otto frustrated stood and said, "Okay." When he turned toward the door he heard Witmer say in Danish, "Beside, your English not enough good." Walking from the building Otto saw that Kurt, dammit, was right. It was a cockamamie idea and to Hell with it! When his term paper came back graded with the A plus as he expected; he resolved he would talk to his cousin about a job. If he could get that it would be the key to a good salary in Denmark.

Within an evening Otto understood Kurt's love of bartending: every night work amounted to hosting a social. There were a few light duties, carrying cases of wine, cleaning up, tallying the receipts, but these were greatly outweighed by the fact that the job was simply fun. On quiet evenings, Otto had an invigorating conversation or two; and when busy, he would be energized by the pace, pouring beer and wine, mixing cocktails in the silver shaker, cleaning up spills took a swipe of a cloth; he lit cigarettes, and stayed ahead of the regulars refilling glasses before they signaled for more. He quickly learned for whom a refill without charge meant an extra coin or two. He made introductions, picked up information and even at this stage of life found he was sought as an advisor to those simple-minded enough to ask for his opinion. That was a rush.

Otto had been looking for Bjorn Johnsson and after two weeks he entered the bar smiling and joking with yet another woman on his arm. Here was someone Otto had yearned to talk with, maybe befriend, because this man understood money; he knew how to make it, and he knew how to make it in Scandinavia, and furthermore, Otto sensed, he knew how to use it to make even more in these tough times. Johnsson had the key to the practical, first hand knowledge that schoolbooks lacked. Simply put, Otto wanted to know how to surmount the most difficult hurdle of all, the first: acquiring the initial capital and backing to start a business.

"Where's Kurt?" Johnsson asked as he settled himself on the barstool.

The blond, expensively dressed woman accompanying him was left to manage on her own. She lay her fur coat on the empty stool beside her.

"Had a problem and wound up in the hospital, should be back in a few days."

"Too bad" Johnsson muttered unfeelingly. He made no inquiry about the possible illness or injury.

In bartender speak, Otto asked, "What'll it be?"

American whiskey, water on the side." And then as an after thought, "Greta, what can he get you?" Greta, a very attractive forty-year old, ordered a glass of white wine.

Johnsson was a large man, Otto judged six-two or three. He carried his weight well, but add a few more pounds and he would be potted-out. Comb tracts were visible in his blond hair that he raked straight back, his blue eyes were surrounded by puffy lids and despite his large nose and full lips, he had a pleasing presence. His suit coat pulled at the buttons as he leaned his forearms on the bar cradling the glass of bourbon in his hands. They looked strong. Like hands that once held the handle of a saw or shovel. Now the nails were carefully trimmed and a large diamond pinkie ring sat on the left fifth finger. There was no wedding band. Greta drank with her right hand; and as was his habit, Otto watched for rings on her fingers. He saw none. So far Otto had surmised that Bjorn was a self-centered, ill-mannered, heavy drinking, rich, womanizing adulterer who knew how to make money. He loved him, admired him beyond all bounds. And tonight he would find a way to talk with him. But first he served the drinks. Bjorn and Greta nuzzled, he put his bulky arm out encircling her slight shoulders and pulling her over to him. Otto stayed at the other end of the bar. By the third whiskey Bjorn had let her go and began staring straight-ahead at the bottles lined up on the mirrored shelves. Greta, sitting upright again and left alone with her thoughts, studied the bottom of her wine glass as if the future could be read in the remaining wine.

"Another whiskey?"

"Right."

As Otto slid the drink in front of the Swede, he began, "I'm studying business, looking for a way to get started." He heard the nervous pitch in his own voice.

"Yeah."

"Yes, trying to figure out what to do. Like to ask you some questions."

"That's easy, go to America."

"I tried that, they won't take me."

"Then go to Canada, they take anybody." With that he reached around the woman again, kissed her on the cheek, put away two ounces of whiskey in one swallow, threw some bills on the bar, took her by the arm and left.

Chapter 11

For Kurt's homecoming the bar and lounge filled up with a noisy crowd of chums, regulars and a group of strangers that happened by. They lined up to pump his hand and offer hugs that he pushed away as his ribs still hurt too much for that. Otto served as host and barman and Kurt, delighted with the reception, sat on a stool with his friends, laughing and waving his arms at Otto to spur on the flow of beer and wine. The beating had changed his appearance, his face still bore several scabbed over scars and he was thinner which made him look younger, his belt pulled in by three holes and the short red barman's jacket that his belly had flared out hung flat. But his nose was straight and his teeth were all there and he considered himself lucky. The beating had brought about one other important change. A pistol, taken from a felon years before, would sit under the bar until closing and then be tucked into his belt for the walk home. By two a.m. when the crowd had dwindled, Kurt ordered Otto to declare the bar closed and shoo the last of the die-hards home and lock up. He leaned on his elbow while he watched Otto clean up, and with the crowd gone and the bar quiet, Otto began to talk while he worked.

"Canada? Jesus Otto, why on earth do you want to go to Canada?" Kurt was incredulous.

"I'll learn good English there and then move on to the United States. Canada is temporary, it's a way in."

"Who gave you that idea?"

"Bjorn Johnsson. We talked about it one night he was here."

"He thought this was a good idea?"

"He's the one who suggested it. So I went down to the Canadian consulate."

"And?"

"And they were very nice. No problem with the papers and they had a list of possible employers. They encourage you to get a promise of work before you go."

"So did you?"

"Yes, it's all set. I have a passport and I contacted a company and signed up to work at a silver mine."

"A what!"

"Not to be a miner, I'll have to run some type of machine."

"What type of machine?"

"I don't know." He paused. "Kurt, it's a start. I can always quit."

"Where is this place?"

"It's near Tuckerton, a town north of Toronto."

"So when do you leave for this wonderful opportunity?" Kurt said over his shoulder as he was about leave.

"In about a month," Otto said to his back.

Kurt took a few steps and turned.

"Look, Otto, I'm not your father, but if you want my opinion, this is a lousy idea. There's no ideal place, Canada included. Certainly not America not since the American stock market crashed. How are you going to be better off at some silver mine over there? Stay here. Don't waste your energy."

Kurt had been back a week or two when wiping the bar he looked up and saw Bjorn Johnsson come in with an unusually ecdysiastic lady who Kurt recognized and had admired for all the wrong reasons, her clothes might as well have been paint; and Bjorn, breaking his usual pattern of sitting at the bar pulled out a chair for her at a small table in the far corner of the lounge where they engaged in a tête-à-tête that appeared to Kurt from a distance to have an intensity he did not realize Bjorn to be capable of. Despite his carefully followed rule against intrusion in customer's conversations, Kurt could not hold back, as some matters are too important for rules. So returning with their drinks, he interrupted.

"Did you tell the kid he should go to Canada?"

Bjorn looked up puzzled, "Huh, What kid? Canada?"

"Otto said you told him he should go to Canada."

"The dumb shit believed that?"

• • •

The fateful day began with a steady drizzle and by evening the rain had progressed to a full-blown downpour. Otto, holding a newspaper over his head ran through the rain to the Dahlberg. While stamping his feet and shaking the rain off his coat in the lobby, Kurt looked up from washing glasses in the bar sink and with a jerk of his head motioned him into the bar. As soon Otto was close enough to hear a whisper, Kurt leaned over the bar and said, "Jacobsen is dead!"

It had been a month, no a little more, Otto thought since the fight, yet from Kurt's agitation he could smell the danger in those three words that they in essence meant he would soon be implicated, arrested, jailed, and tried.

"You have to leave now!" Kurt warned in a whispered shout.

"For where?"

"Canada, where else?"

"What happened to him? How can I be responsible? It's been a month!" Otto's stomach turned over, he tasted bile in his throat.

"He died of a clot on the brain, probably from when you hit him." Kurt had a crude understanding of the circumstances of the Jacobsen's death from a phone call he had from Arne Knudsen and relayed the description to a panicking Otto. The previous afternoon Jacobsen had been taken to the hospital unconscious, following a seizure in the hallway of the courthouse. X-rays showed that his brain was compressed by something, pushed over by something big, a tumor or a hemorrhage. In the operating room doctors discovered a big blood clot from a torn vein, and despite their efforts to save him, Jacobsen never woke up from the anesthesia. He died later that night. Arne called Kurt "just to let him know". But the unspoken message of the courtesy call was clear. Once the creaky justice system made the connection between the clot and the injury from Otto's punches, there was little doubt of an arrest and this time the charges would be very serious, probably manslaughter. At most, Kurt said, Otto had a day or two to get out.

Otto left the hotel that morning, went to the bank, packed, dropped his room key and the rent money on his desk and threw a crushed, unfinished letter into the wastebasket for the police to find that explained to his mother that he had gone to Italy to look for a job. By late afternoon he sat on the deck of a steamer bound for Southampton. Beside him stood his suitcase filled with a few books and the new suit he had planned to wear to the interview with his cousin Niels, and whatever clothes he could stuff in, underwear, socks, and a sweater. In a hurried good-bye to Kurt he promised he would return to Denmark a success and buy him a beer, and Kurt vowed with tears forming in his eyes that, by God, he would hold him to it, in fact a keg.

He took a place on one of the benches that lined the foredeck and bent forward, studied his shoes and thought of the life he was abandoning. The fear of arrest for the moment was replaced by a fathomless melancholy. He pictured the farm where he had spent those months working with Erik to cut the hay that perfumed the air as it dried and they would return to cut some more and then finally when ready the hay was pitched up on the wagon forkful after forkful, arms aching, sweating in the sun; and the gravesite on the hill at the end of the field where Jorgen and Grandfather and so many generations of those unknown ancestors, the Vikings, he had never known lay; and his mother, now happy, her life reclaimed along with Grandmother busy in the kitchen; and the garden laid out in neat rows and the hollyhocks he loved, spires of color, leaning against the gray stone wall by the kitchen door. He would come back there some day. He thought of Kirsten. What a strange relationship they had had. Even so he would miss her. He imagined her naked form that he had never seen again and wondered how many suitors who proclaimed their undying love she would cast off like an old shoe. Funny words to choose he thought, when the ship cast off, he would cast off the life he had known. It was September 8th, 1932.

Part 2
The New World

Chapter 12

In Southampton he bought third class passage on the *Olympic Citizen*, a small liner bound for Montreal scheduled to sail the following day. That night, fearing arrest, he walked the streets anticipating a heart-stopping tap on the shoulder. By midmorning his back and legs stiff and sore he melded into the first wave of passengers up the gangplank and at the top an officious steward scanned his shoddy suitcase and wrinkled clothes and proceeded to examine his ticket with the intensity of a jeweler, turning it over and back. Having satisfied himself that he was not dealing with a stowaway, he gave a sigh of disdain and a quick jerk of his thumb over his shoulder pointed Otto to the staircase that led three decks down. Otto found his compartment located immediately behind the forecastle. Bunk beds lined one wall and the lower had been made up with clean sheets, a blue blanket and three thin towels stacked at the foot. A miniscule bathroom adjoined the cabin. A tin sink in a wooden case folded down from the wall over the toilet and a sheet metal shower stall no larger than a phone booth stood inches away. He unpacked his suitcase into the drawers beneath his bunk and stretched out with a book to pass the final moments until his escape would be complete. Calamity had driven him to the limits of endurance these past three days, so it was but moments before the gentle rocking of the ship as it lay in its berth put him to sleep. It was two o'clock; the *Olympic Citizen* was scheduled to sail with the outgoing tide. He awoke to the repeating ring of dinner chimes.

Assigned to table sixteen, first seating, in the second class dining room located two decks above his cabin, Otto arrived early and joined the crowd of passengers who had gathered in the bar to admire a final view of England, in this case an industrial panorama of docks and sheds, steamers and ocean liners, tugs and workboats moving about a harbor awash in the honey-yellow light of an autumn sunset. The low sun flashed off the rippled water with such intensity it watered Otto's eyes and in solitude amidst the crowd reality struck home, the great adventure had begun. As a tribute to his new world he bought a Canadian whiskey and lifted the glass in the direction of no one in particular and toasted himself under his breath: to perverse destiny, to Canada, and to wealth he would pursue. Neither courage nor love had brought him to this point and already he felt the fierce pangs of yearning for home; gone Denmark, beautiful Denmark, everything, family and friends, a rapid departure with no farewells, all ties cut, and here he stood in a ship's bar, Otto Nielsen, escaped felon, vowing by whatever he still held sacred that he would return triumphant and rich, though he could not imagine how or when. Somewhat fortified by this reaffirmation of his dream and a second whiskey, he put the empty glass down on the bar and walked to the crowded dining room.

Table sixteen was round and sat eight and his dinner companions included three couples already seated, and another single man who took a seat only after searching and finding no other empty chair in the room.

Through the window that looked out across the deck into the growing darkness there appeared a silent hallucination. Otto blinked and concentrated on the buildings along the massive docks as they drifted into the distance; the ship's movement imperceptible until a few moments later when out in the center of the harbor the throb of the engines many decks below rose through the sole of his shoes. He thought of Kristen.

"We're off. Bon Voyage!" twaddled one of the ladies, bringing Otto out of his reverie. Waving her wineglass about, she toasted the trip, smiling and winking at each member of the dinner party in turn. The introductions followed. Otto understood that two couples were Canadian and had toured England and Scotland together, the plain American couple had been to London and Paris and were returning to Saint Louis, and the lone gentleman, an importer of antiques, traveled to Europe regularly on buying trips. Unsure of his English, Otto remained quiet, content to watch the wine make the Canadian ladies silly. Afterward he stood at the port rail, mesmerized by the white bow wave that curled into the ink black sea. He turned in for the night, relieved, temporarily absolved of fear of immediate arrest and for the future, at least as far as he could picture it, free.

At breakfast three days out he sat at a table by a window watching the wave-less gray sea that had flattened down to a heaving gray carpet.

"You're Danish, is that not so?" Inquired a voice paced by the rhythms of a Norse language. Otto turned and found a tall fellow, about thirty, smiling down on him with a plate in hand expecting an invitation to sit. "I overheard you speaking English, which, if you permit me, is atrocious."

"Otto Nielsen, from Copenhagen," Otto replied and waved to the empty chair across the table. "Lars Gregersen" the visitor said as he sat. "Where are you going?" he asked switching to Danish.

"Toronto, I have a job with a silver mining company."

"Business should be good, steady work at least filling orders. Probably more need for silver coin now that fewer people will have the paper stuff, the economy—what a terrible mess." Otto let the false impression that he was headed for a position in the company offices stand. Lars chatted on, "I represent several Danish companies selling to wholesalers in Canada. A comfortable job and I like the travel. I come over twice a year. Start out in Montreal, work down to Ottawa and Toronto … I'll look you up when I get there. The place is dull as Hell, by the way. Montreal is much better, fun, the French *joie de vivre* don't you know." He had a pleasant approach, airy and informative, clearly practiced in the craft of easy greetings that when necessary could ease into a sales pitch. Otto had heard the slick salesmen that passed through the Dahlberg use these opening conversations with great ingenuity before slipping seamlessly into a description of their product line. All the while studying Lars' approach, Otto joined in the banter, trying to turn the subject to the north country without disclosing his purpose and finally asked if Lars had ever traveled up north, fishing or hunting, you know up by James Bay he added casually, as a for instance. Lars demurred saying he had not, but had heard the flies were real bad.

In the quiet of the small library Otto could not avoid the unhappy duty to send word home that he, having seemingly dropped off the edge of the earth, indeed remained alive and well and there was no need for worry. He settled at a small desk, arranging and rearranging the pens and paper until he managed to fabricate, after several false starts, a convoluted explanation for his abrupt departure. His mother and Erik might possibly accept it as partially true, but certainly couldn't swallow it whole, particularly after the police showed up at the farm with a warrant for his arrest. It was more outlandish than brilliant, but it was the best he could do and he ground it out: a simple letter with the facts he could write in a few minutes, but these pages were torture. The letter began with an exhilarated description of a rare financial opportunity in California; beyond any imaginable in Denmark, once in a lifetime, how lucky he had been to learn of it, best thing since the gold rush! Because others were racing to get it, he dropped everything and left immediately racing westward to San Francisco! The golden gate! Please excuse him for not calling or sending a note but there was no time to waste! Now he was passing through St Louis, halfway across America, and would write again when he found where he would settle in California.

His mother would stop Erik from calling it a damned joke and ripping it up, and she, despite the transparent lies would place it in a drawer where she kept those things that meant the most to her, certainly because of the few woeful words near the end where he professed his love for them and his longing for the farm; that part at least she knew was true. Otto concluded the letter with the admonition that if and when the Danish authorities contacted them, and the police needed explanations, don't show them or speak of the letter. He underlined this last sentence, passing the pen under it several times making a thick line for added emphasis. Knowing Kurt would tell the police nothing, probably send them on a wild goose chase to Paris or Madrid, he instructed his mother and uncle to send the police back to Copenhagen, to Kurt, the barman at the Dahlberg Hotel who they could say was the last person in Denmark to have contact with him …true enough. He signed it: Love, Otto. That evening at dinner he asked the couple from St Louis to take the letter and mail it from there, which though puzzled, they agreed to do. He ate lightly as he could imagine the wounding and bewilderment this letter would cause. The thought of it nauseated him.

Otto returned to the ship's library every morning after breakfast. The shelves were filled with heavily used books and thumbed magazines. In the cluttered travel section he found a book on Canada that he took back to his cabin, planning to practice English by reading it aloud. A fold-out map in the back of the book showed his destination, Tuckerton, a mining town located north of Fraserdale that happened to be a short way south of James Bay, which appeared to Otto on the map not too far north of Toronto. Fraserdale sounded pleasant enough; the name spoke of homes and gardens, children and schoolyards. Otto, already missing Copenhagen, began to contemplate weekend trips south to Toronto that he imagined as very cosmopolitan despite Lars' view of it.

Lars, martini in hand, that afternoon sought Otto out at the bar in the lounge before the first sitting. Otto nursed a scotch. The lounge became noisy as it became crowded. They spoke in Danish. "Meet any ladies? They are a lot freer here," Lars asked smiling as he twirled the olive about the base of the empty glass. "My theory is they don't know anyone on the ship, and everyone goes their own way. So nobody is the wiser," he said, poking Otto lightly in the shoulder. Traveling salesman talk, mostly bluster Otto thought as he recalled some jokes, the dirty ones involving the farmer's daughter. Gregersen swung around on the barstool, stretched his long legs out toward the lounge and leaned back with his elbows on the bar and looked over the crowd. Otto regarded his excellent profile as he listened to Lars sigh and suggest, "Yeah, Otto, in fact I may need your help. In case I meet one who is traveling with a lady friend, I'll need someone to entertain her friend. They won't abandon one another, you know." He turned to Otto with a wink. The proposal was not welcome. The boat, foreign soil with unfamiliar rules, did not allow Otto to stray from the straight and narrow; the risk of a misstep, questions about one thing might lead to something else and the reason for his travels might unravel the mystery of his whereabouts. And ships had radios, and, he imagined, brigs. All danger had not vanished when the boat left the wharf; but with only two days left to the crossing, Otto thought the prospective duty unlikely; so unable to resist the persuasiveness of his new friend Otto did not turn the proposal down and he said nothing.

Weather permitting, Otto spent afternoons reading on a wooden lounge in a sunny spot on the deck and Lars found him there. "Otto, I met a lady from Winnipeg. I need your help. You can entertain her sister." Lars stood looking down at Otto in the chair, hands thrust into the pockets of his tweed jacket, brown hair blown by the breeze, a pipe clenched in his teeth.

"Lars, my English isn't that good."

"Otto," Lars turned again to Danish, "all you have to do is walk her around the deck. You can practice your English." Without pausing for an answer he went on. "Typical story, I meet some like this almost every trip. A couple of sisters, father's a cattle rancher. Daughter number one wants to marry some low life, a ranch hand in this case and he is put on the first bus out of town and the daughters are sent on a six-month grand tour of Europe to forget the guy. That's where we come in. We help the old man out. We finish the forgetting process!" He used his big perfect-toothed smile to close the sale and accepting the one-sided conversation as a commitment he walked away before Otto could stop him. In less than ten minutes he strode back, Molly on one arm and Sarah on the other. Pairing had been arranged and as promised Molly had been forewarned that Otto barely spoke English and she would be his coach.

She was twenty years old, smiling and confident and seemed genuinely pleased to meet Otto. She fit the standard set by Kirsten, a standard by which at this time he gauged all women, though her appearance confounded him. He imagined a rancher's daughter from the Canadian prairie to be a modern variation of pioneer woman with dark hair pulled back in a bun and a complexion suggesting a mix-in of Indian blood; a descendant of leather-skinned, work-hardened women standing grim before a sod house against a backdrop of endless prairie. Instead Molly reminded him of a girl in a Hummel figurine with a soft, porcelain white face, rosy painted cheeks and wavy blond hair. They strolled together on the deck, Molly correcting his grammar and pronunciation, teaching him words, asking him to repeat. They laughed at his mistakes. English is never pronounced through the nose she said, and he found that helpful. Lars and Sarah, walking behind, dropped away. In less an hour the missing couple reappeared, holding hands, chatting away and Otto's English lesson ended with a smile and a gentle handshake. Retiring to the bar Lars paid for Otto's drink but remained silent regarding success or failure and Otto presumed his reticence was due to some unwritten code of shipboard chivalry; or at least the details would remain undisclosed until back in Denmark where Sarah's identity would be unknowable and Lars imagination and tongue could loosen over beers with friends. More likely, Otto theorized, based on the constraints of time, an hour, Lars luck had run out.

It had come down to the final night and as his well-informed friend had predicted, the invitation came from the ladies for dinner and dancing in First Class, and according to Lars, whose enthusiasm about his lovemaking prospects spoke without loss of hope, "and who knows what after." But Otto, impoverished by his circumstances and the meager prospects for lessons beyond the limits of pronunciations and the past participles of the new English verbs, could not chase illusionary dreams. He determined his interest that night would be the First Class Ballroom, a space surely finer than Second Class, but he couldn't imagine how; and the wealthy there, seemingly untouched by the great financial calamity, the Depression that awaited them all at the dock … were they all so fortunate as to be absolutely impervious to the economic collapse that would surround them on shore? How many smiles were real, how much would be pretense, who would be playacting, the final act in a charade before facing crushing debt that would engulf them at the end of the gangplank?

They met Sarah and Molly in the lounge and talked as waiters passed flutes of Dom Perignon and crackers with dollops of pate. Lars wore a Tuxedo and the women long gowns; Otto wore the blue suit he had bought for an interview with his cousin Niels that he had ironed that afternoon by placing it under the bunk mattress as he napped. Lars, as if frozen by his impenetrable attention to Sarah did not recognize awkward silence driven by Otto's need for sporadic translations to Danish, and Molly, perturbed by the halting conversation filled with pauses for word searches returned to lesson mode, quizzing Otto with simple questions speaking slowly and enunciating carefully. "What will your job be?" she asked to which Otto answered, "I work with numbers," with no attempt at accuracy as he didn't have the vocabulary for it and fearful of sharing the truth. And she replied, "Are you an accountant or a bookkeeper?" emphasizing the pronunciation of each new word as if he were deaf. By the third simple question Otto had tired of the little game and though he smiled he fought to conceal his frustration with her kind-hearted persistence; he wanted her to tell her "enough"!

Relief came with the opening of the doors to the ship's ballroom that did double duty as the First Class dining room. The room was modern and painted a rosy buff; there were no corners but curves that turned rhythmically around the walls making the space at once organic, elegant, and warmly reassuring. At the windows' edges in abrupt contrast, perfectly pleated drapes fell in place like Grecian columns that stood strong and stabilizing, rooted on red and gold carpet. The clamshell sconces lining the walls provided soft indirect light and from circular cutouts in the ceiling hung crystal chandeliers that gently twisted and sparkled in response to the ship's barely perceptible pitch and roll; that movement the only indication once inside the room that it was contained within the coarse steel superstructure of a ship.

The *maitre de* raised his eyebrows at the blue business suit and with an abrupt turn on his heal led them to a table in the most distant part of the ballroom. Otto's friends, unconcerned by the stares, enjoyed the small display of rebellion made at Otto's expense against the mandatory dress code. A string quartet played chamber music on the bandstand while guests ignored and talked over the melodies. The captain, in full dress whites, circulated among the tables bowing to the ladies, shaking hands with the gentlemen who, to a man, stood in respect. To Otto's great relief he didn't reach their corner of the room before the food service began. How would he have explained his dress at such an august affair? Would he be challenged and escorted out?

Each place setting included an array of forks, knives and spoons of varied guises and three wine glasses of a prescribed shape to enhance the enjoyment of the intended wine. Otto sat back and studied the waiters attired in tails and white gloves as they move gracefully about carrying trays, adeptly serving, and lifting the silver dish covers off with flare. Three wines were served as the courses progressed, each selected for the course by the *sommelier,* a personage who intrigued Otto as he circled about and hovered over the tables of important guests pouring samplings of wine, snapping his fingers at the waiters, ordering them to clear or bring more glasses. Then the lights were dimmed and a dramatic dessert arrived; cherries set in flaming brandy, and that followed by cigars and cognac. Meanwhile the orchestra that replaced the quartet began to play dance music. The four toasted their final night onboard, clicking glasses. Lars excused himself, hitched his pants, pulled his cuffs and walked to the captain's table, patted the captain on the back and began a conversation that ended with a laugh and a handshake. By then couples were swirling around the floor to a rousing waltz but the four of them left, and on the deck, Lars and Sarah silently disappeared again. Otto and Molly simply walked while she did her sisterly duty. He learned a new word or two.

By morning the ship was in the Saint Lawrence Seaway, gliding slowly past bluffs with farms and woods. Finishing breakfast, Otto went below, packed and brought his luggage up to the lounge where it was tagged for unloading. Lars found him as he stood at the rail.

"Well, I guess this is it." Lars put his arm around Otto's shoulders.

"What did you say to the captain last night?"

"I asked him where the dinnerware I had sold the ship was."

"You sold them dinnerware?"

"About three crossings back I ran into the purchasing agent for the line and told him I crossed twice a year and favored this ship, but I didn't like the china. He went through my catalogs and picked out a service."

"And where is it?"

Lars laughed. "They use it in the crew's mess." He looked at his watch. "Let's see if we can find the ladies."

Chapter 13

The four travelers left the ship, descending the gangway together but mentioned nothing of the events of the past two days, only small talk about the sunny weather and if there would be enough taxis. Otto agreed to visit in Winnipeg someday, though he understood this was not an invitation, but something people said when they needed more to say before a good-bye. An invitation when the visit wasn't expected or particularly wanted, that did not set a date or time, or as in this instance, provide an address. The emptiness of it angered Otto but as custom demanded, he thanked Molly for essentially nothing. There were handshakes and smiles. He found his suitcase and with it in hand looked back to see his fashionable friends standing among the first class luggage, pointing to bag after bag that a porter scurried to pick up and place on a cart. Apparently Lars had carried his bag up to the first class lounge as his luggage was there also.

Otto joined the line for immigrants behind an unpainted board fence, essentially a cow chute arrangement that ended at a series of desks. Behind the desks sat uniformed Canadian immigration officials, and behind them, a police officer paced back and forth patting his nightstick in his left palm. Otto trusted that the Danish authorities were unaware of his presence and had not telegraphed ahead that he was aboard; nonetheless, fear gripped him as he shuffled forward a foot or two with each thump of the ink stamps that slammed down on passports and papers. Kurt certainly would have never told them he was headed for Canada and he smiled as he imagined how Kurt would have half the Parisian police force scouring boarding houses.

At the head of the line Otto presented his passport and the Letter of Intent from Higginson and Hughes Consolidated Mining Ltd promising him a job. His casual stance hid the fact that his shirt, soaked with sweat, had stuck to his back; and looking about as the officer studied his papers he felt an uncontrollable panic that at any moment that he would be identified and with a flurry of finger pointing and whistles wrestled to the floor, manacled and led off. But, on the contrary, when the interviewer asked a few questions about his length of stay and if he planned to apply for Canadian citizenship his emphatic "yes" ended the interview with a handshake. He picked up his bag and walked briskly to the street, still dreading a shouted request from behind to return to the desks. On the street he passed the queue forming for taxis. Further up the street three or four buses lined the curb. It had been planned that a representative of the silver company would be there to meet the ship. As he walked, he spotted a man beside a small bus holding up a cardboard sign made from a box top with H&HCM Ltd and NEILSON penciled in crude lettering. Though spelled wrong it had to be him. Three men dressed in wrinkled and ill fitting clothes that looked to have been pulled from a collection bin stood with the sign holder. When Otto approached he was hailed and his bag taken and tied with a piece of cord to the rack on top of the bus that held several broken down suitcases and a cardboard box. Following the others he climbed aboard. The man with the sign drove. No one spoke. The bus lurched onto the roadway. Otto looked back at the taxi line for his friends. They had vanished like a dream.

The yellow paint on the sides of the bus was splashed with hardened gray-brown mud. A spare tire and gas can were strapped to the back. The inside was cramped and dirty. There were two bench seats on each side of the aisle and a seat across the rear making room for twelve. Otto sat alone, closed his eyes and rested his head against the window until the pavement ended and the road became rough. For the entire trip he would struggle to get comfortable enough to sleep. The driver, first in French and then French accented English, informed the passengers they would head west and stop for short breaks when he needed fuel. On to Ottawa and then to North Bay, on to Sudbury and then the bus would turn north. They would reach Tuckerton late the next day having traveled through the night. The driver said it was more than 700 miles. The words struck Otto like a spear, how far? My God, what's that in kilometers? The bus would leave them in Tuckerton, as the last 20 miles to the camp required a high-wheeled truck. It was one in the afternoon.

The bus stripped Otto of any sense of station, and all dignity. These circumstances were not what he had imagined, so dirty, so base, and the land, rough and unfinished, and by European standards, so vast. He stared through the grimy window, and as his distorted reflection came back to him he recognized Otto Nielsen as one more hapless immigrant transported to a menial job; a non-entity, nothing but a strong back, a piece of the world's human rubbish, of no concern to anyone, living or dead. The words replayed in his mind, "Go to Canada, they take anyone."

But what choice did he have, hide out in Paris?

Outside of Ottawa the road passed through forest broken by an occasional farm, on past lakes, over streams, along small rivers and rocky outcroppings. With each hour the landscape became more desolate. Then gradually more houses forecast the outskirts of the city. The bus stopped at a filling station and diner to change drivers. While a gas station attendant refueled the bus Otto ate at the counter, bent over his food to discourage talk though it was clear none of the fellow riders were of a mind to speak to him. Back on board, they rode through Ottawa, on to North Bay as the afternoon light cast long shadows across the road. An hour or so later at a stretch break, driver and the riders lined up along the side of the bus to piss. Through North Bay in the dark and on toward Sudbury, and more gas stops. Otto tried to sleep propped against the window using a coat the driver pulled down from his suitcase for a pillow. A fellow passenger with a four or five day beard slept sprawled on the backbench and threw off the vinegary smell of days-old rancid sweat. The others slept bent forward in the seats, snoring, crooked-necked, chins on the chest. Six in the morning and another diner and a new driver and on through Sudbury and the bus finally turned north. They passed the last of the houses. The roadway turned permanently to gravel and became arrow straight, miles without a bend, mile after mile of nothing but woods and scrub, at times the road became bad and the bus, forced to slow to a crawl, lurched from side to side over rocky wash outs, until once again with a noisy throttling up it regained speed and continued the inexorable plunge into what had become limitless wilderness. With each maddening, desolate mile Otto's bewilderment and helplessness increased; every hour the bus pushed northward magnified his despair. How could he have understood that there would be opportunity at the end of this God-forsaken gravel road? What a monumental mistake! Dear Denmark, how could he have dreamed of leaving? The yearning grew as the bus plunged farther into scraggly bleakness, a place that seemed as remote as the moon. Would the bus never stop? And these coarse men he rode with, who in Copenhagen he would have crossed the street to avoid, they would be his fellow workers. He reckoned by the map from the ship's library the mine would be a short trip from Toronto, but the bus was traveling beyond the end of nowhere! How would he find the money to escape this prison? The thought of it multiplied his determination to get out and he resolved to leave at the first chance.

Finally, Tuckerton, a town with one paved street, Main Street, which looked like a set for a western movie, and a few unpaved side roads lined by rows of two-by-four houses, and that was the sum of it. Under a leaden sky at one end of Main Street stood a white, clapboard church and graveyard reminding him that there was one way out, but no thanks. A little Depression humor brought a faint smile. Looking from side to side as the bus crept along, on the left a row of two story, badly painted wooden buildings that included a general store, barber shop, and between the cinema and diner sat side by side the most prosperous businesses he had seen in all of Canada, two bars with freshly painted signs and light pouring from the windows. Across the street there were several small buildings that housed the professionals: an itinerant doctor, a lawyer, a one-teller bank, a rooming house and the police station where on Saturday nights, he presumed, the drunks slept it off. At the far end of Main Street a one-pump filling station and garage anchored the other end of the town. Behind it a junkyard that contained all the stuff that had broken down there for the past twenty years: the scattered remains of derelict cars, trucks and bins of assorted parts, mostly rusted. Here the bus stopped. It was two in the afternoon.

Parked by the filling station sat a large truck that had been made from a cut off bus. Behind the driver's seat were several benches, and behind them, the back wall that had been welded back on. The truck bed made of heavy planks had been built on the remainder of the frame. The entire rig had been jacked up to increase clearance for the oversized tires. As he approached Otto could see in the truck bed several boxes and bags of food, and three or four new shovels and picks. A tall, thin man with graying brown hair dressed in a red flannel shirt and jeans, a heavy coat and high-laced leather boots leaned back cross footed against the front fender. He flicked the remainder of a cigarette into the street as he pushed off when the four bus riders approached. "Jesus, what a sorry looking bunch," he grumbled.

In the North Country, Otto came to learn, this passed for a polite greeting. The greeter had a half smile and a hard glint in his eye that caught the inclined light of the northern sun. "And Pierre, you old turd, couldn't stay away, hey?" Pierre, as it turned out was the malodorous refugee from apparent homelessness; the one who slept across the backbench, the one who had stood out as the most in need of a shower in this unsavory group. His smile cracked his craggy face and the black stubble drew back revealing a set of broken, brown rotted teeth. Honored even by the offensive recognition, Pierre removed his toque and bowed deep, like a cavalier, and with flamboyant mockery, "Oui, Jon, I have returned to your splendid camp, *chez soi.*" Turning to the others, John muttered, "He's a lying prick, probably running from the law… again."

John introduced himself as the co-director of the camp and eyeing Otto's clothing and shoes remarked that with the first rain the city shoes would disappear in the mud if he hadn't frozen to death first. He ordered Otto to go up the street and buy some boots and if he didn't have warm clothes in his bag, get them. He would wait for half an hour in the bar nearest the filling station.

So Otto drained the last of his hoarded funds for boots, work shirts, pants, thick coat and heavy socks guaranteeing a longer sentence in this bleak prison. As the clerk tallied the bill he felt his throat tighten, each additional nickel hurt and by the end only two dollars and change remained in Otto's wallet. Convinced he would need the clothing for only a short term, six months at most to build a stake for an escape and whatever down-payment he could manage for his future, his frustration was compounded as he watched the clerk carefully bundle the unwanted purchases.

Once on board the rig John shifted through the gears as he steered up onto the gravel road and the truck jolted past the last of the houses. These were not the carefully built and neatly maintained cottages of Denmark, but crude wooden bungalows sheathed with nailed on tarpaper, little black boxes with windows built on dirt plots, lined up in a row, maybe five until the truck past the last and the road turned to dirt and became rutted and uneven. Half an hour later John geared the rig down and turned onto a small track in the woods marked by a sign: SPLIT ROCK MINE, H&HCM Ltd., and the reason for the large tires and raised truck bed became clear. For what Otto estimated to be two miles the track foraged through deep ruts, climbed over large roots, stumps, stones and several streambeds bridged by logs. The rig pitched and rolled at a speed less than a walk throwing the men riding in the bed of the truck against the side rails that they stuck onto like flies to flypaper until it reached a clearing and John shouted, "All out!"

Otto looked about. On the left the main building amounted to a long structure of rough sawn lumber with three metal chimneys, evenly spaced, penetrating a rusted metal roof. Six windows looked out on the clearing and in the center a homemade plank door and screen provided the only way in or out. Straight ahead, facing the rig at the end of the clearing, an immense gray rock formed a buttress against which the camp was nestled. Part way up the rock face, at the bottom of a large split in the stone a wooden frame enclosed a black hole, the mine entrance, from which a tailing of broken rock cascaded like a frozen gray waterfall to the valley floor. To the right of the mine entrance a wooden chute led to a large metal funnel, paint-chipped and rusted, that Otto surmised fed the silver bearing rock into a giant machine that dwarfed the small, rough building built against it. That building had a metal roof and chimney, a crude door, and two small windows made opaque by rock dust. A smaller shed with a padlocked door stood out in the open in clear view from the main building. Looking further to the right a large garage and repair shop judging by the jacks and winches he could see through the open door and the discarded truck and machinery parts scattered about. Parked among the trees were a dump truck and a fuel truck, both modified to accommodate the large tires required to enter the camp. Outhouses, two-holers, were located on either side of the clearing. Neatly stacked rows of split firewood surrounded the doorways of the main building and the two largest sheds.

The group followed John through the door in the main building that led immediately to the dining area. The place was hot and smelled of wood smoke and fried fish, and Otto's appetite, suppressed by the irregular jerks and rolls of the bus and truck he had endued the past few days, returned. A dozen or more men seated at two large picnic tables, their clothes and hair salted with fine gray dust, bent over plates piled high with fish and potatoes; two looked up, and wordlessly lifted a fork as a welcoming salute. As they shoveled the food mouth-ward, Otto was taken by the thick hands that wrapped the fork handles. He thought of some artwork he had seen … was it Pieter Brueghel the Elder or Van Gogh who had painted the potato eaters? Here at the camp the scene lived in the flesh. Beyond them in the kitchen the cook stood sweating over an immense wood-burning stove turning a batch of fish filets in a cast iron frying pan and forking them onto a chipped white china platter. He was a small man by mining camp standards, clean-shaven and appeared bald though he wore a woolen knit cap. Wrapped about his belly he had tied a grease-smudged apron over a stained red checked shirt and overalls. He appeared welcoming because he turned and smiled with a wave of his spatula, the most friendly gesture Otto had received in all of Canada.

Next John pushed the new men to the left, into a room that served as a lounge that housed tables, chairs and lamps apparently salvaged from a rummage sale. In a corner a bookshelf held a small library of pulp paper detective stories and a few hardback books. The dramatic feature of the room, an impoundment marked off by a low railing, was the camp office neatly furnished with a chair and a roll-top desk, closed and locked, a rug, a coat rack, wastebasket and lamp. "You stay the Hell out of there! That's BJ's office." John warned as he herded the new men back through the kitchen to the large room on the right of the kitchen, the bunkroom where he told them to choose a bed. The empty beds were near the windows by the wall. Otto put his suitcase, new clothes and boots on what he thought to be a good choice, then washed-up at the trough sink with four spigots that sprouted from the wall separating the bunkroom from the kitchen. It took only a day to learn hot water lasted only as long as a hot fire burned in the stove and to keep it going splitting wood for the kitchen was a burdensome task shared by the miners; but as everyman was a consumer of food and hot water the woodpile remained high. Cut from a five-gallon oilcan a crude urinal was fixed to an outside wall and led to a pipe that ran fifty feet into the woods. "Welcome to north woods luxury," an old-timer snickered, pointing to the urinal. "Some of the other camps don't have this kind of class … there, if you don't want to take the walk to the outhouse and nobody's looking, you open a window." The rectangular buildings, as Otto surmised, were outhouses, unheated and unpleasant and unavoidable.

The newcomers ate with their churlish host, John, who between bites explained that he was responsible for all the men who worked outside the mineshaft. "That would be Otto here," he said with a flick of his head toward Otto. Speaking to the remaining group, Pierre, and two friends from New Brunswick, both experienced miners, he explained that their orders would come from Big John, or BJ, as he was called, who would meet them at the mine entrance in the morning and make their assignments. Then John set out the rules. "The camp has only two and they are hard and fast," he said: "No drinking. I take the rig to town Saturday afternoons and you're welcome to drink all you want there, but no liquor in camp, period! Rule number two, most important! You are here to work! What your boss tells you is law! Figure he's your god for your own good! Break either of these and I'll march your ass out!" The cook carried a plate over and joined them at the table introducing himself as "Cook" with handshakes all around, and raising a finger like a school teacher making a point, scolded John for omitting the third and " most infallible" rule: no complaints about the food or the cook quits! Despite Cook's smile, it was clear to Otto he was serious about that.

The late September nights were cool, requiring several blankets. The weather was perfect for sleeping once his brain had learned to ignore the sounds of fifteen men in one cabin snorting and snoring and farting in loud blasts. By dawn Cook had already stirred about in the scullery, tossing wood in the stove and the men either slowly awakened with the smell of biscuits and coffee or John beat a large pot with a heavy spoon until the clanging forced the straggler's feet to the floor. Otto and several of the others took the time to shave and brush their teeth, but most men grew a week of stubble and ignored the teeth. Breakfast was inelegant but magnificent, exceeding any breakfast he had known: ham and fried eggs and hot biscuits smeared with soft butter and blackberry jam and washed down with rich black coffee in thick white mugs that Cook walking about refilled from a tin coffee pot.

BJ took the miners out to the mineshaft for their instructions. John and Otto went to the shed that sat beside the big machine, a rock crusher. John explained, "The mine up there follows a seam of silver back into the hill, partway back the seam forks so the mine is like a big 'Y'. There is a team of miners in each shaft. The shafts follow the silver up, down and sideways. They blast the rock around the silver seam. The rock without silver is tossed over there, pointing to the tailing. The rock with silver goes down the chute into the big crusher there and gets broken up. In stages it gets crushed smaller and smaller and finally is ground fine, finer than ocean sand." John muttered "Oh God" when he realized Otto had trouble with English. He began to make his explanation with the simplest words he could use and exaggerated gestures. He pushed open the door of the shed and turned on the light. A potbellied stove stood in the middle of the room and against the wall built against the crusher sat a metal table the size of a billiard table. "That's called the shake table. Your job is to run this. See how the table is tilted up toward the crusher, and also tilted a little to the right, and all the horizontal rows of raised ridges across it that lead to the groove there that runs down the right side. Above the ridges you see the dark shiny stuff, that's silver." He drew a finger along a ridge coming up with dark grains on the tip and held it for Otto to see as he repeated "silver" loudly, pointing and moving his head up and down making certain Otto understood. He reached for a valve. "Now when I turn this on the water runs down over the table, over the top of the ridges." He turned the valve back and forth. "See how you've got to adjust it so that it runs nice and smooth over the whole table, like a thin sheet?" John played with the water tap until he had the desired effect. "Then when we open that sifter up there and drop some of the powdered rock and silver on the top edge of the table, just so, the rock, which is lighter than the silver gets washed down over all the ridges and off the bottom of the table into that big trough there and flushed out the back of the building. The silver gets caught on those ridges.

Understand?" Otto nodded that he did. The process seemed clear to him. John walked over to a switch box on the wall. The building filled with noise as the table began to jerk an inch or so back and forth. John shouted over the noise, "You see how the shaking makes the silver move along the ridges to the groove that runs down the right side there and when it washes all the way down it drops into that canvas bag in the tall bucket." Otto looked into the bag that was about the size of a potato sac standing in the bucket. It was half filled with silver grains. The water that accompanied the silver ran out through the canvas, through holes in the bottom of the bucket, and out a drain in the floor. John walked outside, shouted up to Big John to turn on the crusher. The noise of the engine and rock being broken and ground was deafening. They could no longer hear one another in the building, John signaled Otto to come out. "I'll work with you today until you get the hang of it, until you learn!" he shouted. "Generally we fill a bag or so a day depending on the quality of the rock." John led Otto to the small shed nearby, the one in plain sight of the main building, and unlocked the padlock. "The empty bags are numbered, so keep them in order." Pointing to the twelve or fifteen bags filled with silver piled in the shed, he continued, "When a bag is full, it is closed with the leather belt you see at the top and that heavy wire staple locks it shut." He showed Otto the heavy pliers that he used to bend the staple and looked at Otto again to make sure he understood. "You and I have the key." Otto, amazed by the lack of security, asked, "Can't someone break the door," which was simply planks, "and steal the bags?"

"Each of those bags weighs about a hundred pounds, ehh fifty kilos, or more. You saw the road out of here. No one could get far. No silver has been stolen. No one knows how to do it." John gave Otto a smile and pat on the back. "Another job for you. You cut and split the wood for the stove in this building. We can't let the water for the table freeze in the cold weather. It will keep you strong and if you cut the wood it warms you twice as someone said."

Following lunch Cook gave Otto and John bread dough to plug their ears. By the end of the afternoon, Otto, seated on a small stool in front of the shake table, had mastered the adjustment of the water and separation of the silver grains so that John left him to his own devices and returned to repairing the trucks and buildings.

Chapter 14

Camp life became routine. The job he had dreamed of and traveled so far for he learned was considered the least desirable at the mine, and Drew, who had held it before, told him only a damned fool would stay with it. But it suited Otto well. He had come to learn English. Sitting by the shake table with his ears plugged with bread dough he added the rock and silver dust reaching over to the release lever with one hand and adjusted the flow of water from time to time and checked that the silver washed down into the bags all the while studying his grammar book or reading a novel on his knees. He found a copy of *The Sun Also Rises* on the bookshelf in the parlor and liked Hemingway immediately because the sentences were simple and the plain language helped his understanding.

At first unable to lift the heavy bags of silver, he dragged them across the ground to the storage shed but within a week he learned to hoist the bags out of the bucket and swing them to his shoulder in one motion and stack them in the shed eight bags high. An hour a day with the bucksaw and maul, cutting and splitting wood, made for pleasant exercise in the cold air. The little stove and the split logs he contributed to the kitchen kept him busy.

It became clear as winter approached that to stay warm in his bunk near the wall, far from the stove, would be a struggle. Otto collected the discarded newspapers that the old miners told him were essential for survival. He stuffed wads of paper into chinks in the clapboard and floorboards and tacked it up several sheets thick across the two by four studs by his bed. Useful but imperfect insulation, the papers moved in and out like a bellows on windy nights and every week or two strong gusts would tear his handiwork. As the weather became colder he added layers of newspaper under the sheet on his mattress and another layer between his blankets. By November he slept in his clothes with two pairs of socks and a wool cap. In December he bought a heavy second-hand rug to lie over his blankets and that provided enough insulation for him to be warm on the coldest nights. Buried like a mole, no amount of cold or noise bothered him and he slept warm and well. In the morning, responding to the persistent clang of the spoon on the pot, he crawled out of bed and pulled on the boots he had left to warm by the stove.

For Otto the most enigmatic man in the camp was the cook, who the men called Cook. The name Otto had at first ascribed to a collective lack of imagination among the miners until he learned that the man's full name, Augustus C. Cook III, had been shortened to Cook, an abbreviation that neatly joined his identity and camp vocation. An enthusiastic man with a round face and a baldpate, his dancing blue eyes shone with unusual intelligence. His girth, a testament to his habit of tasting, was wrapped in a butcher's apron and his right hand invariably held a cooking tool: a knife, fork or spatula, which when he spoke making points about politics, history or economics he thrashed about for emphasis. This was no backwoodsman, but someone worldly and intelligent who didn't fit the mold of a cook. But cook he did. Lake trout and pike from the lakes near the camp, the meat and vegetables trucked back on Saturdays from town, and pies and cakes he baked. But it was the fresh bread he baked daily, the thick, hot slices spread with butter and washed down with coffee that kept the men seated at the dinner table for conversation and helped make imprisonment in the Canadian wild tolerable. In return for the food, true to his word, Cook brooked no complaints. "Eat it or wear it" his motto and to the last man they understood he meant it.

The Saturday trips into Tuckerton, anticipated throughout the week, were regarded of such importance that the miners bathed, shaved and changed clothes. Bathing in the tin tub in the open room left no chance for modesty, except for BJ, mine boss, who took his baths in town. Undressing subjected the newcomers to hoots and whistles and loud comments by the old timers who stood around joking about how disappointed the ladies in town would be when they saw "that little pecker." The hot water came through a pipe from the iron stove in the kitchen to a tank that stood on tall legs at the end of a tin tub, which to Otto's relief, the miners picked up and dumped out between each bath. A new square of hard red soap was the camp's principle luxury. Scrub down, rinse off, in and out, no soaking; there was a line. The truck left in half an hour.

For the trips to town a system of seniority determined who would be privileged to sit in the truck, and who rode in back on the open bed. Based on an unwritten formula that factored rank, time at the mine and 'brains'—defined at the camp as respect for job know-how with the explosives and common sense—the system was rigorously applied. Book learning beyond that which directly applied to their work counted for nothing. John drove. BJ, Cook and several old timers sat in the cab. As a new man Otto rode on the truck bed, sitting straight legged against the back of the cab with three or four others huddled under a tarp to fight off the cold, rain or snow. When most of the camp had climbed aboard, the modified bus would lumber out of the camp, tossing the silent riders in unison from side to side until it reached the road and the ride smoothed out. In town the men jumped down with bags of laundry for the women who stood by the filling station to take it in. Then each man went his own way—to the bank, the store, or barbershop—eventually working back to the Crooked Pine or Jenny's, the saloons. As evening approached they filled with miners from the Split Rock and the other mines scattered outside Tuckerton and became loud as the men crowded about the bars two and three deep. The places smelled of smoke, spilled beer, and near the far end of the bar where the whores hung out, cheap perfume.

Otto, working to improve his English, began Saturday afternoons at the town cinema watching whatever was playing several times over, until overcome by sleep or boredom, his concentration failed. As it turned out, the cinema played mostly westerns, Tom Mix and a new cowboy Gene Autry. Then he joined the men from the camp at Jenny's.

Big John, or BJ, or Boss as he called himself, made a point not to socialize with his men, and in fact the only men he spoke to in a friendly way were Cook and John; and the latter, though co-manager, he considered his lieutenant. In town, wordless, he swung his frame off the rig and without a look back, walked with his laundry to a house on the back street. He did not come to the bars. It was clear to Otto from the time he met BJ that his authority garnered only a begrudging respect from his men and certainly no feelings that would pass for affection, because he made no secret of the fact that his demands for absolute compliance with the safety regulations arose not out of concern for the miners but a desire for the stamp of approval he would receive from the Canadian mine inspectors. He tacked the awards and certificates to the wall of his office the moment they came. Pride trumped all friendships, of which he had none. John called him a "starchy shit".

Leaving the truck, Cook and John went off together to buy food and supplies and collect the pile of the past week's newspapers that the storekeeper saved for the camp. When the groceries were loaded on the rig John would sit down with the mechanic at the garage to talk cars by the stove; what General Motors or Ford would be making, how to repair this carburetor or that fuel pump, until the mechanic closed up shop and left for home. Then John could be found at the quieter bar, the Crooked Pine, playing cards until at nine sharp when he would stand and march for the door, purposely making this his only signal to the miners to leave. Tabs were quickly paid with a throw down of coin, and his miners scurried out and followed him and as they passed Jenny's saloon they shouted through the door a warning that the truck was leaving. In less than five minutes, with John at the wheel and Cook and BJ beside him, the rig roared to a start and crept out of town in low gear for the first quarter mile so that stragglers could run it down. Over the years, this had become serious sport. While those on board cheered the laggard on, John maintained a speed that kept the truck bed just beyond the runner's grasp. When he decided the man had been punished enough, he slowed to allow him to be pulled aboard. BJ, as head of operations in the mine, accepted that most of his miners became liquored-up on Saturday and could sleep it off on Sunday; but he did not tolerate fall-down drunks or men with the shakes that lasted until Monday morning. The run for the truck weeded out the men BJ found unacceptable, those who drank too much or had too little stamina to keep up with the rig. They were left behind panting on the side of the road. John called the crude ritual a direct application of Darwin's Principle saying it ensured that the crew at Split Rock Mine would be one of the fittest.

Weeknights the men spent around the stove in the parlor reading last week's papers, playing checkers or cards. After dinner there was little talk; stories and jokes told many times were worn out and other than news of Hitler and the Depression there was little to kindle new discussion and the room quickly fell quiet. Otto, left alone by the men, sat with a blanket over his shoulders by the bookshelf reading

"What are you into now?" John stood behind Otto and bent forward to examine the book.

"*The Sun Also Rises*. Good because it's mostly talk." In five months of reading, watching movies and speaking English, Otto had improved so that he was quite fluent, although a thick Danish accent remained and his vocabulary had become peppered with an unresolved mix of English and French curses and western movie cowboy "lingo".

"Oh, and what's it about?" John asked.

"I can't figure it out. I think the man had his dick shot off in the war. Hemingway doesn't describe it."

"Dick blown away? I never saw that happen."

"You were in the war?"

"I was a mechanic before the war. A piece of luck, that. My time was spent in the back of the lines repairing lorries, motorcars, ambulances, anything with wheels and a motor. Had I been a clerk, teacher or something of that sort, I'd have been in a stinking trench and probably dead now."

"France?"

"Right, bloody grim. Got to Paris some, sat in the cafes drinking wine. The stories you hear about the French women are mostly fables."

"What brought you here?"

"You're curious now to know what an old Brit is doing in this goddamned place? That's a dull story." He paused. He was not willing to divulge more. "And so, what's a young Dane doing here watching silver drip?"

"Learning English." Otto stayed purposefully vague; the question made him uncomfortable. Certainly he could not mention Jacobsen's death and his flight from Denmark and he wondered if there might be similar circumstance from which John would be hiding. In fact none of the men at the mine spoke about themselves, their pasts, wives or children if any, where they were from or where they were going.

"Memorizing those flicks, are you?

"Some of them."

"And then on to some better place?"

"You never know, New York probably." Otto replied, feeling trapped by the question because he was uncertain how the truthful answer might affect his status if he was seen as a short-timer at the mine.

"That's a damn good place to go." John said and apparently gratified by the answer pulled up a chair taking an interest in Otto. "After the war," he began, "I went back to Bristol but the only woman I cared for married someone else. She was a piece of tail and smart. We planned to be a team. That's when I found the little garage but without her it didn't interest me any more and I was spending my nights rotting in the pubs drinking away the time with chums. I wanted something more, money really, a chance at the pot of gold, so it was hard to keep out of trouble. I thought about Australia but it seemed a bit far so I responded to an ad for a mechanic with H&H Consolidated Mining here in Canada. Not gold, silver. At first I was at their mine by Fraserdale then about five years ago they decided to open this place, so I moved down here. BJ and I were the first ones here. We essentially built the place. We hired a few men and put up this building, had the well dug and built the crusher that was shipped in piece by piece. He started the mining; I broke my back putting up the rest of the buildings. At first there were seven of us, but then the vein of silver split and we could keep two crews going. So there you have it. It's a rotten life here isn't it? Someday, when I have enough put away, I'll get out of this rattrap as well, maybe New York or London."

"So now you repair the equipment and buildings?"

"And buy the food with Cook, and take the silver into town every Tuesday, and get the gas and kerosene, and buy tools and lumber, and plow the road, and drive you stinking bums in on Saturday, and get everyone back again. That's all and for a pittance."

Chapter 15

Otto was certain every man in the camp had a story to tell, certainly he did; but the real stories for the most part went untold, and without talk of common experience there was little camaraderie in the group. Each stood alone, the veneer that overlay the identity beneath, in general, impenetrable. He figured what little a man revealed of himself was as often invention as fact. How much of what John had said was true, what had he left out? Not to say that apocryphal tales constructed by others that had been appended to each, a supposed identity pieced together from chips of information picked up from an unguarded reference or momentary allusion to an event or place. In time a rudimentary biography, an incomplete mosaic of indeterminate accuracy, defined each man. This never-ending game of charades concerning veiled pasts was played by some from necessity, by men hidden like Otto in the Canadian North from someone or something. Friendships based on common experience could not be formed, and by default he, too, remained a loner.

BJ's office was hallowed ground, the corner of the sitting room sectioned off by a railing and entered by invitation only. The locked roll top desk held his meticulous account books, time sheets, and careful recordings to an ounce of the amount of silver produced daily at the mine. Like the others Otto had no use for BJ and as far as possible in the close confines of the camp he took extra steps to avoid him. None of the men, at least those that lasted, challenged or even joked with the man. At six foot four, and by Otto's estimate, two hundred sixty pounds, BJ carried his weight well, making him an imposing figure whose fists could speak as loudly as his mouth even at forty years of age. His head, large and square, was crowned with crisp brown hair and his small suspicious eyes, magnified by thick wire-rimmed glasses, stared out blankly, rarely registering an emotion other than disdain. A flat nose spread out above his thin lips and his cleft chin jutted like a stony outcrop. Always shaved and neatly dressed, his gut ballooned his flannel shirt over the leather belt securing the freshly pressed and sharply creased khaki pants.

If appearance and a gruff, authoritative manner were not enough, the diploma from the Colorado School of Mines that hung on the wall underscored his claim to command. Past unknown, family unmentioned, a non-smoker and non-drinker, humorless and unsmiling, BJ had a life dedicated, as far as Otto could tell, simply to mining. On Tuesdays the silver was loaded in the cab of the rig and BJ, armed with a large pistol and John with a shotgun, drove to Tuckerton to meet the collection truck from H&H mining. Afterwards John would wait at a bar while BJ went to a little house on a back street to see the woman he supported for reasons other than the freshly washed and pressed laundry she had for him by the door. It was commonly known by the mine crew that BJ screwed the woman in the little house though neither he nor John spoke of it, and the miners, fearful of being overheard, joked about it only when well out of earshot. And there was more to the story. One Tuesday BJ had been followed to the tarpapered bungalow by a peeping Tom who on the following Saturday night at Jenny's Saloon told a group of miners how he had watched through the window as a big titted red-headed woman, who he now recognized in the green dress standing at the end of the bar, bathed a big man who stood in a round tin tub. "He was like a statue of Zeus or some Greek god except there could be no fig leaf big enough for this guy. She then," the peeper continued, "took off her clothes, one by one, dancing and swinging them about like Salome's scarves though there was no music, and when done, the man bent her over taking her from behind grunting like a rutting bull, her tits swinging like bell clappers, until her red head arched up and they both let out an enormous howl that rattled the windowpane." When the miners stopped laughing they told him just who the big man was and that they'd love to watch the beating he would get when BJ heard of it. According to the version of the story Otto was told, the peeping Tom took off like a rabbit straight out of town.

When Otto first heard John's story about the Great War and his lost love it sounded reasonable enough, but as time passed and the backgrounds of the men became more surreal, Otto suspected that what had encouraged John's emigration from Bristol involved more than ambition. This was not a place that an ambitious man would choose to further his prospects, at least not an honest one. What aroused Otto's interest in particular was that John had given Otto a warning about Pierre that revealed an unusual familiarity with the minds of the criminal class. Otto, John warned, should watch out for Pierre, who, though good in the mine was a petty thief; and but for a lack of talent and opportunity, was capable of grand larceny and worse. The time away from the mine,

John had concluded, Pierre had spent in a concrete cell, and though based on nothing more than a guess; he said he had known too many thieves not to recognize one. "Thieves never reform, they constantly look to steal," he instructed. "They are born to it; you can see it in their eyes, how they look about, always curious for no good reason. And lying, for them, it is instinctive. Believe me, you should trust a murderer first." Otto's most valued possession, a tattered English text snatched from his bookshelf as he left Denmark would be of little use to even the most desperate of thieves. But warned, he began to take note of Pierre, how he slid silently about, materializing when not expected, always on the alert, searching for nothing in particular. Tall and thin, his uncombed greasy black hair trailed over his collar; his long, gaunt, deeply creviced and irregularly shaven face gave him a dark, menacing look and his habit of sucking air through his rotted brown teeth produced a low whistle that had annoyed Otto from the start. The miners needled him, joking and wrinkling their noses, saying that Pierre stank, which he did, forcing him every Saturday to disrobe his waxy white body and fold it like a wadding water bird into the waiting tub. Pierre displayed no humor in return, not a hint that he enjoyed this bunkhouse ribbing, just a look of smoldering rage, which egged his tormentors on. It perplexed Otto, why had Pierre come back to the mine, saying he considered this to be his home. And why would he return to such abuse? How bad could the conditions have been elsewhere to make this camp look good? Prison perhaps; but in addition, what thing of value was there to steal in this place besides silver—yes, Otto thought, it had to be all the silver, bags and bags of it.

For Otto the most interesting man in camp was Cook. Perhaps the most clever imposter—or was he? According to his rumored past, unverified of course, he had been a wildly successful Wall Street stock and bond salesman, *bon vivant,* epicure, all around sport, denizen of the Hamptons and Saratoga horse races rubbing shoulders with the Social

Register, heir to a fortune and also a con-artist who sold worthless shares to the gullible public during the twenties bubble, now escaping his past, pursued by creditors, an angry wife, and especially the Internal Revenue Service. Thought by the miners to be a chameleon, with a talent for adaptation, he was tucked away representing himself as a cook. With a Fanny Farmer cookbook as an assistant he satisfied the unsophisticated palates of a mining camp. Here, as the story went, he hides, sequestered, until the heat in the financial world died down and he was free to return and claim the vast fortune hidden in his Swiss accounts. Of course this was merely a great tale dreamed up and circulated among the men. Perhaps, as he claimed he was indeed an old army cook, here by necessity as no other employment was available, but he seemed too worldly for that. He made no further elaboration of his military past, no talk of the fighting, no mention of his unit or lost friends, and no mementos among his possessions. Otto did not believe the army cook story and became certain the camp's assessment of the man was right and as such, Cook was a man whom Otto became desperate to know, to hear of his past, to learn his money-making secrets and, assuming he was crooked, in legal ways, emulate. Despite Otto's overtures, the barricade around Cook's suspected identity could not be breached. Cook would be pleased to teach Otto cooking, but he claimed to have no other occupation, financial or otherwise.

On the long winter nights lying on his back, deep within the sheets of his bed, Otto's mind was free to range in no predetermined order over his life and his imagined future. He would begin this psychological journey with a trip back to Denmark and then, turning his back to the wall, he would concentrate on plans for his exit. He wasn't helpless, he assured himself. He would leave; it was just a matter of time and money. Once asleep, he dreamed of the future in fragmented, fitful dreams. He saw himself in New York like a character in a silent movie, on the streets among towering buildings in cold, white sunshine and deep shadows; tramping through crowds, jostled, anonymous, alone, moving faster than those around him as if chased by some phantom he couldn't see. Or he dreamed of an ornate dining room, not unlike the ship's ballroom, eating with people he could not recognize their distorted faces that appeared as a amalgam; they were chewing and laughing, and in one dream that woke him, retching. He had erotic dreams of Kirsten, carrying her through the door of the farmhouse or chasing her nude figure through Copenhagen's parks.

One November evening, in a conversation that was ordinary enough, John remarked that Otto needed a haircut, and to ensure that he got one, John would meet him late Saturday afternoon at the barbershop and would even pay for it. Clearly this was an appointment.

Chapter 16

Otto opened the barbershop door at four p.m. and looked around, no John in sight. He eased into the last chair left among the waiting miners and listened to their shoptalk while thumbing an old Maclean's magazine, and tried to read an article about the debates in the Canadian Parliament but after paragraph or two, uninterested, he dropped the magazine back on the table. The barbers smelled tips from the pay in the pants pockets of the miners and worked as fast as the clippers and scissors could drop cut hair on the floor. Tom, the head barber and owner, talked non-stop as he clipped. He also served as Mayor of Tuckerton, and the "tonsorial parlor" as he called it, served him as mayor's office and public forum for discussion of town business and the goings on at the surrounding mines, a subject he inquired about from each miner as the health of the mines was vital the economy of Tuckerton, in fact to its very survival. Otto, with nothing else to do, put his mind to listening and studying the place and concluded the Mayor to be a feckless optimist, a glass half full man. The shop, which projected a level of luxury more suited to a city than a tarpaper town at the end of a gravel road in the northern scrub, boasted big mirrors above the granite shelves that displayed fragrant hair oils in fancy bottles and rows of scissors, clippers and straight razors and two barber chairs with red leather seats, white porcelain arms, chrome footrests and foot pedals that the barbers pumped to raise the seats. A pull on the large, white handle on the side laid the customers back for shaves followed by steaming hot towels from a chrome-topped heater and a splash of cool witch-hazel applied with brisk popping pats that gave the place a smell that a blind man stepping through the door would declare to be a barbershop.

The shop emptied as man after man paid up and left, and Otto, with a fresh haircut sat waiting and returned to picking through the worn magazines that lay scattered on a low table. The faded rays of the last of the afternoon sunlight barely lit the window. Tom flicked on the two lights that hung down from the ceiling and picked up a broom and swept the afternoon's cuttings into a dustbin.

The bell over the door jingled when John walked in and Tom pointed to the back room and while putting on his coat left instructions to turn out the lights and secure the door against the fall winds. In the half-lit back storeroom of the empty shop, seated across from one another at an old table and chairs, the purpose for the clandestine meeting began to unfold. John started by saying he had been observing Otto and liked his motivation and the quality of his work. That's fine, Otto thought. John went on, saying he had considered recruiting Drew for this enterprise, but concern about his intelligence and reliability had led him to conclude that he should wait for his replacement. He paused, drawing a long breath, sitting back and leaning forward again. As luck would have it, he continued, Drew's replacement appeared to be smart and above all ambitious, and therefore a good prospect; someone whose ambition he, John, could relate to; someone who had aspirations and goals like his own, someone clearly planning to leave and go on to something better; someone who would need money. He smiled broadly, more pleased with the compliments than Otto, who, by this point, still worked to grasp the point. He went on. Had Otto considered what an uphill climb he faced, at 12 dollars a week cleared after food and lodging were deducted? Even saving every penny, how long it would be before he had enough to go to New York, let alone enough for a proper start? The phrases in the sentence came out slowly, one at a time with a long pause between for emphasis as John picked his words to uncover his proposal deliberately layer by layer. Between each sentence he searched Otto's eyes for a sign of comprehension, interest or alarm. Then he sprung it. "Working together, you know, we could come by a lot more." Again, his eyes searched for a trace of interest, any evidence from Otto there had been a linking of minds: a slight lean forward, a raised eyebrow, a small smile, indicating the unsaid, what he had implied, was understood. "There are opportunities at the mine." He wanted a sign, any sign from Otto. "Would Otto be interested in a plan that would provide him with a proper start, set him up in fine style?" Otto made a slight voluntary nod, a very small gesture. He desperately wanted a way out of the camp, but he wanted to know more, to hear what John was driving at, what this was that could set him up in "fine style", though, he realized there was only one thing, the silver—and that was a frightening prospect. His slight nod, however, was sufficient inducement. John continued, "Have you ever thought of what one of those bags is worth? Or five or ten?" The implication now unmistakable, his meaning no longer guarded. "Our work would involve putting a hand in the till, so to speak." If Otto was interested he would go on, otherwise "we have never spoken."

Otto considered his dilemma. He had come to make his fortune and understood how serious the odds against that were as word of the collapsed stock market and the growing Depression filtered up to Tuckerton. To succeed in this economic climate he would need to be bold and very lucky. But he hadn't come to Canada to steal or be jailed for theft. Sitting in the harsh light of the hanging bulb, after a moment of reflection he concluded he should listen to John's plan and if it proved to be a good one, in other words, watertight, he would consider it. He did not want to turn the proposal down unheard.

John's voice broke through the fog of deliberation. "Are you interested? Should I go on?" The conspiratorial atmosphere, the dark shadows, softened voices, began to excite Otto. Suddenly tense, alive, alert he was anxious to hear what was either an ingenious plan, or a foolhardy larcenous pipe dream from a mechanic with a questionable past and too much time to think. Was there not a man in camp who hadn't dreamt of a way to steal the silver? Had John come up with the formula that had eluded so many others? Here in the back of a barbershop, would this be the beginning of his fortune or his start on a path to disaster? He sat erect, nodded, and indicated that John should continue. Still more curious than interested, he said he agreed to hear the details, but stressed that he was not able to guarantee participation, adding with emphasis, that he would not divulge a word of what he was to hear. John had become increasingly watchful, frequently glancing about the room and at the closed doors, even though the barber had long since left. The single bulb hanging above the table cast deep shadows, a sinister chiaroscuro, giving John's otherwise not displeasing features an evil look; beneath his brows black shadows accentuated the depth of his orbits, and as he leaned forward, his voice barely a whisper, his face moved out of the darkness.

He began again with a preface that held a strong warning spoken in a tone not present before, "On pain of death mention this to no one." Otto nodded again.

John reached into the pocket of his coat and pulled out three small leather bags of the type that good jewelry might come in, but much heavier, and laid them on the table. "We take a little at a time, not much, just some silver off the top, so to speak. If we get greedy we will get caught. BJ has a very good idea of what each day's weight should be. By my calculations, if silver remains at forty cents an ounce or better, in a year we each could make an additional twelve hundred dollars American, and in two, twenty-four hundred. If you watched your pennies, adding in two years salary, that would give you about four thousand for starters and that's enough to get you to New York in fine style, to set you up in a business, buy stocks, bonds, whatever." He sat back, crossing his arms, and merged again with the shadows. Otto made no response. John sat forward again. "I have planned on this for several years now, just waiting for the right person to work with. Again, are you with me so far? Should I go on?" If Otto was not to be an accomplice in this scheme, John did not want to divulge further proprietary information. Criminal plans had value.

"Continue." Otto realized at this point there was no going back.

"This is how it will work. Every morning, while the mine is running, you are to put three, four, six ounces of silver into one of these leather sacs, put it in your pocket and go to the outhouse on this side of the camp. If you reach under the hole on the right side, way forward and to the right, near the wall you will feel a small shelf I made when I built it. Put the sac there. Later in the day I will retrieve it and return the sac from the previous morning. The amount of silver we take is not enough to change the daily quota and raise suspicion. From time to time, we will be able to take more. The amount of high-grade ore does vary, when it's good we take a lot, when poor less, but greed is our enemy."

Otto began to examine the plan, showing some interest. "And what do you do with the silver? How do we get it out of the camp?"

"The rig has two fuel tanks, the primary under the left side of the truck bed and the auxiliary under the right, both hold fifty gallons. The auxiliary tank on the passenger's side is a dummy, has a dummy fuel line. Anyone who might look under the chassis couldn't notice anything unusual about it. The rig runs off the tank on the left. When I tank up, I fill the left. If anyone is watching, I fake the right. Now the silver you nip each day, I dump down the right fill pipe. By my estimates it will take about a year to fill. At that time the tank will, 'quote', develop a leak and require replacement. I cut it away on the road to town, roll it off the side of the road, cover it, and then, at the garage in town, install a new one. If this has worked well we have another go around, or we pack it in then, retire, sell the silver and go our separate ways. As you see the beauty of this is, BJ won't know the mine has been pinched."

Otto sat back in his chair. He drew a deep breath through his nose and let it out with an audible sigh, indicating his uncertainty. The difficulty he faced was that he didn't have any experience with criminal enterprise and didn't know how to assess the plan; was it workable, or had John spent too many lonely nights in the back woods?

"You think this will work?"

"Believe me, Otto, I have thought about this every day for two years now. I've gone over and over it in my mind and I don't see a problem." Then he added the last of the details. "I have picked the spot to dig a hole by the side of the road. When the time comes, we just uncover the tanks, winch them up on the back of a truck and we are off, free and clear. We need each other to get the silver out, out of the camp initially, then again, out of the woods. We have to remain partners, there is no way we can cheat one another." He paused again letting Otto consider his proposal again and finally inquired. "Now, what do you say?"

"When do we start?" Otto asked.

"Here are the bags, you take two and we start tomorrow."

They left separately, John to take up his usual place at the card table at The Crooked Pine. Otto followed a few minutes later and walked past to Jenny's. Later that night, when he considered his impulsive answer, Otto wondered what in the lessons of his past could be so ignored that he would steal and take such a risk.

Chapter 17

The first winter storm came on gently, no wind. Big flakes floated down like apple petals hazing over the sinking sun, but by dark it had blown up into a blinding frenzy hurling the snow against the camp through the night until by morning, when it crept off as softly as it had come, the buildings were embraced by drifts that wrapped them to the window sills. The thick snow erased sharp edges and the landscape became rounded and soothing, the roofs and ledges made plump and white gave shelter to the bunkhouse from the brutal winds, locking in the warmth of the stoves. The men shoveled their way out and tramped crude paths to the outhouses, the woodpiles, and the mineshaft. The sun when it shone came at a steep angle sparking off chips of crystalline snow, the glare made for squints and teary eyes. The smell of the land, fermenting leaves, pine sap, and the offal of the dump smothered and replaced by the piquant smoke of the wood fires that drifted over the buildings. Otto had feared the coming of winter, thinking that with the darkness and fierce cold it would be the least bearable of the seasons, but the snow brought a welcome quiet to the camp; the roar of the machinery mercifully damped by the drifts piled thick on the roof and around the walls of the buildings. The mood of the men mellowed as their leisure time turned to carving, tying flies, and playing checkers while they lived in the tranquility of the winter interlude before the mud and flies of spring. John fought to open the road out of camp with the dump truck filled with rocks for weight, packing the snow down or pushing away the largest drifts with the scratched and bent orange plow because, despite the impracticability and effort it took to clear a track, cancellation of the weekly trip to Tuckerton would bring an abrupt reversal of the camp's mood, and if repeated, mutiny. They had seen several of those in the past and order restored only with BJ threatening to use the pistol he kept locked in his desk.

At night in bed, bundled against the cold, Otto suffered a recurrence of the attacks of conscience as the lessons of the Gospel and Martin Luther, even though distant both in time and place, had followed him to the Canadian North. He had not given thought to questions of right and wrong, morality and corruption, of Heaven and Hell since leaving Denmark until the meeting in the back room of the barbershop and the decision to conspire with John to steal, in short to become a thief. The last fragment of childhood innocence cast away with some words and a handshake, the old world truly left behind and a return to it made impossible. He was caught up in a new reality, this was a different time and he had let go of one more constraint in this desperate struggle to salvage himself and restart the evolution of the person that Otto had dreamed to be. And like it or not, he would have to find a way to become comfortable with stealing, outwardly and within his own concept of what Otto Nielsen could accept. That was the harsh, even cursed, truth. He had long recognized that at his core it was his desire for wealth that drove him and he had no inclination to control it, even if he could. And as John had said, and the small weekly paycheck confirmed: he could not accumulate enough to support his ambitions—so with no other choice but to escape this Hellhole of penury and isolation he took the opportunity John had offered. The silver provided a golden opportunity, God given or not.

That settled, the fear of discovery continued to plague his sleep. Would someone enter just as he was scooping a handful of grains into the bag, would someone notice the leather bags sequestered in the outhouse, would BJ notice the daily silver weights to be short? But the winter months passed without incident, and encouraged by the seamless transfer of the leather bags, unpleasant as he found placement and retrieval to be, his apprehension waned. In time, rather than question his decision to steal, he began to celebrate it, each transfer of the silver from bucket to fuel tank a step toward freedom. He allowed himself to dream of the future, he would arrive in New York as a young man of substance, travel first class, well heeled, able to shop for just the right opportunity to transform the silver grains into real wealth. The colorful dreams projected on his mind were now in an optimistic hue. The despair that had gripped him from his first steps on Canadian soil had abated, and with each passing day, each pound of silver, his mood lifted. He was on the way out.

With their enterprise running smoothly, the confederates had no need for communication, took no particular interest in one another, and spoke only when required. As far as Otto could determine, John considered his plan faultless and suffered no fear.

Spring, the season of hope and rebirth dissolved the snow and as the ice retreated from the paths, boards and logs were thrown on them and sank in the mire in a week. The paths became mud filled trenches that clutched at the men's boots, which when pulled free, were covered with mud that no amount of stomping and scraping could get off. Mud was everywhere. Once inside the bunkhouse door where boots were pulled and piled, the clots of mud were left to dry, until responding to Cook's shouts to "clean the damn place", a man would pick up a broom and sweep them out the door. The tract out of camp, wet and soft, mired the rig up to the axels. Once stuck, the men would climb down, wrap a cable around a large tree and amidst shouts and curses, spinning tires, exhaust smoke and flying muck, fight to winch it free. That exercise was repeated two or three times before reaching the gravel road and the truck rolled unhampered on to Tuckerton. There the men scattered to the cinema, barbershop and the bars and the liquor, the card games and sought out the women that could be bought.

Following the cinema Otto would stand with the miners at Jenny's Bar, drink a beer, talk and watch the four or five hookers that stood at the end the bar by the staircase chatting together, waiting to bargain with customers. When a miner sauntered over to the women and interrupted the ladies conversation, Otto would bet the man standing at his elbow which of the women the miner would pick and occasionally, if standing near enough, listened to the negotiations that at times became heated and broke down over a dollar or two. When a bargain was struck and the man and woman turned for the stairs to the rooms above a cheer went up. But at times the women could be prickly and brutally rude, rejecting the miner who would throw his arms in the air in mock despair, or as had become a pattern, make a deep bow as he backed away, drawing laughs and catcalls from his amused friends. The dealings with the prostitutes, especially the rejections, amounted to the best entertainment in Tuckerton. Otto called it *Schadenfreude*. He didn't know an English word for enjoying another's suffering.

The whoring didn't bother Otto. He couldn't judge those so desperate for money or for those so deprived of pleasure to pay for sex. He had no interest in joining in, prevented not so much by morals or the prostitutes, several of whom appeared agreeable enough, but by their clientele. He lived with these unwashed wretches who joked of suffering from the "the drip" and seeping rashes and could not stomach sharing a woman with them. Why risk of some infection for which there were no cures. When prodded to buy himself a good time, to "get the pecker up and go for it," he demurred with the partial truth that he was saving his money, and he emphasized to his bar-mates, not wanting to appear a prude; it was as a matter of economy, not morals, that he refrained. "Someday," he would say, forcing a lewd smile. Quietly, however, he did like a pretty young girl with black hair and blue eyes they called Nellie, who sometimes stood at the end of the bar and someday he might do her. He saw that she chose her customers carefully, accepting business only from those who met her standards, which Otto perceived after watching her for several months, as those who were very clean and well heeled.

All of which led to one Saturday when the miners, drinking heavily and looking for amusement, put a challenge to Otto that if he were too cheap to underwrite the project himself, they would buy him a "five dollar whore"—the very best Jenny's could provide. Amid shouts and laughter there began an aggressive fund raising campaign, accompanied by hollers and hoots up and down the bar as the quarters, a half dollar or two and a silver dollar dropped onto the pile. Within two minutes the quotient had been met. Cornered and facing shouted remarks about his manhood or lack thereof, Otto relented and under the scrutiny of the now hushed miners approached Nellie at the end of the bar and made his request. Would she accept? It was like asking someone to dance and he hoped for a refusal. She made no reply, not a look or an indication that she accepted other than to turn on her heel and he followed climbing the stairs behind her to the rooms above, once again to huzzahs and the thumping of fists pounding on the bar.

As a schoolboy Otto had imagined this moment a hundred times; "You can buy sex, wonderful!" and now here it was, bought and paid for, an extraordinary adventure, a time for a surging arousal. But pubescent high hopes did not anticipate the chill reality imposes and with each step his disposition edged toward trepidation. Up the narrow hall in front of a door she stopped with her hand on the knob and told him to wait. When she called him in he found the room lit by candles that flickered on the bureau against the wall and on the bedside table pollinating the air that his quickened breathes brought in, warm and perfumed, seductive. The door shut out some of the noise from downstairs and before him on the edge of the double bed with bedclothes scattered about sat a woman whose beauty far exceeded any adolescent dream. The red velvet gown she wore at the bar tossed on a chair and now she was clothed simply in a short lace gown, her long black hair falling about her face and over her shoulders. She stood and walked barefooted toward him arms outstretched, smiling, with no attempt at modesty. Her breasts moved gently with each step, the lace drifted against her flat stomach and the black mons exaggerated the whiteness of her thighs. With his eyes barely adjusted to the dim light, his reaction to the suddenness of it was distress. She knew that stricken look and had dealt with it before, but once it became clear that a practiced hand working through his jeans could elicit no response, she looked up at him perplexed, unsure if she had been spurned. Otto, deeply troubled by his failure to respond, took her hands and sat with her on the side the bed and saying that his "mind was elsewhere."

"Where else could it be?" she asked, unconvinced that he did not find her unpleasing.

"Oh, there has been trouble at the mine." he said.

As frustration gave way to hurt, she stood, wrapped herself in a robe and ordered him to leave, stuffing a five-dollar bill in his pocket. He retreated, placing the money on the bureau while telling her he thought she was very beautiful and imploring her not to mention his "paralysis" to any of the miners, emphasizing that he would be subjected to unrelenting derision. As he opened the door she threw the bill after him and the noise of the bar drowned out her angry words that followed. From the corner of his eye he saw her pick up the bill again and slam the door.

Descending the stairs he was greeted with whistles and laughter at his quick return "Hey Otto, shoot your wad?" and "Did you get your pants off?" He shouted back "thanks boys" for the "excellent time" and walking up to the bar called to the bartender to treat his benefactors to a drink, which repaid each man some of what he had invested. He was a good sport and his generosity returned to Otto more than he imagined in fellowship. The lessons from Kurt in the small bar in Copenhagen, "be generous with the drinks," applied in Canada and beyond as well.

Heeding John's call from the street, the men prepared to leave. Otto looked back as Nellie descended the stairs. Dressed this time in a flowered cotton dress, a shawl around her shoulders, she appeared as fresh as a schoolgirl, not the temptress he had just encountered. In the truck propped against the back of the cab, bumping along the road, the image of her naked form walking toward him replayed in his mind and now, in the subarctic air, he experienced the unattainable tumescence. Her likeness would recur in dreamy hours of the night and the urges she inspired could not be subdued. Yet, at the bar when he approached she turned away and would not be trifled with, refusing to speak to him.

In May the snow had retreated to the patches of shade under the trees. The conspirators, emboldened by the lack of any indication their thefts had been suspected, began to transfer a pound or more of silver a day, putting them ahead of schedule. The changes in the daily weights had been gradual, increasing over time slowly enough that BJ never questioned them.

Late one afternoon, as he bent down to fasten the lock on the silver storage shed, Otto was slammed against the wooden door, wrenching his shoulder. Turning around with a rush of anger and fear he shoved the attacker off and stood face to face with Pierre who hissed that he knew all along, since he first saw him, that Otto would eventually steal. No man could resist the temptation sitting alone, day after day, with bags of silver and not help himself! It was only a matter of time. Pulling his bony frame erect and with a contemptuous smirk, Pierre announced, his coal black eyes dancing with amusement at having trapped his prey, that he had gone through Otto's clothes for several weeks now, and had found *"Eh, bien!* Curious little leather bags and there, plain as day, stuck to the lining of the little leather bags shiny little granules of silver – evidence that Otto was stealing! Standing there, breathing heavily, his breath whistling through his teeth he flaunted the leverage this gave him and demanded to know where Otto hid the silver because now he was Otto's partner. Or if Otto wasn't in the mood to share, he would expose Otto as the thief he was and jail would be a certainty. Pierre's price for silence: half of the booty.

Otto's right knee smashed into the Frenchman's groin, and as Pierre bent forward in pain, Otto grabbed him by the back of his shirt and belt, and rammed his head against the door. As Pierre dropped to his hands and knees, stunned, Otto took the hunting knife Pierre carried on his belt and flung it over the shed. Staggering to his feet Pierre growled that whether Otto liked it or not, he was going to find where the silver was hidden and, by God, Otto would divide it. And true to his word, over the next few weeks, when not in the mine, the French-Canadian thief dedicated himself to solving the mystery, peering under buildings, wandering about hands clasped behind his back affecting an after dinner stroll, looking for evidence of freshly dug ground, kicking over stones, and, in a tactic that gave Otto the most concern, searching about the outhouses. Otto knew it was a matter of time before he reached far enough under the privy boards and found John's shelf. Otto couldn't sleep.

"Jesus, if I didn't know better, you'd think he's Sherlock Holmes. We should buy him one of those deer slayer hats." John joked, alluding to the resemblance of the tall miner's posture to the famous detective's. Then John said, "Well he shouldn't be at it much longer."

Chapter 18

The Mattagami River, one of the dozens of rivers that snake northward across the forsaken wilderness of Northern Canada, passed within two miles of the camp. Frozen during the winter, in spring it breaks free of the icy clutches and rushes the melt from the winter snows into the massive James and Hudson Bays. A small canoe John bought for a dollar and repaired with fresh canvas and multiple coats of green paint hung from the rafters of the garage, and each year was taken down as the ice retreated and the river cleared. Though prized, the invitations from John to fish with him in the river included an obligation to lend one's back, as the canoe and gear required portage on a narrow, rocky trail where the porter, with both hands clasped on the canoe, submitted to the torment of slashing branches and swarms of flies and mosquitoes that contested the route. The reward would be a day of fishing on the river, an outing that despite the hardship provided relief from mine work and was eagerly sought. And so it was that Pierre left the camp with John one May morning in good spirits happy to have been selected for special consideration, for if there were any individual in the camp that Pierre felt an affinity for, it was John. So without a complaint, he hefted the canoe on his back and pitched forward at the waist to balance the weight. A smile broke the deep lines in his face as he struggled up the trail.

When the police arrived, a day after the drowning, John told the story and, as if carved in stone, the words never varied no matter how often he repeated it. They had stood in the canoe, fishing on the edge of the current casting toward shore, when, despite deliberate pains not to do so, as they understood how tipsy these canoes could be (they had even closed the tackle box and lashed it under a seat in case of such an eventuality John noted), somehow both had cast from the same side at the same instant, which caused the canoe to flip, pitching them into the icy water. Though he swam about searching for Pierre, he never saw him surface. Then he struggled, pushing the capsized canoe to the shore, righted it, and paddled out again vainly searching for his friend using a broken branch for a paddle as canoe's paddles had been carried off by the current. After an hour drifting down the river, calling out, hoping to find him alive on shore there, he gave up. Certain Pierre could not have survived, he returned to camp and called the authorities.

Sergeant Campbell listened to John's account with his brow furrowed, but gave no indication of his private thoughts, asking only that they visit the scene. Taking paddles with them, they found the canoe. After the sergeant inspected the site and canoe for blood, and finding none, he suggested they take the canoe out on the river to search for the body. If John felt a spasm of fear, it would have been then, as he had relied on the current to carry the corpse miles into the wilderness, never to be discovered. For the truth was John had used Pierre's own knife to kill him as the miner, shocked by the icy water, struggled to swim. When the men came together and hung onto the overturned canoe John reached behind Pierre and took his knife from the sheath and grimly pushed it under Pierre's ribs slicing up through his lungs and tearing into his heart, then turning the knife down, sliced down through his guts opening them so the body would not float. The stunned miner, seized with disbelief, sank below the surface amid bloody bubbles.

They searched the brush and snags along the riverbank that might catch a floating body. After several hours it was concluded the miner was lost, and resigned that he had no way to discount the story John told, Sergeant Campbell sat at the camp dinner table and carefully filled in the form pronouncing the episode to be an accidental drowning. As he watched from across the table, John showed no sign of relief, only professed sorrow for the loss of a friend, and once the forms were completed and signed, stood and offered the sergeant a cup of coffee.

Otto never heard a hint of what had happened that day. Even when alone and the loss of Pierre came up, John's story of the grievous event at no time included a wink or smile to acknowledge to Otto something else might be the truth. Perhaps John was generous, seeking not to implicate Otto in the crime or burden his conscience with it. Or the killer simply understood that a secret shared is a secret no longer. He would not disclose what had been a perfect crime, not to anyone. Otto considered Pierre's death very convenient and though he considered the possibility of foul play, John's story to the assembled camp, told with a grief stricken voice, appeared so heartfelt his sorrow and veracity were not questioned.

BJ had little experience writing a letter of condolence, as there had been no accidents or deaths at the mine; however, as the agent for H&H Consolidated Mining Ltd his letter began by saying what great sorrow all the men at the camp felt losing their good friend Pierre. He went on to explain that Pierre had died doing what he loved best, fishing, and that he had drowned a hero trying to save his companion in the icy river. At that point BJ was stuck. He could conjure no more complimentary words about a man so roundly disliked, and chewing on his lower lip managed to add only a brief sentence or two more. The letter was passed around to the men at the camp to sign and add words of comfort should they feel inspired. There were a few. It was then carefully folded and placed with the deceased man's Sunday suit, bank book, gold watch, rosary and missal that appeared unused. The bundle was wrapped in brown paper and tied up with string and mailed the following Saturday. A month later a reply came. In tremulous writing an elderly Aunt thanked BJ for the kind letter and the generous remarks about her beloved nephew. She concluded by saying that Pierre had always told her how much he loved his work and his friends at the mine.

The flies and mosquitoes in the North Country could and did drive men insane, blighting for several months the peace of the unspoiled wilderness. The bugs died away over the summer and the beauty of the country became open to enjoy by the light of the long autumn days. In September gasoline began to spill from the fill pipe of the right fuel tank as the silver went in. In nine months the conspirators had amassed without any indication of discovery enough silver to fill the fifty-gallon tank, and as planned, John reported to BJ that a leak in the bottom of the tank had opened up, and the new tank had been special-ordered by the garage in Tuckerton. One afternoon, by the side of the gravel road, Otto helped John unbolt the tank and roll it into the woods where they hastily buried it and marked the spot with a slash of white paint on the trunk of a tree. Back at camp the new tank was installed. Reassured by how smoothly the exchange had gone and encouraged by the prospects of doubling their riches, John and Otto agreed to carry on until the following spring. It had been a year since his arrival. Otto had adapted to the life of the camp, so much so in fact, that he felt no disappointment in the decision to stay. He could easily withstand nine months more and he looked forward to the tranquility another winter would provide.

The winter passed uneventfully. The silver collections progressed efficiently and plans were made to leave the camp in May or June. In the spring when the gasoline began to climb into the fill pipe John located a replacement tank.

Chapter 19

In April John and Otto bought a truck, or lorry, as John would call it, for fifty dollars—an abandoned 1923 Gotfredson Model 20 that sat behind the gas station in Tuckerton. The cloth top, rotted into shredded streamers; the leather seats, cracked and sprouting tufts of cotton padding; the tires split and flat from freezing and thawing in the mud; and most of the wooden bed rails broken or missing. John and Otto put a chain around the front axle and pulled it free. Saturdays were spent disassembling and cleaning and reassembling. Otto swept the cab out removing leaves and twigs and with rags and a bucket of soapy water attacked the dirt mixed with bird and mouse droppings. John tended to the engine and as the final step replaced the carburetor that he had cleaned as carefully as a watch. Showing Otto how to choke it with the flat of his hand he poured gas down the throat, and shouting curses commanded the four-cylinder Buda engine to fire up. With a burst of black exhaust it roared to life shaking like a wet dog it ran at a choppy idle, skipping beats and backfiring, until John coaxed the engine smooth making barely perceptible turns of the idle screw. Over the din he shouted to Otto with thumbs up, "Behold our transportation!" New pneumatic tires and a spare were added; the seats beyond repair were replaced with a plank and a folded blanket. A tarp was cut and stitched to mend the top. New boards were fitted to the wooden sides of the bed, and as a final touch, the body and fenders were washed and waxed. During the test drive on the gravel road the old Gotfredson ran for fifty miles at almost forty miles an hour without a problem. Their truck, they concluded, would hold up nicely until the silver was unloaded in North Bay and probably well beyond.

On one of his weekday trips to town, John pulled the camp's rig off the road, removed the bolts holding the tank, let it drop to the ground, rolled it down the bank and buried it in the hole under leaves and brush along with the first. He bolted on the replacement tank and reconnected the fuel line. In less than an hour he continued what otherwise was a routine trip to town for supplies.

On the thirty-first of May, John and Otto gave BJ a month's notice. They would be leaving together. BJ unperturbed by news he knew was coming, simply asked if they meant June thirtieth or July first while he licked the tip of a stubbly pencil and marked the date down in a dog-eared pocket notebook. For Otto the month's wait would be barely tolerable; he itched to leave before something went wrong or BJ had some suspicion they were up to something particularly as the two of them were leaving together. He studied BJ's face closely for any sign of mistrust until John, noticing his surreptitious looks warned Otto he had better get over his short-timer's syndrome because no matter how bad the jitters, their departure would be "damned orderly and unrushed". "No one would be the wiser if it goes smooth and natural!" he scolded. The following weekend in town on the pin board in the general store Big John put up a notice penciled in big print for a mechanic and mechanic's helper. The men knew it was a waste of time as the word had been spread around the bars for years that it could be Hell out at the Split Rock because BJ had moods. He was a picky, overbearing hard-assed son-of-a-bitch. He should know better and recruit from North Bay.

Saturday evenings, Otto found himself watching Nellie make conversation with the "ladies" gathered at the end of the bar. She stood apart. She was young, unspoiled. He guessed not yet twenty, and very pretty, her black hair and indigo eyes an unusual and agreeable combination that in his experience only Irish parentage produced. And her name, Nellie, could there be any question of the ancestry. What was she doing here, and doing this, he mulled. The older women clearly were her protectors, especially the plump old red head who appeared to run things, bossing the others about, interrupting, handing out assignments. Nellie must live with one of them. Her? Why did she choose this degrading life? He wondered how long it would take for her to be stamped with the hardened look and flinty sarcasm of the others. The older women that encircled her were toughened, callused, cynical, saucy and insolent. Past masters of the hands-on-the-hips, steely-eyed look and scatological outbursts that cowed the toughest miner. Yet Nellie remained for the moment unaffected and he imagined that in the proper surroundings and with the right clothes, she could flourish. Quietly she had taken his measure as well. Young and fit, he too, stood apart: clearly intelligent though uncertain and unworldly, it was the boyish good looks, his well-mannered behavior and serious air that interested her. But he was a miner, one of the destitute future-less group and that would not do, no matter the appearances ... until that Saturday afternoon when she had heard that BJ put up a notice to replace John and Otto and it was rumored they would be leaving soon. Otto was John's friend. Now she would need him.

Nellie had a request for John. She wanted a ride out of Tuckerton, as far as he could take her. She knew John. He could be hard and unresponsive, not inclined to be friendly or do favors. Unless, she had good reason to know, there was something in it for him. He had a strange, unsympathetic side, even spiteful at times; she had seen it with the miners he had left behind on the road and with the women he had mocked or abused, and a time or two when she had felt his slights herself. Looking up the bar she would turn to Otto. He had worked for months with John on the truck at the garage. She could manipulate this pushover, make him her go-between, and coax him to make John to take her along. So, as Otto leaned on the bar half-listening to the miners' joking and bickering, Nellie drifted by and bent near and whispered in his ear that she needed to speak with him urgently and "in private". He stood and threw some coins on the bar while making a point to his companions that he was about to have one last fling in Tuckerton. At the end of the bar Nellie arranged a visit to her room and passed through the crowd. He followed her up the stairs. This time there was no wait at the door. The seductive atmosphere, flickering candles and the perfume, were gone. She sat on the edge of the bed, fully clothed. He closed the door and rested against the frame, arms crossed. "Otto, sit here," she said, patting a place beside her on the bed. "Sit close. The walls have ears." He sat. He was leery, feared something was awry, his discomfort grew by the second. Why the meeting? What could she know?

"Otto, I have to leave and I need a ride," her voice an emphatic whisper.
"Why?"
"Several of the men have become very possessive. Especially one. I've made no commitments, but he acts like he owns me. I'm afraid of him:

beatings, physical harm."

"So, pack up and take the bus."

"You don't understand, I can't; he would stop me."

"Get the constable to help."

"Otto, are you crazy, he's useless!" She looked around the room, exhaling loudly, exasperated. "Bounce on the bed, make a few moans." Otto complied.

"I know you and John have that truck at the garage. Let me know when you are going and I'll meet you, anytime, anywhere you say!" She could see the discomfort in Otto's face. Though John and Otto had made no effort to hide the truck they hadn't advertised it either. Small town.

"I'll have to ask John."

"I have money. What problem could he have?" The inquisitive tone was purposely taunting.

"I don't know, but I can't speak for him." He said thinking of the two fifty gallon tanks filled with stolen silver that would be in the back of the truck.

She stood up and paced across the room and back, arms crossed, head down in thought considering how she would put what she had to say, forced to play her best card. She stopped in front of him. "Otto, there's talk around here. You fellows leaving together. Maybe you've been up to something."

The words went through him like a lightening strike, he felt his back stiffen, and wondered if she picked up his effort to remain expressionless.

"Where'd you hear that?" using as off-hand a tone as he could summon. The room was warm and the conversation had begun to make him sweat.

"In the bar."

"From who?" This question tipped his hand; she was certain she had a peek at the truth.

"It's pretty much idle talk; a few of them are whispering, 'why would they be leaving together' and 'those two are the only ones with access to the silver' and so on." She sat on the bed again, bouncing the springs, watching his attempt at deadpan with some satisfaction.

"I'll talk to John, but I can't promise anything," his face was taut.

She was serious again. Her bluff became more pointed. "Otto, if you give them time, they will snoop, and figure something out. You had better go sooner than later, and take me with you, that way your secret is safe."

"What secret?"

"Come now, Otto, do I have to spell it for you?" she bluffed.

As he got up to leave she sprayed some perfume on his shirt. "We want them to think we did it, don't we? Now smile." she instructed patting him on the back as he went out the door. He came down the stairs, numbed by the conversation and oblivious to the hoots of approval. "Hey Otto, you lasted more than two seconds, attaboy!" He offered no drinks this time.

They spoke in the crusher shed where the grinding of rock would mask their voices. It was Monday midmorning. They could speak unobserved. "Goddamn it Otto, now we're mixed up with her. If she can make that good a guess, maybe there are others." John appeared more frustrated than angry, but his level of concern had risen. "How can we make this work? If we take her we have to trust her. And then there is no doubt she'll learn what we've been up to. If we leave her here though she'll get to talking, her ideas will float around, make that dumb-ass BJ think, track us down and realize we got some silver out." He looked at Otto for the first time during this speech. "Do we take her?" he mused out loud.

Otto answered, not because he knew the answer yes or no, but because there was something he wanted to learn, more than idle curiosity. "You know her right?" Otto asked. "Yes, for God's sake, I know her, biblical sense! Sometimes I do more than pick up the supplies in town, you know!" and gave Otto a smile that could mean only one thing. Then John repeated out loud to himself. "And she's smart. If we leave her behind she'd plant ideas." He sat on a stool shuffling his feet on the dirt floor, thinking through this hitch in his plan. The bright sunlight coming through the window poured across his face deepening the furrows, darkening the recesses under his brow. His rough hands twisted together as he reviewed the options. After a moment or two he looked up.

"This is what we have to do. I'll tell BJ that we are leaving Wednesday. The story is that you got mixed up with some girl and she has been threatened by her boyfriend and to avoid trouble for the both of you, you need to get out of town; which, come to think of it, is pretty much what she told you. Her lady friends must know about this jealous guy as well, so the story will be confirmed when word gets out that she's gone. It should be okay."

"How is this going to work?"

"We'll load our things on the rig tomorrow and on Wednesday we have BJ drive us in. I have a lot: a trunk full of clothes, several crates of tools, and the drill press and grinder are mine. You have a suitcase and some books, right? In town we transfer them to the back of the Gotfredson; then we go have a few farewell beers and look for an opportunity to pass her a note. That done we head south out of town for a way and pull off the road out of sight. Wait. About 2a.m. we double back, which we have to do anyway, pick up the silver, and on the way back through town we pick her up. Then we are on the way south."

"What if she's not in the bar?"

"I know where she lives. I'll get the message to her. I want her to be out front of her place at four a.m.. If she is there, fine. If not we don't wait; we go straight to North Bay. Tough luck, sister."

Tuesday night Cook prepared a farewell dinner, a banquet of Swiss steak, green beans, carrots, mashed potatoes and gravy. The dessert, a tilting layer cake with yellow icing, confectioner's sugar, flour and butter decorated with chocolate skyscrapers carved from Hershey bars. John and Otto gave him effusive thanks for the "swell" meal, which, as they knew Cook well, he expected. BJ popped the cork on a bottle of champagne, again a rare event as he kept liquor out of the camp. The parsimonious pourings into coffee cups ensured sobriety but led to toasts, mostly rough humor. At one point a miner shouted, "How much silver you taking with you?" Otto's eyes moved cautiously to John's face. He was impressed with the effortless repartee. "BJ has the gun and he and I are going to hold up the mine tomorrow, take a ton out. We're taking Otto along as hostage." Laughter broke the tension. Even BJ thought the joke funny. A few more short speeches and dinner was over. Otto would miss Cook. He had wanted to know him better.

Chapter 20

Sleepless, Otto ached for the start of morning. With the clanging spoon on the pot the miners groaned, rolled from their bunks and pulled on a shirt and jeans. Otto slid his scuffed leather suitcase from under his bed, swept the dust off with his hand, and spread out the contents: one badly wrinkled dark blue wool suit, two yellowed white shirts and a tie, and a pair of moldy wing tip shoes. He shook the suit jacket and pants to get the creases out and refolded them along new lines in the suitcase and pressed them into place by adding underwear and socks and the best of his work clothes. Next he pondered the books and selecting two, dropped them into the suitcase and strapped it shut and carried it out to the rig. Returning he fought the urge to skip; one final breakfast at the mine then they were gone. His heart raced. He bit his lip trying to make it stop. Cook, usually too busy frying eggs and bacon for more than a word or two, took a break from the stove and sat down beside Otto. He wished Otto good luck and said unexpectedly that he would try to look him up if he ever managed to get to New York. Probably small talk, Otto thought. Hoping Cook was sincere he replied he would like to see Cook again. That was how it ended.

After breakfast when the miners had returned to the mine, John and Otto stood beside the business desk watching BJ myopically cipher the numbers in a green ledger book, ticking down columns with his pencil and summing the numbers silently with his lips. Satisfied his addition was correct, he withdrew a large check book from the top drawer, added the figures once again and with what seemed a preternatural reluctance to part with the mine's money, wrote two checks out in a large, clear script. Otto thought the number good and without comment folded the check into his leather wallet, empty except for twelve dollars and his immigration papers. John took the check, looked it over and with an audible exhale and vexed expression, shook his head at the number. But he didn't take the time or trouble to argue. BJ, unconcerned with his partner's dissatisfaction made no indication he had noted it, closed the book, methodically replacing it in the drawer and standing stiff in his neatly starched work clothes, extended a thick hand to seal the transaction. Otto watched, curious. There were no smiles or wishes for good luck, hugs or backslaps between the two men who had worked together to build and manage the camp. It was very businesslike, distant, without an iota of affection.

By eleven a.m. John's gear and tools had been loaded. BJ at the wheel guided the rig as it crept, pitching and rolling, along the ruts, over rocks, across small streams and squeezing between trees for two miles out to the road to town. Like a safe door this unimproved track had protected the silver until cracked by the two passengers who rode along in smug silence.

Positioned between the two men from the corner of his eye Otto could see a trace of a smile on John's lips as he sat, arms folded, lost in thought, oblivious to the swaying and heaving. Once on the smooth road Otto studied BJ's hands as they griped the steering wheel so tight as to strangle it: big and powerful, and so heavy that no veins or tendons showed through the rough skin. He had watched BJ use those hands to smash a drunken miner's face in; heard the pop when the cheekbone shattered. One blow and the man's eye was pushed back and down. When the swelling and purple bruise cleared one eye was permanently lower than the other. The miner saw double and joked that BJ did him a big favor. Now he could look a lady in her face and study her tits at the same time. Otto began to imagine the brutal beating he would have taken if BJ had discovered the stolen silver. He might not survive it. BJ could take them both on. Passing by the spot where the fuel tanks were hidden just off the road, John distracted BJ by remarking that he thought the mine would play out in the next two years; a remark that BJ reacted to with a sideways waggle of his big square head and a snort. Once behind the garage in town they transferred the tools and luggage to the bed of the Gotfredson. Here BJ unmasked his distrust of them and pawed through everything, the boxes, luggage, and tool trunks, opening Otto's suitcase, tossing the clothes one by one on the truck bed. He opened and fanned the books though by the weight of them there could be no silver hidden there. John asked if he was looking for stolen recipes though he knew JB looked to see if Otto had more paper money than a miner should have. John took the opportunity to make a fool of him, opening every bit of the gear with a flourish for BJ's inspection and insisting that he look it over. The mockery became rampant and Otto at a point thought they would come to blows. He picked up a wrench to defend himself. Big John, finally satisfied no silver or the mine's tools were leaving with John and Otto, turned and marched off for the bank and general store. Otto and John headed for Jenny's.

"Still going to New York?" John asked as they slid stools up to the bar. Before he could reply, John turned to the barkeep and him told to send word to Nellie that they had stopped in to say goodbye, then turned back to Otto for his answer.

"That's right, New York."

The habitually laconic mechanic seemed ready to talk. Otto ordered a beer.

"Know anyone there?" The question suggested he might offer a name of a friend or a contact.

"Not a soul." Otto answered and waited for a reply.

His companion let a smile bend his lips, turned silent, and looked from his watch to the door with an unfixed stare all the while drumming the long fingers of his left hand on the sticky bar. All conversation had ended. What little curiosity he had about Otto's plans and contacts had been satisfied. They drank in silence. Otto ordered a second beer and content to watch the bubbles float up to the head, he didn't use the time to ask John where he was going, somewhere west he understood. The arrangement had been business, not friendship, and Otto sat satisfied to listen to the tick of the clock on the wall.

Without a sound Nellie materialized behind them, placed her hand on John's shoulder, nodded to Otto, and asked an empty question designed for the bartender to overhear. "So you chaps are on your way out?" She raised her voice at the end of the sentence as an indication to John that she needed an answer to the underlying question: were the arrangements made for her to join them? For the moment John chose not to answer, his fingers became quiet and he let his hand rest open, palm up, on the bar and he looked at her with glazed pupils behind lowered lids, like in a state of borderline consciousness, appearing not to give a damn, waiting to see her squirm or crack. She fixed a stiff smile across her face and her gaze flipped from John to Otto and to John again, riveting on his eyes for a response. The silence had weight that could be lifted by a word, but John let it hang heavy. The only sound the clink of glasses as the barkeep washed and racked them up by the sink. It had been decided she would go along. The long silence made Otto uncomfortable; had John changed his mind? After a minute or so, John blew an exasperated breath out through his nose indicating that what Nellie had asked for presented a major inconvenience. Then he followed with, "We just wanted to say goodbye. Nice day for a start." He spoke loudly so the barkeep could not help but hear. Then his hand left the bar and he drew a slip of paper from his shirt pocket and slid it under his palm along the bar to her. Otto could read the crude print as she picked it up YOUR HOUSE OUT FRONT 4AM. There was no discernable expression of relief as her fist closed around the note and crushed it. They spoke of the weather and how nice the States must be. With a kiss on the cheek for John and a quick handshake for Otto, she wished them a safe trip and went out the door.

They left bar and John turned the truck south down the road to North Bay. In a while, miles since they had seen any sign of civilization, he backed onto an abandoned road. Hidden from view, they would wait until one a.m. before turning back. Otto slept as the summer twilight of the northern sky dissolved to near darkness. He awoke to the deep rumble of the engine starting. They headed back to retrieve the hidden gas tanks, creeping through the back streets of Tuckerton at the quietest idle the truck was capable of and then, well past the last house, full speed. Working by lantern light they wrapped chains around the tanks and gunned the truck to pull them out of the hole and with added throttle yank them up the embankment onto the road. Using straps they winched the tanks up a ramp of planks to the truck bed and lashed them down in the midst of the gear. The work went quickly. As they headed once again for Tuckerton, John laughed as he recounted how BJ, "that dumb bastard", had remarked about the nice new winch and straps.

With the headlamps off the truck idled down the muddy, treeless street lined with tar papered bungalows that in the gray crepuscular half-light of the subarctic looked like so many indistinguishable black boxes. After a block John slowed to a stop and Nellie's form emerged from the shadows by the side of the road. Otto jumped down, tossed her suitcase in the truck bed and as he boosted her into the cab noted she had dressed in a dark jacket to cover her white blouse and a long black skirt that came down over high leather Wellington boots. He caught the scent of her perfume, the same that had surrounded her in that room above the bar, an inescapable reminder of his failure and her subsequent rejection. As she settled between them on the narrow plank seat Otto saw that she rested her left hand on John's thigh. For his part John gave her no greeting, staring ahead into the gloom as he eased out the clutch; the muted thumping of the engine masked the sound of the barking dog as it trailed off in the distance; the only sign they had been there. At the corner they turned south. Once outside of town, the headlights came on, and the truck at full throttle rumbled down the gravel road that had been laid out on a perfect line by surveyors; the very road to perdition Otto had traveled almost three years before. Now the welcomed pathway out of this place. First stop North Bay!

"Thank you John! I'm finally out of there!" Nellie shouted over the engine noise and leaned over to give him a kiss on the cheek. John, his eyes locked on the road ahead, nodded and let the noisy engine provide the excuse for his apparent detachment, which to Otto indicated, John might think they were not home-free yet. Otto drifted in and out of fitful sleep, mesmerized by mile after mile of packed gray gravel that rushed beneath the headlight's glare. Nellie dozed, her head on John's shoulder.

It was late afternoon before they reached a weather-beaten wooden warehouse on the outskirts of North Bay. John backed the truck against the loading dock, left his companions to wait, knocked on the office door and after a moment disappeared inside. In a while the loading dock door rattled up and with the help of several men from inside John loosened the fuel tanks and rolled them in. The doors closed and John disappeared again. Nellie looked at Otto. "Tell me the truth, there was silver in those barrels, wasn't there?"

"Fuel tanks." Otto corrected, ducking a straight answer.

"So that's how you did it." A smile lit her face, proud that her theory that John and Otto had stolen silver from Split Rock was now proved. Unsure what John would tell her, if he would concoct some lie or other, Otto made no answer; although at this point he could see no reason to hide the obvious.

In an hour John reappeared. He grumbled under his breath something about "bloody bastards" as he swung up onto the seat of the truck. Nellie didn't hesitate to press for an answer. "John, that was silver you took in there."

John shouted an answer: "Right! Over nine hundred fifty pounds of it!" It wasn't her remark that troubled him; it was the deal. "They tried to tell me there was a lot of water and petrol in the silver, so I made them weigh a sample and dry it. That's what took so long. It came to less than a quarter of a percent of the weight. Then they tried to give me twenty cents American for an ounce. I had to threaten to put the silver back on the truck and find another buyer. Finally, I pushed them up to twenty-nine. They knew the stuff was good and weren't about to let it go."

"So how much did it amount to?" Otto asked, looking forward to his share.

"It came to three thousand five hundred sixty-four dollars and they tried to short me a hundred on the money count." He reached down letting off the brake and the Gotfredson bucked forward. "All that goddamned work and I didn't get the four thousand I was looking for, but it will have to do." If Otto made note of the "I was looking for" and instead of "we" in John's account of the negotiations in the warehouse, he attached no significance to it. It had not occurred to him to distrust his partner or Nellie for that matter. His mind was taken up with trying to divide 3,564 by two in his head. As the truck turned onto the street, John added the first considerate words he had spoken since Tuckerton. "I know we are all hungry, but we can't stop here. We are driving straight down the road a way. These people play rough; I wouldn't put it past them to come after us and try to take their money back. That wouldn't be pretty." The truck passed quickly through North Bay and turned south once again. There were more signs of civilization, a few houses along the road. Otto leaned out of the truck and looked back every mile or so. No one followed. After an hour John told Otto to drive, he needed a nap. Follow the signs for Buffalo. Tomorrow they would cross the border.

It was dark when John looked over at Otto and told him to turn the Gotfredson into the next road they came to for a "loo" stop. "Anyone else need to piss?" Otto brought the truck to a stop on a narrow dirt road, jumped down, and walked around to the back of the truck out of Nellie's view. As he tramped back buttoning his fly, he made out John's form beside the truck silhouetted by the headlights against a backdrop of brush and trees. John stood watching for Otto's return. There was a pistol in his hand.

"Otto, I want to thank you for the marvelous helper you have been. I couldn't have had a better partner," and leveled the gun at him. In the reflected light Otto watched a sardonic smile pass over John's face as he amused himself with sarcasm. Otto's response to the treachery was bewilderment and a rush of nausea, and then, like an electric charge, the primal fear of death swept through him as he realized the immediacy of his plight. Death was a possibility he had considered only in the abstract, thinking it remote in his own case and certainly not in these circumstances and with all the plans for his life still evolving in his head. He stared at the barrel that would deliver the bullet, too astonished to consider an escape, impossible at any rate at this range. Stunned, his mind emptied, he had no prayer to offer up, no rapid replay of his life, just a blank. Wordless, he raised his hands as a reflex, as if a prisoner of war, and waited. He watched Nellie jump down from the truck and she—how could she do this?—stood beside John, her right arm around his waist, his arm over her shoulders. Backlit, their bodies coalesced to a single gray mass. Now Otto understood, beside John stood his new partner. John talked on, amusing himself, his voice cheery, rambling, working up to a final joke. "Otto, I'm sorry this has to…" the sentence was interrupted by a flash of light and the loud report of a pistol that bounced through the trees and echoed back from the woods. What Otto saw, he did not process instantly; reality could not overcome the overwhelming expectation of a bullet bursting through his ribs. He blinked, cringed, grabbed at his chest, but felt nothing; and understanding he had been shot, was surprised by the lack of pain. Was that it, was death this easy, so painless? Now the image on his retina focused and sharpened and replayed itself: he had seen the top of John's head burst open in a crescendo of blood, brain and bony matter, the eruption lifted his body off the ground then dropped him, arms akimbo, legs doubled back, like a marionette dropped on the road. Then he saw Nellie standing frozen, her head turned away, eyes shut, teeth clenched in a grimace, her arm still in the air, the sleeve and side of her white blouse spattered with blood and brainy detritus. In her hand a large smoking pistol.

Chapter 21

They stood in the light of a smoky kerosene lantern gazing down at the features of John's contorted face; his eyes bugged and glazed, his mouth agape, locked open mid-word by the shockwaves made by the bullet tumbling through his brain. Nellie slid the pistol back into her boot and without a word, they each took a leg and began to drag the lifeless body into the woods, prying off the snags from the brush and trees that clawed at them, until the lights of the truck were nearly lost. Nellie squatted down and rummaged through John's pockets for his wallet. Otto muttered in a low voice, half to himself that taking the wallet, turning his pockets out, made him feel uneasy, dirty. Looking up, her face yellowed by the flickering lantern he held, she needled him with a smile, "but you are a thief aren't you?" The theft of the cold handfuls of silver from a large, impersonal mining company he had rationalized long ago to be a dangerous game but not thievery in this ugly, haunting way. What he had done there at the mine really hurt no one; the big company would never miss it, after all they didn't know they had it, and almost half a ton of silver was a drop in the bucket to them. But digging through pockets, taking a wallet and money from a corpse was immediate and tactile; and there was a smell to it, the rancid metallic smell of congealed blood; and warmth, John's warmth, fading from the leather wallet she passed to him. A drawing from an old Sunday school book reemerged from memory's mire in full color and detail. It depicted the story of the Samaritan and the ancient roadside robbery, a pair of the thieves, faces etched and sinister in the light of their lamp, bent over the beaten and bloodied traveler in a roadside ditch. Otto and Nellie would leave John too, his corpse hidden and left to rot deep in the brush covered with leaves. This time it was too late for a Samaritan.

On that road by the truck in the light of the emerging dawn Otto shoveled away the bloody dirt and bits of brain and bone throwing them into the weeds. Then he buried Nellie's bloody blouse. With a sigh he threw the shovel into the truck bed. A noisy car approached on the road. The occupants waved as they passed.

Otto backed the truck around and turned back down the main road. Nellie busied herself looking through John's wallet and suitcase finding several stashes of cash that she bundled together without counting and hid in her purse under the board and blanket that formed the seat. As they drove they abandoned John's plan to head for Buffalo because neither of them knew if he was expected there or if the truck would be recognized. Instead they turned east taking the road to Montreal. Otto decided he would sell the truck and tools there and board a train to New York.

In Tuckerton, a town supported by the surrounding mines, Otto had lived insolated from the harshest effects of the Depression. Occasionally at the mine a half starved man would walk into the camp looking for work only to walk out without a job. BJ didn't hire unless the supplicant knew mining work and there was a crying need, and even then, he usually didn't want them. Cook gave them a meal and a sack of food to take along and told them how to reach the next mine so that the long walk into Split Rock wasn't for nothing. Otto recalled the day a union organizer had showed up at the mine and tried to recruit some of the men. Otto had watched as Big John clamped his hand to the back of the man's collar and hustled him out the track, and when he came back his bleeding knuckles warned the men not to get any "fancy ideas". Perhaps Otto should not have felt sorry for the man as the inchoate capitalist that he was, but he did. He held his tongue like the others because at that point the job was more than a job; it had become an enterprise, a silent silver business and his ticket to American prosperity. That night after dinner BJ gave a speech, the only one Otto could recall him giving, reminding the men how lucky they were to have work in these times, any work, and if anybody was unhappy with the deal the mine gave him, he was welcome to walk; there would be ten men to take his place tomorrow. No one spoke up. As BJ said, Otto felt lucky; but Otto thought as the truck bounced along the outskirts of Montreal, BJ didn't know how lucky; he had no idea. Nonetheless, the remote mine in the north woods had hid a lot of the economic realities of the times. In Montreal the financial state of the world was clear. Idle men stood in groups on street corners or sat on a stoop by a store front, some in overalls, some wearing rumpled business suits; unshaven and hungry looking.

Looking for a salesman who spoke English, Otto guided the Gotfredson into a used car lot that had some trucks lined up to sell. This was their third try. As they pulled up to a shed with a sign, OFFICE, and cut off the engine, a small, thin salesman emerged. Yes, he replied, he spoke English. Despite the summer heat, he wore a dark suit, white shirt and tie. His thinning dark hair was slicked back on his head, and a thin moustache striped his upper lip. Squinting into the bright afternoon sun, he sized Otto up noting the Danish accent, and even though Otto towered over him he was sure he was looking at an easy mark. A group of four or five unemployed men drifted over from the shade of a tree to watch and listen to the old pro as he went to work.

"What do you want for it?" He began, a salesman's routine opening pare.

They stood beside the truck surrounded by the disheveled group, who, with nothing better to occupy them, spent a good part of the day watching negotiations at the lot. Otto, clearly a patsy, would provide the afternoon's entertainment. Nellie sat in the truck and looked on as the dealer walked around, checking the tires and listening to the idling motor.

"Five hundred U.S." Otto replied. A laugh went up; the men dug elbows into one another amused.

"Nobody's got that kind of money here—except the bootleggers." The dealer scoffed, cocked his head to the side and narrowed his eyes to a sliver; and as he looked up at Otto, he shoved his hands deep into his pants pockets and spread his legs, assuming a well practiced I-don't-give-a-damn stance rocking back and forth heel to toe.

"Yeah, half the cars in here have bullet holes in 'em from the Federals chasing them back over the border," shouted one man in the crowd to general laughter.

"Eighty, and it ain't worth that." The salesman said firmly as the laughter died down. By now the group had grown, and eyes shifted to Otto as if it were a tennis match, waiting for his counter.

"Two hundred."

The car salesman relaxed and crossed his arms, a scant smile showed at the corners of his mouth. He knew he had his man. No one determined to get his price would come down so much. He saw his opposition was desperate. It was time to thrust home.

"Eighty, take it or leave it." He held his gaze steady into Otto's eyes.

"What about the tools, the drill press and things?"

"Three dollars. I have no use for tools."

Otto was beaten, there was no place to go and his opponent knew it.

"Four dollars and a ride to a hotel." Otto countered.

"Okay." The salesman said and shouted over his shoulder. "George," then looked around until he located George in the crowd. "Show them to a hotel." As he spoke his right hand reached deep into his pants pocket and drew out a fat roll of mixed Canadian and U.S. bills. Pulling off the rubber band and licking his thumb, the salesman counted out eighty-four dollars American. The transaction didn't make a dent in the wad.

George drove. In the city he maneuvered the truck under the portico of the Hotel L'Aquitaine. The doorman, stepped forward and ignoring the de-classe conveyance helped Nellie down with a formality that in better years would be reserved for the well-to-do. The Depression had changed attitudes. Business was light. The bellboy brought in the three suitcases and set them down in the opulent lobby elaborately decorated with oversized Louis XIV furnishings, ornate crystal chandeliers, and thick area rugs on marble floors—and no customers. It was two in the afternoon; it could have been two in the morning. Glancing about, Otto could find no life other than the elevator operator and bellboy in their uniforms, standing against the wall. Ah, memories of the Royal Military Academy and the hours standing in dress uniform against a wall, an ornament at parties or receptions, the duty he hated. How he had suffered that. He felt for them. At the registration desk, Nellie forestalled an awkward pause by speaking up quickly to announce that Mr. and Mrs. Otto Nielsen had arrived and would like a nice room. The clerk, despite having heard and noted the truck through the lobby door, provided one of the finest rooms in the house. Though he requested with well-practiced polite insistence, payment in advance. Otto happily complied, handing him six dollars.

"Otto, you gave the bellhop a quarter, he would have been happy with a dime," Nellie said over her shoulder as she unpacked her clothes folding them into the dresser and smoothing out her dresses before hanging them in the closet. Otto, silent, slowly undid the straps on John's leather grip and laid out the dead man's things on the bed going through the pockets one by one. He was consumed by lethargy, tired and sad. There were no papers, letters, no identification other than a British passport, nothing; just clothes and a gold pocket watch with no inscription. John had been his instructor, compatriot, and though not a pal, Otto had learned working with him for the past two years that, through there were inevitable problems with their scheme, little scares now and then, in the end, by holding steady, they made the plan work—and beautifully. There was a lesson there. The bloody events a day ago replayed in his head, he couldn't get them out, and somehow he couldn't make them believable; his mind fought actuality—it could be a dream. Any moment could there be a knock on the door and John would stride in and with an uncustomary smile would say, "We did it old boy!" That's how Otto had thought it would end, with a smile and handshake, good luck and goodbye. Could it have been John was joking; putting on a big act, just trying to scare him for fun, his perverse side coming out, nothing serious about menacing him with the pistol? Was his head blown apart because he wanted a laugh at Otto's expense? If only things had turned out differently, gone as planned. Regardless, the reality, John was dead.

Otto replaced the watch and absentmindedly closed the bag and dropped it in the corner. He didn't covet John's share of the money. He stood by the window and looked down at the sidewalk five stories below and watched the passersby who were trailed by long dark shadows on the sun bleached cement. For two years sitting in the shed while he monitored the silver trailing down into the bucket or when he looked up from his reading at night he had dreamed of this day, these exact moments, how happy they would be; and what had they become: a surreal nightmare.

"Otto, come over here and look at this." Nellie had climbed on the bed, and sat with her back against the headboard. She had poured out the contents of her purse and had begun counting. He sat on the edge. "All the silver money is yours now, you earned it…" Her voice trailed off as she straightened a pile of greenbacks by her knee. Taking that money, under these circumstances, he wasn't sure he wanted it. He tried to stop thinking about it, but she absorbed in the tally, kept bringing him back to it.

"Otto, there's a lot more here, John had a lot of separate cash in addition."

She counted some more and built another pile. "There's more than nine thousand dollars here." Her news, though delivered with a joyful shout barely penetrated his consciousness. Vacant words that bounced off the walls of the room.

"That's nice," he said.

He stood again, he had to get away from this somehow, clear his brain, wash yesterday away. He walked into the bathroom and turned on the shower. The water streamed down hot and hard like a jet from a garden hose. He stepped in and reveled in it, letting it bounce off his hair and pellet his neck and shoulders like hot sleet. The fragrant smell of the French soap wafted from his skin replacing the stale odor of dust and sweat as he rubbed away the grime from the road. It was joyful. Breathing in the thick, wet air he let the shower run until the room filled with an opalescent fog. The soft towel brushed skin, a simple pleasure, adding to the feeling that it was wonderful to be alive. Then it came to him with emphasis, to be alive. Those words awakened the realization of how lucky he was, how close he had been to death's black abyss from the bullet John was about to send ripping through his chest, to total nothingness. He saw it now, the truth, and anger, raw anger, surged within him! John had planned to kill him all along! They weren't partners at all! The rage grew until he could contain it no longer and the words burst free of the grip of his remorse. "That bastard!" The sound of his shout cleared his head sweeping any remaining confusion away. He saw John for what he was, a liar, thief and murderer. All other considerations faded away. There had been no friendship; he had been deluded, he had been nothing but a tool, and worse, a sap. It was over, thank God. Otto took a deep breath and another and another until he stood tall, ready to go out into the room. The August air was cool and invigorating by contrast.

"Let's get on with the count," he said.

They sat together against the headboard, not speaking for a long time; Otto a towel about his waist, Nellie still dressed in her long skirt, ankles crossed, the pistol handle visible in the exposed boot top. Finally, she broke the silence.

"Otto, what makes you tick?" She turned to look at his face while he peered at the wall opposite.

"Tick?"

"Yes, what motivated you to get mixed up in this? With John? And why were you up there at that mine in the first place? You didn't belong there." He made no move to answer. "I could see you're not one of them," she persisted. "You're no miner or mechanic, you've got refinement, some breeding, there's a polish and class about you."

For Nellie it was more than idle curiosity. She had to learn much more about this incongruous Dane. She had to plan. She had gone this far, done this much; but how much more, how much further, where to next?

Where was he going? What was he going to do? Should she be on her own or with him? She needed an answer.

He slowly awakened to her questions. Gradually his mind was suffused with thoughts of Denmark, the good memories, the farm, Arhus, Copenhagen. As he spoke his mood lightened. He recounted stories of his parents, Uncle Erik, his grandfather, quitting the military academy, Kurt and his work at the hotel and bar. There were some laughs. She egged him on, measuring him, constructing a portrait, cutting short the pauses with questions, urging him to continue.

"Your father was a banker?"

"Yes."

"You must have had a nice home."

"In the city."

"Servants?

"When I was small, but not after the war."

Finally, she asked "What are you going to do in New York?"

"Open a restaurant and bar and sit by the bar and make friends with the customers. That's how you learn important things that can get you ahead." Otto put his head back and smiled as his daydreams once more came into focus. The hotel bar in Copenhagen and the First Class dining room on the *Olympic Citizen* were his models, the blueprints, the schooling that provided the basis for his plans.

"Learn things?" She had picked up on that, not knowing what it implied.

"Yes, learn things. All that time you spent standing at the end of the bar at Jenny's, didn't you learn something useful?"

"Maybe for blackmail, if that's what you mean?"

"No, didn't you learn who was selling their house, what mine was hiring, who was sick or died … who was repairing a truck and planning to leave?" He turned and smiled at her. He had made his point. "Well, in New York it will be the same, except they will be talking about stocks, bonds, real estate, politics. Things that present business opportunities."

"And?"

"And I can learn what is hot, what to buy, what to sell. Who to talk to for this or that. Give favors, get favors, tips, leads, and get to know the right people. Maybe be asked to go in on some deals, not like this, but honest ones. To me bars are like the ancient market places, the agoras, they're the modern equivalent; and if prosperous, well connected people meet there, things can happen."

"Where do you plan to open this place?" Her interest ignited.

"I don't know." Her question had an unanticipated deflating effect. "That's the next job to do in New York."

She thought she knew enough about him, who he was, where he was headed, how he would react, what drove him. He had gone on for hours.

Sensing a break in the conversation, she swung her feet off the bed and headed for the bathroom. As she passed him, talking loudly so as to break through his reverie, she allowed. "I'm glad we talked. I wasn't sure I had shot the right man."

Chapter 22

With his hands behind his head, lying catty-corner across the bed, barely awake, Otto listened to the water run in the shower behind the wall and visualized Nellie's arabesque body slicked with soap and wondered what opportunity he had he missed by showering first. Would she have agreed, a shower together? It had been years since a boarding school know-it-all had announced in the pitch black to a rapt audience of schoolmates during a whisper session after lights-out that the best thing ever was taking a shower with a girl. How this boy came by this libidinous tidbit was left to each boy's imagination. Otto presumed the excited pedagogue had overheard it somewhere, as from Otto's memory of the boy, it was unlikely he had come by the knowledge first-hand. But now the opportunity was real. Nellie emerged from the bathroom robed in a modest, long cotton nightgown and he watched as she brushed out her hair, sitting before the dressing table mirror, hanging her head from one side to the other for stroke after stroke and until her hair dried to shimmering coal-black perfection. She set the brush down, stood, and came over to the bed. Her nipples punched at the thin cloth.

"Roll over, Otto."

He complied.

"After all we have been through, you need a back rub." She swung a knee over his buttocks and sat while her hands like a sculptress working clay kneaded the muscles of his back and shoulders. After a few minutes in the sultry evening air Nellie pulled the gown over her head and tossed it aside. Otto felt an immediate swelling against the mattress in response to the sensation of her moist underside pressing down on him. In a while she leaned forward tracing lines on his back with her hardened nipples, letting her perfumed tresses trickle over his neck. She nuzzled his ear and breathed, "Roll over." As he did, she rose up on her knees and settled down taking him in, and as he pushed up hard, her back and neck arched in a spasm that rippled up her spine and down and through her belly and beyond. The red hues of the setting sun burnished her sweat-glazed skin as she drove on consumed by repeated climaxes. For her such pleasure, surging orgasms, had been rare. In time he took charge, rolled her over and she wrapped her legs around his back drawing in the thrusts until after, sensing the increased stiffening of incipient ejaculation, she slipped free. Otto fell to her side, spent. They lay together in post-coital slumber; she certain he would be unable to resist any request she would make, and he, dreaming of when he was certain they would shower together.

    In the morning at the arched entry to the hotel dining room they were greeted by the tuxedo clad maitre de who led them to a table. He pulled out a chair for Nellie and with a nod beckoned the waiter standing against the wall. Looking about, Otto noted that the dining room was empty, except for a few patrons that had been spaced out among a veritable sea of unoccupied tables, that despite the absence of customers, were set with a full service of silverware, folded linen napkins that stood with four points like a crown, and a rose in a silver stem vase. And Otto considered, why would they set the tables when there were more waiters that customers, other than to keep them busy; or to make the place look as though there would be a crowd any minute, to look finished. He filed that away. Though the menu was lengthy they ordered croissants and fruit and lingered over coffee. The waiters gradually drifted away as the room emptied further.

"That was a wonderful time last night," Otto ventured, thinking a direct compliment of her skill inappropriate, he searched for words to acknowledge his appreciation.

"That was for you Otto, for us. We made love. It was wonderful, wasn't it?" She paused looking around to make certain the waiter was not in earshot. "That was not a five dollar screw I was forced to give out. No one could buy what we had last night."

There was no place for him on this train of thought, he waited.

She looked straight into his eyes, her voice lowered for emphasis. "Otto, you have to promise me one thing. And I'm deadly serious. You must vow to never … and I mean, never ever…breathe a word of my past to anyone. Not a hint. That part of my life is over, gone! As if it never happened. Vanished, erased!" She paused again for emphasis. "It's finished…do you understand?"

He nodded, his eyes engaged with hers, making his compliance clear. Anxious to change the subject he began to thank her for saving his life, for pulling the trigger. But his words, a heartfelt expression of gratitude, a tearful "thank you" sounded hollow to his ears, terribly inadequate for the magnitude of the gift; how do you pay for such a thing, when falling to his knees and kissing her feet would be appropriate? She, however, with a raised palm, demurred, and would not accept his thanks, avowing she had acted in self-defense as John certainly would have killed her next; if not just then, at some later time. "Besides," she added, making light of it, "you are cute, very worth saving."

"Where did the gun come from?" In his experience, thus far, women didn't carry pistols in their boots.

"I'll give it to you in a nutshell. It was my father's." She leaned forward over the table. "My father and uncle are, were, who knows, soldiers, officers, in the IRA and were caught by the damned British. They were sent to prison for twenty years. That has been over four years ago now. I was sixteen, the oldest of six, and with him gone, my mother was unable feed us all." Nellie played with the coffee spoon moving it back and forth with her index finger as she processed her thoughts. "Ma begged my Aunt Mary to take me, give me a start here in Canada. She threatened my aunt, said she could read in the papers that we all had starved to death in Ireland. Hard-pressed, unable to say no, my aunt wrote back that she would take me; but warned mother that in Canada times were very hard too. At that point anything was a blessing." Otto could see Nellie was having trouble telling him this. There were long pauses between her sentences. He perceived her history, painful to live, was even painful to relate. "God knows, if my poor mother had any idea of what she was sending me into, I know she would gladly have had us starve. She thought she was giving me an opportunity, living here and all." Nellie spoke looking across the room as if reading the words off the wall, not meeting Otto's gaze. "My aunt never divulged the real circumstances, how could she? I mean, how could she be honest about what she was about, that her life was not what you would call, how should I say it—wholesome? But she understood how desperate things were in Ireland; she had fled from there herself, escaped, and felt forced to help." Nellie took a sip of coffee and looked down at the tablecloth. Otto noted how delicate her hand was and how perfect her nails when she put the cup down. He wondered how the little hand had fired that big gun.

"She was in a bad way, too. Her husband died ten years ago of tuberculosis. He was a miner. And she had no education, no skills and here she was left with nothing, no savings, no pension…nothing. And Otto, you know in Tuckerton there are no jobs for women, no fancy houses to clean, no real businesses other than the mines, nothing—maybe a little laundry and ironing. She was left with her only possessions—a little money and a tar paper shack." Nellie brought her eyes up to meet his. "You've seen them, they're worth a pittance. For what she could get for it, she couldn't get a place anywhere else. She was trapped in that God-awful town." Nellie drew a deep breath and looked down again and played with the spoon with her left hand. "So, in desperation, she turned to the bars for a living on Saturday nights as a trollop, a common whore. She could make enough in one night there to survive for the week, and I think with time she grew to like it. And on Sunday's she goes to Mass, you know, all pious, stepping from one world into another, slobbering over her prayers, asking for forgiveness. But then, when she passed her prime, so to speak, and the customers fell off, and she went into 'management'." Otto couldn't resist a smile with the image the words "fell off" presented. Nellie didn't look up. "When I arrived she was doing a little still on Saturdays and she still has a regular, a lover you might say, except he pays. A pig, he comes to the house twice a week. She does his laundry, too. He wants his pants pressed just so. But mainly her money comes from managing the girls at Jenny's."

She paused and turned her head to look out the window at the street and passers-by. Otto noted her perfect profile. He was no student of beauty, and was not aware of what elements and proportions of the female face created it, the length of the nose, the shape of the chin, but certainly he recognized she was beautiful. She struggled to continue.

"When I finished school she put me into, what would you call it, service? I should say 'forced', not put. What was I to do? Where could I go? I had to pay my way. Her concession was I could turn down whoever I wanted, and believe me Otto, I became very, very picky. She never let the other girls do that. Other than I had to pay rent and a management fee, I could keep the money I made, but she had no idea how much I made. I kept that well hidden so that some day I could leave. You know, the one benefit I had of all this? There was a lot of time to read; I read a lot."

"Was your aunt Mary the one with the dyed red hair?"

"That's her. How she defiles the name of the Blessed Virgin, running a business like that." She crossed herself with a flash of a hand. "Her name's a joke."

"Defiles?"

"Oh, spoils, dirties or something like that." She went on. "So that's why I had to leave like I did."

"She didn't know you were going?"

"No. She counted on my rent and her cut."

"And what about the possessive men?"

"Oh, there were those too, but one in particular, her lover, the pig. He used to leer at me, and make dirty suggestive remarks. Said I was next. I had to get away. It was just a matter of time before he forced himself on me!"

"BJ?"

"Yes, BJ."

"And the gun?"

"Oh yes, the gun. My mother had heard through the underground that the British planned a house search, so to get rid of my father's gun and bullets she threw them into my luggage as I left." She looked up, "It is a big one and sure came in handy, didn't it?" The impish smile drew back her lips over a row of perfect teeth. "Too bad I can't write and tell her how useful it was."

By now the last waiter had gone. The dining room was empty. Otto went for more coffee from the urn on the buffet along the wall. When he returned she began again.

"Otto, I've been thinking. I want to be your partner in the bar and restaurant. You may think I am forward; but I know you will need some help. I watched you sell the truck. You're too nice, too trusting, people take advantage of you, like John did." Otto made no reaction, surprised by the proposal. "What you need is someone to watch your back. Otherwise, I can see you will be robbed blind in the bar business. At Jenny's I've watched the bartender pocket half the money that came across the bar and the rest of the help stole too, anything they could get their hands on—liquor, food, knives, forks, glasses. If they could carry it out undetected, it went." She chuckled and said, using her smile to defuse any offense he might take, "Just like the silver at Split Rock."

"Nellie, that was not as easy as taking liquor and forks." He said with justifiable pride.

She went on. "I counted the money last night, Otto, and these are the figures." Her tone had now become businesslike. She reached down to her purse and drew out a piece of paper. "There's three thousand five hundred sixty-four dollars of silver money that is yours. John had an additional seven thousand nine hundred and twenty which we should split. I figure I earned half. That leaves me with three thousand nine hundred and sixty and you with, adding things up…you have seven thousand five hundred and sixty-four. Now if we put the money together we have almost eleven thousand five hundred, not counting the truck money, of course."

"That should be enough to get a lease on a good space." Otto said, sounding sure of himself, although he had no idea what the cost would be.

"So you will let me be your partner?"

As she had spoken he had mulled it over. Swayed more by her physical appeal than by any business acumen, he accepted her proposal. "With John dead, we are in pretty deep. We have to stick together."

"Is that a 'yes', Otto?"

"I'm sorry we had to kill him. That's another thing we can never mention, keep absolutely quiet."

"Of course, Otto! Now is that a 'yes'?" her words were emphatic, exasperated.

"Of course, yes, a 'yes'."

Nellie jumped up from the table and ran around and gave him a hug and a kiss. He was startled. He had never known a Danish woman to be that demonstrative. He had sat immobilized, unable to react. Nellie laughed at his catatonic response.

As she sat down her enthusiasm overcame any inclination to hold back. "I have another fifteen hundred to throw in the pot."

"Fifteen hundred? That's a lot of ... how did you get that?"

"Tips."

"Tips?"

"Yes, tips. My customers were big tippers or they didn't come back. Twenty, fifty, occasionally a hundred … at Christmastime; John was a very good tipper."

"Oh, I wondered what there was between you two."

"That was it, nothing personal." She smiled to herself at Otto's double entendre. The breakfast had turned festive. "One always hates to, shall I say, 'discourage', a big tipper, especially with a bullet; but then again, I was leaving the trade anyway." There was a twinkle in her beautiful blue eyes.

Otto had another thousand from his salary, so the total funds came to approximately thirteen thousand dollars.

They spent three days in Montreal, buying clothes and luggage and sightseeing before heading to New York.

Chapter 23

It was six a.m., June 29th, 1934. On board the train Otto put the luggage packed with new clothes in the rack over the seats. They had divided the money and each carried half. The pistol was packed with Otto's underwear. As the train began to glide away from the platform and broke free of the terminal it rocked through the switches of the rail yard and once cleared onto the tracks headed south picking up speed. Nellie settled down with a paperback she had bought at the newsstand in the terminal. Otto fidgeted, worried about this last hurdle, the major one. He checked the breast pocket of his suit coat to reassure himself that their passports and papers were at the ready and easily withdrawn with no sign of nervousness, a routine matter. At the United States border the train slowed to a stop. Two American officials came aboard and Otto watched casually as they worked down the aisle. They paused at each seat, asked a question or two, quickly looked over the passenger's documents, handed them back and moved on. Despite the superficial check the passengers up the aisle received, Otto's mouth dried. He wiped the perspiration from his palms on his trousers leg. In his mind he reviewed again the answers he would make. Nellie sat quietly reading the paperback paying no attention to the approaching officers, or so it seemed; though Otto had come to learn she could be aware of every nuance, any expression of concern by the officials, any danger and had prepared a response. Soon an officer, all business and no pleasantries, stood above them. Otto presented their Canadian immigration papers and passports and said they were tourists who planned to stay for a week or so. The officers passed on without further inquiries. With the officials off, the train resumed its run. Otto settled back watching the trackside utility poles break the countryside into flickering pictures of woods interrupted by the sudden appearance of a farm or small village that, having flashed into view, abruptly vanished. Now and then a clanging crossing gate broke into the soporific tapping of the wheels.

Otto had begun to nod off when her question wakened him.

"Otto, what do you believe in?"

"Believe in?"

"Yes, God and such."

"I don't think about it." He was surprised and peeved by her directness. He turned his head toward the window, taking renewed interest in the passing scenery.

"I can't go into business with someone who doesn't have a good moral compass."

"Moral compass?" He smiled. "Well, we sure have a good start in that regard."

She ignored his sarcasm. "Otto, we are starting over; we have a clean slate."

"If you say so." His tone expressed the discomfort he had with this subject. Talk of God dejected him. The events of the past several years and especially the past week he knew would linger in his subconscious just below the surface and none, good or bad, seemed particularly morally straight. The concept of a clean slate was beyond his grasp. He stared out the window again.

"Do you believe in God?" She persisted, undeterred.

With a sigh, he turned toward her. "Yes, I suppose, but I'm not sure He pays much attention. In my experience I've never seen something happen … it all figured out and made to work, without somebody doing it. So, yes, I suppose."

'What do you mean by that? That didn't make any sense!"

"I mean somebody had to make the universe, so it must be God." He paused and added. "The sky is very big. I just don't know where He is or know if He pays any attention, that's all."

"He's here, all around us, knows everything that goes on."

"That used to scare me when I was small. I was afraid of doing something bad and He would know it, no way to keep anything from Him, He knows everything as you say, and would write it down on a check-list somewhere and eventually, I don't know when, there would be some sort of punishment. I was scared of Him, but I've gotten over that."

"Why? He loves you. Don't you believe in Jesus? Jesus said, 'God loves you.'" She persisted.

"Good God! I don't know, I try to, but that's behind me now. I left it in Denmark," the exasperation in his voice unmistakable.

"Well, I do, absolutely. We need Him. He forgives our sins." She crossed her arms and looked straight ahead, feet planted flat on the floor. Otto was silent and continued to hope she would not persist.

"Mary Magdalene was a prostitute, you know. He forgave her."

"Listen, Nellie, I don't know what I believe. I was forced to go to church, Lutheran by the way, and haven't been back for years. I try to do what is right, that's all."

Continuing to look straight ahead, as if talking to the back of the seat before her, she proclaimed that in New York she would renew her faith and go to Mass every Sunday. She mused that her faith in God and His goodness and mercy were inseparable from her very soul and whatever had happened in Canada, whatever she had been forced to do, He would forgive through the Church and prayer. Otto fearful she would come around to insisting he join her, stood, and reaching for her hand, said it was time for lunch.

Passing between the cars, the burst of noise and challenge of stepping from one car that moved in opposition to the next dispelled any drowsiness that may have lingered. In the dining car, a Negro waiter dressed in a white cut off jacket and pressed black trousers asked if they would mind sharing a table and placed them with a luncheon partner who resembled the pictures Otto had seen of Teddy Roosevelt; stocky, with a shock of short graying brown hair, round wire rimmed glasses, and a bushy mustache. Otto was pretty sure that Roosevelt was dead and introductions confirmed the man sitting across was not he. They had encountered Packwood Parkman, 'Pack' for short, businessman, hard goods. Sitting opposite him Otto and Nellie, between glances at the menu, watched Pack curl his upper lip and sip the chicken and rice soup without straining it though the moustache.

They ordered the broiled pot roast luncheon. It included a glass of red wine.

Chewing and nodding Pack questioned them between forkfuls of dinner. Curious about their accents he quickly pulled from them that they had immigrated from Ireland and Denmark. He pointed his fork at the wine and announced, "You know you couldn't have ordered that a year ago in this country, before the repeal. It was made official last December fifth. That's one day Roosevelt should have made a national holiday!" He laughed and then leaned forward, his voice becoming low. "Of course, you could get all the liquor you wanted anytime you wanted, just not in legitimate places like this." He paused to chew another bite of pork chop, his gaze shifting from Nellie to Otto and back to her where it stayed. He swallowed before continuing. "Hell, the milkman delivered my booze, left it right in the milk box. The police chief in my town was a bootlegger, for God's sake!" He managed to take his eyes off Nellie just long enough to make another stab with his fork at his food and ask Otto what he was going to do in the Big City. Otto cautiously allowed how he planned to go into the restaurant business, but before the repeal, which he added with some pride he had known about, he had worried how he was going to get around the liquor laws … a good bar was central to his plans. Pack, their self-appointed authority on the subject, continued, "The places that went along with the 'powers that be', so to speak, thrived." He made certain they understood what he meant by the "powers that be" by drawing quotation marks in the air with his fingers. "I can tell you there were more bars, that is to say, speakeasies in New York than there were bars before Prohibition. And that's because the average Joe liked the idea of doing something naughty, a little harmless thrill. Wow, there might be a raid!" He blotted his mustache with the tip of the napkin he had tucked in his collar and checked it to make sure it was clean. "Yes sir, it was like belonging to an exclusive club. If they knew who you were they'd let you in. For a lot of folks, that was a special thing."

"Went along with who?" Nellie inquired, making certain she understood who the "powers" were. Even now it might be important to know.

"Yes, went along with the supplier, the illegal liquor provider, kept quiet, kept the police happy and had a way to look clean if raided."

The train had slowed as it passed by a rail yard. A cluster of shacks built of scrap wood and tin roofing were grouped on the far side of the yard in front of the woods. A group of men sat on boxes and or stood around watching the train pass. Pack looked out the window, exhaled loudly, then looked down as he put his fork into a wedge of pie.

"Jesus, look at all them bums. Another Hooverville; they're all over the place nowadays."

"What a waste." Otto remarked, taking an empathetic view of the scene.

Nellie almost simultaneously said they should be out looking for work instead of standing around in a freight yard.

Pack ignored Otto and picked up on her remark. "You're right, Miss. They've had more than enough time to get jobs. No need to stand around doing nothing. Find some work I say; and now, can you believe it, it sounds like Roosevelt wants to put them all on the dole."

As the rail yard passed into the distance Pack removed the napkin tucked into his shirt collar and tossed it on the table, swept his vest off with a quick downward brush of his hands, and laced his fingers across his chest, leaning back to let the waiter clear the table. He started again. "So, Otto, what kind of a restaurant are you thinking about?"

"Something nice, a good bar, good food; I want to attract a high class of people."

"So where are you going to put this restaurant?"

"I thought around Wall Street."

"Do you want some free advice? It's worth what you're paying for it, of course." The brief moment of self-deprecation was meant to imply the exact opposite. His smile drew the bushy mustache above his cigarette stained teeth. Otto could see he was anxious to tell this Danish neophyte a thing or two.

Before Otto could answer, Nellie volunteered. "Otto needs advice, good advice." Otto thought she should mind her own business, but did not respond.

"The well heeled ones don't live down there by Wall Street, they just work there. A lot live up town, the fifties to the eighties, around Fifth and Madison or on the West Side. If you want the dinner crowd, that's where to be."

Otto was trying to process this information, commit it to memory without appearing to fawn. Pack went on enjoying the opportunity to impress this youthful immigrant and especially his attractive companion, who began to take notes on a scrap of paper. He continued looking directly at her and watching her as she wrote; he spoke slowly so that she could get each word. The note taking gave him an excuse to continue, urged him on.

"The Rockefellers are building their Center. It will pull a lot of people into that neighborhood. I would look for a place around there." He paused as he watched Nellie write down "Rockefeller". "They've just opened a big Music Hall there that shows movies and has a stage show. Last year they put up a big Christmas tree, probably do it again this year. It drew crowds"

"Where is this?" Nellie asked pencil poised. Looking up she met his gaze and gave him a smile.

"High Forties between Fifth and Sixth," noting with satisfaction the confused look that crossed the pretty face of his devotee. "Oh, I'm sorry," he remarked with just a whiff of condescension. "That would be Forty-Eighth, Forty-Ninth Streets or so, between Fifth and Sixth Avenues." He watched, bemused, as she carefully wrote down the address not realizing the project was so mammoth it could not be missed.

Otto stared out the window, listening, taking in the advice; but by this time did not feel obligated to give Pack the satisfaction that his guidance was of any consequence. He was annoyed at being talked down to, or worse, ignored.

Pack's interest was sparked. "What are you going to name your place, Otto?" Then without waiting for an answer, he went on. "It can't be 'Murphy's' or some such; you've got to use something French, that's what attracts the swells. There's something high class about a French name."

By now Otto had had enough. If he thought someone had something useful to say, he would try to pull it out of him. But this pompous ass! Unable to find a way to easily break off the conversation, Otto called the waiter over. "We have to go now," he said, paying the check and gently taking Nellie by the elbow. Pack stood and in a practiced move extended his hand with his card. Otto put it in his shirt pocket. By now Pack had Nellie's right hand and pressed it between his hands effusing. "It has been such a pleasure to meet you, My Dear."

Otto walked behind her as they passed through the cars. She stood straight, shoulders back, her carriage assured; and though her clothes were not expensive, she had a sense of style and wore them well, nothing showy, just tasteful. From this vantage point Otto could see how she attracted many an interested glance that flipped up over a newspaper and a few hard stares that though she looked straight ahead Otto figured she had to notice. He now had an enhanced appreciation of her; she did not appear to be what her past would suggest. She had a vitality that bespoke of the status she longed for and a sensual, yet cultured, bearing that somehow she had inculcated from magazines and picture shows in Tuckerton. It was clear her exit from her past had been long planned and studied for, and she had succeeded in both manner and speech. And her accent, though Irish, was soft and refined. She had a disarming charm that she displayed on several occasions in the past few days and that had conquered Pack. No doubt she would be an asset in the restaurant. If Pack had done nothing else, he had affirmed how valuable she would be.

"Otto, you were rude to Mr. Parkman." She said as they sat down again.

"What should I have said? French restaurant, I love the idea?" He replied, miffed.

"You should have thanked him for his help. He was helpful wasn't he?"

"Yes, but he was a meddlesome know-it-all. Didn't he bother you, sitting there like a puffed pigeon, giving lectures?"

"Of course, but we had to draw him out. How else are you going to learn these things? That's what you plan to do at the bar, right?"

She proceeded to give Otto several examples of words he could have used to end the luncheon more graciously. Matters of speech and etiquette came as easily to her as the short witty or scornful sendoffs she had employed at Jenny's. That she had learned these things in Ireland or Tuckerton impressed him and he accepted her lesson, realizing that the restaurant could use her well-suited words, the smooth introductions, the apt sayings, the polite excuses, the necessary interruptions, and the occasional put down.

As the train moved south the landscape had become cluttered with small houses, more and more towns with factories and tenements built up by the tracks. And, there were more Hoovervilles, shanties and idle men. His excitement increased as each mile passed but was tempered by concern over the herculean difficulties of starting a business in the midst of a depression. There were no jobs to be had so what choice was there but to plunge ahead? Trees and fields gave way to more tenements, apartments, and warehouses and passing through the Bronx and over the Harlem River into the continuous shadow of the buildings that lined the tracks before plunging into a tunnel and then Grand Central Station. Finally New York City, home.

Chapter 24

Outside the station, the cabby loaded their bags and looking back over his seat, called out above the street noise, "Where to?" Otto, bewildered by the brusque demand, gathered himself for a second and shouted back, "the Waldorf Astoria". It was the only hotel either one of them had heard of; but stunned by the bill they moved to an inexpensive hotel on Lexington Avenue. There they found a modest room with a small kitchenette for a reasonable rate. At the payphone in the lobby Otto thumbed through the real estate pages of a dog-eared phone book and divined by the name of the realty company listed as Mid-Town Business and Residential Holdings that it would fit their needs. Mel Seiderman, the realtor answered the phone, and upon learning the caller was interested in property "near Rockefeller Center", sat up straight in his chair. The prospect of a good payday energized him. He replied without hesitation that he could handle that. Otto had called near the absolute nadir of the dismal real estate market, at a point where Seiderman would stoop to handle any request for property on the island of Manhattan—cellars, walkups, a hole in the wall. When he heard the customer was looking for restaurant space near Rockefeller Center, Seiderman's delight was unbounded. He roared into the phone he had exactly what they wanted! A restaurant sat empty on Fifty-Sixth between Fifth and Madison.

Mel hollered over the cab's gearing and accelerations that the restaurant they were about to see had the best combination of location and space available, the most desirable in the city. Otto assumed this to be hyperbole and was prepared for anything. As the cabby wrestled with the wheel, checking up short, lane tossing, honking and swerving through traffic, Mel hollered that, "The past occupant was the wrong sort, Serbian or Romanian from somewhere in the Balkans. He made a big mistake by giving the liquor business to his cousin. That doesn't work in this part of town." He increased the volume of his voice to a shout. "Don't buck the system around here if you want to make it." The cab turned the corner and made a sudden swing to the curb. Seiderman employed the kinetic energy of the stop adroitly shifting his bulk through the cab door onto the sidewalk. As he paid the driver, he said over his shoulder with the smile of a diamond dealer about to display the Star of India, "this is it!" and turned and spread his thick arms in front of three large plate glass windows that had been painted with scenes of mountains. Arched over the mountains in gold lettering the name of the restaurant, *The Carpathian House*. "They were small time operators," Mel went on, making his point again, "and when the mob heard they weren't buying from the 'appropriate vendor', so to speak, they dropped off a delivery of ten cases of booze and made sure the cops showed up two minutes later.

The greedy bastard got shut down and the place has been empty since." He looked apologetic, his sweaty round face and bald scalp, rosy from the heat, flushed scarlet, "Sorry Miss, for the bad word."

Mel was electrified and it was catching. His hand shook as he placed the key in the door. Otto was at least a foot taller and looked over his head as the door swung open. Moving surprisingly quickly for a fat man, he bustled into the six by ten foot entryway that simply led to a second thick door with a small glass window, face high. Otto, with Nellie behind him, watched Mel fumble through the pockets of his crumpled suit jacket for the second key. Perspiration soaked the armpits and his jacket gave off a musky smell: cologne, mixed with sweat evaporated by the July heat. "This is the one you had to talk your way past," Mel said over his shoulder as the door swung in. They faced the wall of the coat checkroom. They were not in yet. To the left a claret-colored curtain hung on a brass rod blocking the view to the inner sanctum beyond. Mel drew the curtain aside and Otto and Nellie stared into the restaurant. The place had been shuttered for almost two years and dust lay everywhere. There before the wall opposite stood an ornately carved mahogany bar about thirty feet long. The brass rail remained but the stools were gone. It had been used as a plant stand. Brass pots with dead houseplants were arranged in a line for the length of it, and at each end withered palms stood like acolytes. "The bar was preserved because they thought Prohibition would be lifted. Actually, it looked pretty good when the plants were alive," Mel added. Otto was drawn to it, and shoving several pots aside he swept the dirt and dust clear with his palms and assured himself that the heart of his restaurant, it's vital organ, could be revived; that the rich smooth surface of the bar had not been destroyed and a good refinishing would restore the original splendor. Only then did he bother to look beyond to the large dining room lined with banquettes and filled with a jumble of tables and chairs. Nellie, pointing with her pencil made a hasty count of the tables—more than thirty. As Otto strolled about, Nellie followed with a pad and pencil, making notes while deftly shifting her hips, weaving through the scattered furniture. Padded maroon leather doors in the back led to the kitchen, pantry, and a small office. Stairs led down from the kitchen to a dusty basement that held another large pantry, the bar stools, and broken chairs and tables. As they climbed back up Mel puffing the stale air, asked between breaths, "Well, what do you think?"

The key to negotiation, Otto understood in this new role, as business autodidact and perspicacious bargainer, was to proceed without a trace of enthusiasm. If the intonation of words could be made to sound as bland as milk sopped bread that was how he made them; "It might do," he mumbled. But, as far as he was concerned this place was heart-thumping perfection. He could envision himself ensconced at the end of the bar mingling with customers, the movers and shakers the place would attract. And from there he could oversee the working of an overflowing dining room permeated with the clatter of chinaware and the chatter of New York's cultured and affluent. "Well, you haven't seen nothing yet," Mel retorted.

They followed Mel back to the front of the dining room to the coat checkroom. Pulling open the half door, Mel asked, "Do you see? His eyes sparkled with anticipation as if they were to witness a miracle. As far as Otto could tell there was an iron pipe for hanging coats with dozens of empty hangers. The scuffed walls were painted the same beige as the restaurant.

"There's a stairway behind that wall straight ahead that's concealed by the way the restrooms fit in," Mel explained as he pushed on the panel that would have been covered by coats and released the latch, exposing a set of stairs. He flipped the light switch and led them up into a large, murky, windowless attic that held another long bar, this time with stools. "Behold the speakeasy," he exclaimed. It was a firetrap. Nellie, arms crossed against her chest, took one look and turned down the stairs again. "I want to look at the restrooms," she told Mel as they reemerged into the dining room. The lady's room was pink and black, and in addition to the closeted toilets featured a long makeup table and mirror surrounded by bare light bulbs. "Horrid, this will never do," she said as she marched out.

Mel showed them two more places that day, neither of which offered the potential of the first. They said farewell to the ebullient realtor in front of their hotel, bought groceries, and returned to their hotel room. Sitting by the open window in the sticky New York twilight, listening to the grinding traffic below, they agreed that The Carpathian House was a great prospect. Over the next week Otto dickered through Mel with the owner of the building, some mysterious satrap who they did not meet but who went through each modification of the proposed lease like a truffle hunting hog. It was agreed that the owner would clean and paint the place, except the attic, restore the bar to its original luster, remove the paint from the street front windows, and strip and repaint the ladies room a pleasant rose … a color Nellie assured Otto women like, and install new lights as the subdued light and the rose walls would make their faces glow. All this, Mel reported to Otto would be agreed to—if they would sign a five year lease. Otto had tried every twist and turn, every trick he could conjure up, but he was unable to move his invisible adversary. Otto was torn, undecided whether to sign; concerned the restaurant might fail and leave him with five years of rent payments he couldn't make. Nellie didn't waver; she had the answer for that. "Otto, it's now or never. You can always take the next boat for Denmark." He signed. She chose to be a silent partner.

Chapter 25

After ten weeks the construction work was complete and the restaurant opened. Otto refused to take Pack Parkman's advice to use a French name, as he thought it would give the restaurant an effete image, attracting a "tea room" crowd. Nellie disagreed but said the restaurant was his baby and she wouldn't make a fuss. The new name painted across the clear windows read, Otto's Place; a simple, direct statement of what it was, the brick and mortar embodiment of the vigorous owner, Otto Nielsen, restaurateur, raconteur, and most importantly, young opportunist and expectant laissez-faire capitalist. Now from the street the windows gave a welcoming view of the bar and the tables beyond. His vision for the restaurant had become solidified by the years of repeated imaginings, clear and absolute. The bar, like the opposing poles of a magnet would serve to attract and repel. Discouraged would be the ladies in fancy hats towing whipped men, husbands and otherwise, who would come to drink tea and nibble at little crust-less cream cheese and watercress sandwiches and talk about children, gardens and pigeon feeding in the park. Otto's Place would not cater to them. It stood ready for the men and their ladies Otto sought to meet, the fat cats: businessmen, lawyers, politicians and such. The fine liquor, food and excellent service would draw them.

The bar had been refinished to the original ruddy luster, silky smooth, organic to the touch. Behind the bartender crystalline liquor bottles, only the best brands, lined glass shelves. Above the bottles, a Versailles-sized mirror set in a gold baroque frame spread the soft red glow of the drapery slung across the window tops and falling in a cascade of ruby velvet at the window ends. In addition the mirror reflected the doorway and coatroom, allowing Otto sitting at the bar to monitor the faces of the diners coming and going. New deep red leather bar stools, heavy leather chairs and mahogany cocktail tables gave the intimate lounge tucked in by the bar the aura of Edwardian opulence, which in Otto's mind created the archetypical men's refuge. This would be his businessman's club.

In the dining room the carpets had been removed and replaced. Fresh wallpaper, sconces, chandeliers and table linens conferred on the dining room a separate look that Otto had modeled from the first class salon of the *Olympic Citizen*. They hired a chef, Robert, and let him hire his kitchen staff. In addition they hired two waiters, Carlo and Simon, and a bartender, Jim. Each man picked was the best of dozens of applicants. Nellie would act as hostess and oversee the kitchen and the ordering of the food. Otto would manage the liquor and bar and watch over the dining room and see that every customer's needs were met. There would be no fancy French dishes, or Danish for that matter, but perfectly prepared steak, chops, chicken, fish on Fridays, potatoes, good vegetables, salads, pies and cakes for dessert, cordials and cigars. To set their food apart, it would be presented with fresh-baked, steaming-hot bread accompanied by soft, salty butter, the staple that Otto had relished at the mining camp. The bar would serve two ounce drinks in the finest glassware. Otto instructed he to bring complimentary trays of hors d'oeuvres out to the bar when he noted, peering though the glass window in the kitchen door, that the bar had patrons. This was Otto's formula for success; he would sink or swim with it.

They held a dress rehearsal on a Thursday night in late October. Mel Seiderman and fifteen of his friends were invited for drinks and dinner in exchange for their constructive review of the food and service. Carlo and Simon, both seasoned waiters, did well, serving and clearing with unrestrained aplomb. Various bottles of red wine and several bottles of white were opened for tasting. "Otto, where's your wine list?" Mel shouted as he opened and turned the menu over, examining it front and back with the eye of a contract lawyer. The menu had been printed on oversized heavy linen paper with bucolic scenes of Denmark on the cover, the one allusion Otto would make to his heritage; but was devoid of any listing of wines. Nellie scratched a hasty note to have a wine list printed. Every dish on the menu was presented on small plates that were passed around. The meal became festive, punctuated by a few fake gagging scenes, but all in all, the food evoked rave comments, except for the Brussels sprouts. "Get rid of those stinking frog balls," Mel whispered in Otto's ear between gulps of wine. Following dessert the guests departed. Otto and Nellie, encouraged that no major problems had been encountered, decided they would open Otto's Place the following night. The Brussels sprouts were eliminated.

There was a downpour. Six p.m. found Otto wearing a blue suit, sitting on a stool, with one foot cocked on the brass boot rail. The waiters stood by the back wall. Nellie leaned back against the half door to the coatroom.

Since she had stepped down from the truck in Montreal the evolution of her persona had been linear, straight up. There she stood wearing a form fitting knee-length black dress, short sleeves, scooped neck, pearls and her hair up in a chignon. Otto could see the money spent at Saks, Henri Bendel, and Lord and Taylor on her clothes had been more than an excellent investment; they completed the outward expression of her sophistication, the trappings that achieved the physical transfiguration. There in the proscenium of the restaurant stood the artful accomplishment of her dreams—mind, body and soul. Otto looked across the room at a woman whose intelligence, manners and pluck he was certain would allow her to handle any social eventuality, any awkward contingency, with élan, elegance and tact. She would shine, even here in New York, the place he considered to be the zenith of the American civilization. Certain that his own European refinement and pseudo-polish would carry him through the challenges of the restaurant business, he viewed his newly minted partner to be every bit his equal or more. He loved her for that.

Their eyes met, she smiled and he went over and gave her a gentle kiss on the cheek. "Otto, I don't know how to put this delicately," she said in his ear, "but would you please step back there and tell Simon not to 'claw his cod' while he is standing in the back of the dining room. If he has an itch he should go into the kitchen to scratch." Otto walked back thinking that deep within the recesses this woman had not lost the Irish core, the gift for words. Simon put his hands behind his back.

The street door opened followed by the stomping of feet and the sharp tap of an umbrella on the floor of the entryway. Through the inner door two men emerged, shaking the water off their fedoras and shedding raincoats, all the while cursing the weather. Otto's Place was in business. Eight customers came in that evening, all of whom entered seeking refuge from the rain, and most of whom, seduced by the welcoming hosts and warmth of this new establishment, stayed on after drinks for dinner. The pattern Otto had envisioned—a good bar and food, alloyed with a warm greeting and good conversation appeared from the first to be a winning, if not altogether original, formula. The urbane, affluent, well-connected customers he and Nellie had sought to attract did in time become regulars. Otto's Place grew from this simple inaugural to be, not only a success, but a major member of the city's fashionable dining venues. The restaurant became as well known as Toot Shore's and Jack Dempsey's, identified as a place for the cosmopolitan and worldly-wise to eat, drink and be seen.

That night they turned the lights out and locked the door at two a.m.. The rain had stopped and the wet street reflected the city lights like a warped black mirror. He stood with his arm around her slender shoulders, protecting her, waving at cabs that splashed by until an empty one found them. In the hotel room, lying in the double bed in the dark, tired but too distracted by recollections of the past day to sleep, they talked about the life they had bought themselves, the years they had spent preparing for this time, and the finally the end of all the unmentionable things and the demons that once and for all could be buried deep by good fortune. As an act of will they had risen above it all and now suddenly the good times had begun. Though neither expressed it that night; these things, past and present, were essentially a contract, and for better or worse, they had joined their lives.

Chapter 26

It was a blustery January afternoon. The wind channeled down Fifty-Sixth Street, tumbling newspapers and paper cups until they caught on the grills of cars or piled up in alcoves of doorways. Otto watched from the bar as walkers struggled against the wind grabbing at their hats with one hand and their middles with the other as if reacting to a sharp abdominal pain. And he watched a large man unaffected by the wind other than he held onto his hat walk by the windows and turn into the doorway without hesitation. The restaurant was clearly his destination.

A grizzled hulk of a man, he was enlarged further by the blue camel's hair coat he didn't bother to remove. Hefting his body onto a stool near the end of the empty bar, he threw down his brown fedora on the polished mahogany and put out a paw-like hand for Otto to shake. Part grunt, part wheeze, he gave his name, Silvio, in a raspy basso that sounded as though it was squeezed from a bellows deep in his chest. Though taller, Otto felt stunted by him. Though, no other word was spoken, Otto sensed danger and was overtaken by an elemental reflex, a feral response to a primordial menace; his back hunched, his heart raced, his palms sweat.

The barkeep, Jim, who had become efficient at materializing when needed and then dissolving into the background of routine bar tasks, appeared to ask, "May I get you something, Sir?" The "Sir" was not routine but a wary punctilio added in deference to this customer's intimidating appearance. Jim smelled a rat as well.

Silvio shoved his left arm forward until his thick forearm became locked in the shirt cuff and, glancing at a ponderous gold watch, replied that he didn't drink before five o'clock, in addition, he was here on business. He turned his heavy face toward Otto and wheezed. "Nice place you got here. Open long?" He had recognized, correctly, Otto was the owner.

Sparkles of perspiration frosted the balding scalp between the thin black hairs. His heavy brows overhung his upper lids shadowing the dark, ursine eyes. Rimy stubble covered the cheeks and jowls. His breath, drawn simultaneously through his bulbous nose and slightly parted lips, was a slow and deliberate. The mass of his thick neck and shoulders spread the collar of his overcoat open.

"Almost four months, just getting started," Otto replied. He had been asked a simple question, 'Open long?' and from this Otto had concluded, somehow, he had been guilty of a breech of etiquette by failing to notify the caller that the restaurant had opened.

"I know, I've had my eye on you. I wanted to make sure you had something here that would last."

Silvio paused for a moment as he pulled a few heavy breaths through his mouth. His nose showed external signs of past breakage, bent and barely functional.

"DeTrapani Brothers got your liquor, right?"

"Right."

"Good people, you didn't go wrong there." Traces of a smile raised the corners of his mouth, setting the stage for his sales pitch, as he uttered. "I sell fire insurance."

Otto, not sure he had picked up Silvio's drift, cautiously played along hoping for the best. "Oh, we have fire, liability, theft, already." He flashed his warmest smile.

The corners of Silvio's mouth lifted more, the smile struggled to pull up the pendulous jowls with it and his eyes squinted with amusement. Toying with suckers, stirring them around with his little finger, watching them squirm and melt and agree to anything was what he did for a living, he was a master at it, and he enjoyed it.

"That's for after the fire, I insure before—so you don't have a fire."

Otto, angered by the shakedown, so blatant, so brazen, stared in disbelief, planning a move—take him on? He could count on Jim to jump the bar and help. Otto made no reply.

"One hundred a week." The mobster continued.

"Impossible." Otto said automatically having trained himself never to take a first offer. He tried to figure what he could afford, some small amount that he might buy the extortioner off with, ten dollars maybe. But the squeeze, once it was on, would only grow. It was not a good option. His mind raced through the ways to handle Silvio, to stall, to commit to nothing. He felt perspiration moisten his brow as he locked eyes with the mobster for what seemed an eternity. Cooperation with a criminal, paying him off, he thought must be a crime, and caught between the law and a mob was an uncomfortable place for a young restaurateur, especially one who had come to the States for "a week or so." As far as he could see whatever choice he made, he risked everything.

"Impossible?" Silvio echoed, his sarcastic tone conveyed annoyance with the rash answer.

"Well yes, that's it, burn away, I'll get a match?" Otto turned to look up the bar where Jim was washing glasses. Jim with his eyes askance kept the scene in view. "Jim, toss a book of matches down here." Turning back to Silvio, "If you don't want to burn it now, the address is on the inside cover." He flipped the matches on the bar in front of Silvio

He visualized the restaurant a black, gaping hole, a missing tooth, in a glorious row of businesses on an upscale street; and Nellie and he, having absconded, relaxing side by side in deck chairs staring out at the Atlantic on the next boat to Europe.

Silvio didn't like the message. Thinking his guy was tough or didn't give a damn, or both, Silvio began determining what a good beating would have on Otto's decision making process, when from the corner of his eye, like a wisp of hair, he caught an apparition of pulchritude. Looking up, he squinted scrutinizing Nellie as she walked in holding shopping bags. She read the tension in Otto's face and came over. Silvio, not accustomed to waiting for introductions, turned his attention to her as his eyes swept from her face to the floor and up again. He chortled, his voice a full octave above the hoarse growl, "Well, hello young lady." A broad grin filled his fat face. Turning, he shouted down the bar, "Hey, Buddy, I'll take that drink now". It was like an awakening, like Silvio had fallen off his horse on the way to Damascus and come up goofy.

Otto introduced her politely even though thoughts of a beating administered by Silvio and company some night in the street after closing had begun to play across the back of his eyes. "Nellie, this is Silvio. Silvio, Nellie is my business partner." The image of Kurt lying on the ward in Copenhagen crawled up from his subconscious, except this time Otto would be lucky if not in a metal drawer in the morgue. A smile lit up Nellie's face, a radiant one, a sunburst, a let-me-gaze-into-your-eyes-forever smile. She was an actress. Otto watched her take control of Silvio the feminine way; she worked him over with a charm that evoked in him dreams of those lost nights when love, warm and steamy, was still possible. She said she was "delighted to meet him," and she made him believe it.

By now the bar had several customers, businessmen, out of earshot at the other end.

Jim walked over. "Johnny Black, up," Silvio ordered.

"Two," Otto added, he held up two fingers and looked to make sure they weren't shaking. Nellie passed.

Jim poured generous drinks even by the bar's standards.

Silvio, not a sipper, threw back two plus ounces of the expensive scotch. By now his overcoat was open, and the buttons of the double breasted suit coat strained to hold in the bulk of his belly. He sat looking into the mirror, twirling the glass under his palm, thinking. Jim refilled it. Otto knew better than to interrupt.

"I'll make you a proposition," he said, glancing at Otto without lifting his head. He stared into the clear brown liquid as he spoke, "since you didn't take my original offer."

"What offer?" Nellie's voice was sweet but emphatic.

Otto replied in a near whisper. "Silvio has proposed that we purchase fire insurance from him for a hundred dollars a week as a guarantee our restaurant won't burn down." Nellie caught on instantly, and flashed a fierce glance at the back of the balding, raked-over pate. Silvio caught the expression in the mirror.

"And what did you say?" Nellie demanded of Otto, making no effort to hide her anger.

Silvio looked up, his deep-set rheumy eyes focusing on her in the mirror, "Young lady, your partner here said, 'no'."

She gave Otto a concerned glance.

There was a pause. Silvio stared at the bar, still turning the glass and appeared to be on the verge of some reconsideration, a change in direction, a second proposal, teetering like a suicide on a ledge. Nellie sensing this, smiled again at the mirror, her friendly Tuckerton smile in this instance designed to give him a good push. Finally he fell, his words like flailing arms clawed at the air, his nose and mouth sucking breaths. "I shouldn't be doing this ... it's against my principals to let anyone do business in my territory without payments…For you I'll make this one exception…but remember this…you're a special case." He took another swallow of the Scottish soother and checked the mirror again for Nellie's irresistible smile. It was still there, locked on. "My son, Gino; he's in a tough spot." He wiped the back of his big hand across his mouth as if it were a final attempt to zip it. "Gino, well he uses Gerry, you know, didn't want to seem too Italian, but with a name like Tortorici, what else could you be but a wop?" he returned a smile to Nellie in the mirror. "Well, he's a stockbroker, Wall Street. We're real proud of him…went to Fordham, you know." He stuck a finger up for Jim to bring him another scotch. Silvio took a long draw. His words came easier. "Anyway, he works for Merrill Lynch, but they're selling their stock business to an outfit called Pierce and he's hanging on by the skin of his teeth over there and in order for Pierce to take him on he needs more customers with real money, and that's a tall order in this market." He paused again and watched Otto and Nellie in the mirror for their reaction to what he would propose. "I was thinking, if you put five thousand in a brokerage account for him to manage and leave it there, you wouldn't have to worry about any fires."

"Sounds good." Otto replied immediately with no consideration. The relief he felt was palpable, the tension began to fade, his back straightened, he became aware of the sweaty shirt that stuck to his armpits. He wasn't sure they had five thousand dollars remaining of their original stake or if Silvio's word was good. It was a lot of money, but this was a far better answer than he expected. Nellie, deadpan, shook Silvio's hand without speaking, and went to hang her coat and put her parcels away in the coatroom.

"Christ, I feel good." Silvio exclaimed, shedding the overcoat and throwing it on a stool. "You know, Otto, you're quite a guy. You didn't flinch. I respected that. But do you know what made me change my mind? It was that little lady of yours. My God, she's a knock out." In an instant, Silvio had morphed from a threatening grizzly, not exactly to a lovable teddy, but at least to reasonable company. "At my age, I just gotta look, but I can imagine, just imagine, by Jesus, what it must be like."

He stayed several hours. Jim had instructions from Otto not to take his money for the drinks. Silvio talked with several of the customers, mixing easily, and his belly laugh could be heard from time to time over the noise of the restaurant. As he left he stuffed a hundred dollar tip in Jim's uniform pocket and put his hand on Otto's shoulder. "Here's my kid's card, I'll send him around," he said, and walked out the door, humping his coat up over his shoulders as he went.

Otto figured the hundred was a payoff made that afternoon by some poor sucker up the street.

Chapter 27

Five days after Silvio's visit, Gerry Tortorici came by. He stopped inside the door and studied the setting as he pulled off his kid gloves, folded them neatly into a pocket, removed his topcoat and folded it over his arm. Over six feet tall and rail thin, he had his father's shiny slicked down black hair, coal black eyes, and prominent nose, a feature that though large, did not detract from his good looks. Dressed in the stockbroker's uniform, he wore a blue, hand-tailored pinstriped suit, a Countess Mara tie in a perfect Windsor knot, and black wingtips that peeked out from beneath the break of his cuffs. Looking about, his assessment of the restaurant completed, he determined who the owner would be. He approached Otto with an extended hand. They sat down together at the end of the bar, a spot that had become Otto's *de facto* office. Jim took their drink order.

"My father tells me you are interested in investing in the stock market," he said in a polite, almost reverential tone, a soft sell generally reserved for introducing the newly wealthy to the vagaries of investing. Otto, not certain Gerry was aware of the circumstances motivating his desire to invest, made no allusion to the catalyzing effect the threat of a restaurant fire had on it.

"Yes, I think the market is coming back, we want to get in." The statement, Otto thought, had some basis in fact, but at this point his faith in the stock market was weak. That didn't matter, he was buying fire insurance.

Gerry smiled at him. "I think you're very smart. Most people have been scared out of the market. Then when the market goes up they get excited and start buying again. They should be sensible like you, and buy while it's down, that's the way to win." Otto wasn't flattered by the compliment, realizing it was a standard stockbroker sales patter, designed to sway the unsophisticated. On the raw side of handsome, sincere and earnest, how new widows must have fallen for him. Despite that, Gerry seemed to be the legitimate article, and with no option but to proceed, Otto smiled and nodded gamely. In fact, what he had envisioned Gerry to be had been very much worse. At least he wasn't a goon in a suit; in fact he could easily pass for the scion to the Rothschild fortune habituating the bar at the Paris Ritz. Taking out an expensive gold nibbed pen, Gerry began to fill in a form as he questioned Otto about dates, addresses, beneficiaries, and so on. Finished, he slid the form over. Otto signed and took the form to Nellie for her signature. After checking the facts, she signed as well.

Silvio appeared, almost magically, as if he had sprung up from the floor, and standing behind Otto and Gerry, draped his thick arms over their shoulders. "Well boys, doing some business?" Otto could feel the tug on his shoulder as Gerry pulled away from his father's clutch and stood apart, and with a nod indicating "yes" in acknowledgment to his father's arrival, he prepared to leave. Otto reached into his wallet and fished out a check and made it out for five thousand dollars except for the name of the firm, explaining "I don't know who to make it out to, with the sale of the brokerage and so on." Gerry reached down and took it, assuring Otto that was all right, the firm now went by five names linked by commas, too complicated, he would fill the name in back at the office, and without a parting word, turned and walked out.

"Now that's gratitude for you." Silvio remarked as he signaled Jim for a drink. "I told you he doesn't accept where he comes from." Silvio was clean-shaven, no stubble, his suit pressed and neat, and his manner non-threatening, even jovial. "Otto you just gave a guy you never saw before a check for five thousand bucks that he could write his own name on and cash and buy a one-way ticket to Rio. Man, you're a trusting dumb son of a bitch." He poked Otto on the shoulder with a ham hock fist and gave him a big spaghetti-eating smile that lifted his entire face, jowls to eyebrows. "Well, don't worry, you got nothing to sweat about here; he's as straight as a monk in that Swiss banker suit." His eyes shifted down the length of the bar and recognizing someone he had met last visit, he cupped a hand at the corner of his mouth and called out, "Hey, Doc, I want you to meet the owner." They walked over to a small, gray haired man sitting alone behind a scotch and soda in a highball glass. Silvio gave him a hug, and as he messed the doctor's hair with his fingers, he explained to Otto that "Dr. Weinstein here is a psychiatrist and just imagine, what a great job, he gets paid to listen to crazy stories." Furthermore, Silvio announced, not entirely in jest, that he was particularly impressed with the doctor because, "he didn't diagnose me as a nut, at least not right off the bat," and thumped the diminutive doctor on the back to punctuate the joke. The doctor with both hands attempted to sweep his hair back in place.

The little doctor laughed at the abuse and quipped, "My opinion can be readily revised."

Otto thought what a strange pairing, a curious mix of cerebral with corporeal, brain with brawn, oil with water. The doctor, who appeared about fifty, seemed to enjoy the rough greeting, a male-oriented rite perhaps absent from his childhood; and though he had no option to having been approached, the doctor did invite them to sit. Silvio continued with his description of the physician despite his presence. "The Doc here has an office over on Park Avenue, but lives just up the street. Treats a lot of swells, and fixes them up, isn't that right, Doc?" Smiling, ignoring Silvio's compliment and crude biographical sketch the doctor shook hands with Otto. His hand, cool from the highball glass, was small and delicate, Otto's hand wrapped around it and could have easily crushed it. The doctor was one of those men who appear older than their age; probably gray by the time he was forty. Otto imagined him the bright little boy with glasses who sat in the back of the class and always knew the correct answer and who didn't play ball in the park after school because he practiced the violin and studied French. He had evolved, as if pre-programmed, into the quintessence of a sagacious physician—intelligent eyes behind the rimless glasses, a care-lined face and neatly trimmed white mustache.

"Doc lost his wife a while back." Silvio went on, exhibiting no flare for sensitivity; thumping the doctor on the back again in an oafish gesture of sympathy, then added with a deep, barroom laugh, "Hey, Doc, you can have mine!"

"No thank you, Silvio; I have had quite enough of that revered institution, one wife was sufficient." The soft genteel voice contrasted sharply with his companion's bluster. Then, taking the cautious approach with his large friend, he added. "But, I'm sure your wife is most charming."

"Shit, Doc, she's a dog. We've been together for forty-eight years, and you don't change dogs in mid-stream."

The doctor took a sip of his drink, the *mal apropos* amused him. Silvio was a world away from the refined Jewish clientele that the doctor treated each day, the legions of depressed among Manhattan's privileged class. "That's what I find so enjoyable about my friend here," the doctor said turning to Otto. "No evasive language, and no attempt at pretenses, and most importantly, no sign of neurosis." He didn't stop smiling as he changed topics. "You've done a beautiful job with this place. I came here once when the other people owned it. I had to talk my way in. The bar here was covered with plants so to get a drink they seated me at a dinner table and they brought it out from the kitchen in a teacup. The food wasn't very good either. I never bothered to come back." After pausing to sip the scotch and soda again, he added. "They went out of business, but I suppose you know that." Otto wondered if Silvio would contribute to this account of things, as he must have known about the raid, perhaps even engineered it. But Silvio remained silent for the moment, concentrating on his scotch; then, as if coming out of a trance, he said under his breath, "They had a Helluva bar upstairs, booze and dames by the carload. It got closed down, funny thing."

Whether he heard it or not the gentle physician made no note of the remark and continued. "Mel Seiderman obtained this space for you?" He raised his voice at the end of the sentence which made the remark fit somewhere between a declarative sentence and a question; an idiom that Otto found to be in common usage in New York, particularly when the questioner didn't wish to offend by presuming to know something he had no purpose in knowing. Responding to Otto's nod the doctor went on. "Mel Seiderman and his father-in-law own the building, you know, with some partners of course. Owns my building, too." Otto was uncertain why the doctor would share this information. There could be no motive. Mel had not let on that in essence Otto had been negotiating with him, not some remote, persnickety absentee owner as Mel led him to believe. It should have angered him, but it didn't. In the same situation, in the captain's chair so to speak, he would have done the same, particularly with some wet-behind-the- ears foreign newcomer, a schnook—that was the word they used in New York, wasn't it? But here it was, the information he needed for the next time negotiations were required. Another instance when the bar had performed as expected, providing information that Otto could store and use should an opportunity arise. After a while, his evening cocktail finished, the cultured doctor shook Otto's hand again, excused himself, and left. Silvio quickly garnered another bar mate, and his laugh once again boomed out over the din.

By now the restaurant had a dozen tables with customers. Nellie pulled Otto aside by the sleeve. "Otto, what is that thug doing here again? He acts like he owns the place."

Otto had begun to warm up to Silvio and saw that he might be an asset, breaking the ice with customers, providing some introductions. The positives might in time outweigh the negatives.

"Can't you get rid of him?"

"Nellie, how? I can't throw him out." He moved to stand in front of her so that her voice would not carry over to the bar once he realized to be over-heard was her objective.

"He's gross, Otto, fatter than Murphy's pig," she said looking Otto in the eye.

As far as Otto was concerned, Silvio was boisterous, but so far not all that objectionable. He took her by the shoulders maneuvering her further away.

"Otto," she said again, her perception of Silvio was unwavering; an uncouth loudmouth who was dangerous to boot. "He's a mobster, a crook."

"But, he's our crook. He keeps the others of his sort away."

Unable to make an enemy of a man who could turn on them as easily as he had come around, they had no recourse. Nonetheless she would have the last word. "No more free drinks!"

The matter settled; Otto gave her a kiss on the cheek. He loved her spunk when flashes of anger lit her blue eyes up with the dazzle of a gas flame. He swung around toward the bar again. And Nellie returned to her position, one that she had assumed now habitually for the five months since they opened, near the entrance by the coatroom door. There she could control the doorway, greet customers, hang coats, and fill the tables. The bar she left to Otto. It had become a man's sanctuary and rapidly becoming a men's club, and though women were not excluded, they were usually escorted, guests, not members. Nellie noted the effect on the bar's atmosphere the women made: lowered voices and changed subjects from sports and the markets and business to inconsequential things. If the woman was attractive and gave even a hint of accessibility, she drew the wolves. Nellie had watched all these things before, on a much less sophisticated plane; but the essentials were the same and it annoyed her.

Waiting by the coatroom she passed the time imagining the customer's lives, beautiful apartments overlooking the river or the park, the home in the country, country clubs, horse shows, and elegant parties. In contrast, her work she found demeaning, and strong pangs of envy overcame her. Unable to join their world and with no opportunity for "fancy" friendships as she called them or "lovely" invitations for tea or to shop, she felt once again trapped by the plight of the poor Irish … and here in the entrance of her own restaurant of all things. There were times she lingered by a table after passing around menus to catch snippets of conversations. She listened as Mrs. C. Albert Wickham, Bitsy to her friends, a bejeweled beauty she particularly admired, spoke of growing up with ponies; others spoke of yachts, trips to spas or lawn parties in the Hamptons. Nellie yearned to be there, to mix with the beautiful and fashionably dressed, the poised and commanding. But to them, she conjured she was just another Irish "in service" and in her correct "place", hostess and coat-check girl. There had been no escape at this point. Her past had not released her. She had come far but not far enough.

They argued for the first time. Nellie complained. Her words, though mild, exploded in his head. Didn't she understand their objective to build a stake in the New York and that was on track, he shouted. Yes she did. And how important her appealing looks and her warm welcomes were to the image of Otto's Place, every bit as important to the success of the restaurant as his glad-handing and putting up with the likes of Silvio? Yes but, she reminded him—didn't he tell her how he had chaffed when made to stand like an ornament against a wall at those parties at the military academy in Denmark? Yes he did, but this is different, now they were paying their dues, there was a reason for it and there were recompenses since she could shop for clothes, go to matinees, the museums. Wasn't that enough, didn't she think New York wonderful? She bit her tongue. No, she didn't think New York wonderful. And she had paid her dues, bitterly, and now she had hoped to indulge her dreams, to have something different, yes materially, but also socially, to have some station, to feel at home in a nice, no fine, neighborhood and to put down roots. She didn't see how New York would work for that.

"Everything is for the business, isn't it Otto? Of course, I'll have to do it for the business," she heard herself say as if off in another room. They were the last words; it was an imperfect ending to the quarrel, nothing settled. Her complaints, though heard by him, were not assimilated. He didn't understand her passion and her mounting despair. His love for the restaurant had no limit. Her love for him she thought had no limit; but love for the restaurant, no.

On a quiet Sunday afternoon, she wrote to her mother while seated at the small dressing table in the bedroom and imagined her mother in the bitter cold house, a blanket wrapped about her shoulders to ward off the Irish damp, splitting the envelope open with red chapped hands. Nellie said she had come to New York and was happy to be away from Tuckerton, explaining that she had left secretly at night as Aunt Mary would have prevented her from going, and it was vital, she underscored vital, for important reasons, dangerous ones, that her mother keep her whereabouts secret from her aunt. She wrote on, detailing her good fortune. There was Otto, wonderful Otto, the successful restaurant, the little apartment they rented. But before the ink had dried on the last page she experienced a gradual awakening of shame and regret. The letter had resurrected the apparition of a poor Irish girl and carried her back to Ireland: to the ramshackle row house and the noisy kids, snotty noses, tattered dresses, skinny legs and scabby knees, and now she considered how far she really had come. She could not think of Ireland without a rush of guilt, and though she sought to dismiss it as irrational and uncalled for, it remained tangible and satanic.

As she had told Otto she would, Nellie attended Mass on Sundays, regularly and alone. Otto refused to join her. Prayer and the Church had become her peace-givers, comforters, and the assuagers of the growing demons within. The rhythmic Latin incantations, the sanctification of the wine and Host, and the mystical liturgy that washed over her gave her the promise of absolution, beauty and hope. She prayed for relief from the envy and uncontrolled ambitions and from her frightful new devil—guilt.

Chapter 28

Otto and Nellie had rented a small apartment on Riverside Drive, on the fourth floor of a six-story building with brass mailboxes, a buzzer and intercom to the apartments, and an elevator in a wire cage that clanked and groaned beside the worn marble staircase. Nellie avoided the fearsome contraption and walked the stairs. Otto in need of exercise would sprint up. From the living room window the view was to the west out over Riverside Park and the Hudson River and beyond to the New Jersey palisades. The boats in the river below provided an ever-changing scene that Otto found to be a restful change from the hubbub of the city's streets. From the bedroom the view was less appealing. Ten feet beyond the ally the neighboring building, pocked by windows that stared across, forced Nellie to reinforce the window shade with a layer of heavy curtains.

They filled apartment with second hand furniture, dinged and scratched, "used but not abused" as the salesman pronounced. A double bed, bureaus, tables, chairs, rugs and sofa bought from a store that promised same day delivery. The china, silverware, and glasses came from the restaurant. Soon there were houseplants in brass pots by the windows, throw pillows on the sofa and framed prints that Nellie bought with a specific place in mind. And the finishing touch, as a gift for herself Nellie bought a dressing table with satin skirt and a triptych mirror, and a sterling silver brush and tortoise-shell comb set. For Otto she bought a matched pair of military hairbrushes in a leather case.

Life in New York, as Otto and Nellie discovered, came with troublesome features. Black grit settled on every surface and within an hour or so smudged the inside of shirt collars. There were bugs, not the flies that with the coming of the North Canadian spring flew in a fury at the face and eyes, but cockroaches that crawled about at night and darted behind the kitchen sink the instant a light switch was thrown on. Each morning Nellie washed away black specks, bug droppings, from the counter tops. In addition, feasting on dropped crumbs and sugar crystals, near-microscopic ants that had climbed the brick façade four stories set up colonies under the cabinets. And outdoors, like the paths through the snow at the mine, the city sidewalks became slick with trampled snow that turned to ice and in spite of walking with little mincing steps invited a fall. And the curbside water splashed up by taxis that slashed along with inches to spare. All this, Otto abided and when Nellie fussed, he chided her with a laugh saying that these things add charm to the city he had come to love. The noise, the bustle, the crowds, the changing scene, the lights, his friends and his expectations, they enlivened him. The restaurant, open for seven months, began to turn a profit. He felt victorious.

And there was a pattern to their lives now. Mornings they lay in bed until the building's superintendent arrived in the basement and fired up the boilers. The radiators clanged, then banged and finally hissed and the apartment went from drafty cold to dessert hot compelling Otto to crack the windows an inch or more to control the temperature. Nellie made breakfast, frying eggs and bacon. The smell of coffee and bacon fat lingered an hour or two while Otto sat at the dining table drinking a second and third cup while reading the *Wall Street Journal* and *The New York Times*. Nellie sat on the sofa in her robe and slippers, feet drawn up under her, studying the society pages hoping to spot a customer. When Otto found something of interest, an amusing story or recipe, he would read it aloud. Once dressed and the weather clear and inviting, they would stroll along Riverside Drive or by the river in the park.

On a morning that had turned cold and windy and threatened rain, Otto walked to the kneehole desk that doubled as a sewing table, and despite the lingering fear that the Danish authorities might locate him began a letter to Denmark. He would send the letter to Ireland and Nellie's mother would provide a new envelope and postage and send it on. Like Nellie, he began the letter with an admonition that not a word be said of its arrival or contents, and immediately above his final words he repeated the warning not to speak of his whereabouts. Though he considered himself hardened by the circumstances of his life those last two words, Love Otto, had brought tears to his eyes.

The letter made no mention of Canada. It began with a lie that he had moved from California east to New York City and then he embarked on a description of the new apartment in detail: the white walls, the bedroom with an outstanding view of the side of the neighboring building, the bathroom with a claw-footed tub and dripping shower head, the living room window with the panoramic views of the river, and finally, the kitchen, essentially an aisle between a sink, gas stove and Frigidaire.

Moving on to describe the restaurant he drew a detailed floor plan to show the bar, tables, and kitchen. He related how he and his business partner, Nellie Casey, whom he mentioned for the first time, had leased a prime location in Manhattan, decorated it, and opened for business last October. The clientele had grown steadily, and he credited the early success to serving good drinks, remarking that cocktails for Americans are a national obsession, especially since the end of Prohibition. The food was good also. Some success he owed in part to the patronage of acquaintances of the real estate broker who rented him the place, a Jewish fellow, and also to an Italian-American stockbroker, who introduced the place to his friends and clients. He had met his initial goal to begin to make money. This he related with a measure of pride. As conceived, the restaurant and bar attracted stockbrokers, lawyers, and businessmen and these were the clientele he desired to meet and planned to learn from.

As he neared the end of page eight, he mentioned, as if an afterthought, that he was living with his lady business partner, adding that this was an excellent way to economize because despite his success money remained in short supply. The tease brought chuckle as he wrote it. He went on to say that Nellie and he were married at City Hall in a civil ceremony on February first and boasted that the mayor of New York, Fiorello LaGuardia, had officiated. Afterwards Otto had given the mayor his card and the mayor promised to stop by the restaurant sometime. Knowing his mother and uncle would not appreciate how important the mayor was, Otto added that LaGuardia was the most famous mayor in America because he read the funny pages to children on the radio every Sunday, everyone in the country knew him.

Writing in Danish, Otto rummaged through the Danish lexicon for words that best described Nellie, but in the end his description of her, though not elaborate, summed her up well: Irish, pretty and very smart and they were very happy. He would bring her to Denmark to meet them all and to see the family farm, but for now the trip would have to wait until the restaurant business would run well without them and he was certain it would be safe.

Otto slipped a three by five picture into the envelope taken by a photographer who hung around City Hall to photograph just-married couples. When he gazed at it for the last time, he remembered the wedding picture of his parents that sat on the settee in the hallway in Arhus. Here in New York he too stood beside his bride smiling awkwardly, just as his father had years before. The formal wedding clothes were replaced by a double-breasted suit, and for Nellie, a flowered dress beneath her open winter coat substituted for a wedding gown.

Though he wrote an Irish address on the envelope he visualized Denmark; the green fields, the old house and barns, the cows and horses, and the hollyhocks blooming by the kitchen door. For the first time since coming to New York he was nostalgic, even felt a twinge of regret. At that moment he decided they would eventually retire on the farm, a wealthy couple returning to Denmark with money enough to turn the rough working farm into a show place. He could picture the changes he would make, new fences and barns, flower gardens, and a new orchard. The dream floated up from nowhere.

"Otto, we have to go in an hour," Nellie called from the bathroom. She emerged wrapped in a towel that was held by a tuck at the top. Another wrapped her hair. As she padded barefoot to the bedroom, she asked, "Otto, what do you think of Mrs. Wickham?" Nellie referred to a diner at the restaurant she knew Otto couldn't help but have noticed; she had watched his eyes stop when they reached the table where she was seated. Nellie thought her particularly attractive, and had quietly begun to pattern herself after her, her looks yes; but more her bearing, poise, and a panache that spoke of self-reliance, command, and high birth; the little gestures and expressions, the tilt of her head and the cock of her wrist as she held a cigarette, her laugh throaty and refined; the fashionable clothes she wore. And the jewelry, exquisite, tastefully understated and real. Nellie dreamed of what her life must be.

"Nice," he replied not sure who she was. There were a number he found attractive.

"You know, Bitsy Wickham, she's blond, very classy, and so very aristocratic?"

"A bit snobbish for my tastes." Otto said. He understood who Nellie meant and she had attracted his attention. She was a classic, he thought.

"Not snobbish, aristocratic," Nellie said. "In Ireland you were either born into the aristocracy or you stayed out. Cinderella was about just that, a fairy tale. Here you can be aristocratic simply by appearing to be."

"Aristocrat? For all we know your Mrs. Wickham might be the daughter of some fat, old, tobacco chewing bus driver and happened to marry well,"

"That's my point, why I love America. Almost any goal is within reach; the rules are simply be whatever you can afford. Otto, you know we agree on that. It is the money that counts, not the pedigree. Wasn't that what brought us together, isn't that our philosophical tie?" Otto made no answer; philosophy on any plane was not his forte.

"I like her. I'd like to get to know her," Nellie went on and then let it drop forced to move on to more pragmatic matters. "I have a long list of things to pick up for the restaurant. Hurry up and get showered." As he soaped, Otto pondered one of life's imponderables; women make lists, run their lives by them, planning, scheduling their every move. He never made a list in his life. Shampoo got in his eye and he turned to wash it off his face. In fact he never knew a man who made a list, except maybe BJ. Get an idea and go, works just fine. He turned off the water and reached for a towel.

He walked to the bedroom. Her clothes were laid out in a neat line, she had dried her hair, but she still wore the towel. He pulled the corner and it dropped. "Well, Mr. Viking man, so you think we can manage in ten minutes? I had planned for twenty, but you took such a long in the shower."

"Mirror was too foggy to shave."

"Shave first; don't you plan ahead?"

"No need, I ravage fast."

Chapter 29

Two years passed and by October 1936, Otto's bar had become a noisy standing-room-only, after-work stop for many of New York's cognoscenti, some of whom became shoulder-hugging buddies that Otto made a point to greet at the door with a friendly quip and banter about the news of the day. Here Otto urged on the gatherings that celebrated victories with raised glasses and toasts, shouts and laughter. On the other hand the inevitable losses were silently drowned at the quiet end of the bar. There Otto commiserated with the dejected, adding a conciliatory pat on the back and a few pointers about who to talk to or how to go about getting started again. His advice and tips, when requested, came with free drinks. Just as he had dreamed, the bar had become a market place for stock tips, business proposals, politics and jokes. Otto never tired, going well past midnight because time became irrelevant as the bar amounted to his library, his workshop, his switchboard, and nightly party. He circulated, talked, but especially listened, no subjects in particular, just to the day to day discourse that he filtered; collecting a fact here or there that he made a point of remembering with no set purpose other than someday those words might prove useful to someone. He had become a student of scraps of advice, business news, about who knew who or what, and he gained a reputation for being well informed, perceptive, tactful and especially, useful. The bar had done exactly what he had intended and he was making money, a lot of money, but never enough.

And he drank. Nellie watched Otto at the bar night after night and fretted. One night when Otto had drunk enough to be blurry eyed Nellie trembling with anger spoke out as they stepped inside the apartment and the door had sealed shut.

"Otto, stop drinking so much. You're becoming a souse!"

"I only drink to be so-cible. I have a purpose, it loosens tongues." He slurred.

"I've watched drunks all my life in Ireland and 'you-know-where' and I know a drunk when I see one." She paused for a second or two for emphasis and then shouted looking up into his face, "You're becoming a drunk!"

He blinked free of his languor and shouted back. "I'm not a drunk, Nellie! My drinking, in moderation I might add, is good for our business! We're doing well aren't we?"

"You mean buying all those friends drinks is good for business!" She exploded hurling her handbag across the room. "That's expensive! Liquor doesn't come out of the tap!"

"Nellie, do you know what I'm doing? I'm applying the theory of 'motivational capitalism'," he lectured, his voice now calm and stern. "My friends more than make up the price of the drink in tips for Jim, so you see we save money on salary for him. Here is, my Darling, a perfect blend of good will, and, you might say of, 'what goes around comes around'. It's what's called in the business world 'a wash'."

She whirled around from the closet where she was hanging her coat. "I'll tell you what's 'awash'—your brain, in scotch! Otto, I don't like it one bit! I haven't come this far to stand in that restaurant watching my husband get drunk every night!"

"I'll cut back," he said, with little resolution.

"You'd better!"

She had not envisioned this scene on that hot afternoon in Montreal, sitting against the bedstead with that reticent, quixotic Dane who had spun a web of dreams that caused her to imagine a future life, one with promise. It was on that afternoon she experienced the first time the swell of what she thought to be romantic love, an emotion she could only have dreamed of a few days before. Those sunny days of an early summer they spent wandering the narrow streets of Montreal, the shops, the little restaurants, and especially the bed in that hotel room where sex and love were joined. But here in New York there had been a change, the sudden success of the restaurant had made him over-confident, and less reliant on or responsive to her. She felt devalued. He was blind to the sacrifices, she brooded, she had made for them, and for the restaurant.

But as promised, he drank less, and so on Otto's thirtieth birthday, October seventh, that fell on a weekday, Nellie closed the restaurant and invited forty-five of his closest 'bar friends' for dinner. It was not the kind of party she knew Mrs. Wickham would deign to attend, but it was, for Otto after all, and not for her. The chef cooked a large roast beef and baked potatoes. The liquor and wine flowed and Otto's friends told him later it was a splendid time. Mel Seiderman and his wife Sherri came. Doc Weinstein escorted a perfectly-coiffured, silver-haired lady so delicate she looked as though she would break. Gerry Tortorici arrived, greeted his parents with kisses on their cheeks, but moved away and sat with friends across the room.

Silvio, a regular on Thursday nights, had always come to the restaurant alone. That evening he brought "the little Missus", Tina, whose appearance surprised Nellie because she stood tall, bony thin; hair dyed carbon black and pulled into a bun that exposed gray roots at the nape of her neck. The skin of her face, finely crinkled like cracked glass was glazed over with a thick mudding of powder and rouge. Heavy diamond jewelry hung from her ear lobes and swung from her wrists; large rings turned on her thin fingers. She sat straight and silent beside Silvio who, for his part, ignored her completely, taking command of the food and conversation at a table that had been set for eight.

Nellie had called Mayor LaGuardia's office. Mid-meal the mayor's entourage swept through the door and stood before the diners. The guests, impressed, greeted him with a round of applause, a few raised glasses and "heres to ya, Mayor." With palms up he declined any food, but made a peppy little speech wishing Otto happy birthday and took pains to say what a great contribution the restaurant had made to the city. Then, wishing everyone a good night, he waved and left as quickly as he had come, sweeping out of the door.

For dessert, Nellie ordered an elaborately decorated three tiered cake that was rolled on a cart from the kitchen, so splendid it too drew applause. Ringing his glass with a spoon, Otto stood. His good mood boosted by drinks he rambled. He thanked them all for coming, for their patronage, their constructive criticisms, and for introducing Otto's Place to their friends. Then, turning to Nellie, he thanked "his beautiful bride, for being such a wonderful partner." The applause and "here, heres" that followed encouraged him on. "You know," he said, pointing his glass at the magnificent cake, "our wedding was a simple affair at City Hall; we had no guests, no reception, just a dinner for two and dancing afterward. We didn't have a cake." Otto continued, his voice rising with emotion, "So this cake is our wedding cake, and is very special." He lifted his glass, "to my wife, partner, and best friend, Nellie." Nellie smiled, blushed, and was very pleased. The birthday party was working as planned. More "here, heres" and more toasts followed.

Included among the guests that evening, at Nellie's invitation, was a priest from the small parish she now faithfully attended. As the guests were reseated, Father Donovan or Father Pat, as he was affectionately known, rose with glass in hand. "Unaccustomed as I am to speaking," the avuncular priest gave a wink and a broad smile crossed his red face, "I nonetheless would like to take this opportunity to thank my host and hostess for a most lovely evening here on the occasion of Otto's thirtieth birthday." Otto thought he would sit down, but he continued, having seized the pulpit he expounded on how God had blessed the efforts of this "lovely" couple who had created this "lovely" restaurant. Otto thought he would surely sit now, but the liquor in this case had been far too good a lubricant, the wheels kept spinning. Continuing, he remarked how he was touched by Otto' description, clearing his throat, "of their wedding day," but couldn't help but note that the sacrament of Holy Matrimony was a sacred and "lovely" thing and now that he had the opportunity to meet Otto, it was his most fervent wish that Otto and Nellie, this "lovely" couple, see fit to marry properly in the Church, and soon," making clear the presumption of course that, in the eyes of the church, they were not married at all, and were living in sin.

Giving no indication he was going to sit, Otto was on his feet. "Father, have you heard the one about the Pope and a Rabbi in a life boat?" he blurted. Nellie, now distressed, stage whispered, "Otto, please sit down!" Her glare, which could have stopped a freight train, froze both Otto and Father Pat. They sat. Silvio, with no ear for subtlety or anything that approached it, stood to begin another joke. "Did you hear the one…?" Tina, without a word and exhibiting remarkable strength, grabbed him by the back of his suit jacket and pulled him down into his chair with such force it nearly exploded. At that point the guests, noting that trouble lay ahead, pushed back their chairs from the tables and moved toward the door.

Otto and Nellie stood by the door. Mel and Sherri had already fled. Silvio, working his bulk into his coat, whispered to Otto, "I'll tell you that one next time I see you." Tina, if she heard him, didn't react, just shook hands nodding, without a word. Otto wondered if there was something wrong with her hearing. Father Donovan, vexed by the realization he had precipitated the abrupt end to the affair, apologized for being so lengthy, adding that "gab" was the curse of the Irish. As he departed, he told them they would be in his prayers. Otto was tempted to say "lovely," but not wishing to risk Nellie's wrath again, simply said, "thank you." Doc Weinstein, the last to leave, thanked them for an "interesting" evening. Otto presumed he meant the evening provided unusual insight into the effects of alcohol on group behavior.

The cab ride home had been silent. Peace in the marriage again had become jarred and the wrong words would disrupt the delicate balance as emotions teetered on edge. As he shut the door and threw the bolt, Otto had a foreboding of trouble. Then the words came.

"Otto, why did you cut Father Pat off like that?" she challenged with her hands on her hips.

"I didn't like where he was going and I thought he had talked long enough." It wasn't the best time for an argument; Otto's judgment was clouded by alcohol. When he thought back on it, he wished they had had the discussion on another day, at another time.

"But he was right."

"About what?" Otto feigned ignorance, but knew exactly what

she meant.

"That we need to marry in the Church."

"Listen Nellie, you were perfectly okay with our wedding until Father Pat interfered."

"Interfered! I went to him for spiritual guidance, Otto," she said, exasperated.

"Well, even so, he was out of place. Those remarks were things that are brought up in private, not at a party. He'd had too much to drink!" Her exasperation was catching.

"So now it's the pot calling the kettle black, is it? He was drunk?"

"Not drunk, just enough to make him run on," he said, trying to soften his words.

"Well, will you get married in the Church, or not? Answer me that!"

"Does it mean I've got to be a Catholic?"

"Yes."

"I told you I don't see how I could possibly be a Catholic. All that stuff I can't believe—heaven and saints up in the clouds. You don't want me to be a hypocrite, do you?"

"You don't want me to burn in Hell, do you?" she threw back at him, shouting now.

"I thought you believed in the forgiveness of sins!"

"Of course!"

"Well, just add a civil wedding to the list!"

This last acerbic comment, which Otto regretted the instant it came out, ignited a furious response. She threw the nearest object she could find, a small, but heavy Waterford glass ashtray, ironically the wedding gift from her mother. It missed him but dented the plaster wall and fell unbroken to the floor. As he bent to pick it up he heard the bedroom door slam.

He waited about an hour. Hearing nothing, he slipped out of his clothes and slid into bed.

"Will you at least go talk with Father Donovan?" came a small voice from the rolled up form that was turned away from him.

"Sure," he heard himself say.

"Another thing, Otto, in addition to your, drinking, I hate your sarcasm."

Chapter 30

It had become a routine. Following breakfast Otto would spread open the *Wall Street Journal*, light a cigarette that he let burn in the ashtray, and after reading the morning news turn to the stock pages. Years earlier, lying on his bunk at the mine he had yearned for a time when he could learn the ways of the stock market, the shorts, the puts and calls, buying shares and dumping them for a quick profit. And he would be a winner imagining how his knowledge of the market would be the key to wealth that had been inspired by Kirsten and cousin Niels; someday he would buy a splendid stone house, set on a spreading lawn replete with gardens. There would be lawn parties, money to travel, wealthy friends. At that point he could say he had accomplished his goal, he had arrived.

In America it should be simple. Following his plan he scrubbed pencil lines beneath the stocks he thought would move up, picking them out from the microscopic print covering the financial pages and watched them for a few months before giving up and selling. He had acquired some of the skills of a trader, but often found himself either pounding the table in frustration at the glacial post-crash market or following a steep loss from a tip whispered by a customer at the bar, a so-called Wall Street insider. Tips yielded only occasional winners. The twenties, the highflying heady times he had dreamed of, and wished for again, were long gone. When Western Kentucky Coal and Oil Resources Inc, a tip he passed on as a sure bet working the crowd up and down the bar went under in less than a month, mortified, he apologized; and to save face offered to cover any of his friend's loses, no matter the cost. Not one asked. They weren't suckered in or if they were they knew it was part of the game. From that point on Otto reminded himself, he was there to listen and learn, that was the goal; the harmless act of keeping his ears open made friends of those who could be flattered by his attention and who enjoyed his company and would stay on buying drinks. "First, do no harm" became his motto. By returning to this, the most basic of techniques, his pals remained loyal and most evenings, despite the moribund state of the Roosevelt economy, his customers who he considered friends, remained lined up at the bar shoulder to shoulder. The stock tips flew about and occasionally he quietly bit on a doozy; but for making money, booze was king.

Gerry Tortorici came regularly to entertain his clients at the bar, though once or twice a week, he would escort a woman to dinner. A lady-killer, handsome as Valentino, he had an eye for dreamy blondes and Nellie learned to save a corner table in the back where she could show them off to the restaurant's advantage; but more importantly where they were out of her sight. From the bar Otto would watch askance as Gerry charmed the ladies silly and wait for the right moment to stop by the table for an introduction; a gesture made to impress the date, as if that was necessary, and to gain a close up view. Nellie made no secret of her opinion that Gerry was a shallow skirt chaser and asked Otto to stop "standing at his table eyeballing the girls," as she called it. Although for Nellie, at night in those dim minutes before sleep when she tried to clear her mind, she realized it wasn't Otto's eyeballing that troubled her, but the image of Gerry that floated up behind her eyelids. He brought forth the image of a young miner she had enjoyed whose name she couldn't or wouldn't recall, a rare customer she took pleasure in. And she knew how desirable Gerry would be; she had known too many men not to be sure. The intensity of the suppressed desire troubled her. Painful memories of the past during the daylight cognitive hours she could stifle, but in the dark when the mind rambles they returned with a fierceness that made sleeping a struggle.

But the complaints to Otto about Gerry were of little avail. The "fire insurance" account crept steadily upward despite the dismal market and regardless of Nellie's hesitation to invest with him, Otto added most of the restaurant's profits to it. Otto's own market buys had become trades for quick gains, like rolling dice, a ride on luck. These were made for the thrill of a quick run up and the agony of timing the pull out, like holding his hand over a flame. For him, since the restaurant was a success, small stock losses could be easily tolerated, the market amounted to a lottery and as a result he made little money there. Now he had Gerry. Gerry was an investor, digging deep into *Moody's Manuals* he found companies that he called sleepers, remote arcane businesses—small manufacturers, insurance companies, even banks where the underlying value was not reflected in the stock, and the price of the stocks, as he projected, gradually rose. It was a matter of waiting. "Patience, and her financial offspring, compounding," he would tell Otto, "are the keys to wealth." Otto had spent his ration of patience for things financial at the mine in

Canada, that portion of his investing psyche he had transferred to Gerry. He would play the flyers now and then, Jerry would accrue.

For Otto there were customers in whom he recognized bits of himself, friends that appealed to his expanding interests; no ranking, equally valued: a group of comrades that shared favors, likes and dislikes. The little doctor was one. Doctor Weinstein walked through the doors precisely at five fifteen each evening, and took the stool at the end of the bar with his back to the window, which in time became the "doctor's stool". No regular would sit there until the doctor had come and gone. Jim would place a scotch and soda before him and the doctor would peer into the bubbles that floated up the through the amber liquid, pondering, Otto supposed, what he had heard in the office that day. When the doctor looked up and about, and if the bar was quiet, he would smile toward Otto and raise his glass as an invitation to come over and talk. They began with no subject in particular as there was no subject that did not interest them, from the most salacious of that afternoon's tabloid headlines to their favorite, politics—FDR and Mayor LaGuardia. If time permitted, the discussions became, as Otto put it, heavy, turning to philosophers and drawing on the contradictory theories of Hegel and Kant, Adam Smith and Karl Marx, and Kierkegaard, the latter that Otto, a Dane, had never read, though intuitively he had absorbed the essence of his reasoning. "That's part of being a Dane," the doctor said, "knowing that you are a unique person, pragmatic and realistic." The lonely widower would set forth ideas in a rational succession with insight honed from years of listening to patients, ordinary human stories of rejection and fidelity, loss and gain, guilt and despair. The doctor intertwined these with the metaphysical to explain the eternal values that represent the milestones that gave direction to all civilized life. Despite long conversations, the doctor didn't speak of himself or his own affairs, remaining politely distant and oracular. He had become for Otto a tutor of the classics, of civilized thought; the lessons he taught were the antithesis of the tales of tits and ass Otto enjoyed with Gerry and his friends.

Ed Cutler had become a highly regarded and trusted friend, who above all the financial men that frequented the bar, Otto respected. A dapper member of the Wall Street legal elite, he was a denizen of the boardrooms of corporations that shaped the American economy. Bad as it was Ed never lost faith that the Depression would end—despite the New Deal and the grand betrayer of his class, F.D.R., for whom he admitted he had voted for in '32 and now apologized for having pulled the lever. A corporate lawyer for whom the streets of lower Manhattan were as familiar as the floor plan of his home, Ed could not walk a block without meeting an acquaintance with considerable fortune and influence. Otto realized that he had an intelligence that, if defined as understanding and turning one's environment to one's advantage, was on the genius level. His voice, low and modulated, commanded attention in all matters. And though he had been born to this life, the scion of family of lawyers that used the law to fashion great wealth in the way stonemasons use their tools to shape stone, Ed took the skills to a new level. He had the Midas touch. What marveled Otto was the simplicity of his ideas, spotting concepts that had been out there all along, like pretty shells on a beach no one else bothered to pick up. Ed saw opportunities in the abstract, negotiated them into reality, and then took a healthy deferred payment in stock and a board seat at the nascent business venture, and as it grew, so grew his considerable fortune. If there were shoes Otto yearned to fill, Ed wore them.

Then there were Mel and Sherri, who dined in a different restaurant every night. Sherri didn't cook. Mel kept a standing reservation for eight Tuesday night at Otto's Place. Rotund and jovial, New Yorkers to the hilt, they never climbed a stair when an elevator could be found or walked one hundred feet if a cab could be hailed. "Exercise is for the masses," Mel would wheeze to Otto at the slightest exertion. As a couple they were invariably in good cheer, masters of droll conversation, polite, but with a flare for a piercing word at the right time, and when if needed, a sharp put down. New York was their fishbowl and they had no interest in swimming beyond it.

"Hey Otto, come over, put your backend down." Mel beckoned with a head jerk. Otto pulled a chair to the table. Mel looked around the room and groaned.

"Jesus Otto, this place has gotten too popular, you can't handle the crowd. You're starting to draw the hicks in here from wherever, Jersey even. Why don't you open up the upstairs, put them up there?" His round face assumed a puzzled look, as if this should have been obvious.

"You want people to go up through the coat room?" Otto questioned thinking the idea impossible.

"Look, Otto, you're here four, five years. How are you going to fail? You're turning business away, more tables more money, right?" He rubbed the thumb of his right hand over the pads on the tips of his fingers in a crude gesture, intoning, "money, money, makes the world go around." One look at Otto's eyes and he saw a blank and went on. "We tear out the ceiling up front, over the bar and lounge area, put in a staircase, and voila, an instant mezzanine that extends back over the kitchen and," he grasped Otto's arm and looked directly at his face, "add a service stairs there, and you've doubled your dining space!"

"Look, he's catching on," Sherri chirped, laughing, waving her fork Otto's way.

"Yeah, he may be *goyim*, but he's got talent, look at this crazy place, this is a bonanza!" Mel said in a loud aside.

"Sherri and I have been talking about this. You close down for two months. When's your slow season?" Without waiting for an answer, he went on. "A crew comes in here, redoes the place and you're back bigger and better than ever." He bounced with enthusiasm and the banquette complained loudly under his weight. Sherri clapped her pudgy hands and giggled, the large diamond ring flashed back and forth in the indirect lighting.

"Who pays for all this?"

"We do, well I mean my real estate partnership." Mel took on a more serious tone. They were talking business now and his voice lowered as he leaned forward so that he could not be overheard. "I shouldn't tell you this, Otto, but your restaurant has increased the value of this property, in fact, it has pulled up the whole damn block. What we do to make you better, increase the traffic on the street, helps us. Besides, finishing the second floor lets us raise the rent on the place, a square foot is a square foot, you know." With a wink the big grin was back again. Sherri, laughing, dug her elbow into her husband's side, "Good one, Mel." She turned her florid face toward Otto. "He's joking Otto, in case you didn't know."

"That's a lot to consider and there's Nellie you know," Otto said, uncommonly hesitant about a business opportunity. Their recent fights had a stifling effect on the dreams he shared with her and he had become careful of what he accepted. "But thank you."

"You think about it," said Mel, sensing Otto's discomfort. He abruptly went on to other things. "Otto, do you know who that lady is sitting with those two gents over there?" Otto turned around for a second and shrugged.

"No idea."

"No idea, my God, Otto where you've been, that's Sally Rand! The fan dancer!" Mel blurted. Dressed and lady like, and without her fans, Otto had not taken notice.

"Mel, you bad boy, you!" Sherri laughed, the satin of her pink dress tight around her waist creaked as she moved to give him a swat.

"I've got to get you some fans, my little chickadee," he murmured, imitating W.C. Fields.

"They don't come in my size!" her head went back, mouth open, she tweedled with laughter. By now they were all laughing. In a moment Mel caught his breath, and became serious again. "Otto, do you know who that is over there, to your left?" Otto took another look around. "There must be twenty million bucks at that table," Mel intoned. "The fellow in the gray suit produced 'Tobacco Road'. Worst damned play I ever saw! Who cares about that stuff, God, give me a break. But Otto, he eats here. You know you've got the upper crust in here when people like that are in here. You got to make more room for them. Have a place for the hicks from Jersey. Put them upstairs."

"My friends, especially Ed, point the important ones out and I go over to meet them," said Otto. "I make them feel welcome. In the past month we've had the president of Chemical Bank, Esso, the Music Hall, John and Lionel Barrymore, and even Jack Dempsey came in the other night to see what we were up to. Shook my hand. His place really draws."

"Draws lots of tourists, small timers. He can have it; you want the big shots in here," Mel said, unimpressed.

Sherri dug into her salad again and Otto took the break in the conversation as an opportunity to leave, walked over to introduce himself to Miss Rand and winked at Mel as he bent over to shake her hand.

Otto, still smiling, returned to his customary stool at the bar and Ed turned toward him. He had stayed later than usual and had a drink or two more than usual; Otto understood he was avoiding an empty apartment. His wife was traveling in France. "Otto, Doc Weinstein before he left for home told me there's a new theory that women can talk better than men, are more verbal, but men are better at mathematics. He thinks it's connected to Darwinian evolution; that women being the weaker sex and unable to fight their way out of trouble learned to talk their way out and the ones who weren't good talkers, well over time they didn't make it—so through the millennia the poor talkers were eliminated. Ergo women have evolved as good talkers. What do you think?" Otto uncertain if Ed was serious or not thought it best to conclude that he was, "Well, we have to make some assumptions here. Being a facile talker alone wouldn't be enough: to survive they had to have made a convincing argument." Turning the tables on Ed, he went on, "And, come to think of it, isn't that essentially what lawyers are supposed to do, and if by extension, arguing or putting it even more strongly, fighting with only words and logic, isn't that at the core of your profession? It should follow, therefore, there should be more women lawyers, don't you think?"

Ed went on half in jest. "Well, Doc says women have a strong inclination to be straightforward and honest, so I imagine he would think those qualities would be a drawback in the legal profession. He did ask me how many lady lawyers were in my firm. I had to admit none, although, we have some secretaries who know the law on routine matters better than most of the lawyers."

"So Doc wouldn't think straightforward and honest fits with lawyering?"

"Now, Doc didn't say that or disparage the profession, he did add in a way of a compliment, as he thought he might have offended me, that 'smarts' are what counts. He is very careful with what he says, you know. He has to be with his patients and so on, it transfers. But Otto, as you know lawyers are not all crooks, just the majority," he said with a smile, "so by your reckoning women would do the profession a lot of good, clean it up, so to speak. It was all theoretical with Doc, I had a good time with it."

Otto was about to add, "They're better organized, too." But before he could get the thought out he felt a tap on the shoulder, turned and found

Gerry Tortorici and beside him a stocky, balding man wearing a camelhair Chesterfield and holding a brown Homburg.

"Otto, I believe you know this fellow," Gerry announced.

"Cook!" was all Otto could muster recognizing his friend from the mine.

"Yes, none other than old Augustus C the Third. Well, Otto! I'll be damned! Look what you've done here. This is marvelous!" Cook retorted, making a shallow bow.

"Mr. Cook came by the office. It got late and we decided to go out for a drink. I mentioned this place and he picked up on the name, and asked me, 'Is this Otto fellow a young Danish guy?' I said, 'yes', and he say's, 'you know what, I bet I know him'. And as it turns out, by God, he does!" Gerry marveled, "Small world!"

They found a table in the lounge. Gerry went to the bar to order a round of drinks.

"So Otto, fill me in, what have you been up to?" Cook began leaning forward, his hands folded on the tabletop.

The relaxed joviality of the evening came to an abrupt end. Otto felt the tension as he concocted an answer. "As you know, John and I fixed up that truck and we drove down to North Bay together. John left from there and went on to Buffalo and then to Chicago or someplace out west. He was unclear," Otto got these facts out early so there would be no questions about where they had parted or where John might be.

"You fellows took Nellie what's her name with you too."

"Casey, right."

"That caused quite a ruckus up there, you know."

Otto let that comment go by.

"So you don't know John's whereabouts?" The question doubled Otto's discomfort and trying to sound matter of fact said "no,". He knew he was a lousy liar and hoped it didn't show.

"Nobody does—he seems to have vanished from the face of the earth, not a word from him. His mail stacked up, couldn't forward it." Cook mused. Otto wondered if Cook knew something and was toying with him and he rushed to supply more exonerating detail. "Nellie and I bought the truck off him, drove on to Montreal, and then took the train to New York," he added, trying to put the discussion of John behind them.

"I thought I recognized her, that's her over there, right? She looks wonderful," Cook said, tilting his head in her direction.

"Yes, we're married," Otto declared quickly to prevent Cook from making any allusions to her past, although he was quite sure Cook was decent enough not to speak of it now or later. Gerry returned followed by Jim with a tray drinks and the conversation turned to stocks and Broadway. More than ever Otto was anxious to learn about Cook, who he really was, and intended to get back to that subject, but after half an hour Cook looked at his watch, mentioned he had another engagement and as he stood, promised to be back soon for dinner. Otto was piqued. Why hadn't Cook confided in him at the mine, told him the truth about who he was, about money, making it or not, or at least said enough to dispel the rumors. But then again why should he? At the camp every man had a hidden past. Did he share the truth about Jacobsen?

Nellie, her heart pounding had been watching. She thought she recognized the short man. As soon as the door closed behind him she came over and whispered, "Who was that, Otto, he looked familiar?"

"The cook from the mine."

"I thought so! He didn't mention anything?" she said in near panic. The revelation forced a surge of blood, reddening her face. She reached out and pulled Otto by the sleeve to the coatroom.

As soon as the door had shut Otto tried to calm her. "No, I made sure he knew we were married, so he wouldn't say anything."

"I can't believe he is here! I can't be here with him in the restaurant when he knows— it makes my stomach churn! I can't do it Otto! I can't have him looking at me. It's awful, a nightmare! Is he coming back? If he does, I have to get away."

"He said he would come for dinner sometime, but maybe he won't. We can hope," Otto said bending the truth. He had to see Cook again; there were too many unanswered questions about this enigmatic man. His words didn't mollify her.

"What's he doing here?"

"I think he lives here, in the city. He seems to have struck it rich or was rich all along. He's a client of Gerry's."

"I don't know Otto, I don't know what I'm going to do."

"What do you mean by that?"

"I said, I don't know!"

• • •

That night Otto doubled his pillow under his head so he could look at her. Nellie lay with her head on two pillows trying to concentrate on a book by the light of the bedside lamp. Neither could sleep.

"Mel wants us to close the restaurant for two months so they can make some changes that would open the upstairs and make it twice as big."

Without looking up from the page Nellie murmured, "That's good, Otto. But don't you think it has grown too much already?" She turned the page, uninterested.

"More space, more customers, more money," he said.

Nellie worked to give him no hint of her satisfaction at what she had heard. Mel's plan meant no Cook for two months, and she hoped she could make it longer. This was the wedge she had been waiting for, an excuse to get out of the restaurant, even to get away from New York for a reason that was Otto's responsibility not hers.

"We'll get more help, someone to take over for you and you'll see;

things will be better,"

"Otto, I want to settle down. Why don't we sell it? We could move to the country, somewhere out of the city. You could start a new place there." Leaving New York was no loss for her; she found the city unfriendly, it made her feel small, a place she could not belong, at least not to the class she craved. She had no friends, only Otto's friends; no one would miss her and visa versa.

"What! It wouldn't be the same. There are no people out there. You know what I mean."

"What do you want to do then? Stay here forever?" Her exasperation rode a heavy exhale. "I've said this before Otto, I want to be someplace where I matter, where I'm not taking people to tables. It puts me in the serving class. I'd like to rate, have lady friends, belong to a nice club, learn to play bridge and join the garden club, things like that. I can't do that here."

"Well, we can't move to the country. That's out."

"Then, what about a place where we could go for weekends, get away from the city for a bit, just weekends?"

"We can think about that."

"Good." She turned to look at him for emphasis, folding the book shut holding the place with her thumb. "Now, Otto, I want you to promise, you're certain that Cook fellow isn't going to say anything?"

"I'm certain … and if he does, I'll kill him."

So in a brief negotiation Nellie had obtained her release from the onerous job, a weekend house in the country, and the pledge of a murder to protect her honor. Otto thought of the conversation about women making good lawyers.

Chapter 31

Gerry came in the bar a few days later and the subject of Cook came up immediately. "So what is it you are saying, he hid way up in Canada?" Gerry asked.

"Cooking for a mining camp." Otto allowed.

"Honest to God? So that is true. God, hard to believe. Worked as a cook did he? You know, Otto, the story I heard is that he disappeared a few months after the Crash. Lost a boatload of money, not only a good bit of his own, but also he was investing for a small, select group of people, including his father-in-law. On top of the losses, he apparently told his wife he had to work late because of the market. He told her that a few times too many and she becomes suspicious and hires a private detective who finds him at the Plaza between the sheets with some broad. Events got way ahead of him, his world crashed down around his ears, so he takes off; and it seems to a place nobody would imagine to look. And he was right, you were there, a God-awful frozen place, RFD number one, Nowheresville, Northern Hemisphere. Meanwhile I suppose they were looking for him in France or Italy or on some tropical island in the south pacific, like Gauguin or what's his name, the writer with TB." Gerry took a sip of his drink, "Oh yeah, Stevenson; wrote Treasure Island." He looked at Otto, taking pride in the recollection. "And then, when she couldn't find him she filed for divorce claiming adultery and abandonment. Rightfully so, I guess I should add. It was an open and shut case. She threw the book at him … or at his lawyer and accountant at any rate."

"There was lots of talk in the camp that he was some sort of financier, Swiss accounts, that sort of thing, but he kept his past a secret. I wonder if the time he spent at the camp was like doing penance for him, a situational hair shirt, so to speak."

"You're reading too much into it. I think he just wanted to get the Hell out of here until the heat blew over. It wasn't a matter of penance, just intense discomfort here in New York, like sitting on a hot stove. Her family was well connected. They could put the screws to him, major league."

"So why do you think he came back then… here of all places?"

"His father died. Old Boston family, tons of money, really old money, clipper ship stuff, real estate, lumber, paper, that sort of thing. When his father died a couple of years ago he leaves it all to him, the only child, millions. Congenital wealth, that's the best kind, boom, rich in an instant. So, what does he do, he comes back and pays back what he lost to his investors. I guess a year or so after you got here."

"Well, he seems extraordinarily honest, at least." Otto took a breath, smiled and having thought about it, "in any event, where money is concerned."

"Legally, he didn't owe them a damn thing, he didn't steal it, just lost it in the market; but as far as the business crowd was concerned, it was the only way he could restore his reputation. He's a natural salesman and he had talked people into investments they wouldn't have made if he hadn't pushed them. So he did what he had to do. It was a business decision. Is that honor, or practicality? I don't know, but it was the only way back into the game." Gerry paused, "Otherwise, he should've stayed in Canada."

"Game?"

"Investing, pretty big time. It's like sport to him, and he is good at it."

"By 'big time', you mean?"

The two young men sat, elbows on the bar, face to face, talking in low, confiding tones. They shared an interest in money-making, and in this unusual person, Cook, who they had both come to know. Gerry, *nee* Gino, son of a hoodlum raised in an immigrant family amidst the noise and squalor of the lower East Side of New York, who had worked and fought to leave that behind and become a blend of where he had been and what he aspired to: street-wise and urbane, invariably well-dressed, articulate, and, to no small degree, a lady's man. And Otto, with a Danish accent that provided a veneer of continental sophistication despite the naiveté of an outlander, sitting in his New York bar, choosing his friends carefully from the sharp, the seasoned and the worldly wise that walked in the door. Both men working their way up the financial ladder recognized their common aspiration, a bond of sorts in the pursuit of money. They ran parallel courses on capitalism's track, a stockbroker and a restaurateur. The goal was the same, wealth, and the status it brought.

"By big time I mean, he buys small companies, either outright if he can, or a controlling interest in the stock, with partners, if it's traded. Has an uncanny knack for sizing up a financial statement and for recognizing the future growth of something. He's had a few duds. Bought a company that made cigarettes out of lettuce, can you believe? No taste. But as soon as he saw he couldn't sell the damn things, he mixes in some tobacco with the lettuce and works out a marketing deal with an ad agency for a portion of the profits. Then he finds a buyer for his interest and Bingo, he's out with a profit before the whole business folded! Smoked any lettuce recently? Then he's got a toy company that makes little helicopter things kids shoot into the air with a spring-like thing that looks like a toy gun, does great. It was in the window of half the toy stores in New York at Christmas. Last year he bought a chain of failing jewelry stores for a pittance. Now you would think in this economy, in this freaking depression, even at that price that would be a dumb move with the rents and salaries and all. But he bought them for the good locations. A couple are even in fancy hotel lobbies. The owner had downgraded figuring it would be easier to sell cheap stuff, trying to stay afloat. What does Cook do, he put in only the highest end things and now he has a chain of little 'Tiffanies' on Fifth, Park, there's one a couple of blocks from here. They do really well. The real rich are the ones that still have money, they are doing better than ever, that's who you go after. He knew that. Why try to sell to some poor schmuck who doesn't have two nickels to rub together? Just look around your place here, Otto, your customers have money to spare. By the way, Otto, you ought to get Nellie a nice diamond ring to go with that gold band she has. What are you, a cheap skate?"

Otto was still curious. Gerry's description of Cook's business acumen and his investing skill made his juices flow. These were hardly dealings with Standard Oil or U.S. Steel but it was the type of enterprise he had aspired to, what his bar was about, learning of the opportunities that were out there and getting invited in on them. His thoughts ran like a dropped ball of yarn. He would try to get close to Cook; try again to make him his mentor, perhaps this time he would agree. Who knew what could come of it.

"How did you meet Cook?"

"He was referred to me by a secretary to the president of an investment bank I've been taking out. Had her here once or twice, a platinum blond, gets taken for Jean Harlow, you've seen her." He took a sip of his drink. "But don't let that fool you, it's a façade, she takes short hand and types a mile a minute." Otto could see that Gerry's mind was easily derailed by the thought of any blond. He was sympathetic but pressed on.

"And?"

"Oh, he does business with her bank and was looking for a broker to buy and sell stocks for him, nothing special, just a few fairly large trades so far. She likes me, in fact, has a little account with me, so she gave him my name and filled me in on his family stuff."

Otto's thoughts were on Cook, dreaming how to get him to come around to the bar, have a few drinks and dinner with him, schmooze as Mel would say, sidle up.

"I hear you're closing for renovations." Gerry's remark brought Otto back.

"For two months, January and February. We're going to make the place bigger. With more tables business should increase enough that we can hire a manager. Nellie's tired of the late nights." Otto paused for a sip of his scotch. "She wants a weekend place in the country and we figure with a manager we can get away weekends. We'll be here weekdays, of course. That's the plan."

"Take a ride up the Merritt Parkway, the new road up to Connecticut. There are some nice towns up there." He looked up. "Oh shit, my old man is here." Gerry started to get up, gathered up his cigarettes and matches, pushed them in his coat pocket and signaled Jim for the tab. "You know, Otto, thank you for putting up with him. Coming here keeps him out of trouble, gets him away from those creeps he hangs around with."

"Every Thursday, like clock work. He livens up the place." Otto walked Gerry to the door. "And Gerry, if you get a chance, bring Miss Harlow around again. She's something else, good for business."

Chapter 32

They drove up the Merritt Parkway in Otto's Buick sedan and once they were in the country Nellie scanned the surroundings and when the hills above Farbridge came into view she shouted, "Otto, please turn off here!" because in the distance off to the left rose a hillside where she could see large comfortable homes nestled in the trees, like those she had imagined since childhood. They wound down off the exit and found themselves on Main Street which they followed to a small real estate sales office wedged between the town's grocery store and the Post Office, and there they encountered Mr. Sedgwick reading the Sunday paper. In response to Otto's request that they see quaint bungalows, something with a garden, the realtor took them from little house to little house, none of which filled Otto's vision of a suitable weekend retreat, and certainly not Nellie's more ambitious plans. She would press her case for something more substantial in a way not customary to her. She was not passive aggressive by nature; but in this case that behavior adapted best. She would wait in the car, or if she bothered to enter the house at all, her tour was swift and the dismissal abrupt and uncompromising. She had come to Connecticut to fulfill a dream that had long been the focus of her life, a fine country home, like those of the wealthy landowners in Ireland, not these little servant's cottages! And after half a day of listening to Nellie's expanding frustration Otto surrendered, telling himself that by this concession to her he would avoid another fracture, quite possibly the fatal fracture, in their marriage: that tangled latticework of crime, sex, love and work that bound them. Money at this point could not be an issue … she knew what they had and they had plenty. So by noon Mr. Sedgwick had driven them back by his office to pick up a list of high-end homes, his best offerings. All the while he had been chatting about schools and the town beach on Long Island Sound and drove them by the town green where three churches, the Congregational and Methodist and Episcopal, stood like a row of sentries. The Episcopal Church he exclaimed had been built in 1872 of stone quarried from one of the hills just north of town and like his father before him he served there as an usher and deacon. When Nellie asked to drive by the Catholic Church, if that was convenient, he fell silent and after several blocks turned the car into a modest neighborhood and passed a stone church, less ornamental, but much larger than the Episcopal, in fact all the others. Nellie felt a rush of pride. The real estate agent went on to say that up the road sat Bridgeport, with the factories that employed the Catholic parishioners. He didn't say these factories had made Farbridge prosperous in addition to providing the coins the Catholics dropped in the collection baskets on Sunday—though Otto understood this was his implication.

Then, after a pause, as if that church had reminded him, he noted as he backed the car around in a driveway that they would need to hire help to manage a large house and gardens during the week when they would be in New York. This compromise, a large house in Connecticut Otto would concede to Nellie, though he stood firm on one issue. He would never sell his restaurant. It existed as an extension of him, an expression of his mind and soul, the creative tool for his lifetime objective, the place where his heart lived. He could not leave New York.

It was the first house they were shown and they climbed a path through the rhododendron that blanketed the hillside behind it, and while standing arm in arm on a frigid February afternoon in 1938 gazed down at the large Georgian colonial that sat triumphant amidst lawn and gardens. At that moment, Otto would always recall, they decided this house would be it. To Nellie the house represented the American peerage, which by the mere fact of ownership she too now planned to enter. With their success she would become "established," for indeed they would buy a small estate. They told Mr. Sedgwick, who worked to hide his surprise, to present an offer. It was the finest house on his list and quite frankly, listening to their accents, he thought well beyond their means.

Built of light red brick, trimmed in white, the house was elegant and symmetrical, with chimneys gracing each end. From the street only the upper story windows could be seen over a high hemlock hedge that was pierced by a brick walkway that curved gracefully to the front entry. Further on the road the hedge was pierced again by a driveway of chipped white stone that swept around to the back of the house past the brick porch deck with a green awning to the garage beyond. Here Nellie said they would have supper and sit at night to watch the sun drop through the oaks on the hillside. The lawns and gardens spread to the left and right, the view ending at tall pines marking the lateral boundaries of the five acre demesne; with the sight of the neighboring houses totally cut off, none to be seen, the house stood as a private island. It was the gardens that drew Otto to the place, a private Tivoli; but for Nellie it was the house alone. It thrilled her. She delighted passing through the front door into the grand foyer and looking up the glorious staircase that rose majestically curving around a glittering chandelier to a balustrade balcony high above. And to the left from the foyer a panoramic view down the full length of the living room to the fireplace at the far end framed by white paneling and mantel. There, the perfect setting for a portrait of an ancestor, had there been any. These to her were the essence of a luxurious home, where the photographers in the fashion magazines she had studied captured elegant women descending just such a stairway in evening clothes and gentlemen in black tie, elbow on the mantelpiece, stood before a blazing fire, aloof, champagne cocktail in hand awaiting their entrance. This was a house where she could entertain the likes of Mrs. Wickham and that was the absolute requirement and the deciding factor.

The practical concerns of managing such a place, sobering thoughts, vanished from Otto's mind as he watched with delight Nellie laugh and plan, dancing on her toes in stocking feet on the polished oak floors. Mr. Sedgwick sat at the kitchen table speaking with an elderly lady, the owner. Spread before them sheets of paper with the bid awaiting signatures. The house had been for sale since the past spring, but the work and expense required to maintain the grounds discouraged the other prospects. It is quite unfortunate, Sedgwick quietly thought, the buyers were foreign and Catholics, and that made him uncomfortable; but he reminded himself a number of the latter had moved up onto "the hill" over the years, and certainly, the neighbor, a banker, a bit of a bon vivant who lived next door would overlook such issues once he saw who was wearing the skirt. Sales had been hard to come by, especially for this large of a place, and the owner, a widow, was anxious to move. He would close the deal and take the consequences; he could survive the censuring looks and narrow-minded comments.

Enlivened by her excitement, Nellie and Otto walked about again. Starting once more from the top of the hill, they took it all in, walked down and circled the house, strolling through the gardens, some small with reading benches, coming onto spaces terraced by stone walls, discovering hidden places with a birdbath and another with a little fish pond, and passing through the garage they found a tool shed where tools hung neatly on the wall and outside once again they discovered rows of precisely stacked firewood and concrete enclosures filled with composting leaves cleverly hidden behind shrubs. Inside once again, they climbed up the back stairs to the maid's room and bath, then went room to room ending at the master bedroom suite adjoined by a sunroom that looked out front over the hedge at the narrow county road. Another glance once more into the bedrooms and baths at either end of the balcony before descending the staircase to the living room and through a doorway to library filled with cordovan leather furniture, a desk and reading lamps, and lined floor to ceiling with cherry-wood shelves. They passed into the dining room, and finally into the pantry and kitchen. Every room on the first floor either papered or paneled, and finished with chair rails and wide cornices. Nellie, as she strolled about, studied the home's furnishings that they decided to buy, changing the room arrangements around in her mind. As they walked her words flowed, describing how the house would be used, how they would entertain on the back deck on summer afternoons, how the Christmas tree would fit against the curve of the staircase for holiday parties, and the elegant candle-lit dinner parties they would hold before a crackling fire in the wainscoted dining room. By the end of this tour Otto realized he had bought a house fit for Cousin Niels. For a brief moment he thought of Kirsten.

They offered eighteen thousand two hundred fifty dollars for the house with most of the furniture included. The seller, a widow, who had been enamored by the young couple, accepted the bid, and standing in the doorway as they left, sadly told them how she and her husband had bought this piece of land and built the house hoping to fill it with children, but alas they were childless. With no one to leave it to, she was delighted to know such attractive and refined people would live there. She remarked to Mr. Sedgwick she thought the accents charming.

The headlights cut through the dusk as the Buick wended back along the concrete parkway toward New York. They had bought an estate in a single day. Nellie sat close to Otto daydreaming, her head against his shoulder. It had been the years of hard work at Otto's Place that would buy it and he wondered how the widow would have reacted toward the "attractive, refined young couple" if she had known that a bar and restaurant financed by thievery and prostitution would pay for it. Amused, for the first time he recognized the parallels in his life; he was indeed the modern equivalent of his rapacious Viking forbearers. Thinking to himself how a death by his hand had forced his escape by boat from the shores of Denmark; how he, like Leaf Erickson, had sailed to Canada, stolen silver and a beautiful woman, and how he now spent his life surrounded each night by male comrades, shipmates, and flowing liquor, engaged with them in an unending pursuit of riches. He wrapped his arm about Nellie's soft, warm form, and when he saw a straight piece of roadway ahead pulled her up to him and they kissed with a feeling they had missed for several years. "Otto, let's have a child." Her voice was barely louder than the engine, as if uncertain of her own plan. She had been arranging furniture in the house and now she could visualize children who might fill it.

The sensitive subject required all the tact he could muster, he spoke hesitantly. "But we have done it almost regularly for the last five years now." Not wishing to coarsen the conversation he substituted "it" for the blunt, discourteous words he commonly used for the act of coitus in the bar.

"Do you think there's something wrong?" Her voice was despondent, as if she was certain of it.

"Well, I know we're doing it right. I spent my summers on a farm, you know," he said, expecting some humor would lighten the moment. In their world he had not envisioned children and when he remembered had withdrawn as a preventative. Where would a child, or worse yet, children fit, especially in New York and in their business? They had built a life he enjoyed, why try to change it?

"Otto, be serious, I'm very worried. We've got to do something."

He answered simply "okay"; he couldn't say he was worried too; it would inflame her despondence nor could he say that he wasn't worried at all and risk her wrath. Concentrating on the taillights ahead of them he drove until he thought it was safe to change the subject. "We're going to need a gardener."

• • •

The restaurant reopened in mid March complete with the staircase to the mezzanine floor. Otto hired two more cooks and waiters and a bartender to staff the upstairs and for the first week he suffered leg cramps from clambering up and back to check that things were going smoothly. It was three days before Otto could find a private moment with Doctor Weinstein, who had resumed his customary evening scotch and soda, a ritual that eased the solitude of a widower's life. After describing the home he and Nellie had bought, the doctor agreed it was an excellent investment; Otto alluded awkwardly to the fact that despite trying Nellie had not become pregnant. She was worried they would be unable to have children. What should she do?

The doctor, though he sensed Otto's unease, did not back away from the subject although he chose to illustrate the facts in terms that would avoid any rudimentary anatomic words. The medical evaluation, he explained, was like analyzing a car engine that won't run. "It's either the spark or the gas, except in this case it is either the sperm or the egg. Both systems have to be examined to locate the source of the problem." The analogy, brief and hardly figuratively descriptive, appeared to satisfy his friend who did not press him for details of a more biologic nature. Taking a pen from his vest pocket, the doctor printed a name on a cocktail napkin and passed it to Otto. "This fellow makes a specialty of infertility."

"Thanks Doc. I'll give it to Nellie." Otto said, relieved the doctor had made the conversation go so easily and he tucked the napkin in his shirt pocket. The doctor smiled and looked Otto in the eye, realizing the analogy had been unclear about the timing of examinations. "Otto, you've got to go first. The first thing Dr. Shorter will want is a sperm count. It's far simpler than figuring out what might be wrong with a woman. They are more complex, you know." The doctor amused himself, as he often did, with the *double entendre*.

"How does he do that?" Otto's discomfort redoubled, he thought of needles in unpleasant places.

"I am told he has this little room with picture books from France, nudes and so on." Doctor Weinstein was smiling, deciding now to enjoy the anguish his words produced. "And you make a sample for him."

"Right there?"

"Right there. Needs to be fresh, he has to make sure the sperm swim all right under the microscope."

"Oh, God." Otto looked around the bar, in search of a polite escape.

It was Thursday and Silvio, resuming his weekly visit had made his entrance, dropped his overcoat at the cloakroom and stood looking around admiring the changes. He walked up the new stairs to the mezzanine and back down all the while shaking his massive head, asking who the contractor was, announcing to all within earshot at the bar that he could have had the work done cheaper. Then spotting Otto with the doctor he walked over. Otto was glad to see him, he would change the subject; he always picked the new one.

"The place looks great, Otto," Silvio said, standing beside the doctor patting him on the back. "I see your new manager over there. Hired a wop, you're learning, Jesus you're learning!" Reaching over the Doctor he gave Otto a bear hug. "And a Sicilian, too."

"How did you figure that?

"Does one elephant know another?"

"You know, Silvio, of all the people we interviewed, he was the best, good English and refined," Otto offered in all sincerity though tempted to joke that there had been slim pickings. He held his tongue. This was not a subject for jest with Silvio, friend or not, there were definite boundaries, places you didn't go.

"He didn't tell you I sent him over?"

"No."

"Good, I told him to get the job on his own, no string pulling," said Silvio, turning to look over at the well-tailored young man who was welcoming customers. Nellie, elegant as usual, stood ready to assist by introducing him to the "regulars," her motivation, Otto could see, was to become redundant, and ultimately totally expendable.

Silvio, his face covered by a self congratulatory look, went on, "Otto you needed someone honest in this job. Antonio here, he will look out for you; nobody steals. And, if he gives you trouble, let me know, I'll put him through the ringer." A knowing smile and the subtle rise of his eyebrows indicted Silvio meant what he had said. "Besides," Silvio continued, "he looks very continental, look at the fit of the suit, those cuffs and studs, genuine gold. Adds to the classy atmosphere you got here, the penniless creep. I had to advance him the dough for that stuff. But, you hired the right guy. He'll make you money you didn't know you had. Nobody walks out with anything with him here, the kitchen, the bar, no place."

"Thanks Silvio." Otto felt out-maneuvered, not sure if he was angry or appreciative, feeling a reemergence of the ambivalent feelings he had had toward Silvio from the beginning.

"I look out for my friends. You helped my kid out when he needed it, Otto. I don't forget." Then changing the subject almost in mid-sentence he turned to the doctor. "Well, Doc, you been behaving yourself? I can line you up with a little poontang, a sweet little matzo ball. Send her by your apartment."

Otto turned to walk away as the doctor replied, "Most assuredly, I am doing very well. Thank you but no, Silvio," as he raised his drink in a salute and smiled.

Silvio grabbed Otto by the arm and pulled him back. "Doc, when I walked over did I catch you saying something to Otto here about a doctor that has French picture books?"

"Well, yes." Doctor Weinstein said clearing his throat, chagrinned.

"Doc, you gotta get me an appointment with this guy!" he bellowed with a laugh while applying a gentle punch to the doctor's shoulder.

Nellie had taken a seat in the coatroom watching as Antonio took over, and Otto could tell by the tilt of her head she held a pad of paper in her lap, and he knew, she was making a list. Nellie told Otto that as soon as Antonio was ready to fly on his own, she would go to Connecticut to organize the house. "Otto, I will need a car," she said.

Chapter 33

It had been more than a month since the discussion with Doctor Weinstein and the referral to Dr Shorter. Otto took thinly veiled pride in what he viewed as absolute confirmation of his manhood. "Robust? That's what Dr. Shorter said? They were robust?" exclaimed Dr. Weinstein unable to hide his wonder, though not at the result of the microscopic examination, but that Shorter would use such an unscientific word as "robust." The proper term might have been "satisfactory" or "adequate."

Realizing this was none of his business the Doctor cautiously inquired, "And Nellie is fine?" His way of gently volunteering was meant to be helpful if his friend wished an explanation or had unspoken concerns.

"She was told she probably has scarred tubes, that's all."

The doctor looked around making certain no one was near enough to hear.

"You've known her for quite a while, good Catholic family and all that."

"Oh yes."

"Then the diagnosis is probably wrong."

"Really?"

"Scarred tubes usually aren't a problem for people like her."

"For people like her you say?"

"Yes. Nice people. But there are other reasons," the doctor added to be on the safe side.

A wave of panic passed through Otto. He had no idea what he had disclosed to the doctor had any implication other than this might not be an innocent state of affairs, like she had been diagnosed with big ears or knock knees. Infertility seemed to be a relatively common problem and in Otto's experience nice people had it. The subject must be changed and he wished his disclosure could be erased, or he could strike it like testimony in court. Unable to alter the revelation he grasped at the first thing that came to mind to plug the verbal dike. "Nellie's in Connecticut organizing the new house. She is staying up there full time, at least for the moment, until she has the house settled, taking down wall paper, painting, new carpets, arranging furniture— all sorts of things need to be done. She is very busy. You can see Antonio has taken over here pretty much," he said nodding toward the young man.

"Oh and when do you go up there?"

The doctor, well practiced in recognizing and managing discomfort, had followed his lead and picked up the new subject.

"I go up late Friday night and come back on Monday afternoon." Encouraged by the doctor's apparent interest, Otto went on that he had hired gardeners; Joe, a sage in overalls, and Dominic, his nephew, his apprentice gardener and heavy lifter. In addition Dominic's wife cleaned houses and was helping Nellie put the house together. In time the doctor was sorry he had inquired. Otto rambled on in order to make certain there was no opportunity to return to the subject of scarred tubes, and the doctor, whose work included appearing interested during monotonous patient sessions, unintentionally encouraged him. A question from Antonio about seating arrangements finally broke Otto away. The doctor left shortly afterward.

Otto watched the restaurant fill from his "office" at the end of the bar. A customer, who appeared to be about thirty, came in with several older men. Otto studied his face from across the room because the man looked familiar, enough so that Otto had an uncanny urge to meet him. The customer was thin, fair, with a shock of red hair, and an easy smile. He appeared respectful, yet at ease and confident, talking with the others who were a decade or more older. Otto leaned over to Ed Cutler, New York cognoscenti and now the bar's informal legal advisor. Did Ed know who that group might be? Ed put down his cocktail and studied them over his half glasses for a moment then turned back to the bar saying he recognized Walter O'Malley, the attorney for the Brooklyn Dodgers; but he didn't know the others. By now Otto had decided to walk over and introduce himself, and ask, as had become his pat introduction line "had he indeed recognized Mr. O'Malley?" Inquiries by the owner such as this were not without their price, but a round of drinks or a bottle of wine most often paid off in good will and new customers. Ed had been right and Mr. O'Malley, looking up from his dinner introduced the new announcer for the team, Mr. Walter Barber. "Call me Red, Mr. Nielson," the young man said, standing to shake Otto's hand. His voice was nasal and reedy, almost frail, and the words came with a soft accent, southern, making him as an immigrant of sorts, up from the South. Otto identified with that, yet he couldn't understand why he felt such a strong affinity for the man, and before Mr. Barber sat down he had to fight the impulse to put his arm around him and pull him close.

By now the place was crowded, tables filled upstairs and down, and standing room only at the bar. Otto watched Gerry push through the crowd, breaking the way for the platinum blond he towed by the hand behind him. It was his "Miss Harlow."

Otto sat them at the open table in the back he kept for important guests who might arrive without reservations. Her name was Ruthie and she was the spitting image of the film goddess, but the name Ruthie, and with those looks, good God, Otto thought she had to be dumb as a post. But Gerry had said she was anything but, and during the his visit Otto quickly learned that her appearance, her natural beauty, enhanced by peroxide, cosmetics and sleek clothes, was a carefully contrived affectation, a very effective extra something for a very smart secretary/girl-Friday to have. As Otto sipped a second scotch and soda he learned Ruthie worked as secretary to the president of The Phillips Bank and Trust on Wall Street. From farm country Minnesota she had moved to New York and deduced what it took to land work in an executive suite. Others might have her secretarial skills but what executive wouldn't covet a showpiece for the corporate office to boot? And, for a stockbroker what more valuable friend? A rare find, an information pipeline straight into executive offices of an investment bank. No doubt, in addition to his lascivious interest, Gerry had to be working that angle. She had to know who might be buying what, who was seeking capital, who was having trouble covering interest payments. Here, within this paramount beauty dwelled an incredible source for some winning stock picks, perhaps Gerry's winning stock picks, and by extension money in Otto's account. However when the conversation turned to business she became mum and gave not a hint, not a nod or wink that indicated she knew anything.

"So Otto, tell me something about the restaurant business, your work,"

Ruthie inquired, smiling at him with genuine interest. The lipstick glistened on her lips, her white teeth perfect.

"You mean you would like a job?" Otto said staring into her eyes. He was only half joking. He would never seriously play up to customer's companion, but with her it became painful to suppress the temptation. For her part she had seen the glint in his eye.

"Oh no, I was curious what might draw a person to it, why you choose this?"

He had an answer, but it was not one he wanted to share. He improvised, explained that he had worked in a hotel and learned the business and, despite the long hours, it could be profitable.

"You know," she said, "I see it as more than that, I see it as a window on the world, an opportunity to meet people, to learn useful things, all sorts of things, especially if you spend time with the customers. Of course you would need the right personality, to be outgoing, an extrovert, as Jung would say. I've been reading about personalities and the subconscious mind, how they affect our lives and choices."

She had easily found the nugget of truth he had concealed—that this place for him was a clearinghouse for ideas and information, useful business information, though Otto had no idea who "Young" was. He didn't ask. The doctor would know.

Ruthie gave Gerry's hand, which lay on the table, a squeeze. "Come on Gino, I need to get home. Tomorrow's another workday."

As Otto helped her with her coat she whispered to him. "Otto, get Gerry to use his real name. Gino is so much nicer, and really, Gerry doesn't suit him. If he were more Italian he'd be made of salami."

• • •

Following their departure Otto found a quiet moment at the end of the bar. Jim handed him the phone and he called Nellie in Connecticut. He told her it was a routine night and she told him the house had been measured for curtains, she was going to replace the wallpaper in the dining room, and the books and shelves in the library needed dusting. "Otto, why don't you think about inviting some people up for a picnic luncheon one afternoon in May after the weather has warmed up?"

"Who would you suggest?"

"Anybody but the thug or the cook."

They talked on for a while. Just before hanging up, she noted, "and Otto I like the church up here."

"That's good."

"Yes, I need it. I find I have a lot of issues."

• • •

At eleven-thirty Augustus Cook came in with the after-theater crowd. He looked well. Otto drifted over to say hello, and asked him to come by sometime soon for drinks and dinner; he had some questions for him. They shook hands.

• • •

Heading to the apartment Otto walked several blocks before he caught a cab. It was two-thirty in the morning and Mr. Barber's face haunted him. As he walked his thoughts drifted back to the farm and he visualized the cluster of gravestones on the hill and his skinny little redheaded brother interred there. It came to him. Yes, that's it, his brother Jorgen, had he lived, would have been Mr. Barber's twin! Instinctively he had recognized Jorgen's double, his lost brother incarnate. It had been Jorgen's dream to be a sports announcer and this night Otto had met him as he could have been. Bitter memories made sleep come hard.

Chapter 34

Decoration Day weekend in Connecticut that year began with perfect late May weather. By Saturday morning the rain had stopped and the morning sunshine warmed the bricks of the porch deck turning them from dark red to pink. The temperature was shirtsleeve pleasant. Otto worked in the vegetable garden with a spade, blending a truckload of composted manure into the soil that Dominic brought to him in a wheelbarrow. The grass was freshly cut and the flower gardens were filled with tulips and peonies in full bloom. Banks of rhododendron blanketed the hillside in pink, purple and white. The oaks, just leafing out, played with the sunlight on the lawns. This garden would be Otto's American farm. The smell of the manure as it was blended with the soil, the sensation of the hot sun on his bare back, and the rich green of the lawns in spring reminded him of Denmark.

For visitors Otto and Nellie found a routine that became a pattern through the years. Weekends, weather permitting, Otto worked in the gardens with Joe and Joe's helper, Dominic, while Nellie took charge of the kitchen, and until they hired household help, she prepared the luncheons of small square and triangular sandwiches, salad and desert, usually lemon tort. Guests invited for noon routinely failed to arrive until one or after, and soon the hosts counted on late arrivals. So at noon Otto began his journey in from the gardens bare-chested, back reddened by the sun, wet with perspiration, shirt in his hand; and before climbing the back stairs for a shower would pass through the kitchen and pat Nellie on the rump followed by a light kiss. Returning showered and dressed in golf shirt and slacks he cranked down the green awning over the deck and Nellie laid out silverware in rows beside stacked Lenox china plates and lead crystal glasses on the newly painted table. In the center a blue glass pitcher of iced tea stood like a sentry; frosted rivulets of condensed moisture streaked the sides.

Nellie crossed herself when she heard the tires of the black Cadillac crunch on driveway gravel. The car passed by the deck, coming to a gradual stop before the garage. Otto and Nellie stood on the porch watching as the driver, dressed in black livery, opened the door for the Seidermans and Doctor Weinstein. These friends were certain to be good company, a safe bet to initiate the afternoon parties. Sherri pushed from behind by Mel emerged exclaiming, "What a beautiful place!"

Mel shouted as he hefted himself off the car seat, perspiring from the warm ride, "God, Otto, this is the sticks. The driver got lost twice!"

Sherri shouted back over her shoulder, "Oh, for God's sake Mel, you get lost even when the streets are laid out in city blocks." Uncertain of her footing she walked on her toes in her high heels, treating the gravel like shards of glass. In the city she had rarely walked on anything except cement.

Doctor Weinstein followed them with an amused smile on his face. Their bulk underscored his diminutive frame. Otto wondered if it was a painful ride with Sherri talking non- stop.

"I told the driver to come back at six," Mel called up to the porch as they approached. The car had already turned around and was heading back toward the street. Five hours! Nellie panicked. The moment Otto came into the house she turned to him, "You didn't give them a time to leave? How can we entertain them all that time?" The hard look softened in a flash as Sherri put her head in the door with an offer of help in the kitchen, laughing that she hadn't set foot in one for two years. Despite Nellie's demurral she came in anyway. Just to talk she said promising not to touch anything. At four o'clock Otto substituted gin and tonic for the iced tea, which made the time go quickly and six o'clock work out fine. From that point forward six o'clock became the prescribed departure time. Most guests stayed longer.

The conversation began with Broadway and the shows the Seidermans had seen: *Boy Meets Girl* and Lillian Hellman's smash hit *The Children's Hour*; and a "must see", *The Philadelphia Story*, which Sherri insisted Otto take Nellie to before it closed. They spoke about the radio: Fred Allen, Lum and Abner and *The Cavalcade of America* and the interesting program Gabriel Heater had presented last week… why Madam Chang spoke. How cultured she sounded. Then on to the New Deal and Otto listened, but voiced no opinion, just nodded as the guests spoke of what a boon Roosevelt's social programs had been, especially the minimum wage and Social Security. Nellie served lunch as the subject turned to the interesting column Eleanor Roosevelt had written last week. They spoke of Hitler and what a menace he seemed to be and Otto mentioned the plight of the Jews but his guests failed to discuss it further. Feeling awkward, he suggested a tour of the house and gardens. When they returned the doctor, as he sat crossing his legs, asked Otto if he knew what the name Connecticut meant. Stumped, Otto asked the Doctor what he knew of the theories of "Young". The doctor smiled and gave a discourse on the relationship of Jung to Freud and how their concepts of the workings of the subconscious mind differed. He spoke for almost half an hour giving what became a lecture on the theories underlying psychoanalysis. No one wearied.

From behind the large rhododendron near the corner of the deck a call, "Anybody home?" A sandy haired man wearing golfing clothes walked around the shrub. Spotting the group, he hesitated momentarily until Otto stood and with a wave of the arm beckoned to him onto the porch. In one hand the caller carried a pie. He put out the other—"J. Harland Parsons, or 'Har', to my friends. I'm the neighbor on the other side of the hemlocks past your vegetable garden." Otto had admired the vast Victorian set in acres of grass and trees. He introduced his guests and his wife Nellie, and J. Harwood Parsons taken aback by Nellie's good looks bowed and handed her a pie with the words, "My humble welcoming gift to the neighborhood."

Smiling, Nellie accepted the offering with a little dip of a curtsey, "Please Sir, thank Mrs. Parsons for me."

"Oh, there's no Mrs. Parsons. I baked it myself." His face erupted in a smile. Otto, empty glass in hand, said they were about to have another round of gin and tonic and would Har join them? He accepted and settled into a chair. Handing Har the drink, Otto remarked that the doctor had asked about the name Connecticut. Har said the name was an Indian for "land of the long river."

The Doctor asked, picking up on Har's surname, "And what do you do, Mr. Parsons. I gather you are not a man of the cloth." He had a disarming way of pressing for information.

"Yes, there certainly were some many generations back, but you are right, I work at a bank."

Har didn't divulge he was President of the local bank and along with his father, the Chairman of the Board, a majority shareholder—a fact Nellie learned months later. Instead he turned the conversation to the history of Farbridge, and the type of rhododendron, Catawba, which he had watched the previous owner plant on the hillside twenty years earlier. This land, he did mention, his father had sold to them.

The noisy gravel announced the arrival of the hired limousine. As the car eased into view, Nellie went in. Har, finishing his drink left a few minutes later. Otto picked up the glasses to carry them in pleased that the afternoon had been a complete success.

"Goddamn you Otto!" she screamed as he came through the door. Her voice hit like a spear in the chest.

"What?"

"Dr. Weinstein came into the kitchen and I thanked him for the referral to Dr. Shorter. And he said, 'you might want another opinion. I can arrange it for you' and I said, 'Do you think I need one?' and he said, 'It didn't seem to fit with your circumstances'!" her words began in a hissing pianissimo building in a crescendo to furious shouts. "You told him Dr. Shorter's diagnosis? Scarred shut fallopian tubes! And in the bar for God's sake Otto! What were you thinking! Or were you too soused to think!"

"I'm sorry, it slipped out. He won't tell anyone."

"Slipped out! Scarred fallopian tubes slipped out? He knows what's a cause for that, gonorrhea! How could something like that 'slip out'!" She paused as if deciding whether to open the floodgates on a sea of feelings. "You know Otto" she went on, her voice lowered, "I'm beginning to think the only thing we have in common is the past."

"We have the restaurant."

"Don't you realize I hate the damned restaurant? I've told you that a dozen times! Didn't you see me standing there night after night, bored silly half the time, watching you carouse with your friends, egging them on with drinks, on the verge of intoxication yourself, 'gathering information'. You don't care do you? You don't have any idea what you have become or how I *feel!*" She shouted the last word.

"Of course I care!" What gave you that idea? We get along. We love each other! I think you are beautiful, wonderful. We're a team. You do a great job in the restaurant. It wouldn't have been half the success without you!" he said treading water, grasping at anything that might float.

"Feel, I said feel! Do I have to spell it?"

"About what!"

"Come on, Otto! What does Dr. Weinstein think? I feel dirty! Some miner up there may have infected me. I never had symptoms. If there is any infection left, the sulfa pills Dr. Shorter gave me took care of it, but it's the shame! The shame Otto! There is no pill for that! And just when I think I have left all that behind me who walks in the restaurant with one of your buddies, but that pudgy little cook from the mine, dressed up like a millionaire, and you're fawning all over him! One word from him about my past and all I have struggled for is gone, my life ruined! Now there are two people in your restaurant who could ruin my life."

"He knows we are married! Believe me Cook's a gentleman; he would never say anything. He's a friend!"

"You know, Otto, I think I can understand my Aunt Mary now. Sometimes I wish I had stayed in Tuckerton, a prostitute, not having to hide who I was, no pretense, no worry about exposure. By now I would have lost my looks, some drunken miner might have knocked my front teeth out, but what I was, I know in Jesus' eyes, was forgivable. Like my aunt I could have gone to Mass and begged each week for His forgiveness and He would have given it."

She paused and looked at Otto blankly as though her words had exhausted her. "While we are on the subject of feelings, don't you have a conscience? Can't you understand how shooting John might affect me? Doesn't it bother you? The murder?"

"I'm over it. I thought you were over it. It didn't seem to bother you at the time. Nellie, it was necessary, and besides it wasn't a murder in that sense, it was a justifiable act—call it a shooting, a justifiable homicide."

"Whatever you call it, I'm not over it, Otto! And I'm certainly not over it anymore since coming here to this beautiful place. I can't get away from it, Otto, it stays up front in my mind, the guilt; it's always just under the surface."

"You saved my life. He was a murderer. It's not like you killed an innocent person or a child."

"That I absolutely couldn't live with, killing a child, that would be the worst crime of all, like putting Jesus on the cross!"

"Can't you go to confession and ask for forgiveness?"

"Good God, no! I can't confess that or the prostitution here. I just confess little things. I can't have another person on this earth know these things. Don't you know how it would change the way the priest looks at me? The subtle ways, his behavior around me, and then people would notice, and somehow it would get out. I'd be shunned. Here! After all I have done to get this place!" She took a breath, crossed her arms and leaned back against the kitchen counter. "And do you know what else, Otto? This house and how I love it, and everything I plan to do here… the auxiliary at the hospital, and we can try to join the Country Club…it all makes me feel guilty. I feel guilty like I've stolen it; like a poor little Irish girl shouldn't have these things … doesn't deserve this life! I spend time everyday on my knees talking to God about it."

"Sounds like you are taking the Protestant approach, talking straight to God," he said smiling, trying to cheer her up. "That's good!"

"I give up! You really don't get it, do you?" She started up the stairs. After three steps she turned. "I'm not coming back to New York, Otto. I'm not showing my face in that restaurant again. I'm living up here and you can come up weekends. We can try to work things out."

"Oh come on, for God's sake, Nellie!"

"Otto I can't make you understand! You don't understand me! How can you love someone you don't understand? Am I just something to look at, a piece of cheesecake, skin deep, without insides, no essence, no thoughts, no troubles, no feelings, no needs?" She spit the words, Gatling-gun style. "What is it about me that you love? My looks or the screws or my help at the restaurant?" She waited a few seconds for an answer and hearing none, drew a breath and went on, now with resignation. "I thought I understood you and maybe I did once at the beginning but I didn't see it all. Either you have changed or I didn't know you well enough but I know now I don't like what I have learned. The goddamned drinking, your boozy friends, mister big shot, and that damned restaurant! I'm... I'm not sure I love you any more."

She turned and went up the stairs to bed ignoring his shouts, "Nellie! Nellie!" Otto thought of following; he had begun to fight an impulse to shake her, to win the argument physically that he couldn't win with words. Instead he walked to the kitchen and reached under the kitchen counter, pulled out the scotch and sat in the living room until long after there were no sounds in the room above. The killing of John had generated remorse but not a moment of guilt for him, she had pulled the trigger; but that was of small consequence, they both are glad he is dead. If the roles were reversed he would have pulled the trigger. Taking his money, that bothered him at first but what other use was there for it? Leave it to rot in the woods? It had been put to a good purpose, financed their restaurant and bought them a life they could only have dreamed of. Guilt about John he didn't feel, why should she? And the prostitution, she was forced into that, why feel guilty about that? It was gone and over as soon as she could escape. But, her fear of disclosure, here is what he could see as real. Living always vulnerable to disclosure, constantly susceptible to ruin, he could understand that. It could be stressful, even agonizing. Especially now that she was beginning a new life, her dream life … that's what she had said isn't it? Here the fear and guilt came back because there was so much to loose.

Praying so hard she was asking God to remove the risk. Otto saw it clearly. Nellie was wrong! He did understand her.

Nellie slept with a light. On the wall a crucifix hung over the bed. It had bothered him—but he understood more than ever why she wanted it there. He was sorry he had told her that he felt inhibited by it…not that he didn't love Jesus. But sex with the Lord watching made him uncomfortable, spied on, though he never suffered a twinge of guilt about the sex they had for no reason other than the pure pleasure of it; he overcame that hurdle years before in Denmark thanks to Kirsten and good old Kurt. Lying there in the dark he thought about Kirsten and wondered what she was doing.

Chapter 35

By September the last of the tomatoes had begun to ripen, the summer squash and cucumbers were over-planted and given by the basketful to the neighbors, and the pole beans, which proved tough and stringy, joined the compost pile. Trial and error; Otto appreciated that a garden is dynamic, always evolving, and he planned to thumb through the seed catalogs some winter night and order a better variety to plant next year. Joe and Dominic worked three days a week mowing the lawns, edging and weeding the flowerbeds that they planted, tore up, and replanted with new varieties, progressing according to a calendar determined by the flowers.

Har wore a path through the hemlocks that separated the wide lawns of the homes. Sitting on the garden fence watching Otto weed and cultivate he spoke of the neighbors, the comings and goings that made up Farbridge politics and of the news of the town that week, mostly trivial. To Otto the politics here seemed more rancorous than any in the city. As Har spoke he kept an eye out for Nellie glancing at the kitchen window hoping for a glimpse of her. There was something unexplainably erotic about her; the silhouette of her form, the tilt of her head, the way her hair danced on her shoulders when she moved. She aroused him. He made no attempt to analyze his feelings, or had any idea where things might lead; he had simply succumbed to the surreal magnetism that drew him to his neighbor's garden and cocktails on the deck. Her wedding band offered no deterrent, in fact provided an attraction for the bachelor: he knew married women didn't talk, an essential requirement in a small town where gossip spread fast as lightening over the phone lines. Nellie occasionally caught his protracted looks, and these looks from most men were unwelcomed, but she liked Har and socially he was an important friend. Nonetheless, she made a point to give no encouragement to any advances, just sterile smiles, rarely looking him in the eye or appearing to take an interest in his visits with Otto. She had no desire for a dalliance and steeled in these matters, she had fended off many an amorous approach in Canada harshly, and at the restaurant delicately, and she would handle Har. Adultery was not a sin she cared to add to her list that she worked so hard to expiate.

For the most part the Saturday afternoon gatherings that summer were a success. The exceptions led to minor flare-ups in the artificial quiet of the marriage, that like a pot below the boil remained hot to enough to burn should the subjects of the restaurant, Otto's friends, or his drinking come up. These were the ones that would destroy the marriage and they were avoided.

Gino Tortorici brought the blonde secretary, Ruthie. The Packard convertible, top down, pulled into the driveway, resplendent, the paint burnished black and the white walls like chalk. Gino waved and stepped out wearing a tailored white linen suit and a new pencil-line moustache while Ruthie untied the scarf that covered the serried waves of platinum hair, freeing them to glisten in the afternoon sun. She wore a sleeveless blue silk dress. Nellie's greeting was cool and quick before returning to the kitchen, pretending she had left the sink running. Otto invited them to sit. Within minutes Gino stood and insisted on a tour of the gardens, stripped off his suit jacket and brown and white saddle shoes, rolled up the cuffs of his pants, and walked barefoot down the steps to the lawn and strolled beside Otto, holding Ruthie's hand, stopping to admire the plants that he named, some by the Italian name, some by the English. As a boy he explained he had spent two summers working as a gardener's helper for an uncle in Italy. With no effort to hide his envy he complimented Otto and mused that someday he would buy a place such as this. "Does the house have a name?" Gino asked. "In Italy all the fine houses like this have a name." Otto thought about that for a moment, but couldn't come up with one that he could repeat; the house and the marriage were inseparable, and therefore it too was pervaded by an uneasy ambivalence: Unrest Home, Discomfort Harbor, and Tension Place were what came to mind. He simply said, "no."

Nellie's guests that day were the O'Conners, acquaintances from Church she thought to be respectable people, conventional Farbridgers, a judgment she made as they went out of their way to speak to her after Mass. She noted they made interesting conversation at the church coffees about cruises taken to the Caribbean and Hawaii and their recounts of the wonder of sailing through the Panama Canal had been enthralling. But paired against the New York guests their stature quickly diminished, the comparison a stark contrast in sophistication. And suddenly Nellie thought them plain, even peasant-like, and most of all distressingly dull—how could she have thought their descriptions of cruises interesting? Within fifteen minutes she cringed with embarrassment every time they spoke. On the other hand, Ruthie thought nothing of the sort and found common ground with the O'Conners, connecting easily, remarking that traveling was one of her goals and telling them she was a transplanted Minnesota farm girl revealing that beneath the glaze resided a spirit as plain as any. Otto watched her and thought certainly she had come to New York to escape the farm, maybe run-off by her parents like his mother had been a generation earlier to find an easier, more secure life. Wasn't that the American way, leave the farm to seek your fortune in the city? But it was her adaption that interested him, how flawless, she was at home even though nothing grew in New York but street trees, some grass in the parks, and weeds in the cracks in the sidewalks. Otto swirled the ice about in his glass, giving the idea further consideration and mused, this was not Minneapolis or Chicago, but New York, a tougher place that grew the finest and most abundant of harvests: marriageable men. So where better to select a rising prospect with unlimited potential but in the corporation offices and banks of this city? And, as proof of his premise, she had picked from the crop of rising stars her suitor, Gino, who appeared a bit of a wild rose, perhaps, but one Otto thought she could handle with some skillful pruning. That afternoon on the porch Ruthie had Mrs. O'Conner enthralled. They spoke of banana bread recipes and how to put up vegetables in Ball jars making sure the seal was absolutely tight, and that larkspur was best planted in September for spring blooms. Otto took note of that. Everyone was beguiled except Nellie, who remained mum until the guest had gone.

"Otto, her hair looked like crushed straw," she said, referring to Ruthie.

"But you invited her," Otto replied, referring to Mrs. O'Conner, who had light brown hair, flat and trimmed off at her neck. Otto thought he could get by with a gentle needling. After all they had been on fairly good terms for a few weeks.

"No, stupid, not her, that Ruthie woman!" She said "woman" with an intonation that underscored all the pejorative implications the word could possibly contain.

"Woman, she's the same age as you," Otto gave back as a compliment, as Ruthie was young and fresh and the comparison was favorable. She let it pass unanswered.

They did the luncheon dishes. He washed and she dried because the soap irritated her hands. After a while the quiet clicking of dishes and clink of the silverware induced him to break the silence and from somewhere deep in his cerebrum, his suppressed anger broke free, disguised as a boyish jibe, "Mrs. O'Conner's dress did appear to come from a hardware and feed store," referring to the dress that may have been purchased from a the Sears Roebuck catalog. Nellie threw down the dishtowel and stormed from the room. He shouted after her, "I thought she was very nice." He followed her into the living room.

"Otto, do you ever stop poking fun, making caustic remarks? Not everyone can shop at Saks."

"I apologize."

"I saw how you watched Ruthie, are you really all that interested in canning peas? How well do you know her, anyway?"

"Barely, met her once before,." he replied, stretching the truth a bit.

"Barely', that's not one of Dr. Weinstein's Freudian slips, is it?"

"Hell, why would I give a damn about her? She's nice, that's all, period!"

"Better be!"

Otto let things drop there. Whatever he said she would counter and things would escalate. He had learned from the start she always had the last word. He regretted starting this spat and vowed to speak only positively of her friends in the future and if that was impossible, say nothing.

That summer Nellie's mother had written from Ireland that she had cousins that lived in Bridgeport, and if this was anywhere near Farbridge, Nellie might ask them for a visit. Even though obligated by filial respect, Nellie was excited by the prospects and called them with an invitation for a Saturday luncheon. Her cousin would bring their children. "It will be wonderful for us all to know one another," Nellie said, putting down the phone in anticipation of finding extended family in the New World. There would be introductions to an expanded circle of friends. She envisioned holidays together, picturing a Christmas tree and presents and well-mannered, neatly dressed children. Otto set up the croquet game on the lawn.

They arrived, not announced by the usual pleasant crunch of the white gravel, but signaled by the rude noise of an abused, flatulent Plymouth that gunned around the corner of the house and skidded to a stop mid-driveway by the porch well short of the turnaround by the garage. The original color of the car was unrecognizable, faded by the sun to into splotches of color that resembled a swirled oil slick and the fenders, cracked and dimpled by the hammering of broken snow chains, were eaten through, cannibalized by rust. With the last turn of the tires, all four doors flew open and children spilled out. Four boys and an adolescent girl had been stacked into the back seat; Mr. and Mrs. McCarthy and the baby rode in the front. The boys, ages four to twelve, spied the croquet set and set on it like dogs on raw meat, and within a minute were fighting over mallets, tripping over wickets, and sending balls beyond the grass, bouncing onto the driveway, ricocheting off the car and the base of the brick porch. Though they swung the mallets like golf clubs coming within inches of their heads, neither parent paid heed. After collecting diapers and bottles scattered about the floor of the car, the McCarthys strolled to the porch deck with the baby. The girl, the oldest of the brood, walked behind her parents, head down, hands behind her back, clearly wishing she were somewhere else. Introductions were made in the shade of the awning. Mrs. McCarthy, Patty, pulled the baby off her left teat and covered up so she could shake hands. Francis, the father, was a slight man, outweighed by his wife by about fifty pounds. His long oily black hair combed straight back on his scalp and his Irish features, quite pleasant, placed charitably on a face that had been creased and fissured by time and worry … and freshly scraped by a razor. Under his closely bitten nails black grease was imbedded so deeply that no amount of scrubbing would suffice. They labeled him a mechanic by trade. Otto thought Patty to be the incarnation of "Tugboat Annie," heroine of the stories he enjoyed in the Saturday Evening Post; she had short red hair cut dust mop style, and the figure of a stump. She looked as though she could pick Francis up and throw him against the wall, which Otto figured she probably did when ticked off. Nellie stood paralyzed, her vision of a well-bred, cultured family exploded, no fancy holiday parties, that dream ruined. Stunned, she pulled a chair out from the table for Patty, who hooked the baby in the crook of her left arm and sat opening the top of her dress to nurse again, agilely throwing a diaper over the process in respect for the refined surroundings. Nellie disappeared into the house. Francis sat cross-legged with an arm draped over the back of his chair, absentmindedly admiring the view. Otto gave the boys a croquette lesson and then sat down next to the girl, Molly, and asked her about school. She wore a Sunday dress, long black tresses tied in a red bow, white ankle socks and patent leather shoes. She clasped her hands in her lap, and she had locked her knees together and tucked her skirt tightly under her thighs. In a soft voice she answered that she was in tenth grade at St Ursula's School. Before he could inquire further Nellie appeared with a tray piled with sandwiches, peanut butter and jelly and tuna fish. The crusts Otto noted remained on. He followed her back into the house to carry more food to the porch.

"Otto, don't you dare offer them drinks! They'll probably get drunk and never leave!" Nellie's voice had the ring of desperation.

After a lunch with the children that resembled a medieval banquet, Otto played tag with the boys and showed them the paths up the hill and the "fort" where neighborhood boys smoked cigarettes under the rhododendrons. Nellie talked with Patty while Francis, probably sitting down for the first time in years in a relaxed setting, silently studied the birds and squirrels that scampered through the oaks. After three hours with the dishes cleared and no hint of further food or beverage coming from the kitchen, they gathered up and left. Nellie stood on the porch to make sure they were indeed gone, listening to the noise of the car dissolve into the distance. With the last audible sputter tears flowed down her cheeks.

"Thank God, I thought they would never leave!"

"They were fun, a bit wild though."

"Didn't you see?"

"What?"

"The girl, Molly."

"Yes," Otto said, puzzled, his smile vanished.

"I was that child!" she cried. "Fifteen years ago, that was me!" The child's image was like an apparition to her, a terrifying vision of her haunted, repressed past, a reminder of how her childhood abruptly ended, how she was forced to leave Ireland and confront the unspeakably ugly life in Tuckerton. Her response to the sight of the child had been a tremor and a palpable thumping of her heart that she fought by breathing slowly, controlling her breath all afternoon. She could not make herself speak with the girl and unable to look at her directly sat with her back turned as she talked with Patty, feigning interest in the baby.

Over the course of their marriage Otto had surmised that an affectionate response to a crying woman at moments like this was a trait genetically absent in the male of the species, especially Scandinavians who turned to wood in these circumstances. Even to touch her in a tender way, if that at one time had been inbred, by now it had become bred out. It occurred to him only a woman could truly, with real empathy comfort another crying woman. He stiffly put his arms around Nellie trying to gather up the appropriate words to say. Nothing came … he let silence be a token of the sympathy he felt, signaling that though he stood clumsily holding her he understood her despair. He resolved that on some quiet evening at the bar he would talk about this failing with Doctor Weinstein. What was lacking? Then he thought of his father and felt a wave of nausea as the parallel across time became clear. Nellie broke free and he followed her, hands in his pockets, back outside to the porch where he watched her yank back chairs and with a broom sling the half-chewed crusts, bits of lettuce, stepped on tomato and bits of tuna fish, the scattered luncheon spillage, from the porch onto the lawn there to be left for the squirrels.

"And she had the nerve to tell me I wasn't doing enough for my mother! Thought fifty dollars a month wasn't enough, and especially when she saw this place, said it 'was like a drop of piss.' How unbelievably crude! How disgusting!" The tears flowed again, falling from her cheeks staining the brick. Then her anger roiled. "That fat bitch doesn't know what I've been through, what I have suffered! She can burn in Hell!"

Needless to say that was the last time they saw the McCarthys, though Otto suspected some of the times Nellie hung up the phone saying the caller had reached the wrong number the person on the other end had been Patty calling to make plans or amends … if by some chance she had been perceptive enough to recognize Nellie's politely suppressed shock and disappointment with her American relatives that fateful afternoon. Surely he hadn't recognized her suffering, and who knew Nellie better? That night Nellie redirected her pent up fury into sexual exertion, which made for an exceptional time inducing Otto to hang a silk scarf over the crucifix at the head of the bed as soon as he realized there would be some gymnastics that might not be sanctioned by the Church. In the obstetrician's office three months later, when they counted back the weeks, they realized the McCarthy's visit had produced an apparent miracle. Nellie was pregnant.

By fall that year the guests had been categorized as of the outdoor or indoor variety, the latter decreed by Nellie as socially refined enough to occupy a seat at the dining room table. Otto's New York friends did not qualify. The couples came from Farbridge, hospital volunteers and church members that Nellie selected from her appraisal of the women's appearance, style, and refinement. They made the invitation list unless she learned of a reason for elimination, usually from gossip in the beauty shop, such as the husband drank too much or could be a crashing bore.

In addition there were two notable guests that summer who became regular visitors indoors and out. When Nellie first told Otto she had invited Father Lombardi and Monsignor Callahan from the Farbridge Catholic Church, he groaned audibly. Nellie, of course, was one of their favorites, a gold star parishioner, and though Otto never attended Mass the issue of his piety during the many dinners with the priests came up only once. In a flash Nellie interceded, fearing the enormity of Otto's incipient gaffe should the unsuspecting priests encourage him to expound on his history with the Lutheran Church or his interpretation of religious duty, saying that Otto "was conflicted on matters of faith." The good priests, interpreting her words as an unambiguous warning quickly dropped the subject. Easy to talk to, full of good humor, Otto found the priests excellent company, particularly when the subject of current events and political philosophy remained the staples of conversation. But most importantly, in his view, they made Nellie happy by listening to her sentiments and appearing to value her opinion, as it strayed little from theirs. This she found to be an endorsement of her intellect and reinforcement of her conclusions about affairs secular and devotional. Otto gladly endured conversations about the church fair and the women's guild as his silence in this instance was appreciated. After a time, particularly when the conversation had turned to these subjects, Father Lombardi took a drink that Otto assured him was weak, fibbing as he surreptitiously poured heavy ones that the good Father pretended not to notice, a little secret they enjoyed together. Over the years they became fast friends. When the little purple book with questions and answers about the Roman Catholic Church appeared on his bedside table one winter weekend, Otto understood who had left it and forgave them with a smile, but dismissed the effort, dropping the book in the bedside table drawer. He never cracked the binding.

One day Otto spoke gingerly of the McCarthy's daughter Molly and perhaps helping her. Nellie did not respond though it was clear she had heard.

Chapter 36

In anticipation of the birth of their child, Nellie moved back to the apartment for the last month of confinement and the change erased Otto's weekday loneliness and soothed the irritation he felt from Nellie's complete conversion to chatelaine of the manse in Farbridge and her preoccupation with the Church. Even the weather welcomed her back with a sunny day accompanied by brisk April zephyrs that gathered up off the Hudson and swirled about the streets.

On warm mornings before Otto left for the restaurant they strolled in the park by the river and talked. Nellie was excited, her face radiant with the roseate hue of pregnancy. Otto was unsure about the trials of child rearing and the effect on his life. Toward noon, when he had set out for the restaurant, Nellie resumed her war on bugs reducing them to an occasional survivor that she smashed with a rolled up newspaper. As time grew short her prenatal nervous energy grew in intensity. She made the bed, cleaned the bathroom, the kitchen counters, the refrigerator, the living room rug and floors, and attacked the dust and grit on the tabletops with an oily cloth. She sorted through the piles of newspapers and magazines, *Life* and the *Saturday Evening Post,* stacking the recent ones under an end table and hurling the others down the chute to the basement incinerator. The sound of them banging against the walls of the tin chute had a finality to it. She was satisfied, the cleaning was finished. One day she washed her hands and lined up bottles and rubber nipples by the stove that would stand ready to be placed in a large pot that served as the sterilizer. In the bedroom a white wicker bassinet waited at the end of the bed and by the wall the changing table piled with diapers. With preparations for the child complete, and if the afternoon breezes off the river were warm that day, Nellie lifted the window sashes and let the curtains balloon with fresh air and rested reading the new book with rave reviews, *Gone With the Wind.*

At five Otto returned from the restaurant. Nellie prepared dinner and he, recognizing her effort, pulled a chair out for her at the table saying how wonderful the place looked, so cleaned up and polished. They talked of only pleasant things laughing about the gossip in the papers. Do you think Wallis Simpson "seduced" Edward the Eighth, maybe slipped him a Mickey. Nellie swooned over Walt Disney's movie Snow White that she saw two times before she was able to pull Otto to a Saturday matinee. They made travel plans. Nellie dreamed of Paris and planned to take French lessons. "All truly cultured people must speak French," she insisted, adding, "Otto, your French needs work." The thought of Paris reconnected Otto with the abandoned memories of Kirsten, and while he half listened to Nellie's imaginings about sidewalk cafes and intimate hotels where the tourists didn't go, his mind wandered with a trace of regret to memories of Kirsten going there and what a clumsy, hesitant lover he had been. But Nellie's plans for a train ride across the Great Plains and through the Rockies to see San Francisco and the new Golden Gate Bridge brought him back. He could look forward to new places more easily than Europe, especially with the troubling news from there. Their lives meshed as they had at the start and Nellie felt a peacefulness she had never known.

Her name would be Margaret Anne. She was born at the Presbyterian Medical Center at 168th Street and Broadway on a warm May night at two a.m.; a perfect blond, and blue-eyed child. They would call her Maggie and joked what a battle it must have been for Otto's genes to win the struggle for dominance. When the ten-day maternity stay ended, Otto took a small suitcase with baby clothes to the hospital and brought mother and child to the apartment in a cab. Despite Otto's appeals that Nellie and the baby stay with him for a while, Nellie insisted that no child should remain in the city with all the dirt, and bugs and tuberculosis and other "scabby" diseases. Her mind was made up weeks before when a neighbor told her a woman with leprosy sold cosmetics door to door. "Otto, you can't see it she hides it under her clothes. You know there is no cure for that!" They would sacrifice for the child's sake.

That weekend the Buick turned onto the Merritt Parkway headed for Farbridge with Maggie in Nellie's lap and baby gear piled in the back. Planning on occasional short trips to New York with no dates in mind, Nellie left three dresses, a coat, shoes, several hats and a drawer with undergarments and a sweater in the apartment. The conversations about a life filled with travels and shows and the outlandish personalities of the Royals and Hollywood's swells vanished.

As soon as the baby was settled, Otto drove off to pick up the new maid who had been hired as a matter of small coincidence. At a morning social the colored maid, Virginia, spotted Nellie's gravid state and when the opportunity arose inquired if Nellie had "help" at home. Her younger sister needed work. A maid, Nellie had come to understand, especially with a newborn, was considered *de rigueur* in Farbridge. By the end of the party she had assembled eighteen dollars from her purse for a bus ticket. The sister would come up from North Carolina. The maid's room above the kitchen and the maid's bath, which had been used for storage, was emptied, cleaned and freshly painted. New towels, sheets and blankets were purchased and piled neatly on the bare mattress at the end of the bed—Nellie would not make a bed for a maid.

Geraldine was a slight girl that Otto guessed to be eighteen or so. Wearing a cotton print dress, her hair in pigtails, brown tie shoes and socks, she carried a cardboard suitcase. Greeting her, he felt a bond comparing her day to his painful landing in Canada, but his attempts to put her at ease fell flat. Soon he realized it was impossible to conceive of her dread and mistrust of this white world. He had paid little attention to Southern culture and of the life prescribed there for the coloreds, as he called them, accepting by not questioning the injustice of segregation. Geraldine's reticence for conversation, the polite "yes sirs", told the story of the cultural and social divide. By the time the car turned onto the driveway only the motor breached the silence.

As Nellie had instructed, Otto led Geraldine into the house through the kitchen door, the servant's entrance. She was not a trained domestic. Nellie understood that. In America the domestic work was not looked on as a profession like in England or Ireland where employment as house staff imbued one with a certain middle station in life, a home in the servant's quarters of the finest houses and a view into the private lives and domestic secrets of the wealthy and influential. In America the work generally was left to those who could find no other and training was left to the employer. And in that capacity, Nellie planned to train Geraldine.

The middle child in a family of ten, Geraldine knew about caring for babies and settled in fully at ease with Maggie, changing and bathing, cuddling and cooing and keeping her "fat and sassy," as she liked to say in her gentle drawl. But the duties Nellie had scheduled for her, cooking, setting a table and serving guests required instruction. There were lists of "do's and don'ts" and repeated lessons and drills before her mistress would be satisfied. When Otto suggested that informal dinners be taken in the kitchen, "family style" with the baby and Geraldine, Nellie threw her arms up. "For Heaven's sakes Otto," she declared in a whisper so as not to be overheard, "you don't ever eat with the servants!" The age-old subjugation of the Irish people had embedded in her psyche a rock hard concept of class and status. And now that the circumstances had changed, and it was her turn to savor privilege, savor it she would. Remembering the restaurant and all the women who looked past her when she helped them with their coat, escorted them to a table, pulled a chair out and seated them; how they never saw her, a lowly hostess … that she had put that behind her for good. And now at long last this is how Mrs. Wickham would have had it at home…service. But unlike Mrs. Wickham, Nellie's status came with a gnawing exception, guilt. Did she deserve all this? Had she suffered enough? "Oh to be able to give such matters no thought," she said out loud to an empty room. So from these days forward Nellie prayed more fervently, conveying deeply felt thanks that she could have this life, and each day rising off her knees becoming more confident that these eager prayers should suffice. They would be served dinner in the dining room and she would feel good about it.

Otto assumed that Geraldine had grown comfortable with her duties, as she remained unfailingly cheerful and unerringly polite. She made it a practice not to be too sociable; or as Nellie put it, she kept her place. As such she remained a fixture in the Nielsen household for seven years.

When Otto passed pictures of the baby around the bar, Ed Cutler, after making the obligatory white lie that she was the cutest baby he had ever seen, he chided Otto. "Now you've got to buy life insurance. That's a big responsibility lying there in that crib."

"Bought a twenty-five thousand dollar policy last week," Otto said, mentioning that he bought it from a salesman who kept an insurance and real estate office in the little group of stores in Farbridge.

"You trusted that guy, didn't get quotes and shop it around?"

"Ed, there are no crooks in little country towns. There's no place to hide. Everybody knows everybody."

Ed shrugged and let the conversation drop. But Cook, who had become a "regular" by then at the bar, put down his drink and picked up on the lecture.

"Otto, for a man in your circumstances an insurance policy is not enough. You need proper instruments for the distribution of your estate, not just insurance and a will." He took a sip and looked Otto in the eye. "You have a will I assume, right? Well, what you really need are trusts. Otto, otherwise you will hand your money over to the government! For God's sakes, don't give your money to Roosevelt! He will throw it away on some socialist scheme!" Turning toward the lawyer, Cook implored, "Ed, be a pal and help Otto out here. Have one of your men at the firm draw up some papers?" Ed lifted his glass in acknowledgement, reached in his vest pocket, took out his business card, and on the back wrote the name of the man Otto should see.

Several weeks later on the attorney's leather topped desk, Otto signed the documents that left his worldly possessions in trust to Nellie and the baby. The trust included funds for his mother and uncle and a special provision that upon his death his remains were to be returned to Denmark with instructions that they be interred in the family graveyard. Copies of the papers were left at the lawyer's office for safekeeping.

"That's an unusual request," the young lawyer said.

"Going home." Otto quipped.

Divided by miles, the gulf in Otto and Nellie's lives widened. She preoccupied with Farbridge social events and the status of her soul, and he with the bar and the status of his investments left only the child as the durable mutual interest between them. They talked about Maggie, and when that subject exhausted, the nightly calls to Farbridge from the phone at the bar ended. Weekends in Farbridge, Otto played with Maggie on the lawn, or during winter afternoons, on the carpet by the living room by the fire. When Nellie hadn't arranged for guests for dinner or garnered an invitation out, Otto spent the evenings reading, listening to the radio, or playing cards, as often as not, solitaire. Nellie would retire early. She replaced the double bed with a twin set from one of the guest rooms, saying she changed the beds about because he moved so much she couldn't sleep. He pretended he didn't regard it as significant.

Each year a tall Christmas tree was placed in the curve of the stairway that reached high enough that the top could be decorated from the balcony. Draped with lights and tinsel the fragrance of the balsam filled the house. Nellie sent invitations to the "nobs and toffs" of Farbridge that made it onto her guest list for what had become an annual affair, the Christmas party. She hired caterers and decorated the house with candles and sprigs of holly. In the library a bartender dressed in a tuxedo stood by a bar. The dining room table was decorated with a sprawling arrangement of pine bows and Christmas balls. Plates, cups and silverware were arranged at one end and the remainder filled with trays of sliced ham and smoked turkey, oyster dressing, small sandwiches, and rolls and butter. Salvers piled with cranberry bread, miniature fruitcakes and Christmas cookies sat on the sideboard beside silver urns steaming with coffee and tea.

Otto in black tie and Nellie, with her hair swept up and wearing one of her chic New York dresses bought for the occasion, greeted the guests at the door until the house filled. Then Nellie moved easily among the friends, aware of envious eyes that followed her. Geraldine, smiling in her black and white formal uniform, passed a silver tray with cups of hot glogg and flutes of champagne. Otto who felt unsure of names of the guests he may have met at one affair or another stood in the library near the bar, familiar country. There he had a straight on view of Har and with no other preoccupation, studied him noting how his rust brown hair had become streaked with gray, his jaw line had begun to sag, and giving him the look of a classics professor, he wore round tortoise-shell eyeglasses.

From Geraldine, his wellspring for uncensored news of the weekday events, Otto had heard the warnings. She said, "Mr. Har has a craving eye and finds 'scuses to come by until Miss Nellie told him he should come only when Mr. Otto's home." Otto sipped his scotch and thought Har Parsons understood the request. Otto understood Nellie's determination to provide Har no opportunity to interfere in or risk her new life: Connecticut required absolute propriety in the true sense of the word. And anyway Nellie took pride in appearances, who she was matched with, how they looked together and he was sure Parsons didn't measure up. But Otto knew what would be the existential reason: her Confessor had urged her to separate herself from any and all temptation if she desired to qualify for a life in the hereafter.

• • •

In September 1939 Hitler's armies swept across Poland nullifying the Munich Pact signed by a deluded and outwitted Neville Chamberlain. There would be no peace in this time. Otto, in the quiet moments before sleep thought of the evenings while the Great War raged when as a boy he had listened to the little group men assembled in the farmhouse kitchen speak of the news from the front. His grandfather, talking in a hoarse whisper, as if spies listened at the door, recounted the stories of the fighting as the Germans advanced into France. And how life had changed for the Danes! Now years later and miles distant, the gnawing fear he felt as a child recurred. He worried for the family he had left behind. Astrid's last letter described her concern that Denmark would be overrun. Her intuition proved correct. His apprehension grew as he read newspaper accounts of Nazi control of Denmark and Norway. All contact lost.

Cook had watched the military buildup in Europe for several years with the eye of an opportunist and over drinks advised Otto to "buy stocks, heavy industry." He pointed out at a near shout that as the country struggled to emerge from the Depression now it was vital, in this time of great threat, that Roosevelt forget the silly programs and spend money for tanks and planes. Proclaiming that it was everyman's patriotic duty to support the preparations for the inevitable American involvement in the European war, Cook drew looks from up and down the bar. "Buy stocks for victory and for yourselves," he shouted back. Otto bought, patriotic yes; but with an unspoken desire to cash in.

Chapter 37

In the sunroom Nellie basted a skirt hem and talked with a mouth full of pins, her voice a muffled garble as if speaking into a pillow. She coached Geraldine from her chair, telling her how to hold the cloth stiffly to guide it under the jittering needle of the portable sewing machine. Geraldine, bent over the work, intent on making the seam straight, ran the line of stitches in jerky bursts joining the cloth for a skirt. While they worked the shadow of the house had slipped across the lawn to the hemlock hedge that bordered the street. On the radio the oily voice of the announcer had just welcomed them to this afternoon's episode of Oxydol Soap's *Ma Perkins* when the door chimes rang. The chimes rang again, twice, insistent. Geraldine folded the skirt she was working on, laid it on her chair and trotted down the staircase to the front door. Nellie put her sewing aside and pulled the window curtain back and searched the front walk and the patch of road she could see beyond the hedge. She saw no one. A black Chevy coupe parked across the road appeared empty.

"There's a gentleman here to see you." Geraldine shouted up.

"Ask who it is, please," she shouted back in the pleasantest voice she could muster.

"An old friend from Canada."

Before the sentence was finished Nellie stood, ran to Otto's bureau, pawed through Otto's socks and drew out the old pistol. Holding it behind her back she walked to the balcony and looking down she recognized the square head on the large form silhouetted black, blocking the sunlight of the open doorway. She pulled shut the door to the room where Maggie lay napping, and started down the staircase; and as she did, she laid the pistol on the balcony floor behind the newel post.

"Geraldine, you can go back to your sewing now," she said controlling the panic in her voice.

"Well Nellie, fancy this place, real nice, you sure got a palace here," BJ said while she stood blocking the entrance. The huge mine boss looked over her squinting through thick, smudged glasses and grunted approval of the artfully furnished entryway and spiral staircase that swept up from it. She had always feared this man, BJ, or Honeycums, as her aunt called him. Every week when he came with his laundry and stayed for a "visit," Nellie had taken her cue and fled the tarpaper house sickened by the thought of what her aunt, bound by the desperate circumstances had come to and sickened the more that she made no secret of her love for him. Back then, when Nellie walked to the door he looked at her with a longing as he dug into his pocket for a dime for the picture show that she watched two times through, making certain that the Split Rock rig had roared back out the gravel road to the camp. Only then would it be safe to return. From the first she understood why he lingered and why he overpaid so generously for washing and ironing those starched shirts and khaki pants, why there was a puddle of water on the kitchen floor, why the house smelled of his sweat and soap and her aunts dime store perfume, why her aunt's bed was a jumble. And now after all these years in veritable safety of this sheltered place, years without a thought of him, here he stood, and the stench of his nauseating sweat invaded the doorway ... in a flash all the fear and ugliness and hate ... the sordidness of that secret existence came back.

"My God, what are you doing here?"

"What are you doing here? The mailbox says Nielsen. Looks like Otto struck it rich. So you married him after you run off? Or are you the cleaning lady?"

"I said, BJ, what are you doing here!" She held the door, closing it slightly she braced her foot against it.

"Now, now, there, aren't you going to invite an old friend in? We're practically family. I drove all the way down here to tell you your poor sweet aunt passed on and bring you her things." Before she could react, he pushed the door open brushing her aside and stepped into the front hallway. He stood looking about with a brown paper package under his arm uttering, "My, oh, my."

"You could have written, mailed the package," she said, backing away, not taking her eyes off him. He ignored her.

"How did you find me?"

"It was like you and John and Otto vanished into thin air. Do you know what happened to John, I never heard from him again?"

"No."

"You never wrote your aunt. She claimed she didn't know where you were but after she died I put together her things there and in her missal was a scrap of paper with this address, no name, just this address—but I knew it had to be you. I admit I was curious, thought I would find you in a little shack down here, maybe in a whorehouse."

"Get out!"

"Let's not get uppity. Don't you want to know how she was after you left?"

"My mother writes several times a year, she sends me her letters."

"I bet you love reading those, all about the fancy social events in Tuckerton? She wouldn't write the truth. She started to drink more and got fat as a pig, a big fat red headed whore pig."

"I told you to get out!"

"I'm not finished! I didn't come here to get thrown out!" He put the packages on the hall table. "I came in one Tuesday afternoon with a load of silver and after I got rid of that I went over with my laundry and there she was on the floor lying in a puddle of puke and blood, her face and hands all swollen and purple. She'd been there a day or two and begun to stink. That's what happened to her! Not that you would give a good goddamn!"

Nellie moved toward the staircase. He grabbed her arm.

"Where are you going? Those Tuesdays before you left while I was plugging your aunt I know John was fucking you at that whorehouse. And after you were gone, and she got so fat I used to dream about you, your pretty little whore cunt—thought about it all the way down here."

His hand reached out fast as a viper strike and ripped open her blouse; the buttons popped off and scattered about the floor. With his hand over her mouth he forced her down on the staircase.

"Now's my turn. It'll pay for my trip." His other hand lifted her skirt and tore down her silk underwear. As he lay against her he panted, fumbling with the buttons on his pants.

The iron corner of the Singer sewing machine hit him in the small of the back square on the spine and bounced with a crash down to the marble floor. He rose up with a cry in pain, freeing Nellie enough that she could spring out from under him and race behind Geraldine to the top of the stairs. She picked up the pistol.

"Now, get out!" Aiming down the stairs at his chest.

Groaning, he rubbed his back, standing straight, working it around as he rubbed. "You wouldn't use that pistol would you?" Backing toward the door he smiled. "You want to know something I didn't tell you, Nellie? Huh? After a while some people were looking for John, from where he was supposed to go. He never showed up there and they came by the mine, checked at the bank, checked out his forwarding address, no John. Wonder that. And you know what? They never did find him. Not a word. Strange isn't it? Then maybe five or six years ago the police bring me a little rag of cloth and asked if I recognized it, wondered if it belonged to John. Found it along with a skull with a big hole blown in the top, with some bones and bit of clothes scattered about, the animals had chewed them up pretty good, no doubt. Nice burial, don't you think? You know what I think, Otto blew John's head off, stole his money, and that gave him a start on a thing like this? Interesting question, makes sense, don't it? Sweet little Danish boy; I'd like to see the asshole. Oh, pardon me … Mr. Nielsen."

"Where is he anyway, at work?"

"I expect him any minute."

"Good, I'll wait."

"By God, BJ, if you don't leave this second I'll kill you! I have a witness you tried to rape me. But I'm giving you a chance to leave, and you had better take it, or I swear I'll pull this trigger."

"You wouldn't do a nasty thing like that, an uppity bitch like you."

"BJ I know how to use this thing and I'll put six bullets in you before I'm done!"

"I'm going." He had his hand on the doorknob. "But I'm sure now what happened to John."

As he went through the door she shouted, "If you come back BJ, I'll shoot you! Swear to God!"

"I think you would, you little Irish whore."

She raced to throw the bolt on the door. Geraldine went to the phone.

"Should I call the police, Mam?"

"No! Don't call the police!" Nellie pulled her clothes together. "How much did you hear?"

"Hear what, Mam?"

"What he said to me?"

"I tried not to listen."

"But you heard?"

"Yes, Mam."

"Geraldine, if you so much as breathe a word of what you heard or saw to anyone, I mean anyone at all, I'll blow your head off, understand? By all I hold sacred, I will." Nellie held the gun up and shook it in Geraldine's face to emphasize her words.

"Yes, Mam."

Nellie checked on Maggie, who slept and called Otto. He would come right away and told her to keep the gun with her until he got there and to put some bullets in it. There was a box of them in back of his sweaters on the top shelf of closet. The following day he bought a small pistol she could carry in her purse.

Then he tried to locate BJ. He phoned Ed and asked him to have one of the secretaries in his office find the number of H&HCM Ltd and see if BJ still worked there, and find him. The secretary got the number of a mine and put in a person-to-person call several days later. When BJ answered she spoke long enough to confirm it was he and then hung up. Otto stayed in Farbridge for a week until he was certain Nellie felt safe enough to sleep alone, though she kept the new pistol under her pillow. And Otto vowed to her he would kill the bastard if he came back. He would shut him up once and for all.

"You would do that for me?" she asked.

"To save your honor," he said. That night she suggested they take the bedside table out between the twin beds and push them together.

In the dark she asked. "Do you still love me?"

• • •

At the bar the members of the little investment group were incredulous.

"Someone broke into the house so you bought her a pistol? In Connecticut she should need a pistol?" the doctor asked.

"She carries it with her all the time, even to church," Otto replied.

"Imagine that," Ed said.

Silvio added, "In my neighborhood half the old ladies at morning Mass are packing." Otto thought he was joking. He ordered up another round for his buddies.

Chapter 38

April 1942. Silvio sat with his elbow on the bar, his heavy head against his closed hand. He looked askance at Otto when he came over. "Gino's joined up," he said, barely audible. Any effort he had made to call him Gerry had been scrapped.

"I know; he called me." Otto said adding to the pall.

"That pig Mussolini and the fucking Fascists," Silvio hissed through clamped teeth. His huge hands rolled into a tight fist, the knuckles white. Otto wondered how many flattened noses and broken faces they had produced. "The Army wants him to be a translator or interrogator or some such thing. You know, Otto, his Italian is perfect, speaks like a native." He took a long draw on his drink. "He never spoke a word of English before grade school. His mother still can only say 'Hello, goodbye and how much', for Christ's sake. It's like she never left Italy." He took another drink of scotch and went on. "The neighborhood is like an Italian island, she never goes out of it." He pulled in a sonorous breath through his nose, kind of a reverse sigh, a non-verbalized "oh, what the Hell". Otto had grown used to the noise the twisted nose made. Someone got in a lucky punch he thought.

"You know, I thought she was deaf." Otto now amused at his lack of perception, risked a weak smile.

"Deaf? What the Hell's the matter with you?" Silvio was lightening up slowly.

"Yeah, the night you brought her here, years ago, my birthday, she didn't say anything. I figured she was deaf, reading lips or something."

"Jesus Christ, Otto. And I thought you Danes were smart." He had brightened some more.

"When does he go?" Otto continued, looking to fill an uncomfortable pause in the exchange.

"He's gone. I put him on the train a couple of hours ago, heading for Basic Training. Then he gets a commission. Told me they told him, a lieutenant. With his education and Italian they should make him a general."

Otto bought Silvio a drink and they drank to Gino's good health and good luck. It was left unsaid, but they both knew he would need it.

The restaurant had lost half the staff to the draft. Antonio and Simon were gone. Carlo was too old and Jim was forty-two with five children. They stayed. Business was down so the remaining employees could handle it. Otto closed the upstairs except for an occasional party. There were blackout curtains that were pulled across the windows every night. The mayor had said the city was vulnerable to sabotage and who knew what else, maybe even air raids. Pictures of London on fire were not lost on New Yorkers.

Silvio broke the silence once again. "Otto, are you going?

"The FBI was in here a week ago." Before the sentence was out, he realized his words were charged with a threat to the mobster. Silvio's head came off his hand as if a gun had gone off by his ear. He sat bolt upright. Otto's response when the agent showed his badge had been muted panic, a racing heart, an affected calm; the visions of John's corpse, scattered bones and rags that BJ described loomed. Why were they here! Silvio's reaction was far more acute; Otto imagined he instantly tallied his list of criminal acts, perhaps even remembered a jail cell or two.

"Yeah, what did they want?" Silvio insisted, trying to regain his composure, feigning a lack of concern.

"There were two of them. They asked me questions about where I lived in Europe, who my relatives are and whether Nellie had any ties to Ireland anymore. Things like that." Otto had tried to answer his companion's unasked question of whether they were here investigating some crime or other. "Nothing about my customers or friends," he added. Silvio understood, or at least appeared to.

"You're a citizen, right?" Silvio asked, still seeking other reasons for the visit.

"Both Nellie and I for a couple of years."

"So at least they won't deport you," Silvio wisecracked.

"No, they want to clear me so I can translate things they get that are in Danish."

"That was it?" His eyes locked onto Otto's as if to squeeze information from them like juice from cumquats. In a few seconds, satisfied Otto held nothing back, he appeared to relax, "Well, that's good, nothing serious. You never know what those sneaky shits are up to." Taking what remained of his drink in one swallow, he picked up his coat and without a word walked out. Otto never saw him again. After several Thursday nights had passed without his friend's regular visits, Otto realized the law had come too close for comfort.

The FBI clearance came through after a month. Otto began to work three days a week at an office building downtown near Wall Street, translating Danish and German materials, nothing of importance as far as he could tell. At least he was contributing, in small a way. He remembered a line of a poem he had heard somewhere to the effect that "they also serve who stand and wait" or was it "sit", anyway he put himself in that category.

Months later, as Otto was going through bills at the end of the bar, a tall woman accompanied by a young girl came through the door. She wore a print housedress with white buttons down the front, black shoes and white cotton ankle socks. Otto stood and reached for his wallet, contributions, assistance, a helping hand or whatever they called it went with the business. The woman pushed the girl forward and made a stop gesture with her hand signaling that she wasn't looking for a handout.

"Have you seen Mr. Tortorici?" the girl asked in a small voice.

"Not for a long time," Otto responded, not understanding the significance of his words. Then he recognized the woman, Silvio's wife. The dyed black hair piled up on her head, the thick lipstick, rouge, powder, and heavy jewelry—gone. Stripped of all ornamentation, she was doughy pale. Stringy gray hair hung against her face like a dirty wimple, her black eyes peered out with dispassionate dejection. Without a word she took the girl by the hand, pulled her around and pushed her away toward the door. Before following she looked at Otto and uttered in a heavy accent the only words he would hear her speak, "in the river". Otto spent an afternoon at the public library going over newspapers searching for an indication of his friend's fate, a mob hit or the name Tortorici in the obituary columns, but nothing.

• • •

The limitations imposed by gas rationing required that the Buick remain in Farbridge. It became Nellie's car. Friday noon Otto took the train to Connecticut. On rainy or cold days Nellie met the train. On nice days he would walk the mile or so to the house with his suit coat thrown over his shoulder. He wandered through the little town square looking in an occasional store window and beyond to the streets where the sidewalk ended. From the edge of the road he studied the houses and lawns and what flowers bloomed in the gardens. This little route was essentially all he knew of Farbridge.

Once home he would pick up Maggie and carry her piggy back up the stairs, toss her on his bed, rumple her hair, change his clothes; then outdoors they would roll on the lawn or he would push her on her tricycle until naptime. Then he worked with Joe in the gardens until supper. Now that Maggie was five, she ate at the dining room table perched on a booster chair with a small silver fork and spoon. Conversation included the child. The war was not mentioned; a world away it could and would be ignored. At her bedtime Otto told Maggie stories, listened to prayers and tucked her in. Then in the library bent over the radio he listened to the resonating baritone of Edward R Morrow reporting from London with the sounds of the blitz in the background, or the high pitched nasal staccato of H B Kaltenborn's reports as he relayed word of the struggle to the home front. And Otto read the papers. The newspaper accounts of the war were discouraging. Reports of the German advances in Northern Africa and Japanese successes in the Pacific forced the scraps of good news off the front pages. He scoured the back pages for news of Denmark, but details of events there were rarely mentioned. Nellie wouldn't discuss the war, it gave her nightmares she said, and idle talk of the restaurant and Farbridge had limitations. Most evenings passed in near silence.

Chapter 39

The bar was quiet. The only customers were a little group of the regulars huddled together, Ed Cutler, Doc Weinstein, Mel Seiderman and Cook. Otto joined them and stood behind, spread his arms over their shoulders, and bent in to listen. Cook explained he had heard the military had a serious shortage of khaki underwear and was looking for a supplier. Forced to raise his hands and shake his head to cut off the guffaws, he went on. "The little manufacturing outfits can't handle the big orders, someone has to organize it. We can get the contract," he enthused; but, he needed his friends' help because he was about to sign a lease on an old factory building in the Bronx. He went on, explaining that most of his own money was tied up in a company his cousin organized to broker fuel oil to the military. Mel retorted half in jest, "Why don't we get in on that deal, who needs underwear, besides what's the matter with white?" "Camouflage" Cook said, brushing off the comment with a quick glance and proceeding to say he needed capital and offered his friends a "buy in". "Fifty thousand dollars from ten investors and we've got the contract." Without bothering to hear more details Ed Cutler slipped a checkbook from his breast pocket and wrote a check for the amount. Otto loved Ed's insouciance that he perceived as the investing equivalent to grace under fire. The move, the confidence Ed exhibited in the proposal reassured Otto and whetted his appetite, his pulse quickened while his mind sifted through his accounts figuring how he could pull that much together. Cook's voice, the distant Siren's song, related how they would buy up all the sewing machines they could find and induce as many of the Seventh Avenue shops, whose businesses making ladies fashions were on hold anyway, to partner or lease their sewing equipment. In his building they would set up an immense sewing center with hundreds of sewers. Rolls of cotton cloth would come by rail to the adjacent side spur. They would need cutters, sewers, packers, shippers—Cook went on and on. Laughter broke thorough Otto's reverie. Cook had declared what was needed most at the moment were khaki brassieres. Tough to make, he added, "Lots of sizes and lots of finicky little seams, takes skill to make one of those things."

Otto cobbled the money together selling stock and emptying the joint savings account he shared with Nellie in Farbridge. Unsewco, a sewing company, was born with ten signatures on half a dozen papers and with his investment Otto was assured a place on the Board. They would meet the first Wednesday of every month. The two story building from the outside appeared to be a derelict. The irregularly laid brick of the outer walls had been worn and faded by decades of weather. The large windows made up of dozens of small dirt caked panes had many that were cracked or replaced with plywood. The inside presented a very different picture.

The cement floors were clean and polished to a shine. The freshly painted white walls reflected the light from the bulbs suspended on a wire over each worker's table. Otto walked through the building that reverberated with the whir of sewing machines. He stopped to marvel at the seamstress who took pieces of precut cotton from a pile on the right side of a sewing table and in a few moments with a number of nimble motions dropped a finished undergarment in a basket on the left.

The meeting was held in a cement block room adjacent to the managerial offices in the back of the sewing plant. Cook seated the ten board members in scarred folding chairs around the director's table assembled from three card tables. Otto concealed his disappointment in the surroundings and listened to the plant manager's concern that the plant's monthly output had not met the prescribed quotas following an influx of new orders. That brought Cook to his feet. "Don't stand there and tell us you have a problem, tell us your solution! More machines, more sewers! Tell us when and how we will get them. We can't lose business to another outfit! Get on it!" With the final shout and a thrust of his arm toward the door the manager was excused. Otto could imagine the colonic distress the man must have felt as he backed out of the door. Cook took up the Balance Sheet and the Income Statement that showed the government guaranteed revenue lined up against the expenses, principally labor and materials. The numbers looked very good. It was no small proposition. What had started as a plan to manufacture cotton underwear would expand rapidly over the months and years to include the sewing of uniforms, coats, caps, even tents. Truckloads of finished goods rolled off to the training bases and to the docks. This was the first time Otto had made "big money". He thirsted for more.

Doctor Weinstein had listened, but could not be tempted by Unsewco or any investment in the spring of 1942. No thought of an investment could break through his withering melancholy. During the day his patients recounted tales of what would come to be known as the "final solution": stories of missing relatives, arrests, narrow escapes, that came as little scraps of news that somehow made it out of Europe. Countless descriptions that overwhelmed the strongest coping mechanisms and evoked symptoms of deep and unremitting depression that like a grisly plague spread among them paralyzing, stupefying, and imprisoning; and consuming their psychiatrist as well. Many evenings Otto listened in disbelief to the doctor's accounts of the massive pogrom, unable to comprehend the magnitude of what was occurring. Common sense told him it couldn't be that bad, but the little doctor knew the stories were not exaggerations, and indeed, he had been spending his money to finance as many escapes as possible from Germany since kristalnacht when it became clear that the Nazi policy of Judenrein, merely forcing Jews to emigrate, had been superseded by something far more sinister.

On this particular day, when Otto returned ebullient over the financial reports at Unsewco, the doctor's tales were beyond bitter: stories of ruin and theft on a grand scale and increasing knowledge of massive deportations to concentration camps thought to be death camps. "Otto," he said, "I don't treat psychosis. I can't treat that. That's what the mental hospitals are for. I used to treat neuroses, but when unbearable angst is brought on by a reality so shocking as to be incapacitating, how can you call it a neurosis any more? It's reality! Can anyone treat such a terrible comprehension, such an awful truth?" He didn't expect Otto to answer. "Anxiety, no more than that, dread, unthinkable frustration, bottled-up anger and hatred, all of that; I hear it all day long, session after session, patient after patient. They slam their fists; they cry out, scream, nothing but flowing tears, futile tears. And what can I offer? Nothing! A few platitudes, so-called words of comfort that can't possibly heal or even soften the pain; platitudes that are so inadequate they stink the air they are spoken into. I embarrass myself as I say them and think, 'you

...inable charlatan pretending to treat. Give it up!' But I go on, what use is there? I'm all they've got." He paused for a sip of scotch, gathering his thoughts, contemplating whether to go on, whether to shed the mantle of professionalism further laying bare his vulnerability to a friend. "But do you know what is most bothersome, Otto, what grinds me down day after day? What makes me want to plug my ears and stop listening to it all?" Otto, jarred by the impassioned outpouring from this ordinarily reserved man, sat mute, shaking his head in an indication of the only answer possible—no.

"It's the helplessness! The utterly complete, pathetic, abject helplessness, especially when help might be possible." The words came out, one by one. Otto watched a tear teeter on the edge of his eyelid magnified several times by the rimless glasses and finally fall and splash on the bar. "Not to be able to do anything; not to fight, to organize, or even die for them—just powerless with no means available except the impotent letters I write to the government, to Roosevelt, filled with their stories, begging for help. I'm reduced to a pitiable state by it all. How can I treat them, even comfort them any more? There are no words. Sometimes they just sit and cry, come in, sit down and cry and say not a word—and I with every ounce of strength I have try not to cry with them, but I do."

Otto put his arm over his friend's shoulder in an awkward embrace. He didn't know what to say and said nothing. They sat that way for several minutes each lost in his thoughts. Otto's mind went to the farm. He imagined German troop carriers passing by it on the road.

The doctor broke his silence. "How could a people who gave us Goethe, Schiller, Bach and Beethoven become so insane as to follow a murderous lunatic?" They spoke for a while longer until finally the doctor wondered out loud, "To what purpose are a whole people being put through the trials a thousand times greater than those of Job?" Again Otto had no answer. With this question, spent by emotion, the doctor took off his glasses and wiped his eyes and glasses and thanked Otto for listening "to the ramblings of a discouraged old man." Otto turned on the bar stool to watch his doctor friend wander off into the teeming heat of an August evening.

Otto had looked out scores of times through grimy windows of the train at the bleak backside of little Connecticut towns, the warehouses along rail sidings, the backdoors of businesses, trash cans, barred windows and the duplexes, the small houses and little board-fenced yards lined up against the tracts. He sat, an open newspaper on his lap, caught up by the thought of the greeting he would have as Maggie charged at him, a wide-armed welcome that would end with a clutch. Nellie would kiss him on the lips and as his hands slipped down over her firm bottom she would break away from his embrace, turning as if she didn't notice, like a sexy prioress, back to managing the kitchen. Geraldine, at the sink peeling potatoes, would turn to smile.

Nellie had asked if he didn't mind if Father Lombardi and Monsignor Callahan came to dinner, implying their presence might be an imposition, even though he had assured her he enjoyed their company and in fact he looked forward to their visits. It annoyed him, why couldn't she believe him? He found them entertaining, and strangely enough, less, what he would call "religious" than she. They took a glass of wine, and Father Lombardi an occasional drink, and he could tell a good joke. They liked to laugh. Tonight he would ask them what they knew of the Jews' plight in Germany and what they thought of it, what could be done to help?. Perhaps something helpful might come of it, a crumb of solace, a fresh idea he could convey to his tortured friend.

The trio shared a glass of wine under the awning on the porch while Geraldine fed and bathed Maggie before Otto broke away to tuck her in for the night. At Nellie's beck they filed into the dining room. A candlelit dinner. Red and yellow dahlias from Otto's gardens were arranged on the table. Nellie wore a modest dress, but the cloth was not up to the task and could not hide her well-sculpted body. Otto wondered how Father Lombardi, a robust forty, endured sitting across the table from her, how he, a vigorous man, repressed his cravings. Cold showers? At the Academy Otto had heard that the army put saltpeter in the food to slow the troops down in this regard. On the other hand, the old Monsignor was gray, soft-spoken and wise, and Otto could see he was at complete peace with himself, almost as if he had reached a higher stage of understanding of life and the great beyond. He appeared to project a comfortable understated holiness, what Otto thought might be meant by grace, a word he had a poor understanding of ... not having met such a uniquely committed person before. The conversation was directed to church affairs. Otto let it run and delayed discussion of the war until dessert, mindful of Nellie's dislike of the subject. Then he would risk disrupting the evening for his friend.

Over sherbet, cookies and coffee Otto asked, "Father, what have you heard of the struggle the Jews are having in Europe?" He used the euphemism, struggle, purposefully for Nellie's sake, hoping she would let the topic get by.

"Just what's in the papers," Father Lombardi replied, but his interest was kindled.

"A friend of mine in New York, a psychiatrist with mostly Jewish patients tells me that the Jews are not only placed in concentration camps, but the word he has from his patients is, that it is likely, Jews by the thousands are being murdered."

"Otto, please, that's absurd!" Nellie shot back with a look of alarm that asked, how could you spoil my evening? She began collecting the dessert dishes, something Otto had rarely seen since Geraldine was hired. The conversation had ended as quickly as it had begun and the Father had no chance to reply, except as the priests were leaving he softly pronounced,

"There are things in this world that defy explanation."

She lay in her bed and he in his. That beautiful body wasted for another night but there was no point in suggesting, he had known the risk. Before he turned off his bedside lamp, she put the dinnertime look into words that served to warn and punish, "Otto, you ruined a perfectly good evening." Otto rolled over; there was no answer to any of that.

Chapter 40

October 1943. Otto spent the afternoon translating Danish and German to English in a large, dusty room in a government building at a desk piled with messages typed on yellow paper. He printed his rendering on white forms that were picked up as quickly as he wrote them. When the work was complete, he was free to leave. It was a bright Indian summer day with a refreshing dry wind that channeled down Madison Avenue. He walked from lower Manhattan to the restaurant. He had learned to savor a day like this, for in October zesty weather lasted only a week or two. Soon the harsh winter winds would slam down off the buildings, tearing open his coat and like ice water the cold of the frigid cement would seep through the soles of his shoes and cramp his feet. There were fewer cars on the streets now, less noise, the urban din muted; the war had returned the city to earlier, less frenetic time—time moved back in an agreeable way that a visitor would not perceive. And Otto reacting in synchrony with the surroundings, the city's slowed vibrations, relaxed his steps. He had become a part of the whole. He was a New Yorker. Weekends in the country, he realized, would remain a leitmotif, a weekend break; he could never live there. His major work: running the restaurant, managing investments, overseeing Unsewco, hobnobbing with friends would always be here in New York; fixed, unmovable.

He turned off Madison Avenue to walk west, the low afternoon sun reflecting off the windows blinding him. Squinting he entered Otto's Place. As his eyes adjusted to the dim light he made out Jim drying glasses and talking with the lone customer, a woman. From a little quirk of posture, or from some other fragment of his past perception of her, he recognized the darkened silhouette of Ruthie. The platinum hair was gone; a blond pageboy fell onto a pink cardigan that hung over a pleated tartan skirt; for her uncharacteristically demure clothing. When he sat down beside her and she turned, he noted a transformation adapted to the times or changed circumstances; but her voice, the manner in which she held her cigarette, the milky gaze and playful smile reassured him the change was superficial.

"Otto, how are you?" She said bending forward to give him a light kiss on the cheek.

"Doing fine, and you?" Wishing he could ask what happened. His glance down at her clothes conveyed the message.

"Oh, these. I teach now at a secretarial school, Katherine Gibbs. They have a dress code. Like it?"

"You left the bank." Otto had long since adopted the declarative sentence technique as a respectable way to pry.

"Less pay but better hours and no lechers," she said, taking a sip of her Manhattan. Her reply was a topic killer, lechers, he couldn't go there and she knew it; so she continued with an off-hand clarification, "I became tired of those prurient old men pawing me with their eyes," and then she dropped the subject. His mind had wandered a bit. Looking at her he surmised that there had been more difficulty than she had foreseen managing the consequences of her former heady style; she had gotten what she wanted from it anyway, Gino, so then her choice then became, quite literally, take it or leave it and she left.

"But wasn't it a great job, being in on the happenings of high finance?" A job he would have killed for, he thought to himself.

"Lots of temptation for the big shots, but with Roosevelt's SEC boys around, things aren't like those good old days, before Joe Kennedy." Speaking with her was like playing verbal leap-frog. Her mind was quick and tended to pick up an understated meaning before the connection was clear. He took her answer to indicate she didn't pass stock tips to Gino as he had suspected.

"How's Nellie?" she asked changing the subject.

"Still full time in Connecticut." He didn't know how his answer had anything to do with how Nellie was, it just came out. Nor did Ruthie. He saw her eyebrows dart up and down. Again she took from his words more than he had intended.

"Everything okay?" She looked down at her drink, tactful not pressing.

"Oh, yes, fine, no problems." He didn't know if she knew of Maggie, and for some reason, he didn't fathom he didn't want her to know. She didn't ask about children.

She ordered another Manhattan. Otto looked at the beautiful amber liquor set like a cut stone in the long stemmed glass, the maraschino cherry a perfect red accent. It was a work of art, a jewel of a drink. He ordered a scotch.

With fresh drinks they began a new page.

"The reason I came by is to tell you I got a letter from Gino." She glanced up at him thinking he might have already heard the news. When he made no response, she continued with emphasis, "a Dear Ruthie letter."

Nonplussed, he didn't have a reply, just mumbled "Oh yes."

"Writes me this epistle about how much I meant to him, but he has met this girl, a WAC, over there and he plans to marry her." She reached into her purse and took out a two page single spaced letter typed on onionskin airmail stationary. It crackled as she unfolded it; a snapshot fell onto the bar.

"I'll bet he made ten carbons of this thing. There're probably girls crying all over the city." She laughed at her own mordant humor. Picking up the picture and holding it out for Otto to see, "at least she's great looking. I wouldn't want to lose out to a—umm, you know what I mean." He did, she had pride. She looked from the picture to Otto to get his reaction, smiled, "Nice set, huh?" She had read his mind.

By the third Manhattan she was well past Gino, her mood rising. Otto was feeling good as well. The conversation had turned to amusing things. She had a sharp wit; they were laughing, toasting the betrothed, one toast nastier than the next, making light of the situation. He drank more than his custom; each swallow of scotch tumbled warm and pleasant, like a delightful tropical waterfall through his chest. Tonight there was no pacing. They were celebrating, strangely, celebrating hard luck.

Locking eyes with Otto, she picked the cherry by the stem from her glass and putting it to her pursed lips sucked the juice from it before taking it behind her lips and rolling her tongue around it. Then baring her teeth, she pulled the stem off and squashed it against her palate.

Otto made the nightly call to Farbridge then signaled to Jim they were leaving.

She lived seven or eight blocks from the restaurant. They walked as a unit, his arm over her shoulder, matching coordinated steps, talking about little things. No spoken invitation, he simply followed her into the hall, up the little elevator and into her apartment, a one bedroom, completely white: the walls, furniture, carpets, and drapery. She disappeared. He sat. Adultery didn't matter. New York was a different world, a different life to be lived separately. He had desired Ruthie from the beginning, brains and spice, refined yet erotic, worldly yet unpretentious, the complete package. He thought of the fight with Nellie over Mrs. O'Conner and "canned peas". That sealed it. There was no uncertainty this woman would be his.

She emerged from the bedroom in a red dressing gown. An invitation sent and accepted. She was the only color there, red emblazed on white, as if projected on a movie screen until he stepped into the picture. They bathed Hollywood style in a tub spilling scented bubbles over the side and shared a towel before falling onto the bed. He was reminded how she had played with the maraschino. "Cherries are the best part of Manhattans," she said.

Chapter 41

Friday afternoon Otto phoned Nellie to tell her that a large batch of documents had come in and required urgent translation and he was expected to be at the federal building until all hours, even over the weekend. A clumsy lie; and this became the first of many. Lying wasn't easy; he hated it—and time and practice did not improve his comfort. Ruth and Otto spent the next ten nights together. She dropped the 'ie' as a requisite for her position as a teacher of shorthand. A whirlwind romance, she on the rebound and he no longer inclined to resist temptation. Otto moved into the white apartment by bits and pieces, unsure of his intentions or what the goal might be. First a shaving kit, then suits and shirts; he was cautious, prepared to back away at any time. Neither participant had a glimmer of insight into how it would develop or end. Later Ruth joked that at first it, this spontaneous thing, was "a meeting of the loins, not the minds; an irrational corporal spontaneous combustion of sorts." She enjoyed words. Did the *New York Times* crossword puzzle every Sunday. But as the days passed she found a reason for the growing affinity, the things undisclosed at first, substantial, intellectual, noble even, that they had in common. She could not have said simply, as Otto did, "it just happened." It had to be more than that and as the days came and went, as she predicted, the allegiance grew stronger with each new discovery of some unexpected compatibility, as if each had just the part to fit the other's incomplete puzzle. Formed as it was; piecemeal, unplanned, the conclusion of the affair left unaddressed, the obligate questions they postponed or avoided altogether—how would this work in the long run with the possibility of years of deceit and the potential for harm? Neither knew, and at some point, neither cared. There was no proposal, no formal agreement, their arrangement as it evolved would leave all else always unchanged: weekdays together in New York, weekends he would go to Connecticut, a divorce never an issue. Ruth, intelligent and realistic, expected nothing more. She assured Otto on that first Friday before he left, when he had become apologetic for leaving, that she had salvaged a portion of her lost dream and was satisfied with her decision that "though imperfect this was surely better than nothing." Otto had a mistress and the companionship, humor, and lovemaking and the ornery trials of a double life that came with her.

•••

On the last Saturday in October he rode the train to Connecticut, a beautiful fall day. The woody scent of smoke from piles of burning leaves drifted skyward. As he walked home from the station he stopped to speak with the homeowners who stood with rakes watching over fires lit by the roadside. Otto didn't waste leaves like that. Raked onto tarps they were dragged to the compost piles to rot and nourish the gardens. Once leaves were cleared there followed the fall chores: the window screens came down and the storm windows washed and hung, hoses rolled and stored, and the logs that lay by the garage he would split for exercise and stack next to the backdoor.

Otto raked leaves off the hill down to the edge of the porch deck, building a pile for Maggie and a neighbor boy to jump into inventing spins, scissor jumps, flying eagles and then crawling free, leaves stuck to their clothes and hair, they raced back to jump again. Nellie and Geraldine, drawn from the house by the squeals and laughter, stood arms crossed and watched the antics along with Joe and Dominic, who taking a break, leaned on their rakes.

Tired, the children sat on the edge of the deck. Maggie begged Dominic to do his funny walk, a show Nellie detested. She turned and went indoors. Since the Gela Beach landing in Sicily where an exploding shell shattered his right kneecap and tore the joint apart, Dominic had a limp. The army surgeons with no choice but to fuse his knee leaving him with a fixed joint and shortened leg. He wore a thick-soled shoe. The Purple Heart and a Bronze Star that came with the knee he left in a dresser drawer. As the children had requested, he straightened his good leg and did a high kick march, goose-stepping about. Otto admired him for making light of the wound, but imagined the pain and terror he must have endured. Joe, going back to raking, didn't watch.

The raking done, Otto, Joe and Dominic sat on the porch and nursed beers, wringing the wet bottles with their hands, enjoying the cold against callused palms. They called him Mister Nielsen, which bothered Otto and despite his protests they persisted, as he was their employer, a man of a higher station; and they were working class men, not equals. They talked business: talk of the gardens and lawns, what to plant next year, what shrubs would be wrapped for the winter against the coming snow's weight, who to call to trim off the dead branches high in the oaks, nothing personal, nothing of their life beyond the hemlock borders of the property. He knew they were married, attended the same church as Nellie, good Catholics, and Dominic had children; but no more. He didn't inquire. They didn't speak of these matters and he wouldn't presume to intrude. He assumed their lives were simple, uncomplicated; a little house with a yard, simple business concerns; no affairs, no mistresses, no deception, no guilt as he had begun to feel. And these men were respectful of him! As he sat with them he suffered the invalidity of a sneak, a cheat, and an adulterer and the duplicity made him even more estranged; more out of place than ever, more like a transient, a weekend visitor that in essence he was. The truth weighed on him; he had taken on another load, self-imposed. Yet he knew the discomfort, the perfidy and remorse that he felt as he sat there would evaporate, clear like the morning fogs over the Hudson as soon as he returned to the city.

The backdoor swung open. A girl dressed in a princess costume skipped through and tugged on his arm. Halloween night and it was time to start. Joe and Dominic, after carefully placing the beer bottles in the trash, as if the neatness of the trash was an important matter, left.

Otto and Nellie stood on the road and watched Maggie run up the neighbor's walks, ring door bells, hold up her sac for candy or apples, and run on to the next. After an hour they turned toward home, Otto carried Maggie; Nellie carried Maggie's bag. At bedtime again their ritual, Maggie would say her prayers and Otto would tell her a story, he knew lots but mostly he made them up. Nellie would listen before she gave her child the last kiss goodnight. Nellie said Otto should write the stories down; he never did.

Sunday dinners were quiet affairs. Two immigrants, thrown together by circumstance, had built a life without family or close ties. No Grandparents or crazy uncles, sisters or brothers to fill the empty space, to break the silences, to boast or complain about, to let the fresh air in.

They sat at one end of the long mahogany table. There were Irish lace placemats under the silver settings, candles burning in silver holders, the last of the garden's chrysanthemums in a cut glass vase. Maggie the center of their lives sat between them on a booster seat in a new dress. The child's closet burst with clothes and little shoes that Nellie was unable to resist buying for her little princess, her sun and moon, the center of her life. And when outgrown, Nellie took the flood of clothes that flowed through the house to the church, fueling in her a grand sense of noblesse oblige. A wonderful feeling knowing she had relieved some, if not suffering, at least humiliation for some child who otherwise attended school in a shabby dress. She took pride in handing down to the less fortunate.

For Otto and Nellie, every material need had been fulfilled but the human needs had become insatiate, the place for love between them empty, the marriage an illusion, an act. They stared into space while they ate, the lethargic, uninspired conversations polite but mostly monosyllabic. Nellie's customary question, "How was your week?' brought a rush of blood to his cheeks he hoped she wouldn't see. The thought of the companionship and sex with Ruth gave him palpitations. The week had been great. Uncertain what answer would ring true; he nonetheless fabricated a triviality about the chef, his wife was sick. She nodded, not interested enough to inquire what the problem was. He suspected she knew it was concocted. The clink of the silver on the china ricocheted about the walls. Nellie spoke more than ever of the Church. Otto thought of his parents and the silent dinners in Denmark and then he thought of Ruth some more.

• • •

Ruth met the train Monday morning. She took that day off. They ate lunch at a special place, the Plaza, before wandering about museums and galleries for several hours. She loved art and had spent many of her lonely hours after Gino had left for the army strolling the halls of the Metropolitan, contemplating the great collection of paintings, many, she told Otto, she had studied in the Art History classes at Saint Olaf's.

"Where?"

"A college in Minnesota. Named after the Norwegian Viking king."

"I know Saint Olaf. Boy oh boy couldn't they think of a better name?"

"Otto, I loved the school. Founded by Lutherans, you know. They gave me a scholarship that made my dream come true. I got off the farm."

"Well, there are two things we have in common, we're both off the farm and both bad Lutherans … at least as far as the Lutherans are concerned." He laughed.

"Well, a bad Lutheran is better than nothing, don't you imagine?"

• • •

Later he walked her to the apartment and went on to his restaurant, but stayed only until the dinner rush had cleared and the money was counted before eleven. Once "home" they played a hand or two of gin rummy and listened to the latest war news on the radio before turning in.

Switching off the light she said, "Otto, I don't think we are bad. I mean, what you said about being bad Lutherans. If we love each other, it can't be bad, can it? Love is what life and God are all about, at least for me."

"You know, I can't think of things in absolutes: good and bad, right and wrong. For now what is is, and the ups and downs that come with it." Then he added quickly, "and we sure do love each other". Good thing,

Chapter 42

Despite the complexities of Otto's dual life, the subterfuge became less difficult with time, almost effortless, and once back in New York during the week he barely gave Nellie a thought. In fact his life ran smoothly for several years. Time, Otto learned, did heal, or in his case dissolve most of the apprehension and guilt that, like pine pitch, stuck to him at first but came off with wear. The cheerless marriage helped. From the beginning of his affair he rationalized Nellie and he were a mismatch emotionally and spiritually, unrecognized early on, and from then the disparity had grown, and now manifest. Her discontent with him began with his friends, his drinking in New York; and now in Connecticut things grew worse. Summer weekends he worked in the garden like a day laborer in shorts and shirtless, his sunburned back covered with oily sweat. Every hour he walked to the kitchen to pour another gin and tonic, tracking dirt and suffering the complaints. Nellie detested the chumming with "wop" laborers and reminded Otto that their friends, the "proper people" as she called them, spent their weekend afternoons at the Farbridge Country Club playing golf and tennis and sitting on the veranda overlooking the practice green sipping iced tea. Why couldn't they join? Weekdays Nellie lived for the invitations for morning coffees and afternoon sherry parties held by the countless "Mrs. C. Albert Wickham's"… her new friends from the Protestant churches, the garden club, the Junior League, the Florence Crittenden Society. A large chalkboard mounted on the kitchen wall served as a social calendar and scoreboard listing upcoming teas, parties and charity balls she would insist that they attend. Otto conceded that. As she had dreamed she was at least to some degree, "established".

Otto thought Nellie was far too pleased with her status in Farbridge to risk throwing it away. He reasoned if Nellie learned of Ruth and his double life she would accept it, see it as a loathsome matter but nonetheless a fact of life; a result of their separations and that he, weakened by loneliness and weekday celibacy, had fallen prey. And that she would see this discrete arrangement as acceptable despite her prayerful life. Her past was worldly enough to understand these matters. Hadn't she seen enough in Canada? Taking a mistress she would regard a venial sin and not make it grounds for divorce or whatever the Church prescribed for an unhappy civil marriage. Of course for him, the perfect solution would be that they could face facts openly and each have their own silent, secret weekday world. He would happily forgive her any quiet affair; certainly like he, she too must be in need of fleshly release. Wouldn't such an adventure be a gratifying diversion from the doldrums of Farbridge?

And think of the financial considerations. Didn't he support her; keep her in a style appropriate for this fancy Connecticut town? Here she would not be capable of taking the bold steps she took in Canada when she had nothing to lose; there would be no pistol shot. Instead, her only weapon, almost as fatal, would be to drive him to the brink of madness with little cuts, lacerating words and gestures, but only to the brink. He would withstand these because he had an inviolate reason to: their child. His response then to the eruptions and arguments, like always, would be apologies and good humor. At this point he thought he would enjoy the challenge.

So as a practical matter, weekends Nellie worked in the kitchen or retreated to the sunroom to sew or read. Otto in winter spent hours in his basement workshop building a large dollhouse or a little puppet theater; Christmas surprises for Maggie. He could hear footsteps upstairs. Nellie would be reading to Maggie or playing dolls or go-fish. And when the spring flowers emerged he returned to the gardens to work with Joe and Dominic until the afternoon guests began to arrive to sit on the deck for cocktails and conversation: Nellie's well pedigreed DAR type neighbors that Otto intermixed with his New Yorkers, mostly Jewish, and from time to time the reverend Fathers, who appeared tolerant if not amused by the social chemistry. And of course Har Parsons, their attentive neighbor who stopped by unannounced, bearing pies for Nellie and gin for Otto. If Maggie had no friends, Nellie let her sit on her lap and swing her legs and listen to grownup talk.

Despite Otto's view of Nellie's situation, for her part she simply looked to her faith for solace, taking Father Lombardi's words to heart that a marriage, no matter how unsatisfactory, is sacred and that she must work within it to make it better. A task she found less and less tolerable because as time passed their marriage had become, as far as she was concerned, as unsatisfactory as it was unsanctified; and she fretted because Otto had no interest in correcting either failing. She had given up hope it could be improved. Even so, she did worry that the fragile marriage could fly apart with an uncensored word, a verbal blow as effective as the axe that Otto used to split the dry ash logs on winter weekends; words she struggled not to speak. Her faith wouldn't allow it, and for Maggie's sake she would maintain the artifice of a happy home. And there was her love for the life in Farbridge. She would not lose that.

Through smiling brown eyes, Geraldine watched as she worked about the house, never hinting of what she knew. She had seen Mr. Parsons follow Miss Nellie into the kitchen with his pies or on some errand, and more than once she had found them talking softly in a the corner shielded from the doorway. His eyes searched her face; she turned her eyes aside, her arms crossed on her chest in a gesture of resistance. Geraldine listened intently as she worked at the sink, turning off the water to catch snippets of what was said, "Why not?" he whispered, and "How would it matter?" He forced a short kiss and she pushed him away breathing, "No, no I can't, not now."

But then there was Otto's laundry brought from New York each week. The shirts once stale with tobacco smoke now carried a hint of perfume that drifted up when Geraldine lifted the top of the suitcase. The sweet scent of jasmine any Carolina girl would recognize. More than once she plucked off a long blond hair that clung to his clothes when she placed them in the washtub. Satisfaction, that's what she felt, and power to end this marriage, and pride in her generosity not to do it; a small recompense for this life of servitude. As she ironed in the sunroom listening to soap operas, she smiled and hummed old gospel songs.

With profits good at Unsewco Otto made Jim restaurant manager. As bartender and factotum the action was a natural evolution, but for Otto the desire for more time with Ruth was the pressing reason for the change. Jim absorbed the responsibility easily and despite the war and reduced numbers of customers the restaurant responded to the new energy. Otto came in at four, sat at the end of the empty bar, checked the books, went over the receipts, and paid the bills. By the time his cronies Mel, Ed, the doctor, and Cook filtered in after five, the ledgers and checkbook were stored under the bar and Otto, with scotch and soda in hand, wandered about picking up on whatever news they brought. Cook had developed several other schemes for the little investment group, most successful, but none so much as Unsewco—the mother lode that earned Otto three hundred thousand dollars that he reinvested in the new projects. At seven, Otto would excuse himself and call Farbridge. Nellie realizing it would be his call let Geraldine answer. He would spend twenty minutes telling Maggie bedtime stories and then blow a goodnight kiss through the phone before slowly putting the receiver down, listening to hear if she had something more to say. Goodbye sometimes took three or four tries.

With Otto's help, Ruth rented a larger apartment in a better building. There was an awning and a doorman, an elevator with brass doors and hallways with wallpaper and a thick carpet. The apartment door opened onto a living room that spread out to a wall of windows and a view of Madison Avenue far below. There were two bedrooms and marble baths, twelve-foot ceilings with crown moldings. In the second bedroom they lined the walls with bookshelves to make a library and comfortable place to talk, read the newspapers or books, and play cards as they listened to the radio. They talked about the farm in Minnesota, eight hundred acres, planted with soybeans, winter wheat and corn and the farm in Denmark where he would one day take her. Their life had taken on a pattern; Ruth worked three days a week, which left Monday and Friday for them to explore Greenwich Village, take the Staten Island ferry on nice days, find small restaurants for lunch and afterward wander about galleries they found. If they found a painting they both liked, which tickled them, and if the owner gave them his best price, at least ten percent below the price on the frame, Otto would buy it. Once home Otto took off the string and brown wrapping paper, together they picked the right spot on the wall, and with two blows of the hammer he hung the new trophy. The walls of the apartment gradually filled with art bought on impulse and soon they were rearranging paintings, crowding them together, putting some above others, making room for any new ones they were unable to resist. He bought her clothes and jewelry; she surprised him with new ties, a pen set and a leather brief case.

The apartment on Riverside Drive stood empty. Otto took a cab there once a week to pull the mail from the crammed box. He walked about and looked in the small abandoned kitchen noting that even the ants and cockroaches had migrated in search of food. He glanced into the bathroom and bedroom, and paused to stare across the river out the unwashed window. The place was cold, gray and silent, a dreary warehouse of memories. He pulled dollar bills from his money clip to leave on the dining table for the cleaning lady who came once every two weeks to dust. Then he pulled the door shut and listened for the dead bolt to fall with the turn of the key. It was like sealing a tomb.

Until the Allied invasion of Normandy it was difficult to tell how the war for Europe was progressing. The news of casualties and suffering was appalling but after D-Day, a pattern of victories gradually emerged. Otto and Ruth listened with interest to word of the liberation of Paris, the Battle of the Bulge in the Ardennes, the fall of the Siegfried line, the crossing of the Rhine, Hitler's suicide, and finally the German surrender. At the end of the war in Europe, Otto wrote home. His letter to Denmark passed his mother's somewhere mid-Atlantic. She had written she could no longer manage the farm. Grandmother was ninety-three, Uncle Erik had died in the war. She did not elaborate. The farm had been sold to the neighbors across the road. They had two daughters with families and needed the land. She and Grandmother moved to an old folk's home. The letter ended with the new address, written in large, quivering letters that magnified the shaking of her hand. More than her words the handwriting betrayed how she had aged, how the deprivations of the occupation had withered her. He had written with pictures of Maggie and said that he would buy the farm and arrange to have it managed, though to what purpose other than to ensure that the life in Denmark he loved would go on unchanged. But the war had changed everything, down to the last detail, everything. And now the farm, his anchor to Denmark, gone.

"Otto, how could you have possibly known when you left there, there would be a war? That Hitler would last, that common sense wouldn't take command," Ruth pleaded.

"I could have done more there than here, fighting or in the underground."

"I believe you were more valuable here, translating those messages and things. There's no way to say for sure, but you may have saved thousands of lives," She looked at him and smiled. "You need cheering up. There's a Braque exhibit at the Metropolitan."

"All right, let's go."

Chapter 43

June 1946. Cirsonrad Inc, a company that made parts for military radar and sonar systems: circuit boards, vacuum tubes, cathode ray screens; the brainchild of MIT professors, was for sale privately. Thorston G. Hallowell finishing his coffee after Sunday dinner looked through the shear drapes that hung at the heavy walnut framed windows of the dining room out across several hundred feet of lawn that divided the homes on a narrow winding road in Lexington, Massachusetts. Noting a familiar car in the neighboring driveway, he excused himself from the family group chatting there, picked up a folder from the front hall table and walked across the grass to the home of his long-time neighbor, Augustus C. Cook III. Hallowell, or "Thor" as he had been known since playing end as a lanky student on the Exeter and Harvard football teams, was one of the principals of Cirsonrad. An athletic sixty-eight, he bounded up the worn wooden stairs to the porch of the big yellow Federalist house, rapped on the door and addressing Cook by his given name, Augustus, asked if he had a moment. Cook thought he was collecting for the Red Cross or American Cancer Society, and glad for any company on this, one of his weekend visits to check the family home in Lexington, welcomed him in. Sitting down in the parlor, declining coffee, Thor first discussed the weather, then looked up casually and with no further preamble, asked, "Augustus would you and perhaps some partners be interested in purchasing a controlling interest in Cirsonrad for 10 million dollars?" Cook was taken aback, having expected a request for a donation to some cause or other, the customary reason for these awkward Sunday visits when a visitor would sit upright on the edge of the sofa cushion, not comfortable enough to sit back.

The corporation was well known to Cook. It was housed in one of the large plain buildings surrounded by a chain link fence and security gate that had mysteriously sprung up in 1942 west of Boston. It had been assembled rapidly and covertly as part of the war effort to build the advanced radar and sonar systems that had been developed at MIT and the University of California for the detection of enemy aircraft and submarines.

"You know the building?"

"Oh yes, Thor. Passed it many a time."

"Some friends and I underwrote the costs, set up the company."

It had been for them the equivalent of the Cook's sewing company, a cash cow, except on a much grander and complex scale.

"Well Thor, I can tell you right off that I am very interested."

Thor Hallowell, comforted by the eager response, sat back, crossed his long legs, and pulled several sheets of green lined ledger paper from a folder.

"Augustus, you need to understand the profit figures on these statements no longer apply." There was a note of concern. He would make sure that his friend understood.

He laid the sheets on the coffee table and taking out a pen began pointing out some numbers and crossing out others.

"The numbers here reflect payments from government contracts that have dried up, and in addition, the patents and manufacturing rights for the radar and sonar technology we sold to Raytheon. But, and this is the key to the offer, Augustus, the plant is well equipped for the manufacture of circuit boards, resistors, capacitors, vacuum tubes and so on and with proper direction could be modified to produce electronic devices for the retail market, radios and so forth."

Cook saw the potential instantly; and, he knew full well if he declined the offer the shares would be sold in a matter of hours following a phone call or two. A few more sentences regarding the need for an inventory of the machinery and an engineer's report certifying the suitability of the building and equipment for the manufacture of radios, and Thor had a deal. Cook agreed to buy a major portion of G. Thorston Hallowell's stock with a handshake, that ancient press of the flesh in Boston remained a covenant, a pledge of honor; lawyers and contracts served only as a formality to satisfy state regulations and the paper pushers. Here in blue blood country one's word was his bond. The transfer, they agreed, would take place in ninety days.

On Monday morning Cook, having clarified assignments and gone over the accounts with the housekeeping couple who lived in the caretaker's apartment over the garage, and assuring himself the big yellow house would be well maintained until his next visit, took the train back from Boston. The following day, calling from his New York office, he arranged for the engineers and accountants needed to assess the plant and finances of Cirsonrad Inc. At five p.m. he walked to Otto's Place, and smiling with drink in hand, his round face flushed with enthusiasm, called a meeting of the informal "Otto's Place Investment Group", namely Mel, Ed, Otto, and Doc. In the relative privacy of "Otto's office" at the far end of the bar he said there was big business to discuss. Clearing his throat as if making a formal presentation he announced with some pride that he, Augustus Cook, had been offered a controlling interest in Cirsonrad. Noting that this proclamation drew blank looks from his companions he went on to add that once more he was looking for business partners. He planned to put up five million dollars himself, but had to raise the rest.

Only Ed had heard of the company. For the others benefit Cook carefully explained what it did: namely, build radar and sonar systems. The small group, trying to understand Cook's pitch about the market for and manufacture of electronic components sat silent, nodding.

Looking from man to man, he explained, "Their military business has dropped to near zero. There's little call for military radar and sonar now that the war is over so that business, the core business of Cirsonrad, has been sold off and now the original partners are prepared to sell control of the remainder. They made their killing and are moving on," he said. Otto searched for the logic in Cook's proposal.

"Then why buy it? What's left? Is the building any good, good location?" Mel interrupted. For him real estate was always the best investment. He was looking for a good building for the group to buy.

"Point well taken," Cook responded, as if teaching a business seminar by the Socratic method. Mel like a star pupil received a pat on his thick shoulder. "Why buy it, I was just getting around to that." Cook paused to take a sip of his drink. "The beauty of this company is that it can make car radios. Can you imagine how many cars are being bought now? All the pent up demand? We will go after subcontracts with Philco, Delco or Emerson or make our own brand." He paused again for effect. "I can see down the road a way, people will begin buying television sets. Television has got to catch on. When it does it will be big. Imagine all the circuit boards and vacuum tubes there. I tell you, this company is a potential bonanza!" he barked. By now Cook was standing as if beckoning customers into a carnival sideshow, but quickly sat down when heads at the other end of the bar turned. Otto's blood boiled. In the space of a few minutes Cook had convinced him. Here it was, the opportunity to make a real fortune looking him in the face. This proposition had to be another one of Cook's winners; no it was the biggest. Otto hadn't been that excited for years. The effect was alimentary, his guts churned. Unlike Unsewco, there was no end in sight! This thing had no dependence on wartime contracts. It could grow with the post-war economy. It had unlimited potential.

"This is preferred stock, voting shares?" Ed asked, exhibiting a lawyerly concern for details of the agreement.

"Absolutely," Cook replied, his wide grin revealing yellowing teeth. He slid the green ledger papers along the bar for Ed's perusal.

"What are we talking about here?" Ed persisted peering over the half glasses set half way down his falconoid nose.

"Two hundred and fifty thousand minimum, five hundred thousand will get a seat on the board." The numbers made Otto blanch, but there would be no denying him, somehow he would be a director, have a voice in something bigger than a restaurant where he dealt with small suppliers and the headaches generated by the kitchen and wait staff. He wanted to blurt out count me in; but the numbers, those high initiation costs to get in the door. He could feel his pulse pound in the arteries that ran up his temples by his ears. He pictured the dignified, no-nonsense board meetings every month in a fancy boardroom, big numbers on the profit and loss sheets, voting on new directions for a major business, responsible for decisions that meant millions. And from there where else would it all lead but to more of the same? Money, big money. This would make the American dream come true, what he had envisioned since that dinner in Copenhagen when he tried to impress his rich cousin that he would do well, what all the effort had been about, the nights he spent in the frigid bunkhouse at the mine dreaming of money, the years building the restaurant business. But half a million? Listening to Cook, he had no choice, he would raise it somehow: business loans, a new mortgage, sell the restaurant, anything.

"Who would like in? I need your money within ninety days, but you've got to let me know as soon as possible so I can spread the word if necessary." Cook concluded. No one committed on the spot and the subject was dropped as lightly as if they were discussing ball scores. On to Harry Truman and how could Roosevelt have picked such a bonehead.

That night Ruth listened as Otto paced back and forth across the Persian rug in library, like the captain on the deck of his ship of fate, navigating the new, uncharted course of his ambition. He would sell all he had in the stock market and borrow another two hundred thousand, using the restaurant, the Farbridge house, and his insurance policies for collateral. He would get this by Nellie, promise her anything, make her see what a deal this is. To Hell with the risk, there's no risk, he was going to do it. There was no going back. Ruth sealed the decision saying, "Go for it, that's what you came here for, isn't it, the gold and silver? And, oh yes, for the women," she added laughing.

Ruth had listened, humored and encouraged him, and asked nothing from him, no divorce, no marriage, no share in all this; she felt thankful for the measureless pleasure their time together had given her. He healed her disappointment and filled the emptiness. Somehow without a sensual word, the thrill of the decision, the muscular body of her lover, inflamed her desire for a conclusion that only dissipation, inventive and exhausting could satisfy.

Chapter 44

Nineteen forty-six turned out to be a year of summer dreams. While Otto dreamed of directorships and newfound wealth, Har had quite another. He hired a pool contractor in April who began to dig in a sunny spot in the back lawn, far enough from the trees to avoid shade and the leaves that would drop into the water. It was completed on a late June afternoon. The swimming pool was more complicated than Har had imagined. What appeared to be a simple rectangle of crystal blue water surrounded by a concrete deck he found to include a pump house with such a frustrating array of pipes and valves that he forced the contractor to come back and label them so he could manage to circulate the water, add the chlorine and, trickiest of all, backwash the sand-filled filter. In addition, it came with a test kit and the requirement to measure chlorine and Ph levels every week. He understood, though the salesman failed to mention it, the pool also came with algae, drowned frogs in the skimmer, and the need to vacuum the bottom clean of accumulated dirt. Har put up with it because this pool had a higher purpose, a purpose worthy of the expense and trouble. Declared to have been built for him to swim laps and for a place to lie in the sun— he kept his five foot eleven body in reasonable trim and worked on a deep tan each summer—and in the evenings a place to gather about for cocktails. But there remained the unspoken, all-important intention: invitations for a swim designed to entice a child, a specific child, Maggie. Har was determined to compel Maggie, with this elaborate carrot, to beg, cry, and whine until she would force her comely mother to walk with her through the hemlocks that divided the houses for swims on lonely summer evenings. Har's vision: Nellie clad in a wet bathing suit, reclined on a lounge chair, turned toward him, one leg drawn up under the other, an arm brought up behind her head, her eyes lit up like sapphires in the setting sun. Though the immediate allure was sensual there was much more about her that excited him. He had known sexy women before and many like she, unwilling and unyielding. What made this woman irresistible was the mystery. She would not speak of herself or her past, not a word about her family or jobs, and the omission generated an irresistible aura: what was there in the hidden past, something implausible, alarming, so unspeakable that neither she nor Otto would speak of it? She had dismissed his indirect inquiries with a laugh and a natural agility with words that steered the subject elsewhere. He was driven to get an answer.

Not to say Harwood Parsons didn't get around. At forty-five, a prosperous, childless widower and for more than seven years a confirmed bachelor, the banker didn't want for introductions or opportunities. When he drove off each morning in his new Cadillac (at the war's end he had been at the top of the dealer's waiting list as the bank held the dealership's notes) he prepared for a day of decision-making interrupted by customer visits and civic luncheons. Evenings he returned to his empty house and following a shower and change of clothes, he left again. There were drinks and dinner at the Farbridge Country Club or there were dinner parties. Busy matchmakers provided introductions to attractive women, a constant reminder that he was highly prized game. The mandatory discretion the small town climate demanded became his forte, a fact he thought that Nellie knew and should appreciate. In his experience religion, even her religion, was not a deterrent that couldn't be overwhelmed with persistence and ardor. He wasn't picky, Catholics, Protestants, agnostics; it didn't matter. He had had several affairs; one lasted almost a year and he could easily have more, but they were put aside by Nellie's presence.

As it turned out Nellie and Maggie swam only on weekends and always accompanied by Otto. When they did come Nellie would swim briefly and then rest lying on a lounge chair, her coal black hair slicked back, her dark blue eyes alert for trouble as she watched Otto play with seven-year old Maggie in the water. Finally, wrapped in a towel, a tired Maggie would climb on the lounge with Nellie. Otto would then swim up and down the pool, first the crawl, then the butterfly, puffing like a seal. Har took this chance to sit by Nellie and talk. Then as the Nielsens left, he stood and watched her. Otto, barefoot, picked his way back along the path through the hemlocks between the houses. Nellie followed with her arm around the shoulder of her child. Har would wait. She knew.

The conflict Nellie endured was beyond the scope of Har's imagination, the reason he could learn so little of her; why her past was never a subject of conversation at the picnics on the deck or evening cocktails on his patio. When the stories of amusing childhood exploits were tossed back and forth, what did she have to tell? Raised poor and hungry, educated in strict Catholic schools, a scrawny impressionable Irish girl in a faded dress; it was a bleak, humorless trap with nothing amusing about it.

Between spelling and ciphering she had listened in cold classrooms to the starched nuns' instructions that sin was as much the result of thought as deed; that Hell awaited those who stepped off God's narrowly prescribed path— these were uncompromising lessons pounded deeply into a fragile psyche that even years later she could not be overcome. The warnings were persistent, echoing in her head, recurring in dreams that would shake her awake. Nightmares despite her unrelenting belief that Jesus would forgive her. Now more than ever, that her early trials were long ended and she lived a life of fortune, privileged and sheltered, the specter of her past sins came back to haunt her with increased intensity. How could she deserve all this with her record? Enfolded by the towering trees and the clapboard homes of Farbridge, she struggled for redemption, making restitution the only way she knew through daily communion, prayer, and gifts of time and money to the parish. The maintenance of her marriage to Otto she came to see as added penance; an obligation for absolution. Despite the temptation her attentive neighbor created with his indelicate suggestions she would endure the lonely weekdays and the stale relationship on the weekends.

Nineteen forty-six was the summer Geraldine gave a week's notice. On her day off she met Eddie, a soldier back from the war. Where once there had been a high-spirited presence, humming and smiling, a sewing and cooking companion, there remained an empty place at the kitchen sink. She left, as she had entered, by the kitchen door. There were embraces on the steps and 'do writes' while Eddie waited with the car motor running. Geraldine held a new suitcase in her hand and wore her best dress and a stylish hat festooned with colored flowers. Nellie gave her the sheets from the double bed she and Otto no longer used and the towels from the maid's bath. Otto slipped two hundred dollars in her hand. They watched her go sitting bolt upright, eyes straight ahead as Eddie steered out the driveway. Her departure left an eerie quiet in the house. They never heard from her again, not a word. Nellie thought that she had gone back South.

Otherwise, Otto's summer was untroubled. He bought the maroon Buick Roadmaster sedan he dreamed of. It came with a white plastic steering wheel, white wall tires, the big V-eight, and gray velour seats. Friday nights, after Ruth turned in, he drove the empty roads fighting to stay awake, lighting Old Golds from the pack he tossed on the dash, windows open, the radio turned up full. When he reached the driveway he kept the engine at idle, the crunch of the big tires on the gravel the only sound as the car rolled to a stop. Closing the driver's door softly, he would wander back by whatever light the stars and moon provided to inspect the vegetable garden. Then he turned toward the house. First he went to Maggie's room to kiss her on the forehead and tuck her in again, and then to the bedroom to undress in the dark and, clad in his underwear, slip between the sheets. Nellie, curled up a few feet away, might stir.

Distracted by the prospects of Cook's proposal, Otto stopped amid the plants in the garden to lean on the handle of his rake, his mind adrift contemplating the riches the Cirsonrad deal would bring and how they could be parlayed into something bigger still. He had taken Ruth on a drive to Boston. They toured the factory with one of the engineers. As they walked amid the idle machinery in the cavernous building, the engineer expounded on how quickly and easily a conversion to the manufacture radios for the mass market could be made. Otto had driven up there with the possibility in mind that reality might take hold, that he would recognize Cook's proposal to be a cockeyed pipedream, and that then, he could politely tell him he would pass this one up. The trip had the opposite effect; it magnified his appetite for the deal beyond the point of reconsideration.

Otto and Ruth stayed at the Parker House and wandered about Boston for a day. They found a jeweler and to celebrate the new prospects he bought her a diamond ring to go with the gold wedding band she wore for the benefit of hotel clerks and nosy neighbors. Their union, the "New

York marriage" as they called it, was happy and fun and in their minds required no licenses or sanctification. It was strong and felt permanent. That evening, they had drinks and dinner at Lockobers; Manhattans, oysters, creamed spinach, fresh haddock and Indian pudding with a glass of cognac. The next day on the ferry to Martha's Vineyard they stood on the deck as it pushed through the chop, the cool wind shifting about blew their hair every which way. They stayed at a bed and breakfast with thin walls and a bed that creaked. They stifled their laughter at the challenge that presented. In the morning they walked the beaches and explored the shops that sold souvenir lobster buoys, sailboat pennants, paintings of cottages and dunes, and always, homemade corn relish and muffins. The next day they drove on to Newport and toured along Atlantic Avenue, peering over the walls at the grand 'cottages' before turning the car toward New York, where they arrived Thursday night tanned and tired. Friday Otto checked in with Jim and spent a few hours in the "office" ordering meat and liquor and going over accounts before returning to the apartment for a light supper. They read, played cards, listen to records that dropped from the changer before he kissed her goodnight, walked to the garage and drove to Farbridge.

Assured that the project was a good one, Otto went about raising the money in earnest. His stocks came to almost two hundred fifty thousand. His credit was good. A loan from Grandover Trust was granted and though the value of the restaurant didn't cover the loan, the agreement was sealed in good part by his reputation as a businessman, a pledge of Cirsonrad stock and the friendship he had developed with a vice-president of the bank over drinks. Nellie signed the loan papers only after Otto took a pen and scratched the house off the collateral form. With no further interest in his business affairs and without so much as a wish for "good luck" she signed. With half a million dollars at his disposal he would be a director of Cirsonrad, Inc.

Chapter 45

It was the end of summer. Maggie had a lingering cold. Otto never considered it could be anything more. Nellie worried Maggie would miss the first day of school.

Otto drove to New York the day after Labor Day secure that the transfer of money from his broker and bank to Cook's account had gone smoothly. The weather was hot and dry. An occasional cloud drifted high across the empty sky. He threw his suit jacket on the back seat. All the windows of the Buick were down. The whistle of the wind through the open windows blended with the cadence of the tires on the concrete. He drove with his right hand on the wheel, his left arm on the warm windowsill. He stayed to the right letting cars pass, content to follow, thinking of the radios and televisions the factory would turn out. They would need a supplier for the fine wood for the cabinets and an ad agency; the ad campaign should be ready to go. And they needed a brand name. Something catchy and easy to remember like *Transend or Clearceive*. By the time he reached New York and the traffic demanded his attention, he had thought of a dozen names and had turned to thinking up slogans.

At three a.m. that morning the dusty phone in the dark apartment on Riverside Drive rang twenty times; an hour later it rang again and then no more. Nellie called again in the morning and no answer. Then she called the restaurant at ten; she knew when the chef and manager came in. Did they know where Otto was? No one knew. They wrote Otto a note and left it on the bar by the phone. "Mr. Nielsen call home." The note gave no reason. He found it that afternoon when he came to sit at the end of the bar to go over the accounts. Jim set a scotch and soda on the bar while he dialed Farbridge; he took a sip listening to the ring tone, but no answer. He called again at seven, and looking at his watch excused himself from a conversation with a customer to call at eight and no answer. At nine he called from the apartment as Ruth sat quietly reading, the Victrola that routinely played classics or show tunes turned off. He finally reached Nellie.

"Otto, where have you been?" Her voice a veritable shout suffused with frustration.

"Where have you been?" he replied needling her.

"Maggie's in the hospital."

The words, meant to shock, did, and he couldn't ask fast enough, "What happened?"

"She fell after you left yesterday, by afternoon her whole side was one big bruise. I took her to the pediatrician. He took one look at her and sent her straight to the hospital."

"What's wrong?"

"At first he said it might be something called...." she hesitated and he heard papers rustling as she looked for a note she had written. He could feel her irritation at not being able to pull the note quickly from the scattered papers he pictured on the table by the phone. At last she breathed one word, like a terminal exhale, into the phone, "purpura." She wanted to go on but her voice cracked and she stopped for what seemed an unending lapse to choke back tears, "but the blood count came back and its leukemia. I know the doctor knew it all along. He just couldn't tell me that right away."

"Jesus God." He grunted into the phone. "I'm on my way up there."

Relieved he had avoided a ticket, Otto reached Connecticut in record time, pulled the car into the driveway stopping by the deck not bothering to park in the garage. It was eleven p.m.. Nellie sat in her robe in the kitchen. When he came in she lifted her eyes from the coffee cup; her hair uncombed tumbled in strands about her face. In the fluorescent light it took on a green cast.

"They want to transfer her to a medical center, either New Haven or New York." Nellie said, barely above a whisper. "I told them Columbia-Presbyterian so she'd be near the apartment."

• • •

Nellie rode in the ambulance that morning with Maggie down to the city. Otto followed in the car. By noon on the Pediatric Service the high side rails on the big bed fenced in Maggie's body that made a small mound like a mole tunnel under the green blanket. The intravenous that dripped from the bottle into her thin arm seemed to wash all color from her skin, now chalk white. They sat silently while Maggie slept, reading the newspaper and magazines and listening to the sounds of the hospital floor—ringing phones, overhead pages, the rolling carts, and muffled medical discussions. The nurses in their starched white uniforms came in and out to take a temperature or adjust the drip of the IV. When Maggie awoke, Otto pulled a chair to the bed and softly read from a worn copy of Winnie the Pooh. How different from those carefree times when he read to her at home. There, her room glowed a warm pink, lace curtains on the windows, rugs scattered over the floor and a comforter and pillows on the bed that she shared with dolls and teddy bears. Here, in a windowless cell, with light brown walls and dark brown linoleum, a grim struggle for life would be carried out. On the wall opposite the bed an amateur artist had painted a scene of a miniature village with mice walking about dressed in fancy clothes. Above the village a mouse flew off waving from a hot air balloon.

Nellie and Otto spoke barely a word. Any thought of Cirsonrad vanished. His mind, brimming with optimistic numbers, names and slogans, like a blackboard had been wiped clean. At five o'clock the Chief of Pediatrics, Dr. Allis, entered he room, trailed by three house officers in short white coats and white pants. He sat on the bed by Maggie and asked her how she was and told her how pretty she looked and then he listened to her lungs, his fingers danced over her skin as he felt for lymph nodes in her neck and under her arms and finally he gently tapped the outline of the swollen spleen that loomed in her left belly; all the while asking the house officer who held the chart about the number of "blasts", temperature readings, and if a transfusion had been ordered. Otto tried to follow the conversation, hoping to hear a word of good news, anything positive. Following a few questions, the doctor swung his body upright and in one continuous move jammed his hands into the pockets of his white coat. Small and round-shouldered, his plump face retained the fine features of a boy as though he had not passed that stage. With an automatic sweep of a hand he brushed back the brown bangs that had fallen over his brow. Otto thought he resembled Napoleon. In a softly modulated voice, at once authoritative and sympathetic, he explained with a sigh, that Maggie had acute lymphocytic leukemia, her body had made millions of white blood cells. There were experimental drugs they could try; she might go into remission. "Never give up hope," he said with emphasis, "miracles do happen." After three minutes he was gone.

They agreed to tag-team; Nellie would stay with Maggie days, Otto nights. Shortly thereafter Nellie left and hailed a cab for Riverside Drive. She worked the mail free from the stuffed mailbox and took the cranky little elevator to the fourth floor. Opening the door, she realized the apartment was more than empty, it looked and smelled unlived in; there was no sign of life, no magazines about, no coffee cups in the drainer by the sink. Anger welling up, she pulled open the refrigerator door, a lone catsup bottle. Marching to the bedroom, she opened Otto's bureau drawer, empty. In the closet a few of his old suits and her abandoned dresses. Enraged, she yanked the dresses off the hangers that were sent clattering across the wooden floor. She rammed the dresses in the wastebasket. Slamming the door behind her, she went down the hall, not caring if the door had latched, which it hadn't, and took the last commuter train back to Farbridge.

Otto sat in the chair, going over to Maggie and stroking her forehead when she awoke, otherwise he read the paper or strolled up and down the hallway; but mostly he sat with his forearms on his thighs, his head hanging. He wondered if it would do any good to pray. He tried. It seemed futile; the words didn't seem to go anywhere. He had read in the National Geographic that astronomers had figured the universe to be millions and millions of light years large and wondered how God could hear him when his prayers didn't produce a sound that could be heard in the room. Sometime after midnight the gate on the elevator clanged open and the quiet of the night in the hospital ward rudely broken by a bed that rattled by. The nurses came in and out. He gave up. He went to the lobby and called Ruth from a payphone.

Nellie arrived early the next morning with nightgowns, books and stuffed animals. She asked Otto where he was living. He said he had found an apartment closer to the restaurant. She looked away in disbelief and after that she ignored him. He went home to rest during the day returning by five to see Dr Allis on his evening rounds. This pattern continued for almost four weeks.

Chapter 46

Since the war ended, Otto's Place had been on a run, customers were abundant, profits were up, the future looked golden. Barely a pessimistic word had been spoken in the bar for six months until on Thursday when Otto shared the news of Maggie's illness. There were mumbled words of condolence and gentle pats on the back before his friends, silenced by the news, wandered off and circled about to find an empty seat down the bar. No one would say what he thought, that they had never heard of anyone surviving that disease, that leukemia was hopeless. Before leaving that night they gave Otto lukewarm encouragement expressing wishes for a miracle that none of them remotely believed in. The torrent of balloons and stuffed animals that quickly filled Maggie's hospital room they agreed were the sum total of what could be done by anyone, the doctors included. It was true that as Ed said, there was no limit to what they would spend if it could possibly help; but these men were businessmen, in the essence pragmatists who knew a hopeless case when they saw one.

On the following Monday, Ed Cutler quietly relayed more bad news. Gathering the investor group at the end of the bar, he reported in a somber tone that forebode trouble that there had been a call to his law office that caused his secretary to drop the phone and run into his private office waving a paper message interrupting a meeting with a client. "It said," Cutler paused and continued with carefully measured words modulated for their gravity: "Augustus Cook dropped dead over the weekend." The startled group looked at one another. Otto absorbed another blow, his face a frozen blank, his lunch came up into his throat. Ed went on. Said he had followed up with a phone call to Lexington and the housekeeper told him she had found Mr. Cook dead at the foot of the stairs, an apparent heart attack. True to form, Ed was unruffled. His demeanor affirmed his cool interior, a sang-froid that Otto thought could be patented and sold. Otto's life, everything he valued most, suddenly in grave danger, first his child and now his money. He had sent Cook half a million dollars to place in Cirsonrad stock less than ten days before and now the originator, the prime mover behind the deal, the only one of their group with the expertise, connections and time to see it through, lay in a crumpled mass at the bottom of some stairs!

Ed looked over his half-glasses and reacted to the group's alarm. A broad smile crept across his face. "Cook had not bought the stock! He and Hallowell hadn't closed the deal! They were to meet in the lawyer's office in Boston this very morning!"

Hallelujah! Thank God! Otto had never known anyone to jump for joy, but with this news it was all he could do to keep his feet on the floor. What a turn of events! His spirits shot skyward. He wanted to dance and forgetting the solemnity of the moment, he couldn't resist joking, "By golly, Cook had a knack for doing things right, if it had to happen he got it done in a nick of time!"

The little investor group had dodged a bullet and drank to that. For the first time Otto felt a modicum of relief from his sorrows. The rush of emotions tumbling to the depths and then up again he found strangely exhilarating. They raised a second and a third glass to their departed friend. "God bless good old Cook!"

He arrived at the hospital as Dr Allis entered the room. "Would Mr. and Mrs. Nielsen please step out, there is a small procedure I have to do." The nurse rolled in a little cart as Otto and Nellie left. In the grim cafeteria Otto bought two coffees and they headed for a table in the most remote corner. The tray was awkward, some coffee splashed over the rim of the thick china cups onto the saucers as Otto put it down. Nellie put paper napkins under the cups.

"You've been drinking." The blue in her eyes turned steely as she looked at him.

"Its part of my job, I drink with the customers. You know that I pace myself."

"You've more than paced yourself," she spit out.

"I had some bad news and then some good news today," he said, almost smiling, showing just a crinkle of the crow's feet at the corners of his eyes. "Poor old Cook died over the weekend, but luckily the Cirsonrad deal had not gone through. Our money is safe."

"I'm sorry," she said, meaning she was sorry that Cook was dead even though she had never liked him. She had no interest in the deal. They were silent for a while, looking out of the window at the lawn between the buildings sipping the coffee and watching squirrels chase up and down the trees and the pigeons peck about in the dirt. Then she began again. "I hired a private investigator." Her eyes studied his face for any hint of discomfort.

He wasn't sure of her intentions. Why?

He breathed an "Oh." A declarative fragment designed to exhibit a detached interest, hiding his concern, of which there was plenty.

"He followed you to an apartment in the Fifties, said you were living with a woman there. I have pictures of you and her going in and out of the building, Ruthie isn't it?" she continued as calmly as she might have been reading the social page in the local paper out loud—Mr. and Mrs. So and So are returning from a three-week trip. He gave the only reply possible, a nod to the affirmative. Then she said simply "I want a divorce."

Otto felt a wave of nausea; he blanched white, the drinks and coffee swirled about in his stomach. What response could he have? His stared at his hands, then wordless he looked at her hoping some reasonable words would come to mind. There was no explanation that she could possibly accept. They both knew that. She stood, he heard the scrape of the metal chair legs on the granite floor, and he watched her back as she walked away, head up, the sordid bit of business finished. She was beautiful and he had to admire what she had done. He respected her, she had done it with class; no shouts, no tears, no curses; he had been skewered neatly, cleanly, and properly. She had conveyed her message. They were done, period. And that made him ill. Her unexpected grit and determination easily overcame the risk of losing Farbridge, that with a few simple words she made it humiliatingly clear that his rationalizations on which he had relied were dead wrong. She would not stay in the marriage no matter the consequences, and it was not that surprise, stunning as it was, that burned him to the core, but her absolute resolve. How he admired her for that … and the unexpected, sudden, world-shattering sense of loss he felt as soon as she spoke the words. The words hurt beyond all measure. He had not calculated the cost in those terms: sensate, demoralizing, and regretful.

In the men's room he splashed cold water in his face then took the elevator back upstairs. The procedure was over. Dr Allis was leaving.

Maggie slept, apparently sedated. They talked with the doctor. More guarded optimism. Otto and Nellie stood together, as though nothing had occurred, as if it was just one more sorrowful day nodding and listening to the doctor's message that was always the same: don't give up hope. When he finished speaking Nellie gathered her things and left for the night. Their life together in that room remained unaltered, but in every other respect, it was over.

That night Otto had a nightmare. He rarely dreamed. In the dream the apartment shook, he looked out at a street. He saw flashes of flame, people running through the dark, buildings crumbling, facades breaking away, crashing down hurling up dust. He didn't know if he was in London or Berlin or New York or who was bombing the city or why. He found himself running barefoot in the street, falling walls bursting into rubble behind him. The dream woke him up.

Over drinks that afternoon, he asked Doctor Weinstein about it.

"Your subconscious is reacting to your life in crisis, certainly not news to you."

"Bad things happen in threes, don't they?" Otto asked.

"That's what they say," the elderly doctor replied.

"Well, the third shoe has just dropped, so to speak." Otto went on to relate how Nellie had discovered he lived weekdays with his paramour, lived a double life. And hearing of the encounter in the hospital cafeteria the old doctor asked, "Are there more shoes?"

"No. But I feel rotten, ashamed that it has come to this."

"You should," was his unsympathetic reply.

"You know at first when the affair started three years ago I had a hard time with it, the guilt I mean; but I gradually resolved it, took a year or so."

"Is that so? Resolving guilt is my job. It often requires professional help," Weinstein said without a hint of humor.

"I saved you the trouble. But now I have to deal with the consequences."

"So will she," the doctor said, not a bit consoling.

"You think it was wrong? It didn't hurt anyone, at least until now," Otto pleaded.

"That's right, until now."

"Doc, I'm not making excuses, but Nellie chose to move up to Farbridge, she has her friends and the Church up there now. You know she didn't like the restaurant and the drinking, especially my drinking. Which, Doc, you see, isn't all that bad. And the conversations around here didn't interest her, either—business, politics, jokes, things like that bored her." Otto searched the doctor's eyes for some small sign of understanding. Seeing none he went on. "She has become more and more introspective and devotional. Our marriage went downhill long before anything happened between Ruth and me. Nellie and I were essentially separated, estranged. She's the one who left me here. She wanted twin beds for Pete's sake."

"So? You work on it and fix it." The doctor realized his advice was too late to be meaningful so he changed tacks. "We all knew, by the way, we've seen you around town with, Ruthie, isn't it?" The little doctor had a trace of a wry smile.

"Ruth. She doesn't like Ruthie; it's too unsophisticated, childish." Otto corrected and then went on, "So why didn't you say something?"

"Interesting question. You know, I don't know. I presume there's an unwritten code of conduct among male friends for addressing or not addressing one another's adulterous misadventures." The doctor amused himself with that concept.

"So, you think I was wrong,"

"You want the truth?"

"That's what I'm paying for," Otto said nodding at the doctor's scotch and soda.

"Then yes, absolutely."

Chapter 47

Otto couldn't place when or precisely why his mind had changed. He thought it must have been her arms. They had become covered by black and blue blotches and scattered with bright red needle marks. At night sitting by Maggie as she slept he shifted about to get comfortable in the grimy chair in the corner and for weeks made unfocused prayers, hoping they were not futile, that there would be some miracle, that somehow this was all a bad dream and he would wake up and life would return to what it had been. That she might live. But now he had begun to pray she could die, that the suffering would end. He was certain these bitter prayers would be answered even without divine intervention; but his plea was for more, that it would be soon. Father Mike had come in on the day Maggie arrived and pinned a Saint Christopher medal on her gown and prayed with Nellie each afternoon. And somehow Father Mike always smiled. Otto reasoned the priest truly believed that there was a caring God who called this child to a better place, following, so to speak, an angelic Peter Pan to a heavenly Neverland; otherwise, Otto thought dealing day after day with such misery would have driven him crazy. Otto wished he had a grain of faith such as that, how it would help him now. But for Otto the afterlife, if he gave it any consideration at all, had consisted in the past of the rough and tumble land of the Nordic folk tales. Certainly Valhalla wasn't a place for an innocent child, filled as it was with rapacious thugs. She had to go to a better place. And he, if nothing else, was certain of that.

    Near the end Nellie stayed later, taking the last train back. Otto couldn't remember when they had spoken together that soulfully, opened up, and made apologies of sorts. At the same table in the back of the cafeteria, they spoke of the life they shared and how, ironically, at this time when they stood so united, that circumstances had been unalterably changed and when Maggie died they would part. No looking back. Neither could express it directly, but in so many words that evening they came to realize how they had stood in their marriage back to back, looking out, not inward for solace and support; Otto looked to the bar and his friends, she to the Church. Was it that big a deal for him to join the Church, to bend a bit, to pretend, to feel like a hypocrite for her sake? And maybe not drink so much? And couldn't she give it up a little, get over this guilt thing, give the Church a break? Maybe help at the restaurant several days a week, take an interest in his business affairs and friends? Looking at her he wanted to reach across the table and take her hand, but didn't. He had let go of it a long time ago.

    Though they had weeks to prepare, the end was a shock, the finality of it, the last ember of hope gone cold. Maggie had difficulty breathing about eleven p.m.. Otto called the nurse, she came in and out and called the house officer, a sandy haired kid who studied Maggie's breathing with a stethoscope wrinkling his brow as he strained to hear the faint breath sounds. He stood and walked out without a word. Otto sat in the dark wondering what was to happen next. Magically in ten minutes Father Mike appeared. He nodded to Otto and leaned over the bed to speak with Maggie. Otto couldn't hear what was said, just watched the priest's head bob up and down in response to the child's whispers. Father Mike motioned to Otto and they went into the hall. "She wants to be confirmed in the Church," the priest said. It was the first time Otto had seen him frown. "That takes a bishop. I can't promise but I'll try." Alone again with Maggie, drifting in and out of sleep, Otto was awakened by the crash of the elevator door and clang of the gate at the end of the hall. It was two a.m.. There was a commotion, voices, and footsteps. He looked out of the room and recognized Father Mike with another priest accompanied a short man in a black cassock with a red sash about his waist. Like a whirlwind they swept down the empty hallway and stopped at the child's bedside. Otto stood against the wall as she, barely able to swallow, received the sacraments. The Bishop turned and spoke with Otto, expressing his sorrow and wishing him peace. Then just as suddenly, with a clank of the elevator door, they were gone and Otto and Maggie were alone again. In a while Father Mike came back and leaned in the doorway. "Do you know who that was?" he asked smiling. Otto bit his tongue. He was tempted to wisecrack "the Lone Ranger," but shook his head. "Cardinal Spellman, can you believe he came out in the middle of the night!" Father Mike grinned from ear to ear. He, a simple priest had pulled off an ecclesiastical coup. Otto concluded he had no idea what to believe any longer, but understood he had witnessed the essence of what this great religion was about, what gave it beauty and meaning.

  She died late in the evening two days later. Otto and Nellie were with her. She wasn't afraid. Father Mike and the Cardinal had done that for her. Otto had come to understand that quite simply that was their job. The sandy haired house officer had been called. This time he looked up, lifting the stethoscope off her chest and said she was gone. That was it. No crash of thunder or peeling of bells. Nellie straightened the bedclothes about Maggie, arranged her hair on the pillow, packed up her belongings and said good-bye. Her countenance was stone-like, marbleized in an expressionless pantomime, unchanged by the pain that she somehow internalized; her eyes as she walked out as unseeing as those in a sculpted face. She walked up the hall toward the elevator, past the nurses' station, not seeing or wishing to recognize Father Mike who looked up from the chart he was reading with an expression of sympathy. At the elevator she turned down the stairway and with each floor she increased her pace until reaching the lobby she broke into a run to the cabstand. She took the train home, silent and impassive as the scenery clicked by.

Otto cried for the first time he could remember, sitting in that chair he had hated so. The nurse came in, cleaned off the bedside table, and left. In a while she came again and asked if there was anything she could get him. No, he just wanted to sit there. Now he couldn't let it end. A gurney with a yellow drape over it rolled up outside the door. The sandy haired house officer in a whisper asked to speak with him. "Would he permit an autopsy?" Then he recited a well-practiced speech about "that's how we learn about disease, help others, and advance medical science." Otto felt sorry for the poor kid having to ask this stinking question, but couldn't suppress his anger at it; the thought of it turned his stomach. No! He wouldn't allow that final indignity. He sat once more. Events in the room became frozen. The nurse came in again and asked if there was anything she could do. She said they couldn't take Maggie away until Otto left. He wouldn't leave. He sat in the chair with his daughter. Tears ran down his face. After an hour of so Father Mike came and took him gently by the arm and led him out.

By then it was five a.m.; the sun was beginning to cast some light on the street over the buildings. He walked over one hundred and twenty blocks down Broadway to the apartment. His trench coat was open, the belt hung loose, he looked down as he shuffled along, counting the cracks in the sidewalk, kicking trash to the curb. When he found an open bar he stopped. He drank until he ran out of money; local bars, black bars in Harlem, hotel lounges. He reached the apartment that afternoon thoroughly drunk. Ruth opened the door, he didn't have to say what had happened; he couldn't have spoken the words. She helped him with his clothes, put him in the shower and into bed.

The funeral was small; the hearse and a limousine and four or five cars followed out to the Catholic cemetery on a hill in Farbridge. Nellie had bought two plots there. He stood with her for the last time by the grave as they buried their child. Afterward he went to the house and packed his things. He looked in the bedside table. There was the little purple book on renewing faith in the Church he had tossed there. He thought he might look at it sometime and flipped it into the suitcase. He carried out boxes of books and armfuls of clothes to spread across the back seat of the Buick and when he passed with the two suitcases, he looked into the living room where Nellie sat on the sofa in her funeral clothes, talking quietly with some neighborhood ladies. There was an untouched plate of sandwiches on the coffee table in front of them. He leaned in the doorway to say good-bye. She looked up from her conversation, smiled and made a little wave. That was it, the last act of their marriage, absolutely trivial; as if he were going to the corner store for cigarettes.

• • •

At the bar he spoke with the doctor. No bullshit there.

"Oh God, Otto, you're asking me that, a Jew."

"I'm serious, how can a just God let these things happen? Her suffering was so wrong, so unfair. Where's the justice, the goodness?"

"That's the oldest question in the book, a tired old cliché, and Otto I have heard it in one form or another everyday for the last twenty years. Why do the innocent suffer?" The little doctor paused, and then said, "You would think I would have an answer by now. There's no answer. God only gave us gravity, not fairness and justice."

"How's that?"

"Otto, He gave us the laws of nature and the ability to reason, and to figure them out. He lets us learn what works and what doesn't, which has led to physics and biology and so on. In other words, he gives us a chance to make things better, if we choose, for ourselves … human advancement and all that. Part of that package of course is the ability to tell right from wrong, good from evil, and that choice is ours, from here, not from somewhere way out there. But, I'm getting off tract." He moved his glass in circles and studied the wet tracks it made on the bar, then he began again, "to answer your question, He made things fair only in the sense that those natural laws apply to us all equally, nature has no favorites, doesn't distinguish good or bad, just what works and what doesn't, as Darwin demonstrated with his finches. As for justice, whether He metes out justice in the long run we'll have to wait and see, won't we."

Otto patted him on the back. The cost of another free drink well spent.

In a few weeks life had begun to equilibrate. Without the weekends to worry about, things were simpler for Otto though he could not speak of Maggie, even in the years to come, without his voice cracking.

Chapter 48

Upon returning from the funeral, Nellie sat in the living room and listened to Otto's footsteps in the bedroom above as he packed. She waited for him to leave, keeping her distance, dreading the awkward goodbye. The doorbell rang. Still dressed in black from the funeral, she answered. At the door, two neighbors held plates of sandwiches. One was the mother of the little boy Maggie played with. Nellie didn't want company, but trapped, she opened the door widely, and summoned a smile inviting them in. They sat together in the living room and talked softly of Maggie. This visit, this quaint custom, so different than the boisterous wakes of Nellie's childhood, permitted her to talk and recall the happy times with Maggie and soon the conversation became easy and pleasant, the memories comforting, and in the end she was glad they had come.

When Otto, with two suitcases in hand leaned through the doorway to say good-bye, Nellie didn't get up. The ladies helped with that too. There would be no opportunity for a difficult, drawn out farewell. Careful not to give the impression that the marriage was anything but over, she made a small smile and waved from the sofa, as if he were running to the store for cigarettes.

In the empty house that night the dark was darker, the shadows deeper, the creaks and groans of the boards that broke the silence louder. She put the big pistol under her pillow. No Maggie, no Geraldine, she even missed Otto. She felt small and alone in her bed. Reading was futile. The torment started. The same irritating question seethed within, the one with no satisfactory answer turned over in her mind: how could He let this happen to her child? Hadn't she prayed enough? Was this her punishment? Flinging down the book and leaping from the bed she screamed into the empty room. "Is this it, have I finally paid the price now? Damn You!"

As a child, sitting in the cold church while the parents cried, she had accepted unquestioned the liturgical explanations for a child's death in the sorrowful homilies that accompanied the scene. But the vision of her child in a coffin under the mound of fresh dirt made them ring hollow, irrational and intensely cruel. "Damn You! Damn You! Damn You!" The screams came and came until she was bent over and breathless and her spent voice grated her throat. She lay down once again, but was far too agitated to sleep. She left the bed and in the kitchen found Otto's scotch and at the table under the harsh fluorescent light she stared at the bottle, making herself squeeze three or four gulps down until the repulsive taste made her put it away. For what seemed hours, she sat with her head in her hands, pondering what all this had meant. Then came the rush of nausea. She ran and knelt before the commode, vomiting the little sandwiches and the scotch, retching until there was nothing but green bile and icy sweat. Back in the bedroom, she took down the crucifix, and along with her missal put it in the bedside drawer and slammed it shut. The table jumped, crashing against the wall, throwing the lamp and phone to the floor. She carried the little table down two flights to the dusty basement and set it roughly beside the furnace. When she turned to climb the basement stairs she stubbed her toe, a small cut bled. "Damn you!" she shouted again. "Can't you ever stop? Can't you leave me alone?" It was eleven p.m..

She showered, dried her hair and changed into white silk pajamas, slippers and a robe. She would not stay in this skeleton of a house, cloistered for reasons she now questioned, praying to a God she couldn't understand, that enraged her, that at this moment she hated.

At one a.m. she turned the last of the lights out and left through the kitchen door carrying a flashlight. She picked her way past the garage and vegetable garden, through the path in the hemlocks, across the big lawn by Har's swimming pool, onto the flagstone patio, up the back stoop stairs and rang the bell. When there was no response, she rapped sharply on the windowpane in the door. A light went on upstairs, tossing light onto the patio. Then a light on the staircase at the other end of the big house dimly lit the interior. She watched Har, in a robe, pad toward the door and leaning forward peer myopically through the glass at her. The latch clacked and the door swung open, no words, he stood aside to let her pass.

"Har, may I stay here tonight? The house is too empty."

"Of course, the guest room is made up."

She followed him back upstairs as he turned the lights out one by one. He headed past the master bedroom but she stopped in the hall where the light from the bedside lamp spilled out of the doorway. "May I join you?" she asked as simply, as if she were asking to share a table. "I can't be alone, not tonight."

That morning, Har made bacon and eggs. They talked over coffee. He learned of the private investigator's report of Otto's secret life and of Nellie's plans for divorce and took no joy in it; in fact the news of her pending divorce and the new freedom that allowed for the relationship to become more than a dalliance panicked him. He wasn't sure he wanted someone to dry the dishes he washed when the drainer did perfectly well.

Later that morning, at the large antique desk in his office, Har Parsons looked into space and rhythmically turned a pencil over and over, sliding his fingers down to the eraser then to the point. Unable to concentrate on the documents before him, he called in his assistant and asked him to read through them and put a check mark in the margin where there were questions. Now he realized he was playing with fire; his mood intermittent, swung from delight to alarm. Since boyhood his life had been carefully programmed—he had been sent up the road to boarding school in Wallingford and then on to Yale, and if he chose to stay in line he would be safe, nothing in his life left to chance or effort or merit for that matter and, as expected, he moved through the prepared steps to his birthright, to the presidency of the bank. His social life was decreed in a similar manner; his wife he had known from private school tea dances and coming-out parties, all part of a veritable caste system that strove to make introductions only among members of the social select. How abruptly the tables had turned on him; this situation with Nellie had reached a place he hadn't planned on, she had taken control. He chided himself. The flirtations she had spurned, the little overtures that she seemed to reject absolutely, he now realized she had understood very well, and now she had in effect last night called his bluff. But most troubling, he realized she had the one weapon he couldn't fend; she effused a remarkably classy sensuality, an erotic fantasy he was unable to resist.

At this stage of life his second bachelorhood had provided a pleasant milieu. He had watched as the warm marriage next door turn frosty over the years; gradually, like a skim of ice slowly thickening on the surface of a pond, and he wanted no part of that, marriage again was not for him, not without serious consideration; it would require lengthy evaluation like a very risky loan, the ones with high potential that were hard to pass up he dealt with from time to time. He resolved to proceed cautiously, if the question of matrimony came up, he would have figured a way out, an exit plan if necessary; but then he thought of how they had lain together, two thin layers of cloth between them, the perfume in her hair, his arm draped over her side in a half embrace, brushing her breast, and the promise of more, the incredible more. And that could be a permanent picture?

"Mr. Parsons, Mr. Calmotti is here to see you," his secretary announced.

His mind snapped back to the business at hand. One of those upstart Italian builders raising money again, he thought, getting rich putting those tacky little tract houses all over the landscape.

"Come in Mr. Calmotti, please have a seat." He heard himself say. "Can my secretary get you some coffee?"

Chapter 49

Two weeks after the funeral Otto received a letter that had been crumpled into a ball, then smoothed out, unevenly folded, and stuffed roughly into an envelop with a stamp pasted askew and posted to the apartment on Riverside Drive. He concluded Nellie had read the letter, wadded it up and then in a flash of remorse pulled it from the wastebasket having decided, after all, to send it on. Otto smoothed out the creases on a tabletop with the palm of his hand, and read the scrawl written in large, careless script across the letterhead. She would not give him a word of greeting or sentiment, it read simply: "This came. You should read it. N." Her bitterness tightened his throat as if bile had run up.

W. Rosser Wilson

Dear Mr. and Mrs. Nielsen,

I wish to express my sincerest condolences to you on the tragic loss of your beautiful daughter. My heart dropped when I made early morning rounds and looked into her room and saw the empty bed. The house officers told me she died last evening. I am so sorry we couldn't do more for her.

She was a very special child. Did you know I purposely saw her as my final patient on afternoon rounds? She always had a smile for me, no matter how much pain or fear she felt, her smile could lift my day. I took that smile home with me and it often helped me get through the night.

There are some patients a physician never forgets. When I am old and sitting by the fire some winter evening and think back on my years as a doctor, her face and smile, I know, will come back to me through time.

Again, my condolences to you both and I am grateful to you for giving me the privilege of participating in your daughter's care.

Sincerely,
Frederick C. Allis MD
Professor of Pediatrics

• • •

Otto read the letter twice, and then because he was alone, out loud in a voice infused with emotion wavering and raspy. After Ruth came home, he controlled his voice and read it to her, and then walked to the bookshelf, hiding the tears that blinded him, and tucked it in the little purple book the priests had left and that for some reason he felt compelled to keep. He had no plans to open it. No disrespect to his clerical friends. He simply had no interest in the Church, any church, though if he had a bible he would have put the letter there. Ruth set down her reading in her lap and watched Otto as he read; she saw the tears and recognized his shame at what he had been taught to be weakness. She pretended not to notice them. She had brothers and knew well from them the earliest lesson of manhood, buck-up, boys don't cry, had been impressed into Otto's nature and only when he was alone he would let this affliction be overcome. With the last words of the letter she lifted her book again and adjusted the light and said the letter was "eloquent" meaning poignant, heart rending, moving, though those tender words were not words Otto would appreciate and were left unsaid.

These were troubling days. He loathed mornings most and let sleep, like a pool thick with molasses, pull him down and hold him until noon when he forced himself free. He could not defeat the sleep and felt degraded by the need, but with sleep he fought the depression. By late afternoon he walked to the bar again. Jim poured him a scotch and after two or three refills the anguish would be suppressed and he could once more play the part of host. When the rays of the setting sun emerged from a gap in the buildings across the street and burst through the windows of the bar and lit up the room with a rosy light, the gloom faded and once again he was at home in the temple he had built and dedicated to companionship and prosperity. And by this time, a few weeks later, his pals in the little investment group had shucked all signs of mourning, no more long faces and useless words of sympathy; the laughter and bear hugs, jokes and banter returned. They spoke with enthusiasm again…business and politics mixed in air made aromatic with tobacco smoke. By evening the icy highball glass in his hand had a lovely, hard, sensual feel that he craved as much as the restorative contents. All the while, among the chatter and turmoil of the bar, he followed the operation of the business, the organized efficiency of the waiters and busboys doing their work threading among the tables. He had returned to Nirvana. Only the quiet of his garden suited his psyche more. There in the solitude laboring for hours in the bright sun among the rows of plants, if he had conversations with God, that's where they spoke. But at the moment he had nothing to say to Him at all and as for the garden, it lay fallow in Connecticut filling with weeds. Someday somebody would make it a lawn.

By nine o'clock Otto began to watch the door for Ruth to come and join him for dinner, a ritual that energized him because she loved the place so and he shared in her delight, seeing it through her eyes, new and exciting once again. Her arrival was anticipated by his assembled bar buddies because once again she enjoyed her flair for style and every now and then wore a mad innovation that she knew would evoke a chuckle or a clever remark. Ed Cutler, assuming a fatherly manner, would look over his half glasses to greet her with a kiss on the forehead and hold her away at arms length like a child and mutter, "My oh my, what do we have here?" And she loved it. After a few words Ed would look about to see if there were guests in the restaurant who could make the evening an event, somebody she had read about in the paper or a magazine, somebody she could dream about the next day. He would point them out, so that she and Otto could drop by the table with a short word of welcome, a Hello from the host and hostess, owners of Otto's Place, usually a few sentences and occasionally, if invited to sit down, a visit. Writers they found to be the most receptive, celebrities who went unrecognized on the street, the printed word more revealing of character than a face, except for the exalted few like Hemingway, Fitzgerald and Menken.

One night Ed gave a nod toward a table with unfamiliar faces, and whispered in Otto's ear the names of Andy White and Harold Ross. "Writer and Editor," he said. Seeing no indication of comprehension in Otto's eyes, he added facts, *"The New Yorker,* the magazine, you know." That did strike home. Ruth read the magazine each week, copies piled up beside her reading chair and bedside table, some reread before they were discarded. Otto took Ruth's hand and led her to the table to make introductions and offer a bottle of wine. The encounter lasted less than five minutes.

After the visit leaning forward over her dinner while she watched Andy and Harold from Otto's table in the back of the room beside the kitchen door she said, "You know who they are don't you, Otto?" Andy wrote *Stuart Little* and Harold started *The New Yorker* from scratch, she enthused. She called them by the first names from that time forward. Ruth reminisced for months.

"From now on, Otto, make sure you and Ed point all the writers out."

"How do we recognize them? How are writers supposed to look?"

"Pale and stooped from spending days and nights bent over a typewriter in a dark room. Oh yes, thick glasses, definitely thick glasses. Nearsighted from reading all the small print."

Late one afternoon Gino Tortorici strolled in. He stopped and squinted for a moment while his eyes made certain that the place was the same. Studying the dim outlines of the patrons he recognized that the bar was inhabited by the same inmates he had left behind when he headed off to war. Nothing had changed, same crowd only larger. Mel saw him first and shouted, "Hey, look what the cat dragged in, Mr. Vitalis, beautiful as ever!" There stood the new mid-Manhattan Branch Manager for Merrill, Lynch, Pierce, Fenner, and Bean dressed in a handmade suit, chalk striped navy blue with vest, that fit as if molded, French cuffs peaking out the sleeves. Handshakes and drinks around.

"Who the Hell is Bean?" Mel was shouting now over the din.

"You kidding. Nobody even knows who Fenner is," Gino shouted back.

"You get them to kick one of those creeps out and put Tortorici in there."

Gino came in regularly after that, several times a week, just for a drink or two, before heading home to his twin boys and wife. Gino had pictures and she was the well-endowed woman Otto remembered from the picture Ruth had shown him before ripping it up and stuffing it in the trash. On a quiet, overcast afternoon when Otto and Gino found themselves alone, the bar dark and empty and Jim out of earshot, Otto, suspecting the worst, asked about Silvio. "Your Dad hasn't been in for a while," he said. Gino looked aside, swallowed, his larynx rising up and settling back in over his tie, and said in a hoarse whisper, "the mob killed him, disappeared, never found him." Otto bought Gino several drinks and they talked about old times. Thumbing through a catalog of events, a child's death, Otto's bitter divorce, until finally Gino asked how Ruthie was and said he was glad she was happy, that with Otto she was better off. They had come to the final page; the past had been revisited and put in order. Now that he was in charge, Jim scolded Otto for giving drinks away. Otto slid ten dollars over the bar to put in the till.

When alone at the bar Otto pictured Nellie in the living room, the fireplace roaring, feeding old photos or any flammable detritus from the life he left behind into it; her features in the roiling light a study in grim satisfaction. Good riddance to you Otto! There had been brief notes written as lovers, but their courtship had no separations that generated love letters worth saving, so there would be no ribbon-wrapped packet of envelopes for her to toss into the leaping flames. The imaginary scene of the cleansing bonfire provided a conclusion for him. Had he had any, he would have thrown her letters in the trash as well.

A letter arrived from Denmark, postmarked Copenhagen, from Kirsten. She had been his first love lost and set his standard for beauty, station and wealth, the ideal that he had duplicated in America. Ruth had replaced her in Otto's earthy dreams. Her news, at first, a bland recounting of domestic events: the entire family had survived the war, Niels retired, put Hans in charge and she had married Hans' best friend, a man Otto imagined her father promoted up through the corporate organization always, of course, a step behind Hans. Kirsten had three children but she correctly assumed that would hold little interest for Otto and skipped over any details. The paragraph ended at the bottom of the first page.

Otto laid the letter down and closed his eyes, he could not suppress the feelings that had been exhumed; the old rage, the jealousy, the disappointment, the aspersions of inferiority his cousin's family cast upon him. He turned the letter over and began to read the writing on the back. Here he found the purpose of the letter. It was a sympathy note. She was writing to express her sorrow upon learning that his Uncle Erik had been arrested and shot by the Gestapo for hiding Jews in the loft of the barn. She assumed Otto knew. The news struck him as incredible and he read the sentence over as if somehow it would be different the second time, that he had skipped over a word that would change the meaning. Erik wasn't a moralist or interested in heroics. Otto had never heard a word from him that spoke to one man's obligations to others or any particular concern about the plight of anyone, troubled or poor. Astrid in her letters hadn't let on and Otto had imagined his uncle dying in bed from a heart attack or some mysterious infection much as his Grandfather had, cursing Deaths' angel from between clean sheets. And Astrid and Bente there to nurse and attend to the internment. Now it was clear his mother kept the truth from him to spare him, he need not know the truth, secure as he was on the other side of the Atlantic. Why disturb his peace? And for her own sake, she had dealt with pain as she had always had, the Danish way, compressing the fury in her heart, refusing to speak of the details of it. Otto imagined the scene. Erik shot like a dog, his crumpled body face down in the dirt by the edge of a field. He was certain his mother trembled as she fought to exclude the details from her letters. Rage at the Germans yes; but also rage toward Erik, her rash, imprudent brother, for doing such a foolhardy thing. They could have all been shot. At a minimum he had left the two old women abandoned, bereft, and for whom or what, some strangers?

Otto tore off the return address from the right hand corner of Kirsten's letter and put it in his desk. He had no reason to write. What could he say, "Thanks for the letter?" When he returned to Denmark, having conquered America, with his treasure, Ruth, by his side, he would look her up, make the comparisons, measure his success, and determine his score.

• • •

Christmastime brought bad tidings. Ed Cutler had been negotiating with the lawyers representing Cook's estate, an old Boston firm that had protected the principal at the nucleus of the family's fortunes since the whaling and China trade days. He worked to wrest free the large advancement of funds forwarded by members of the Otto's Place Investment Group to Cook for the purchase of Cirsonrad stock. Cook's family's tight fisted lawyers, tested and hardened by attacks on those assets for two centuries were not willing to give up a dime. Indeed they welcomed the financial boon of a legal struggle, especially as they had little risk of losing, figuring the New England courts to be inbred and friendly.

The estate's attorneys informed Ed that Augustus had parked the checks in his personal account where on that fatal weekend the money sat awaiting the opening of business on Monday. The difficulty to be overcome, one that appeared nearly insurmountable, was that Cook's will left everything upon his death to a trust and that trust in turn directed all the funds to be divided among a list of schools and charities. Ed's attempts to exclude the Otto's Place Investor's funds from the estate and direct the Probate Court to the return the monies to the investors had gone nowhere. The raffs of legal correspondence, phone calls pressing one point or another had come to naught and so by the end of the year, December 31st, the funds would be dispersed to the beneficiaries. Once that happened, the only recourse: to sue the beneficiaries—a dismal prospect, at best. As Ed put it, "The schools and charities will cling to the money proclaiming a pressing need for every cent." Then his voice rose in a high plaintive tremolo imitating a prospective opposing lawyer. "Oh, judge, please, please think of those poor widows and orphans and the penniless students. What in heavens name will they do deprived of their rightful gift, a gift Mr. Cook rejoiced in making?" The group's suit, he concluded, will appear to be the equivalent of theft from the most weak, hapless and deserving members of society. The bleak prospects of regaining any of the money he had struggled to make made Otto ill. For weeks he suffered stomach cramps, headaches, and a tremor that shook his morning coffee cup. Now sleep became elusive. He drank more. Doc wrote him a prescription for a barbituate.

Not unexpectedly, Nellie sued for divorce; grounds adultery. Otto was to drive to Farbridge after the first of the year for a meeting with her lawyers. Ed's firm drew up papers. She would sign over her interest in the sale of the restaurant, and Otto would exercise a quitclaim deed giving her the house. A Connecticut court would set the alimony payments he would pay. There were no other assets unless Ed's efforts against the Cook estate proved successful. Otto's income from the restaurant just covered living expenses and the interest on the loan Grandover Trust lent to buy the stock. He saw no way of repaying the principal. His friend at the bank became nervous. There was no recourse; the court would order a settlement. That was it. What could he do?

Otto and Ruth were broke. They hunkered down, watched every nickel. She said of the predicament, "Boy, don't we have all the luck!" But they were still in New York. Finding free things to do became a game. They haunted the museums, galleries, parks, and for a treat went to Radio City or the Roxy. When melancholy set in, Ruth and the city were his salvation. With Ruth by his side, Otto could be distracted. She made the days bearable.

Otto drove to Farbridge on the last Monday in January 1947. It was one of those rare winter days during a January thaw when the sun shone warm. Whipped cream clouds floated in a china blue sky, and the melting snowdrifts sent black rivulets across the gray macadam of the roads. He didn't need a coat. Otto pulled up to the Nellie's lawyer's office at eleven. He looked for Nellie's car in the parking lot, but didn't see it there. Inside he found Nellie, hair up the way she knew he liked it, elegant in a pink suit, silk blouse, a pearl necklace and earrings he didn't recognize. The pin on her suit jacket he thought must be costume jewelry; those couldn't be real rubies. She sat beside her attorney, her defender, and it was clear from the richly paneled surroundings they would not be defeated. In the hush of the little conference room the papers made a soft sanding sound as they slid back and forth across the table for signing. In fifteen minutes it was finished, they stood, shook hands, very antiseptic, and very final. No longer welcome, he left alone, alone as he had ever felt. He took his time putting the papers in a folder on the front seat and then fumbled for his cigarettes and lit one waiting for her to come out; he wanted to see which car was hers. They were all expensive, beyond her price range. And he wanted one more look at her, a final depiction, like a last snapshot to take to carry in his mind. She didn't come out. She had more business with the lawyers. He could only guess at what that business could be; already she was better off without him! He put the windows down in the Buick, and headed for the cemetery.

    He tossed his cigarette out as he gunned the V-eight up the long hill to the cemetery gate. Walking to the gravesite his shoes sank in the cold wet ground. The gravestone they had ordered for Maggie was up. MARGARET ANNE NIELSEN cut into the gray granite. He read the dates to make certain they were correct. Then he stood and looked at it wondering how this could have happened, how all his expectations for this life in America had collapsed.

He heard a shout. "Hey mister, your car's on fire!" a cemetery worker yelled across half an acre of headstones. Otto looked up to see black smoke pouring from the windows of the Buick. As he ran up he realized the cigarette he had thrown from the driver's window had flown back and set the back seat on fire. The cemetery worker pulled a hose from the shed, screwed it onto a garden hydrant, turned the spigot, the water burped from the nozzle. He aimed the spray through the back window of the beautiful maroon Roadmaster and in a few minutes the flames were out. The inside of the car was covered in black soot. Otto borrowed a rag to clean the windshield, gave the worker a dollar, and drove back down the hill. The incline made the icy water from the back of the car run under the front seat and fill his shoes. By now a sheet of steel gray clouds blotted out the sun and the rare warm January day vanished. It was winter again. When Otto reached New York his feet were numb, he couldn't feel the pedals. He traded the destroyed Buick for a used robin's egg blue Nash Rambler he hated. A cheap piece of junk, he called it. Ruth took the news with a shrug; though she told him it did strain her good humor more than a bit. "Otto, you should stop smoking," she said, and he did.

The little doctor had listened to many a tale of woe, and this one resembled, he said, as pitiable story as he had heard. Otto's buddies in the bar thought the story amusing and bought him drinks and a carton of cigarettes. Later, he confided to the doctor that he wasn't able to pay the capital gains tax on all the stock he had sold and the IRS was after him. "Now I feel like that Job guy."

"You're right on course." The doctor shook his head.

"Well, it turned out all right in the Old Testament, didn't it?" Otto asked.

The doctor winced, "In a manner of speaking."

Chapter 50

Unable to afford the apartment in the fancy building on Central Park West, Otto and Ruth gave it up and moved to the old apartment on Riverside Drive after a fresh coat of paint was put on the walls. Otto hired the building superintendent for eighty-five dollars, including materials and labor and got a "superintendent's special": the windows painted shut, the switch plates and switches painted over, even the crystal glass doorknobs covered by a thick layer of eggshell white. Scraping the paint off the knobs and the window glass he cursed himself for not coming up with the cash to hire a painter. "I think he drinks," Ruth said, scrubbing a switch plate in the sink with steel wool.

Certain that times would be better, Ruth would not to let their good furniture go, arranging it to fit in less than half the square footage gave little apartment the appearance of a second hand furniture store. Many of the paintings they had wandered the galleries to buy they sold at a loss. Otto nailed up what remained filling the walls practically frame to frame. "The South shall rise again," Ruth would say, wrapping her arms about him clasping him in a hug. "I don't want to hear any more discouraging words."

The bank forced the sale of the restaurant and Jim bought it with the chef and some partners. The money from the sale went to pay down a portion of the Cirsonrad loan. Otto never saw any. With Otto gone from the bar, the "gang" drifted away. Otto figured Jim wanted it that way. He made changes Otto didn't like; but in truth there were no changes Jim could have made that Otto would have liked; Otto understood that much about himself. Jim picked a new name that to Otto sounded like a French town or something. He didn't remember it on purpose and he couldn't make himself go back.

Otto worked for Mel now. The Real Estate firm was located in one of the buildings Mel's firm owned. Otto had a desk in a large basement room with ten or twelve other sales agents. Mel's desk, covered with leases and settlement sheets, sat behind a partition at the far end and there he spent much of the day with a phone pressed to his ear. Upstairs on the first floor there was a fancy office with a clear desk top Mel used for meeting customers, signing deals and closings; but the basement was where the action was, the "war room" they called it, and that's where Otto wanted to be. Detailed maps of Manhattan, ten block swaths in each, filled with colored pins marched along the walls circling the room. Stanley, Mel's most valued employee, had worked in the city Property Tax Office and knew every piece of real estate on the island. His job: to look for distressed properties in good neighborhoods, buildings that might have a tax lien or owners who might want to sell or trade. The smoky air in that dusty cellar reawakened Otto's capitalist passions, the reason he had come to New York in the first place. It was stuffy, it was hot, there was noise, phones rang, shouts, curses, laughing, thumps on the back; Otto's kind of place. He loved it! The doldrums began to lift. There was a lot of money to be made, and they were making it. He saw the way real estate fortunes were built, slowly, steadily, property by property, and every now and then a bonanza, big money that was turned right back into more property. If you were alert, one deal could bring in a bundle, like finding a nugget at Sutter's Mill. Here he would begin again, make it back, become a player. He was a believer; America was still the land of opportunity. He agreed to start at the bottom, on commission, showing apartments to would-be renters; one step above sweeping the floors and emptying the trash. He took apartment hunters around and stood quietly by the hallway door as they wandered about, looking out the windows to check the view, usually a dark courtyard or neighbor's window, opening the closets, and turning around in the living room with arms out measuring the space by eye and figuring how their furniture would fit. He had a knack for showing, which for him meant he kept quiet letting the place sell itself, until, and most importantly, if there was a particle of interest and he put the lease agreement in front of them and asked them to sign before someone else grabbed this "beauty" from under their nose. They usually did. Soon the small commissions began to come.

This helped, but the financial hole was far too deep for take-home pay based on rental commissions. He needed more. He studied for his real estate license. And in the meantime, Ed Cutler was taking the Otto's Place Investment Group's case to court. There lay a remote hope for financial salvation.

The case was to be heard in the United States District Court for the District of Massachusetts. The three of them, Otto, Mel and Ed, hired the Boston law firm Fellows and Whelps, known in the trade, Ed said, as

"Bellows and Yelps." Otto drove to Boston in the Nash for a deposition. "Answer only the questions asked, and be brief," Ed had coached him before he left. When Otto walked into the office suite it was apparent why the Fellows and Whelp's fee was so high; somebody had to pay the rent in that big space with parquet floors, oriental rugs and a view high over Boston Harbor. Otto was in the business, he knew what it cost: plenty. The receptionist took his coat and hat and led him to a conference room, offered him a cup of coffee, and left him there to wait for the deposition to start. He watched the boats pass up and down the harbor. First the stenographer came in, then a group of lawyers representing the schools and charities, then Thatcher Fellows, his lawyer. After introductions and handshakes all around, the proceeding began. Not knowing what to expect, Otto thought it was all very cordial. Mr. Fellows posed the questions.

Their case rested on the fact the group established a precedent over ten years of relying on oral contracts while doing business together as the "Otto's Place Investment Group". The evidence for this were the verbal agreements used for the establishment of the uniform sewing company, Unsewco, a multimillion dollar business, and a number of other smaller businesses in which the group had interests over the years. He testified further that the group's checks to cover the purchase of stock in Cirsonrad Inc had been deposited by Mr. Cook in his personal account apparently so that Mr. Cook could provide guaranteed funds with a cashier's check for the stock the following Monday. The Monday appointment to purchase the company could be corroborated by Mr. Hallowell's lawyer, who was to administer the sale. Neither Otto nor his partners had authorized Mr. Cook to comingle funds for the purchase of the stock with his personal funds and they had no knowledge that it had been done. Finally, Otto recounted, prior to Mr. Cook's untimely death, he had drawn up a list of names and a corresponding list of the number of shares that were to be dispersed to the each of the purchasers and this list was in the possession of Mr. Hallowell's attorney. Throughout the deposition the defendant's three lawyers sat doodling, twirling pencils, walking about, looking out of the window. They raised objections for the record, but had no questions for Otto. He figured at one hundred dollars an hour apiece, this was costing the "widows and orphans" plenty. It took over three hours. Otto drove the Nash back to New York that night, pulling in after midnight.

• • •

It took a year for the case to go to trial. In the meantime, Otto's divorce was finalized. Otto and Ruth were married in a chapel at Riverside Church on a sunny Friday afternoon in September 1947. The assistant minister officiating read a passage from the Old Testament: *Ruth, i, 16,* that began, *Wither thou goest, I will go…* apparently picking up on her name. Otto had heard the passage years before, probably in Danish, but had no idea until then where it was from. It was appropriate, he thought.

They held a little reception afterward in the apartment. They fit the guests in by moving some of the furniture into the bedroom and some out the door into the hall. Mel and Sherri came in addition to some the friends from the office, a few ladies from the secretarial school, Doctor Weinstein, Gino, Jim, and Ed Cutler. Ed took Otto aside and reminded him to come by the office and change the beneficiaries in his will. Otto interpreted the reminder as a rare sign of optimism on his lawyer friend's part, because unless the suit was successful, Otto would have only debts to pass on. In the morning, Otto and Ruth left for a weekend honeymoon at a resort in the Pocono Mountains. Before they left Otto took a picture of Ruth smiling and waving standing beside the blue Nash. She wore a corsage on her new suit jacket, a hat with a veil, and white gloves. It was enlarged and sent to her family at Swenson's farm, Rural Route 1, Sandquist, Marshall County, Minnesota. Otto hadn't told his mother of his divorce, so he couldn't send her a picture of his new bride. He would get all the news to her later.

• • •

Attempts at an out of court settlement having failed, the case was assigned to Judge Elijah K. Holt, a wizened old man who peered intently over the edge of the bench like a gnome with thick glasses. It would be a jury trial. Thatcher Fellows served as lead attorney for the investment group. A professorial looking man, he had a thin, hare-like face, adorned with round horn-rimmed glasses and a habit of blinking and sniffing at the same time; that for a reason Otto couldn't grasp, made him appear extraordinarily intelligent. He wore a bow tie and a Brooks Brothers' suit styled to narrow his naturally narrow shoulders. This studious demeanor, calculated to underscore the fact that his abilities lay in the dialectic rather than theatrical approach to jury persuasion, added to his effectiveness. Counselor Fellows stood alone, like David before the jury, not fearing whatever Goliaths the defendants might muster against him. No junior lawyers sat with him at the plaintiff's table. He was opposed by a team of lawyers from three separate firms; the lead firm Sheets and Unwite was represented by B. Arnie McGraff, known familiarly in the legal community as 'Blarney' McGraff. This man, Otto thought, had a remarkable resemblance to Clarence Darrow. He proved to be a rough and tumble courtroom battler who strode about waving his arms as he talked or shouted or cajoled, even cried. The jury paid attention.

The testimony given by all three plaintiffs was the same and supported the testimony they had given in deposition. Cross examination by counselor McGraff consisted of one question twisted into several forms, namely, were the plaintiffs aware when they made this "so called" oral contract with the deceased Mr. Cook that contracts under the law must be written to be valid. But the wily lawyer held his most effective weapon for the closing argument where he intoned in a resounding basso stressing over and over that the plaintiffs "were rich businessmen from New York who sat in a bar making shady deals over drinks." The words rolled out slowly and separately so that without using the words shysters or money-grubbers, his meaning was clear. "They are interlopers, trespassers in our community coming here for the purpose of extracting money from two deserving Massachusetts schools, shall I say, venerated institutions, and from our worthy charities that serve our needy and our dispossessed children here in the Commonwealth." The trial lasted for one day. Otto was certain they had lost.

Otto, Mel and Ed were joined by attorney Fellows for supper at a small restaurant near the courthouse, The Ends of Court, a lawyer's hangout. Ed, unusually chipper, asked Thatcher, as he now called him, what he thought.

"Well as Samuel Butler said, 'In law nothing is certain but the expense,' however, I think we have an excellent shot at winning." Otto leaned forward, anxious to hear where this was coming from, what this seasoned jurist saw in that courtroom he had missed. "The jury," he continued, "were for the most part poor and the ones who were not, middle-class women. Not to disparage the poor, but in general the poor have little regard for the letter of the law, nor for the elitist institutions of learning Cook gave the money to. And in this case I think they will be swayed by common sense." He took a sip of water and went on. "Now the middle-class ladies, if nothing else, are fair." He looked up and smiled at Ed who nodded in agreement. "The Cook Family Trust distributes funds to worthy causes on a case by case basis, hospitals, boys clubs and so forth. But, the jury saw that your monies amounted to a small fraction of its value, and it wouldn't be substantially affected by returning your funds. "The schools" he paused, "on the other hand, I have some trouble with." Otto felt his spirits drop. "Because," the lawyer went on, "like the late Mr. Cook, I am an alumnus. When the Alumni Fund managers learn that I am responsible for the school's loss in court today they will come after me to make up what I made them lose, or better yet, if I am lucky, they will throw me off their fund raising rolls." He looked up with a big smile. Otto noticed his front teeth were abnormally long; they went with the rabbit-like sniff and blink. "Baxter, my prep school, caters to the wealthy, although I wish to note here for the record that I was a scholarship boy. And the college, oh my, that poor, poor, needy institution sitting on the banks of the Charles River that is known to have the largest endowment of any school in the United States. I don't think the jury will be concerned about its welfare." He paused for effect. "So, gentlemen, that's why I think the jury will see through Blarney's blarney and we will win our case." Otto realized Thatcher Fellows Esq. had it all figured out from the beginning.

The Jury returned a verdict before noon the following day. Judgment for the plaintiffs. The money was to be returned by the beneficiaries of August Cook's estate, but the plaintiffs request for interest on the funds was denied.

Chapter 51

Har took Nellie to dinner the next night, choosing a dark corner of a restaurant several towns east of Farbridge where it would be unlikely he would be recognized. He searched Nellie's eyes for the barest hint of interest in him; and she, feigning disinterest, carefully turned her eyes away, preoccupied with the menu. Looking up she commented on the art that hung on the walls, and when the conversation lapsed she introduced an unusual topic for her, gardens and landscaping. Neither Nellie nor Har mentioned the previous night. For his part he told a few funny stories about complications with the pool, a squirrel in the attic, and then in a moment of inspiration, an offer to take her sailing on the Sound undoubtedly in the grip of indecision, fumbling, unsure, all the while measuring the risk of revising his plans for a freewheeling bachelorhood against a life enriched by this beautiful woman.

Motoring back to Farbridge he remembered his father's advice to "sleep on any important decision before making a commitment" and chuckled inwardly and answered in the silent confines of his mind, yes Dad, that's exactly what I plan to do by substituting an "on" with a "with." But how to accomplish this while avoiding any irreparable damage: namely commitment? She sat on the far side of the car, a challenge to Har's sporting appetite. He hated to lose. It would be he who would control the process moving forward, decide whether to continue on, but only after the night of sex he imagined. With no prior announcement he brought the Cadillac to a stop by the back stoop, explaining as he opened her door, "Nosey neighbors, you know." He reached for her hand and led her into the house, through the labyrinthine hallways to his library, the inner most sanctum of the rambling interior, where in that room redolent of leather and dust, he left her amidst oriental rugs, heavy draperies, brass lamps and his books that she noted he kept in alphabetical order by author. Placed in a commodious red leather chair, Nellie looked across at the paintings on the wall opposite and among the landscapes and hunting scenes, horses and hounds, one painting stood out, far out of character for the room, a nude that the artist, carried away by his model's beauty, had failed to shadow out any detail. When Har returned from the kitchen, a wine glass in each hand, curiosity bested her. She asked why he had it.

Handing her a glass, he responded apologetically, "Oh, my mother doesn't like it either."

"I didn't say I didn't like it, it just seems different, doesn't fit in with the others."

"It's called Persephone, a painting by Thomas Hart Benton, a famous American artist," he added unsure she had heard of him. "It's only a print of course, but a good one." By identifying of the painting as a serious work of art he intended to legitimize it and, somehow, excuse its presence.

"It's very erotic," she commented, studying it through the rim of her glass as if there was a caliper there with which to gauge the proportions of the nude's anatomy. She took a sip of wine. Her comment regarding the eroticism, delivered offhandedly, caused an uncomfortable lull in the conversation. Har thought carefully about what he would say, gathered his courage, and decided to follow through.

"I saw it in a gallery and it reminded me of you." He looked over at her hoping his smile wouldn't look too lascivious.

"Oh?" was her only response; she let the silence get to him before she said anything more. She, like a cat toying with a trapped mouse, would enjoy his futile efforts to extricate himself; his awkward intentions had become a shambles. She had an advanced degree in man handling and would make allowances for his clumsy sexual advances under these circumstances; but this was amateur stuff.

"She was queen of fertility, crops really, in Greek mythology. That's why there is a grubby old farmer in the picture leering at her. Symbolism," he stammered, not sure how this was going.

"The old farmer sort of resembles you," she quipped, smiling at him to soften the insult.

"Oh, yes?" he nodded, too shaken for a comeback.

"What would it take for you to take it down?" she asked matter-of-factly.

"Take it down? I don't know," he murmured, not picking up her gist.

"What if I took my clothes off, like the painting. That would be the real thing, now wouldn't it?" She watched the color rise in the face of the bank president, the man who was used to control and had lost every particle of it. His discomfort had reached the level she desired; she had him in check, stumped. Standing, she went over, bent down and kissed him softly on the lips. Took him by the hand and said, "Come on, silly boy, it's time to go upstairs." She led him up in a way practiced long ago in that mining town in Canada. He had no idea what fate had brought him: the devout Irish Catholic woman, the beautiful prioress from next door who spurned his advances, seemingly uninterested in sex proved to be a master of the sensual arts and tonight he would be given Lesson One.

• • •

As she wished, a proposal came quickly. This marriage she would make work. No compromises; she would devote her life to their mutual happiness. Unlike in the past, she could look into the marriage for sustenance, no longer dependent on a priest or the scriptures. She would look to Har; they would stand together to face the problems that surely would arise, a team against the world and for her, the universe. It was a calculated decision based on reflection that all the prayers she made, and there were many, hadn't arrested Maggie's illness or prevented her death. Nellie had for her entire existence put her trust in a Force that when she cried for help, wasn't there. Now she would take command of her life! It took a child's death to set her free; free of reliance on a Power that she now considered arbitrary and unfeeling. Finally freed of the gnawing guilt in her gut she spent years trying to purge, and vomited out; now it would be God's turn to accept some guilt. He was guilty, wasn't He? Hadn't He let a child fall sick, suffer and die? For six painful weeks she had stood by Maggie's bedside praying with Father Mike to no avail. And during the lonely train rides at night back to Farbridge, she kept asking, "God if you have a higher purpose then tell me what it is? What purpose for Maggie could there possibly be?" Finding no answers, she concluded that here on earth she alone must control her destiny, at least so far as any human could command. She thought of her Aunt Mary for the first time in years; hadn't she made that choice long ago?

Harwood Parsons had his foibles; she knew that, his privileged ways, his self-centered outlook, the entitled attitude that permeated his shadowy house wrapped in the protective limbs of massive oak and ash.

It was a trade, Otto for Har, marginal in some sense, as the new marriage lacked passionate urgency on her part, not loveless or non-caring, but would require her to rely on her powers of deception to make him happy in every regard. The Club, his stuffy friends, and his social church, the Episcopalians; they suited her. Only fine old families passed those portals. And this new church had seat cushions. There would be some raised eyebrows on both sides of the spiritual fence, of course. She wasn't certain how her Catholic friends would react, disdain she supposed. And Harwood's parents—they unerringly spoke his full name—the alarm she imagined they must have endured. Their son marrying a divorced immigrant girl and a practicing Catholic, a status they would term as most "unbefitting"; but they must have bucked-up because they took it graciously. She understood that for all practicing patricians, above all, decorum is what matters. All disparagement, any hint of opposition to the union, had been sealed off behind bedroom doors. No matter the circumstances, they would stand by their son.

The Parsons Senior held an engagement party and stood with Nellie, introducing her to their friends in their home: a H.H. Richardson brownstone manse with a portico, stained glass windows, heavy wood panels, library, music room, a dining room that could seat thirty and a lawn that gently rolled down to a small lake over hung by an immense weeping willow. Nellie thought the champagne punch and hors d'oeuvres were perfection, though she dared not take any; the risk of a fleck of watercress stuck to her teeth too critical. All the best people were there, more than a hundred. This marriage she would not let fail; she was strong, case-hardened by life. Harwood, as she too now called him, would be her final challenge. She had a family, one she could only dream of, an old family, an American family, an aristocratic family.

They were married in the stone church on the town green. Harwood's parents, a few close friends, twenty in all, stood with them. She wore a white suit and carried a bouquet of yellow roses. Har had reserved a room at the Club for a wedding luncheon afterward. On the way, Nellie and Har stopped at the little grave on the hill. The grass had healed the rectangular scab of dirt in front of the stone, but nothing else. Yellow roses were Maggie's favorite. Nellie left them for her.

"Harwood, doesn't it seem they always build cemeteries on hills to be nearer to heaven?" she asked, tears in her eyes.

"Nellie, I think it's for good drainage. You don't want caskets floating up."

Well, she quietly acknowledged to herself, he is practical.

Chapter 52

Forced to redirect his ambitions, Otto veered from successful restaurateur and major shareholder on the ground floor of a corporation guaranteed to skyrocket, to that of a minor-league real estate investor. Badly rattled especially during the blackest, most sinister hours of the night when he couldn't imagine a win in court, he vowed he would never give up his quest, he would come back strong, no compromises, no short-cuts, just a program of steady investing, step-by-step, property by property until as he would awaken one morning a real estate titan with office buildings, apartments and even hotels in his portfolio.

During the years of tight budgets and self-sacrifice and the inevitable second thoughts and grieving over the rare events that robbed him of what would have been a sure bonanza, Otto scratched out little commissions here and there that provided some relief from the daily "watch every dollar" existence. Finally, the check the court settlement had promised came and Otto walked through the door of the little apartment smiling and waving it over his head, holding it up like a trophy. Ruth hugged him and then breaking free, twirled round and round her arms out in a tarantella tumbling through the crowded furniture like a pinball bouncing off bumpers, and finally, dizzy, she collapsed on a sofa. Otto stood with his head thrown back in laughter watching the celebration. They had won! They had won!

The victory had been costly. The remainder of the loan from the bank was paid off first. Of the original two hundred and fifty thousand of his own he had invested Otto would receive one hundred and nineteen thousand; legal fees, court costs, and taxes ate up the rest. But still, in 1949 that was a lot of money. Otto hid his disappointment at the final figure, but Ruth saw the settlement as sufficient for a move up, a restart. That evening they returned to the Waldorf Astoria and dined and danced to love songs at the Starlight Roof, just the two of them, the brutal luck, the dreadful sorrows, the stormy season past and for those elegant, blissful moments, forgotten. The youthful, hyperkinetic plans for conquest, the Viking-like dreams, finite and fixed, the grandiose valuations set as markers for conquest, he modified. Without anger or contempt for himself, he would pursue opportunities as he found them and live life as they could afford it, no more envy. He would avoid the pitfalls of reckless ambition. He was forty-six and starting over. And the magnificent dream of a fortune won in the contest of life had become more difficult now; time had changed sides and no longer stood as partner, but a challenger who lengthened the odds. With a loyal cheering section in Ruth and Mel, an ember of ambition continued to glow. Didn't he work in a smoky cellar where fortunes had been made? Not all the old dreams would die.

But first they would splurge. When a two-bedroom co-op with a view overlooking Central Park came on the market Otto snapped it up and at a good mortgage rate. The apartment on Riverside Drive was sold. Ruth hired an interior decorator who sniffed at most of the furniture Ruth had saved there. Threading through it, pointing, she exclaimed, "this won't do, that won't do, junk that, very unsuitable." The decorator bought a large Persian rug and a new couch and chairs, lamps, tables, and bedroom suits. Ruth was sorry she had hired her. Otto was indifferent. It was only money he said. At breakfast, skipping past the stock pages, he scanned the ads for Bergdorf's and Saks Fifth Avenue, and taking a sip of coffee told Ruth, "It's time for you to buy some new things." Ruth put aside her reading and mused, "Do you mean like 'there's a time to sow and a time to reap' and we can reap a little more?" "Reap away," he said. The remaining ninety thousand he invested in real estate.

Evenings they had cocktails in their apartment before the two large windows that looked out over the street and trees to the lawns of Central Park where New Yorkers, strollers and ballplayers took their exercise. Ruth quit teaching shorthand; dictating machines had made taking dictation unnecessary anyway. To keep busy she took a job working three days a week selling paintings in a small gallery a few blocks from the apartment. One benefit, she carried paintings home to try on their walls for a time; another, she met local artists, most Bohemians, and as an artists' representative, she and Otto were invited to oddball parties in Greenwich Village. There were dinners out, restaurants to try, shows to see, Sunday brunch at Tavern on the Green, and always the crossword puzzle in the Sunday *Times*. New York was exhilarating once again.

Otto had earned a real estate license. He made a good living on rental commissions but now he could sell. Although in real estate, owning, not selling is the answer. Mel advised him on what properties to buy. "Start small and parlay," he instructed, "figure how to use the proceeds from one building not only to pay down the mortgage but to have some left over to build another down payment. Start with tenements and go from there." Otto took his advice and bought six in Spanish Harlem in a block near 110th and Lexington Ave. He would be a real estate mogul, he dreamed. Mel approved but said in any tenements there are problems, drugs, gangs, and collections. If you have to go up there, don't go alone; take one of the guys here with you.

It was the happiest time of Otto's life. It lasted two years until October 1951. But as Mel said owning tenements wasn't all roses. Furnaces and hot water heaters broke, plumbing failed, vandalism, skipped rents all came with the property. There were constant repair bills, plumbers, electricians, painters and of course the mortgages. The rents came by mail. Every month Otto would sit at his desk with his green ledger book and make entries, trying to balance the accounts, maintain a margin of profit to reinvest. There had been negative balances last winter. Looking back through his books he noted that some of the December, January, February and March payments came weeks and months late, mailed from Puerto Rico. He asked Mel if he was aware of this phenomenon; if Mel had had this problem.

"Oh, lots of the Puerto Ricans go back for the winter and lie on the beach. The checks are late because by the time the welfare check gets forwarded to them and they might decide to send you the rent, it is long past due." Mel smiled knowingly; just one of the perils of the business. He had been there and knew of what he spoke. "Otto, the answer is you've got to get tough with freeloaders." Mel, standing over him in his shirtsleeves, his girth pushing over his belt, he realized his friend was not inclined to take that advice, and he started again. "Otto you are too trusting, too nice a guy, this isn't your cocktail bar, you've got to be tough, get nasty sometimes. Hire someone to go out there and knock on the door of the ones that stiffed you last year and get payment in advance, and threaten them. If payments are more than sixty days late they will find their furniture dumped out on the street." He paused for a moment for effect. "Otherwise, every year it will be the same damn story; and you'll get payments late and short." Otto didn't answer; he studied the green ledger pages looking for another way to handle it. Mel walked back to his desk behind the partition. His phone was ringing.

 Otto didn't discuss his day with Ruth. They had theater tickets that night for *South Pacific*. He put off thinking about collecting the rents until the morning when he picked up his briefcase, keys and a list of apartments from the table next to the door. He took a cab up to 111th St. and found one of the buildings he owned. As he pushed open the door, he noted the mailboxes in the hallway were broken; the brass covers bent and the locks popped open with screwdrivers by thieves looking for checks. The entryway floor made of quarter sized white tiles was dirty and cracked. The smell of urine rose up from a wet patch in a back corner. Where the Hell was the building superintendent? He turned up the marble staircase, the center of the treads were worn thin by years of foot scrapes, the gold paint on the ornate balustrade chipped away. It had been a proud address once, a building that had passed through waves of immigrants, Jews, Italians and now Puerto Ricans and with each, new stages of neglect and decay. The building looked to be near dead, unsalvageable. As he turned to climb a second flight to the third floor, he saw the plaster of the dun walls broken as if hammered in a fit of rage producing large gray splotches in the dreary hallway that appeared like the menacing animals in crude cave paintings. A solitary sixty-watt bulb that hung from a broken fixture threw harsh shadows on the grimy scene. By the time he reached the apartment he sought he had decided he was getting out of this end of the real estate business. No ambiguity here, it had a stench that couldn't be perfumed over, he was a slum landlord; an avaricious, uncaring lowlife; nothing heroic or noble about this form of capitalism. He regretted he had ever considered it and clearly he didn't have the stomach for it any longer.

Otto stood in front of the apartment door and considered turning around and heading back down the stairs. A door slammed on the floor above, two teenager boys rushed full speed past him down the hall, loping down the staircase three stairs at a time, running perfect low hurdles down to the street. He raised his hand, hesitated, then knocked. There was the shuffling sound of footsteps inside and from within a sweet voice inquired, "Quien esta?" He could feel her eyes crawling over the skin of his face as her scrutiny bore down on him through the peephole. He counted five locks on the door starting from the top to the bottom and saw that they were necessary as the metal of the door had been bent back in several places by pry bars. Clack, clack, clack the locks echoed through the stark hallway as each of the deadbolts snapped back. A pretty young Latino woman stood in the doorway and looked at him over the chain lock. Her foot was planted like a wedge against the door bottom. She switched to English. "Yes, mister?" she inquired.

Otto could see over her shoulder the apartment was nicely furnished. From the appearance of the outside of the building and the hallways, parts he was responsible for, he expected a disheveled dump within filled with torn, stained secondhand store furniture. Quite the contrary, he could see a new sofa, end tables and lamps, curtains neatly hung at the windows, a nice rug on the brightly polished wooden floor.

"Hello," Otto began, "I am from the management of your building…"

Cutting off his sentence she turned her head and called, "Carlito, venga aqui, por favor." never letting go of her grip on the door or making any gesture to let him cross the threshold.

"Que pasa?" a sleepy voice asked as a small bronze skinned man, hair uncombed, shuffled barefoot to the door while tucking his undershirt into his belt-less pants.

"Hello," Otto repeated, "I'm from the management of the building. They sent me here to ask that you pay your rent on time this winter." His words were met with puzzled looks.

He started a third time. "What I have been instructed to do is to ask that if you plan to go to Puerto Rico this winter, that you pay your rent two months in advance. The management has adopted a new policy." The door shut. He never got to the threat about putting their furniture out on the street if the rent was behind two months. He stood there looking at the chipped paint on the black metal door. Only one dead bolt clacked. He took that as a sign they intended to open it again. He felt like an idiot. After three or four minutes the door opened a few inches and the man said he had enough for one month's rent in advance handing him a small assemblage of tens, fives and ones. Unable to stand this unpleasant duty any long Otto said, "Thank you." The door shut again and the five dead bolts clacked in rapid order. Otto put the money in his brief case and turned down the stairs.

As he left his building the sidewalk ahead of him dazzled in the bright morning sunlight from little particles of silica in the pavement that sparked up the light. Squinting he noted a gang of boys standing across the street. He had not walked twenty paces, his eyes still accommodating, when from behind someone ripped the briefcase from his hand. He yelled "Hey" and as he began to turn he felt a sting in his left lower back and heard a simultaneous "pop", not loud, but like the familiar sound of a campaign cork coming free. He fell backward, striking his head on the sidewalk with a smack that made his ears ring. In an instant the pain in his gut grew white-hot, like an expanding ball that throbbed with every heartbeat. Unable to move he looked up at the sky, a broad river of blue running between the even roofs of brown tenements. He heard shouts "a man's been shot!" and a call for an ambulance and another for a priest; a small crowd gathered and peered down at him. A heavy brown skinned woman knelt down and cradled his head in her lap. He could feel a sharp pulsing sensation from the tear made by the tumbling bullet in the wall of his aorta. Blood pumped into his belly. Someone asked, "Are you all right?" He wanted to laugh but was only able to nod, yes, and lay there. Then slowly that pain in his gut began to abate, colors began to fade, the blue of the sky turned white, the brown buildings, black. Soon all color washed out. He relaxed; comfortable, resigned. A priest arrived. The brown woman opened his shirt looking for a cross on a chain. "I don't know if he's Catholic, Father," she said in a worried voice. "Oh, we are all Catholics today," he replied. The last sound Otto heard on earth was the voice of the priest incanting the soothing words Father Mike had said over Maggie and with those words Otto knew God would take mercy on his non-believing soul. He would see his little girl again. Then the black corners of the buildings, the last images on his retinas recorded, he recognized to be the prows of Viking ships. He was gone, gone home.

• • •

He was late for dinner. Ruth called the real estate office. "No, he hadn't been in all day." She called Mel at home. Sherri's happy chirpy phone voice quickly switched to a crisp call for Mel when she heard Otto was missing. Mel, in an easy chair, dropped the newspaper, and hefting himself out felt his face blanch as he took the phone. Otto might have gone out collecting rents. He was concerned. Taking the phone he told Ruth he would make some calls and call right back.

"Yes," the man in the Coroner's office said, "a man answering that description was brought in this afternoon. Shot in the back. Probably a zip gun, one of those things the gangs make out of pipe." He went for the file and returning he said in a non-emotional bureaucratic monotone: "According to the papers in his wallet, his name is Otto Nielsen."

Otto's remains were cremated. There was a short memorial service at the chapel where he and Ruth had married. Ruth asked Jim if he could close the restaurant for a few hours for an after-funeral gathering of Otto's friends. He did. They put a tall scotch and soda in front of Otto's stool at the end of the bar and toasted the spirit that had once held reign there. Ed Cutler told Ruth Otto's will stipulated that his remains were to be interred in the family gravesite on a farm in Denmark. She arranged for the funeral director to send them, though she felt abandoned by the gesture.

• • •

The box of gray dust about the size of a shoebox arrived at the Danish farmhouse mid-December. The weather had been cold and it had rained for three weeks straight. The letter accompanying the ashes requested they be placed beneath the soil in the Larsen burial plot in the grave marked Jorgen. In the dark, ancient kitchen, with the thick stonewalls that had sheltered countless generations of Larsens, the letter was read out loud by the girl from across the road, Johanne, who had bought the farm with her husband, Rudi. "Poor Otto," she said. "I shouldn't tell you this, Rudi, but my sister and I, we had a crush on him. He was my first love, I was six; we were naughty together, I saw his weeny." Rudi, not unexpectedly, didn't discern a trace of sentimentality in this, being a farmer with thick hands and a very literal mind. Looking at his uncomprehending face she realized how inappropriate she had been and was sorry she had said it. Recovering, she instructed: "Rudi, please take the ashes out and bury them as he asked on the hill with the others."

Rudi held the box in both hands staring out the open kitchen door. The fields were soft from all the rain; if he drove up to the gravesite his tractor would make deep ruts that it would take all spring to heal. There was a steady drizzle. He opened the box of fine gray ash and with a muscular arm, reached around the thick stonewall of the doorway and poured them onto a bed of low green plants that huddled dormant there. Then he walked to the horse barn and threw the container in the trash.

That June, Grandmother's hollyhocks erupted from the soil, grew tall and bloomed with new splendor.

• • •

Ruth closed the apartment and flew to Minneapolis. Taking a bus on westward, she leaned her head against the window as she watched the great barns and round silos that stood on the great Northern plain like the colossal stones of Stonehenge pass by. At the farm, the place she had left to conquer the world, beneath the picture of her smiling, waving by the robin's egg blue Nash that hung on the wall, she told her brother and parents in the dim glow of the kitchen window the story of her time and love in New York.